For Troy

a native of Barwick
and a fellow returnee
~~to~~ South Georgia.

Bill

6 - 16 - 12

A World of Deception

The Memoirs of "Philipp Devon"

A Novel by

Bill Raiford

ONE

Permit me to introduce myself. Philipp (with two ps at the end) Devon is the name I'm currently using and I'm writing this memoir because friends have begged me to. They wanted to share the excitement and adventure I experienced this past year. They keep asking me about "what I really do" in my job. I say that I'm a courier, a person who hand-delivers important documents.

Some of my friends are convinced I'm a spy. I can state with complete honesty that I'm not a spy, certainly not in the conventional sense. I see myself as a collector of information, which I then pass on to the bosses of two "collection agencies", one in Washington, D.C. and the other in London. My role is a vital one and my work is dangerous, sometimes even life-threatening. My submissions have contributed to the arrest of major drug dealers, assassins, moles, counterfeiters, and other unsavory characters engaged in the sale of highly classified documents that could, if they fell into the wrong hands, disastrously affect the balance of power in the world.

Before I go any further, I want to tell you something about my past.

When I was growing up, I was strongly encouraged to attend the same schools my father and grandfather attended. I reluctantly did, but only lasted two years in college. Standing 6' 4", lithe and well-muscled, I liked sports. I swam and earned several letters and medals. I was a good dancer and was popular with women. I read spy novels and became acquainted with a life of intrigue. So I quit school at the end of my second year and joined the Marines. My five-year tour instilled in me a sense of duty and purpose. It also calmed down some of the rebellious nature in me. After being honorably discharged, I applied to the Agency. Even though I didn't have a formal education, I was accepted and sent to a Russian language training program. When I discovered that I had a gift for languages in general, I studied several others and became quite proficient in all of them.

My first assignment with the Agency was in New York and it was there I met Arlene Fulgham. At that time, she was in training with Z's group and was attached to the British Delegation at the U.N. After dating for several months, I went with her to London where she introduced me to Z. With permission of the Agency in D.C., I was allowed to train under Z. He acted as my personal mentor for two years.

As head of British Security, Z deals with matters of spying, pilfering of State secrets, counterfeiting, forgeries, murders and other troublesome goings-on. He has been one of my bosses for the past fifteen years. My American boss in D.C., Charles Tufts, heads a similar Organization. My training under each was similar: learning to read quite fast using a tachistoscope, a machine designed to get one in the habit of recognizing longer and longer numbers in shorter and shorter periods of time; learning to code and decipher rapidly; and learning to be properly dressed so as to fit in unobtrusively on every assignment. Under Z, however, there was a "continental flair" associated with each assignment and, while under his tutelage, I came in contact with many heads of State, attended many upscale social affairs and gradually assumed a more British persona. To obviate a paper trail, I was paid for the expenses of each assignment, plus several thousand for my expertise, by a deposit in my Swiss bank account, which carried with it a card for withdrawals.

Arlene Fulgham was the most sophisticated woman I'd ever known. Her brains matched her beauty. She was in great physical shape and always perfectly gowned and coiffed. Men were drawn to her like bees to clover. When I first met her, I was immediately infatuated with her conversational skills as well as her beauty. I learned that she'd been educated at private schools in London, had come from a fairly wealthy family of which she was the only child, and had recently been a Dior model. Her coterie of friends was vast, yet she seemed to be able to make time for me whenever I asked. Our conversations were intellectual as well as sexual. We hit it off immediately and became quite an item in New York and London, as well as lovers. I could write a whole book about her but I'm eager to introduce you to my world of deception.

My past assignments have taken me into many countries. On some of them, I feared for my life. I've been shot at in Moscow, mauled in Naples and captured and tortured in Kiev. Had it not been for my excellent physical condition, I might still be hanging by my ankles somewhere in Ukraine, although my more recent assignments have been less dangerous as I grow older.

Arlene was also involved in similar assignments. We worked well together.

My world of deception began years ago, but, in this writing, I'll only relate what took place in the years 1984 and 1985. I kept a diary in cryptic code of key words and abbreviations that would prompt my memory to re-envision details. This is an honest account and reconstruction of the events.

In 1984, I found myself in Tangiers, the northwestern Moroccan seaport at the western end of the Strait of Gibraltar where the

Mediterranean and the Atlantic meet, and only five minutes from the Pillars of Hercules; an enchanting, storied haunt for spies and smugglers and con artists; an old world land of dark people and cloud white buildings.

"How much you think to pay?" Rashid the rug merchant wore his traditional loose fitting white dishdashe, the kaffiyeh skullcap covered by a cotton smagh headdress held in place by a white agal rope. He leaned as if in a casual pose on carpets from Persia to Afghani war rugs and Kazaks, Iranian, Pakistani carpets—and even durries from India. Rugs stacked like a colorful silk deck of cards. Some hung from a wire to reveal their tribal source and prayer themes. The one on top of a pyramid of rolled rugs would do for my purpose. Rolled back a bit, a tongue of it stuck out. I turned up a corner to ascertain the vividness of the pattern underneath. A tight weave, the backside was a rich repeat of the front, only in a slightly lighter hue.

"Not more than alf (one thousand) dollars," I said. "It is a small Baluchi rug."

"Valuable rug, made by the best," Rashid responded.

I spoke in measured words. "It is a beautiful rug but I will not pay more." I should explain, my friends, that my language may sound a bit stilted and formal. Arabic does not use contractions. I spoke to him in English with as much of a British accent as I could muster in order to hint that I was the master, he the servant. Although I'm very much an American, here I was disguising myself as a Brit.

I swiveled my head, scanning the souks slowly. "I see many rugs," I said in my best feigned anger and crossed my arms.

He turned his left palm out. "Good price last time, but now . . ." He turned his right palm out, "inflation . . . storage . . . personnel costs—"

"Alf," I said even louder to ensure his competition wouldn't think he was undercutting their agreed-upon price limits. I did an abrupt right face and took a step, prepared to play the vote-with-your-feet trick and walk to the next merchant. It was all a game, anyway, a show for the others.

"You hard bargainer," he said loud enough for everyone within earshot. "Alf. Only American, with green backs."

As I counted out ten 100-dollar bills in a fan on another stack of rugs, he ducked out like Casper the Ghost through a beaded-curtained doorway to wrap my purchase. When he returned, the rug was rolled tightly and secured with two jute cords. I slowly poked the corners of the ten bills, counting them aloud in Arabic.

I left the bazaar with my heavy-for-its-size purchase over my shoulder.

The 1977 Cornish Rolls Royce Silver Cloud with silvered bulletproof windows that had been provided me by Doris, my hostess, idled with its bolt-like clanking engine and stream of dark colored pipe exhaust.

The driver floated the car away from the Bazaar and slid into the lazy stream of afternoon traffic. He stopped at the gate to the wharves where several yachts were docked. Not a word was spoken until I said *"shokran (Thank you)"* and bid him *"masa'il kher (*Good evening).*"*

The blindingly white hull gleamed. It reflected the water so cleanly that the only way to tell the difference between appearance and reality was to focus on the thin line where the mirrored image started. The hull and its reflection sparkled and flashed the late afternoon sun in spokes and sprays of golden light at the line between the world of water and ship. High up on the bow, painted in money green, was *37*. As some of you know, I'm always conscious of details and the difference between truth and deception. I have to be in order to stay alive. I live in a world of deception.

I clanked over the gangplank and boarded the *37*, the largest of the three yachts moored at the wharves, and the second largest privately-owned yacht in the world; so large in fact that it occupied the entire eastern side of the dock where normally four or five good-size yachts could have tied up.

My hostess, Doris, or as she prefers to be called by all but her closest friends, Madam Thirty-Seven, the owner of the yacht, was a mathematician manquée who wanted to teach college, but her Down East father felt that she was destined for bigger things. Her grandfather died when she was five years old and thus she became the wealthiest female in America. She loved and was fascinated by the history of mathematics. Prime numbers consumed most of her interest and she spent much of her leisure hours poring over ancient texts and treatises and creating some novel diversions for her mathematically-oriented friends. Doris has for many years been "forty-nine" 'though she could pass for a woman in her early forties. Her hair and her eyes are brown and her figure shows the many hours spent with her personal trainer.

I locked my stateroom door, untied the scratchy new jute and unrolled my carpet. The manila envelope was there. I checked the contents to make sure they were what I expected – confirmation of the identity of a suspected mole in the American Embassy in Paris -- and placed the envelope in my briefcase along with the itinerary given me when I boarded in Copenhagen—a schedule of the daily shipboard events with a suggested "uniform" for each event.

The low hum of the side thrusters warming up told me to go topside. I joined the other thirty-five guests and our hostess standing at the port rail. The thrusters vibrated and pushed the *37* into the harbor channel exactly at eight o'clock and into the rapidly advancing dusk. They stood, each of them with a hand on the rail, all the men in black tie, the ladies in sherbet print evening gowns and white cork-soled patent peep-toe wedges.

I should explain that through study and experience I learned much about labels and style. I had to. My bosses were sticklers for details in debriefings. My codified notes had to contain such minutiae or I'd be chastised "humorously." In fact the more I learned, the more I enjoyed this aspect of my life. It had served me well through the years. I might as well tell you that much of it I learned from the women who wore the dresses which lay on the floor by my bed during a night of passionate love-making.

The crew wore black high cut waistcoats with a deep V and silk lapels, black bow ties, and white shirts and duck trousers. They could've been on the cover of *The International Yacht Registry* if it were still in existence.

In a matter of minutes, we were in the Med and then the Atlantic. With the yacht's stabilizing gyroscopes, we rode the seas as though floating on soggy clouds.

The city lights shrank into firefly flickering. We engaged in small talk pleasantries. A couple of the guest pointed out fading historical landmarks.

Waiters magically appeared with trays of cocktails and hors d'oeuvres. The sweet aroma of canapés, empanadas, skewered Mediterranean shrimp and ceci fritos (fried chickpeas) and other tapas was bettered only by the out-of-this-world taste in my mouth and the vision of beautiful women. A steward in seagoing livery announced dinner would be served promptly at nine.

The *37* left Stockholm three weeks earlier with only five guests, the others boarding at Copenhagen, Amsterdam, Le Havre, and Lisbon, totaling 18 men who would be seated alternately with 19 ladies in the dining room. Doris was not superstitious; she just made the most of numbers when she could—including money. Besides, what meaning could underlie 19, another prime?

Casual breakfasts in the salon, buffet lunches poolside on the main deck, weather permitting, were the order of the day. The yacht incorporated every modern convenience, from a beauty salon to wine cellars, seawater desalinization ice making machines, and even redundant electrical wiring that could be switched by the tap of a button.

I hoped to have a tête-à-tête with Stockholm Sven, a gourmet chef internationally known for his lox and lobster bisque, who boarded with me in Copenhagen. As large as the yacht was, I still couldn't corner him. He was tall and fit and had an engaging personality; we'd worked well together on several assignments.

Arlene boarded at Le Havre. She was known throughout Europe and the Americas as one of the most stunning and important women in the world of high fashion. She and I also worked together on several assignments in both France and Belgium; working with her was always a distinct pleasure. She was thirty-five, four years my junior, but in my arms she was much younger. Neither of us had ever been married and each time we were seen together, the tabloids reported the story of a rumored engagement. She made me proud as a barnyard cock to be seen with her.

At Le Havre, I'd greeted her with our usual "paparazzi" kiss, while photographers and several of the crew popped bulbs and strobes like winking stars. She was outfitted in a Vera Wang fallow crepe suit with a Fendi diamond bangle, and matching Mikimoto black Tahitian pearl necklace, earrings, and ring. That outfit helped get her on the cover of *Vogue*.

I escorted her to her stateroom and after her luggage arrived, I made sure she hadn't forgotten our last meeting in Paris. She always smelled as sweet as freshly dewed lilacs. I held her closely and whispered "Dearest

Arlene" into her ear. She melted in my embrace and kissed me on my neck, chest, and lips and everywhere else on my 6' 4" body both above and below my waist. We looked into each other's eyes and it was clear we could've made love again and again until we finally fell asleep in each other's arms, but we both had to change for cocktails and for the formal greeting by Doris.

She leaned back into my hands at her waist and said, "Did you get my cable?"

"I was delighted to know we'd be working together in Paris for a few days."

"Plans have changed," she said.

This was nothing new. Sometimes it was just to throw anyone off in case my whereabouts might be anticipated by unwanted parties. Even I occasionally didn't know until the last minute.

"We're going directly from Le Havre to Baba's château in Normandy. She'll pick us up at the dock."

I knew better than to ask about the change of plans, for it often occurred when Arlene and I were on the same assignment.

From the beginning of my trip in Copenhagen, I was introduced as "Philipp Devon." I'd used this name so often that I'd almost forgotten my real name, which didn't seem important anymore.

The first night out was spent by almost all the guests in the casino. The medium of exchange was the dollar. I'd brought with me sufficient cash to enjoy several hours at the tables. Routinely, in Washington, I withdrew four hundred dollars with my bank card and then converted the twenties into hundreds. Thus I established the level of my weekly expenditures. Since I lived alone in D.C. and took many of my meals at home, I rarely used my credit card, certainly never on assignment.

At the end of the evening in the casino, I took my winnings in 20-dollar bills. With my mathematical mind and excellent memory, I find it easy to keep track of cards played. With only 4 suits, and 11 values to count and calculate odds, I was often the winner of the evening. I've a secret compartment in my briefcase and a crotch pouch, a discreet rounded money belt; I divide my paper equally between the two.

Arlene and I spent quite a bit of time together aboard the yacht. We were photographed at poolside by several members of the crew and guests. We played the "tabloid item" to the hilt. Arlene looked like a caped three of diamonds in her pink peek-a-boo tunic and bikini. No one could resist checking her every feature. I noted that the women especially gave her the three-over.

She'd been a Dior model in Paris for several years and had often appeared in the European press. A brunette, 5 feet 6 inches, she was a frequent visitor to Cannes and Monaco and had appeared on the cover of both *OH LA!*, a French *People*-type magazine and *POINT DE VUE,* the other French celebrity magazine. Whenever we met someone new, she somehow worked into the introductions that I'd been a model for *Gentlemen's Quarterly* and also had a national swimming medal and that I was in the best physical shape of any man she knew. Then she would turn and reach as high as she could and try to tousle my hair. We do make quite a couple, I must say.

At dinner, Arlene was seated between Sven and me. Since the death of his wife two years prior, Sven Christen was known as a man-about-town. He had earlier in his life dated Doris who now made no excuses for her attention to his every need. He was about fifty-five and in superb physical condition. Doris always asked him to assist with the mathematical entertainments, for he was also quite good at numbers.

At dinner, the tender squab; bouillabaisse with a hint of saffron; an Israeli couscous with lemon zest; and cranberry salad with walnut vinaigrette; a clean smooth Mâcon-Lugny white wine to complement the seafood; and a refreshing orange cake in a Grand Marnier sauce—all made for constant "oohs" and "aahs" and dabbing of lips and sips of wine to clear the palate before the next bite.

We three lapsed into talk about favorite dishes and restaurants around the world. Sven's mention of my favorite Paris restaurant—La Ferme Saint-Simon—was an agreed-upon signal that I'd be receiving a note from a mutual friend when I arrived in Paris. The envelope would also contain additional dollars to tide me over until I got back to an ATM.

As the *37* neared Le Havre, we saw our luggage stored near the gangplank. Arlene and I busied ourselves saying our goodbyes to the other passengers and to our hostess. We two were the only ones debarking at Le Havre. I had my briefcase in hand and Arlene carried a small Louis Vuitton traveling case.

My luggage was plain vanilla but my briefcase was one of a kind. Engineered in London, it had ordinary-looking clasps, but if the correct combination was not entered in the dials by the second number, the entire case became galvanic.

As we walked down the gangplank, I noticed a Silver Shadow in the receiving area. The liveried driver stood at rigid unsmiling attention.

"I shall retrieve your luggage," he said in a quiet, confident voice.

When the driver opened the left rear door, the occupant in the rear seat leaned forward and spoke in a sultry, rich contralto. "Bonjour, mes chers amis. Bienvenue." It was Baba. Her brandy-soaked voice filled my soul with a cozy-warm sense of familiarity. We'd met in Brussels, Paris, Madrid, and D.C. An American who had married a Spanish nobleman, she was a gorgeous brunette in her early forties, about five feet five. She'd worked closely with Arlene on several assignments. It'd be her choice whether or not to acknowledge our previous meetings.

After she and Arlene had exchanged cheek kisses, she extended me a gloved hand. The ritual of kissing her hand without having my lips touch her glove was a most important public act which I'd learned to do effortlessly.

Arlene and I joined Baba on the couch-like back seat of the Rolls. She nodded to the driver, who closed the glass between him and us.

The Norman countryside was beautiful with rolling gently-nodding red and yellow poppy fields—just as I remembered from my last visit to Honfleur two years ago.

As we approached Baba's château, a building reminiscent of the Château de Giverny, a gatekeeper stood aside for the heavy iron filigreed gates to swing open. They began to close like pincers, seemingly pushing the car through. I'd forgotten this measure of security that prevented more than one vehicle at a time passing through the gates. As we drove along the white gravel driveway, footmen appeared with wide sand trap rakes to erase our tracks.

Under the porte cochère, six people in servant attire with colored epaulets indicating their stations in the household stood at attention on the steps, lined up like dominoes. Ah, the old world wealth that spared the wealthy from the detritus of daily existence.

The driver opened our doors and snapped to. Two men unloaded our luggage and disappeared within the château.

Baba greeted each of the servants by name and thanked them for their cordial welcome. She then introduced each of us. Arlene and I followed her into the library where we found sherry, a rich, dry Spanish Pedro Romero Amontillado, awaited us. It was quite refreshing.

The Countess nodded to a footman who closed the pocket doors to the library. Baba informed us that Z would arrive later in the evening. Z was on everyone's A-list of guests. Arlene and I'd worked with him mainly in London and Paris. Baba suggested that we address her as "Countess" whenever servants were present, but when alone, we should call her "Baba."

So here we were: Baba, Arlene, and I sitting in the library of a magnificently restored 16th century château in Haute-Normandie. I felt

embraced by the green leather library reading chair, the six-foot wide

slightly arched fireplace, and all the books that I would never know even

the names of. We waited for one of us to tell the other two why we were

here. Baba spoke first.

"I asked Arlene to re-arrange your schedules and come directly here

before we all go to Paris tomorrow afternoon. I have some very interesting

information I want to share with you before the arrival of His Lordship."

(No one knew his real name, though I discovered why he was called Z the

first time I reported to his office. He had a son, now deceased, who as a

small boy would try to say his name, but only "Z" would come out of his

mouth.) She turned her focus directly to me. "I assume, Philipp, you

picked up the envelope in Tangiers, and you, Arlene, received yours

before you left Paris."

"We did," we said simultaneously. I delighted in how quickly Arlene

and I slipped into our old habit of speaking in unison, with one mind, you

might say.

Baba leaned forward a bit and cupped her fingers for us to come closer

and listen up. "The Ministry of Defense in Paris, has asked the three of us

to assist them in capturing a mole who is stealing secret information from the Ministry."

Moles were a real problem. More and more they popped up in surprising places. "Fake documents were planted for him to steal. Covert cameras got good photographs." She sat back and took a lady-like sip of sherry.

"As you know, my brother works in the Ministry as liaison from the U.S. State Department in Washington, and it was through him that the request was conveyed to me.

"The mole is an Arab-American and the information which you, Philipp, received in Tangiers is confirming background data from our friends in Morocco. You will turn the envelope over to His Lordship during our discussions this evening."

She faced Arlene. "The package you received in Paris contains our invitations to the American Ambassador's Ball on Friday evening. It also reveals the contacts at the Ball and by what means we shall know them. The three of us must memorize these details before Z arrives. We shall be traveling with him to Paris tomorrow and to the Ball as his houseguests.

"After he arrives and we have had an opportunity to review all the details, we shall not speak of this to anyone, not even among ourselves until after the Ball and our duties have been completed." Baba always spoke in this formal manner.

The Ball was being held on American soil so the subject could be arrested by American authorities. The waiters serving that evening would be from the Embassy Security Force. At the appropriate time, a nod from His Lordship would signal Baba to ask the suspect to dance; and after a reasonable interval, Arlene will ask to cut in.

"I will protest the interruption," Baba said, "and, rather than make a scene, Arlene will suggest that the three of us go out on the terrace for a smoke."

Once on the terrace, they'd head for that portion of the terrace nearest the steps to the garden. When waiters had discreetly ushered any other guests on the terrace back inside, the two waiters we met earlier would approach us and quietly place the suspect in handcuffs. They would scurry him down the steps to the rear garden gate where additional Embassy Security Forces would whisk him away.

It sounded simple but we were all trained to look for chances of screw-ups. I wondered why the suspect was being arrested at the home of the Ambassador and not within the Embassy itself; we'd videotaped him taking documents. Suppose our suspect doesn't want a smoke at that time? Baba could insist and plead that she needs a light. If the suspect senses something is amiss, Baba was to fake a faint. What if the other guests declined to leave the terrace? There were too many "ifs" for my comfort.

The projected interval from the arrival on the terrace until the suspect was handcuffed was calculated to be no more than three minutes. With the suspect out of the way, Baba and Arlene would express total astonishment at the happenings on the terrace when they go back into the ballroom. Baba would be visibly upset and declare a headache, and the three of us would take her home.

My thoughts turned to a similar experience in Brussels several years ago. Baba, Arlene and I were on assignment to assist Interpol in capturing a German art dealer who had stolen works of art from private collectors as well as art galleries. We were attending a ball in a fashionable hotel and knew the suspect was infatuated by beautiful women, so Baba and Arlene together invited him to join them upstairs for a "good time." I was on the room's balcony awaiting their arrival. When he made his first pass at Baba, I rushed into the room and began what turned out to be a real fist fight. He knocked me down with a one-two punch and stomped on my stomach. Had I not been in such great physical shape, especially my abs, I'd have been a goner. Immediately the Interpol guys rushed into the room from the hall and cuffed the target and took him away.

When one of the doors slid into the wall, His Lordship entered the library and greeted each of us like the old friends we were: two-handed shakes and cheek kisses for the ladies. A distinguished, six-foot, sixtyish white-haired Scotsman with a fatherly air and the aura of a nobleman, which he was, having previously served both as an Ambassador and as a member of the House of Lords.

A servant closed the library doors. Baba locked them, and the four of us moved to the center of the room to a sunken area with overstuffed chairs. His Lordship began the briefing, asking each of us if we understood our particular role in this encounter. We discussed the "what could go wrong" subjects in detail to everyone's satisfaction, especially the one about the place of the arrest. Z explained that the mark was being arrested at the home of the Ambassador rather than at the Embassy itself because our case will be stronger if we confront him after he has stolen the documents and left the building.

Z asked for the envelope I'd received in Tangiers. I unlocked my briefcase on my lap. He glanced at its contents before placing the papers in his briefcase. We four then moved to the sitting area in front of the fireplace. Baba unlocked the library doors and summoned an attendant to bring wine. The cocktail hour lasted until 6:15, when the maître d'hôtel announced an informal dinner would be served in the small dining room off the library.

The conversation at dinner was casual, friendly small talk with nothing about any of our doings or the library briefing. We enjoyed a meal of goose liver pâté, pheasant, and champagne. For dessert, we were treated to flambéed bananas with cointreau. Baba called it a simple meal. Compared with my own preparations at home, this was a grand repast.

After dinner we savored Moroccan coffee and liqueurs in the library before we all retired for the night.

Baba had arranged for Arlene and me to have adjoining suites on the top floor of the château. How thoughtful. And the door between our suites was not only unlocked, it was open.

When I stepped out of the shower, I saw Arlene, completely nude, stretched out on my bed a la Goya's Nude Maja!

She was in a playful and commanding mood. I was instructed to lie on my back and not say a word or move my hands from the headboard. I always obey instructions, especially when they come from someone so . . . full of charm. My hairy-toed feet hung over the end of the bed.

The moon shone through the open windows and over our bodies. I did as I was told, the details of which a gentleman would never reveal. Suffice it to say that the licking and the probing was rapturous for both of us.

When the first rays of dawn pierced the darkness of my room, I slipped from bed. After I'd shaved and showered, I stepped back into the bedroom and found an empty bed and our mutual door closed. The shower in the adjoining suite rattled as Arlene sang "O, What a Beautiful Morning." Yes, it was and I was hungry.

I slid into slacks covering my money pouch and tucked in a polo shirt (with no insignia or logo), and wiggled my feet into my Zelli loafers.

I descended the three flights of stairs, ending up in the echoic entry hall. I was greeted with a cheery "Bonjour monsieur" by one of the femmes des chambres. She bowed slightly and swept her arm toward the breakfast room.

The curtain-filtered sunlight was easy on the eyes. The aroma of food salivated my mouth. Baba was perfectly coiffed and gowned in a pink dining negligee—just right for the early morning at a European estate. She was seated at the head of the table with His Lordship on her immediate right.

A hearty good morning and an inquiry about my night's sleep set the pace for a rousing breakfast with much talk of Honfleur, the poppy fields, and our upcoming trip to Paris. Not a word about our mission or the fact that we were to be the houseguests of His Lordship.

The attendants quietly buzzed about bringing food and keeping full our crystal water glasses and elegant white bone china coffee cups with deep saucers. A bountiful breakfast transported me from the dangers of our mission to the pleasures of the moment.

The coffee was typically Norman, strong and rich with heavy cream. As I was having my second cup, Arlene entered the room. His Lordship and I rose to greet her. Baba said, "You look flushed. Are you feeling all right?"

She had a glow about her that appeared on the surface to be angelic. I knew why she glowed and, after our lovemaking, that she was no angel. With all of her charms and sophistication, when we were making love, her sexual appetite was ravenous.

"Never felt or slept better. The play of the full moon through your bedroom windows was enchanting." She looked at me and said, "Everything about last night was enchanting."

Arlene joined us at table and requested only one biscuit, some French jam, and coffee. I looked at her and found myself smiling about her coy allusion to our night together. I wanted to shout at the top of my lungs what a wonderful night I'd spent in the arms and between the legs of this amazing woman. Calming my enthusiasm by sipping my coffee, I managed to look at Baba and His Lordship without, I hoped, revealing anything.

His Lordship wore a double breasted blue blazer with the crest of The Arts Club, a club for men of letters and great accomplishments, in London. In addition to his service in the quiet world of secrets and discretion, he was a gifted poet and musician. His trousers were gray and his ascot was red, green and gold, the colors of his family's coat-of-arms. I'd once commented to a friend in London that I couldn't comfortably wear an ascot, to which he replied, "One does not wear an ascot unless one has been there."

Our departure for Paris was set for 1:00 P.M. Baba, Arlene, and I would be traveling with His Lordship and his driver in the Bentley. His Lordship dropped a comment at drinks last evening that his Bentley had been souped up for rapid departure if the need should ever arise.

Last evening in bed, Arlene and I discussed the possibility of a trip to Mykonos when our current assignment was ended. So far as we both knew, there was nothing on our respective calendars for the next two months.

The Bentley was a behemoth compared to the tiny cars jamming the

Paris streets. Bicycles whizzed past.

We went directly to His Lordship's flat on the Avenue d'Iena. Our luggage was unloaded and deposited in the service lift. We four proceeded to the 6th floor in the other lift, the walnut-paneled one, deep with age and care.

The door opened to a foyer tiled in black and white marble. Pushed back pocket doors revealed the drawing room, which burst with Impressionist paintings—Matisse, Monet, Manet, Mary Cassatt, and a Klee thrown in for variety, I supposed. We enjoyed a glass of 1982 Montebuena Rioja before dressing for the ball. His Lordship always made a point of having my favorite wine on hand.

We were shown to our rooms where, in mine, a valet awaited to see if my tuxedo needed touching up with a steam iron. I assumed the ladies had equal amenities. I quickly shed my clothes and took a shower, after which I lay diagonally across the bed. I thought about last night and tried to persuade myself that I'd rather stay home with Arlene than go to a stuffy Ball where someone was going to be arrested. But duty calls, so I got up, dressed, and was about to put on my jacket when there was a knock at my door.

"Come in," I said. My valet entered and asked if I needed help with anything. He scrutinized my complete attire and removed one or two pieces of lint before pronouncing me ready.

"Monsieur is quite handsome in his formal wear," he said in English with a French accent. "I have dressed many of His Lordship's guests but you are the most trim."

I thanked him with a Gallic phrase I've used many times to impress the listener: "Merci beaucoup, monsieur; merci mille fois (Thanks a million)."

"Je vous en prie (You're welcome)."

We four gathered in the drawing room for a quick mutual inspection and then took the lift to the waiting Bentley. His Lordship and Baba sat on the rear seat and Arlene and I occupied the fold-a-ways. The short drive to the residence of the Ambassador took about ten minutes. When the Bentley pulled up at the curb, an attendant opened the right rear door; we exited and proceeded through the entrance of the residence. After depositing our wraps with the "ladies-in-waiting", we joined the other guests already queued for the receiving line.

The Ambassador and her husband were most cordial, addressing each of us in the appropriate manner: "Your Lordship, Countess, dear Arlene and Philipp. It is so pleasant to see each of you again. Thank you for coming."

After leaving the line, we were met by two waiters with trays of champagne.

"Your lapel buttons are the color of the champagne," noted His Lordship. "You must be new here. I don't recall ever seeing champagne colored lapel buttons before."

"We two have been designated as the personal attendants on the Ambassador and her honored guests, Your Lordship. Enjoy your evening."

We mingled with the crowd as best we could; we knew no one. The canapés were hot and delicious as we sipped our first and only glass of the bubbly. Presently, I caught His Lordship's eye as he nodded toward the entrance to the room through which we'd recently come. A darkly complexioned man of an indeterminate age was leaving the receiving line. As the four of us wandered into the ballroom where dancing had already begun, this newly arrived stranger followed. At the end of the current dance number, the Ambassador took the microphone and said, "I have invited many of you this evening some of whom have never before been to our residence, and many of you do not know very many people here. So I ask you please to introduce yourselves to each other and join with the music in dancing. I hope you have a wonderful evening."

There was polite applause as heads began to turn, looking for an appropriate dance partner. Baba stepped up to the darkly complexioned man and introduced herself as the Countess de Bollo. He in turn gave her his name and kissed her hand. When she asked him to dance with her, he replied, "I am not a very good dancer, Madam, and I fear that you would be embarrassed to be seen with me on the dance floor."

"Nonsense," said Baba. "I have already targeted you as a wonderful dancer with whom I would love to be seen." He smiled.

Taking her hand, the two of them joined the other couples and mingled into the crowd quite unnoticed. At the completion of that number, again there was polite applause. I noticed that Baba had maneuvered the two of them in the direction of Arlene and me. When Baba asked for another dance, her partner appeared to be flattered and readily agreed. About eight measures into the number, Arlene stepped forward and said, "Countess, with your permission, I would like to dance with your partner."

"You may wait your turn, my dear; he's mine for now."

Her partner appeared to be highly honored being "fought over" by two lovely women, neither of whom he'd ever seen before.

"If you will promise me a future dance, Monsieur, I will be patient.

Will the two of you join me for a smoke on the terrace when this number is finished?"

"Of course," Baba replied. "Now run along to the terrace and we shall join you shortly."

The two of them finished the dance after which everyone again applauded. Baba and the mark walked through one of the doors to the terrace; I promptly followed. There were no other guests on the terrace. As the two waiters approached the mark, he sensed what was about to happen and made a run for the garden stairs. I tackled him at the top of the stairs and held him until the two waiters could cuff him. They then escorted him to the rear of the garden where additional Embassy Security personnel were waiting. Baba, Arlene and I re-entered the ballroom, both of them appearing flushed. Each asked for another sip of champagne as His Lordship approached.

"Are you both all right?" he inquired.

"Yes, but we have had a harrowing experience," said Baba. "I feel that I need to rest and would like to be excused so that I may return home and lie down."

The couple nearest us heard what was being said since Baba was speaking rather loudly for the benefit of any nearby ears.

"We shall all go together after we have said our farewells to the Ambassador," said His Lordship. He turned and led the three of us toward the small group arrayed around our hostess.

"Madam Ambassador, I regret that we must be leaving your delightful party but the Countess has become somewhat flushed and I feel that she needs to return to the house for some rest."

"May we be of any assistance?" inquired the husband of the Ambassador.

"No thank you. I shall be fine. The closeness of the crowd and the champagne were not compatible with my plans to enjoy such a wonderful evening. Please pardon our departure, Madam Ambassador. It was so good to see you again."

After gathering our wraps, we left the residence and, after only a few seconds, the Bentley pulled up. Silently, we got in and returned to the home of our host. When we were once again in the 6th floor drawing room, His Lordship, asked for a full report. We later learned that the mark had been taken to the Embassy for interrogation and a full confession of the pilfering of the documents and the selling of them to the enemies of America. Arlene spoke up to say that she rather enjoyed the whole affair.

"It was hell", said Baba looking at me as I dusted off my jacket.

His Lordship poured each of us another glass of Champagne after which we parted for the evening with sincere thanks from our host. I gave Baba a peck on the cheek and a similar one for Arlene but with a long look into those lovely blue eyes.

When I was awakened at precisely 8:30 by a knock on the door, I threw on a robe and opened it to find my valet holding a breakfast tray, which he put on the small round table between two overstuffed chairs. He promptly left the room. Shedding my robe, as was my custom of being nude whenever possible, I sat down and picked up the two papers, *La Monde* and the *Herald-Tribune.* I didn't feel like reading French at that hour so I glanced at the headlines in the *Tribune.* On the second page was a brief blurb. It was reported that there'd been a minor altercation at the residence of the American Ambassador last evening. One of the guests had had too much to drink and became unruly. The notice was short and matter-of-fact. There was no mention of the incident in *La Monde.*

I turned to my food and found, under the plate of eggs and ham, a sealed envelope. In it were ten 100-dollar bills, two airline tickets to Athens and the following note:

"On our trip to Paris from the country, I overheard you speak of Mykonos. These tickets are for this morning's flight to Athens, which leaves Charles de Gaulle at 11:10. Have a nice vacation." The hand-

written note was signed "Z."

TWO

I knocked. Arlene opened her bedroom door with an aromatic Arabica cup of coffee in her hand. Like me she was in her traveling clothes. I hadn't told her anything about my plans for the morning. A marvelous woman, always ready, on time, and thinking about her next moves. As I bent to kiss her on the forehead, she moved the coffee in an outstretched arm and rose on her toes like a ballerina. When I told her we had two tickets to Athens, she said "wonderful" and asked for ten minutes to pack.

I went to the drawing room to thank Z for his assistance with our mini-vacation only to find a note informing me that he'd left for the Chunnel and on to London and that Baba had taken an early morning flight to Cannes. He left a taxi telephone number. Ever the British gentleman, he signed off with "In grateful appreciation for your work, your friend." No name.

I phoned for the taxi, went to my room to finish packing, and found

Arlene ready to go, looking like a movie star.

"Charles de Gaulle à Lufthansa, s'il vous plaît."

En route to the airport, we talked of Mykonos. When I leaned into her ear, the light but potent aroma of lilacs flooded my senses. Looking at her I felt a stirring in my loins and lightness in my head.

I told her when we landed in Athens I'd call Sophie, the owner of the hotel where I'd previously stayed. We could hardly wait to spend real time together without interruptions.

When we got to de Gaulle, I offered the driver a 50-dollar bill, but he said in perfect English, "Your fare has been more than taken care of by His Lordship, and he instructed me by no means was I to accept anything from you. His Lordship said, 'God speed.'"

At the check-in counter the attendant gave Arlene a slip of paper and said she'd had a telephone call. Arlene went to a nearby booth. When she returned she said the caller was Colonel Davis from the American Embassy and that the Ambassador had scheduled her for a one o'clock luncheon at Pré Catelan (my second favorite restaurant in Paris) in the Bois de Boulogne. An Embassy car would be waiting at the curb.

This was a change in plans that carried our mini-vacation off in the wind and threw cold water on my libido.

I suggested she take her plane ticket back to the Embassy and try to re-schedule her flight. If she couldn't, she should ask the Embassy to return it to Z with a proper explanation.

I walked her to a limo with a diplomat tag, rapped on the driver's window and asked who he was waiting for and who sent him. I was sorry he had the right answers. I knew there was no way out.

Arlene melted into me with a hug, pushed back, and kissed me long. Her nectar-scented breath filled my lungs. I couldn't speak but pulled her close and gave her a last hug. I waved as the car drove away, then returned to the check-in desk, received my boarding pass, and called Mykonos Sophie. I explained to her that I had a few days off and wanted to spend some at her hotel, if there be "any room at the inn." She sounded pleased but must have heard hesitancy in my voice. "Just a recent disappointment," I said, almost an apt word. "Dis-assignation" would be more like it. I told her I'd take the ferry from Piraeus tomorrow evening.

At the gate the plane was already boarding. I settled into my first class seat. I didn't feel like eating or drinking anything so I pushed the seat into "horizontal" and covered my eyes with the *Status* magazine I'd picked up at the airport. I recalled how I'd come to know Sophie.

She was a former girlfriend of Dimmie, an Officer in the Greek Air

Force whom I'd met in Washington. On my last visit to Athens, Dimmie and I took the ferry over to Mykonos for a two-day visit, staying at Sophie's hotel in Chora. Sophie was forty-five, widowed by the last Greek-Turkey war. She and her younger brother, Nikolas, ran the hotel. Dimmie informed me that Nikolas was known on the island as "the stud."

The island is a vacationer's delight. Almost everything and every building are whitewashed. The streets are mostly cobblestone and narrow, and walking was *de rigueur* in Chora, except for a taxi to one of the more than twenty golden sand beaches—always pristine and populated by people of every race, creed, color, sexual orientation, and status in life. On some, they sunbathed, burned their privates and frolicked in the Aegean.

The taxi ride to the port of Piraeus, some thirty miles southwest of Athens, was filled with both centuries-old and brand new buildings.

The ferry didn't leave until 9 PM. I purchased a round-trip ticket and, after telephoning Sophie to reconfirm my arrival the next morning, I sat down to read *Status*. Occasionally I looked up but didn't recognize any of the others waiting for the ferry. Was I really going to be incognito on this trip? Free, without an assignment from Z?

The *Express* departed the dock at Piraeus on schedule (a rarity) and I settled on one of the many benches in "the lounge." I've slept on cramped planes, in cramped buses and waiting rooms, but this was elbow-to-stomach tight.

The Aegean's gentle mood caused slow rolls from one side to the other and soon people were lining the rails hoping not to vomit on themselves when the ferry rolled back. Pretty soon the rancid-sour cloud of vomit was followed by the dry heaves. The rock and roll finally put me to sleep. It was a fitful sleep but evidently the two obese tourists on either side propped me up.

I was awakened by the bump of the ship against the dolphins. The sea had turned angry and docking wasn't smooth.

At the pier on Mykonos, I looked up at the windmills, phallic reminders of the virility of the area. Behind them the pale blue sky and streaky white clouds scudded with the gusty wind. But nary a taxi, so I phoned for one. When I told the driver in Greek I needed to go to Sophie's hotel, he asked, "You are American?" I told him I was and complimented him on his English.

As he handed me my luggage I wished him a *Kali mera* (Good morning) and gave him a dollar tip. He thanked me profusely with a sincere *efkaristo* (Thank you).

As I walked into the lobby, Sophie greeted me like an old friend.

Nikolas was behind the desk. The hotel was a modest establishment but quite clean and friendly.

I signed in by the name they knew me by and Nikolas hefted my luggage and showed me to my room He gave me the key and as he turned to leave, I offered him a five-dollar bill. He was somewhat taken aback but accepted the money anyway.

I changed into a comfortable white shirt and trousers and went downstairs to ask Sophie about getting something to eat. She told me of the nearby Aroma Café where I could get a light meal. She suggested Pasta Nostra for the evening meal. I invited her to join me as my guest.

The café was a short walk from the hotel. I ordered Greek coffee, currant bread and a dish of ródi (pomegranate seeds) and grapefruit sections.

The compote that lay before me was a picture worth taking. The pink grapefruit dotted with cherry red ródi in a pedestaled cut glass bowl promised a sweet sharp flavor. My palate—mouth and cheeks—puckered as soon as the waiter set it before me.

He brought me another coffee to replace my cup of muddy grounds and returned with a piece of phyllo pastry he called *bougatsa*. He said it was like baklava but was filled with Greek custard.

"Special treat from Sophie," he said. Sweet with a hint of lemon, more than special, it was perfection.

After the meal, I went in search of a loom-made hand-sewn shirt at one of the many boutiques and found one that made me look less the tourist. Back at the hotel I asked Sophie to spend the day with me at one of the beaches of her choice. She said perhaps we could go tomorrow but today she had many chores. She asked Nikolas to accompany me to a beach. He agreed. So we made plans to leave at 10:30. Nikolas said that he'd have a taxi waiting and we should take only a towel and a few dollars for the taxi. When I looked at him quizzically, he said we should go to one of the "clothes optional" beaches.

I remembered on my first visit to Mykonos with Dimmie that he and I and Sophie had gone to one of the family beaches. However, not wanting to appear prudish, I agreed and went to my room to rest for a while.

I went down to the lobby at 10:25. Nikolas was distributing mail in the room slots behind the desk. Sophie looked up from the desk and nodded.

Nikolas said the open-air taxi was out front. He told the driver where we were going. The ancient rocky rutted roads stretched the trip. We finally arrived at a spot where a serpentine path disappeared from view before it turned into the beach. We wended our way down a heavily trodden goat path. As we rounded the last curve on the path, I could see the beach was full of naked people, men and women of all ages and physiques. Some were lying on beach towels and some were sitting directly on the sand. A few were in the water. A group of young men and women were engaged in a nude volleyball game in the center of the beach. The bouncing breasts were hypnotic, the flapping penises were not.

At the far end of the beach we tucked our sandals and clothes in a crevice in the rocks. Before leaving the hotel, I'd taken off my crotch pouch and put it in my briefcase. I had a few dollars in the pocket of my trousers for food and the taxi.

When Nikolas disrobed and faced me, I knew why he had the nickname. His genitals dangled halfway to his knees. Impressive, but people on the beach didn't pay much if any attention to all the naked bodies. He and I spread our beach towels parallel to each other and sat down to chat. We sat with our arms about our knees.

He said, "Do you travel much?"

"Some."

"Where have you been?"

"My home is in the U.S. but I have business in England and the mainland." As soon as I said it, I knew I'd used the wrong word. It was a slip I'd never made before, probably because no one had ever asked.

"Business?" he asked. "What kind?"

Apparently the social rules about privacy and not asking about one's business didn't apply—perhaps after one takes one's clothes off, all is fair game. I said I had various interests that required travel from time to time.

When he asked what some of my favorite cities were, I politely said that Chora was at the top of the list.

He chuckled. "Nobody comes here for business. They come for the women." He swept his arm panoramically around the many naked women on the beach. Indeed, the island is a paradise.

"You never know," I said in a slightly sing-song way. I added: "I gather data for a travel agency in the States." Questioners like direct answers and this was my "cover."

He seemed to be satisfied and switched to his favorite topic—women. I marveled at the wide variety of females he'd encountered on the island. The population of Mykonos was only about 5,000 but they were outnumbered by the 900,000 visitors that swarm the streets, nightclubs, and beaches each year. "Young rich women far outnumber the men," he said. "Here they're anonymous and we want them to spend their money and go home raving about what a good time they had. I can't do it all by myself but I do what I can. I take them shopping and they take me to bed."

He carried on about body types and differences in attitudes and how the gays would stroll over to gawk at him and make small talk and lewd innuendoes. He stressed how usually one of them was bi. After he seemingly had exhausted his braggadocio he stood up and suggested we get wet. The warmth of the sun and the sexual talk had clearly lengthened and fattened his penis. Never one for jealousy, I counted on my well-muscled physique to attract notice. Besides, as fascinated as people might be with his family jewels, most women would be afraid to do more than stare. We ran into the surf. The water was warm, clear as glass, and most pleasurable.

As we came out of the water, he asked if I'd like to walk along the shoreline to the other end of the beach. I said I really preferred to lie on my towel and absorb some rays. His departure gave me an opportunity to look around the beach to see if I recognized anyone, but more importantly, to view the naked women and girls all around me.

On one of my glances toward the far end of the beach, I thought I recognized a familiar face, that of a portly man I'd met, perhaps in Paris, within the past year. Through the protection of my silvered sunglasses, I stared at him. I became convinced that we'd met, but since I didn't remember the circumstances, I delayed pursuing it further.

After what must have been an hour, Nikolas came back from his walk with a very young blonde on his arm. She couldn't have been more than twenty. I knew he was at least my age if not a few years older. He introduced the young lady as a former Miss Scandinavia. I could certainly see why she was selected. Her caramel-colored hair hung loosely about her face and shoulders, a few strands caressing her pink puffy nipples. She was gorgeous and very sexual, not just sexy. She sat down on Nikolas' towel saying, "Come; sit." He sat.

She turned to me and her blue eyes stared hungrily at my manhood and said, "Hi, I'm Helga." I was beginning to feel like a third world alien. I crossed my legs under me and stood up. I excused myself by saying I'd had enough sun for my first day out.

I asked Nikolas how I could get a taxi. He said to go back to the spot where we'd been dropped off, that taxis patrolled the road and one would come by soon.

I retrieved my clothes and dressed and said goodbye to the adorable Helga. She looked into my eyes with the softest, sexiest look I'd seen in a long time. Nikolas gave me a hearty handshake and I proceeded to climb the goat path. No sooner than I'd gained the road but a taxi stopped and within twenty minutes I was back at the hotel.

I checked my briefcase and my crotch pouch. Everything was just as I'd left them. Having had little sleep on the ferry last night and being well-heated from the beach, I stripped off, took a cold shower, and lay down across the double bed. I quickly dozed off and dreamt about my recent visit with my dearest Arlene and how much I missed her at the moment.

I slept for several hours. When I awakened, I heard voices downstairs in the lobby. I looked at my watch. 6:05. I'd better get up now or I'd miss cocktails and dinner with Sophie, although we hadn't set a time for our evening rendezvous. I took another shower after shaving a two-day stubble. After putting on my white trousers over my "companion" pouch and the sheer white, embroidered shirt I'd purchased, I walked down to the lobby. Several guests were getting directions to various tourist sites from Sophie. Nikolas was nowhere in sight.

When Sophie was free, I asked her about our dinner plans. She indicated that 8:30 would be an appropriate time since Nikolas would probably be back by then. I walked around awhile and looked into several of the small shops hoping I'd find the perfect something for Arlene.

But, as I was leaving the hotel, I saw Nikolas. He was alone. He appeared to have been dragged backwards through a keyhole. I don't recall ever before having seen a man so completely washed out. I greeted him with "Well, don't you look happy?" He smiled and said he and Miss Scandinavia left the beach shortly after I did and took a taxi to her hotel room where they spent the next four hours exploring every inch of each other's body in every possible position. He admitted he was getting a little old and short of breath. However, he must have performed well, for he said they had another date for tomorrow afternoon, again at her hotel. She just loved older men and called him "Daddy." He said he would take a shower and be ready to take over for Sophie so we could go to dinner anytime after 8:00.

I resumed my exploratory tour of the boutiques, again thinking about Arlene and how much I missed her company at that moment. Walking on the wavy narrow cobblestone streets was rather tricky in my thin-soled sandals, but nothing would deter me from finding a gift for my Arlene.

Coming toward me was the same man I'd sighted on the beach earlier in the day. Since we both were wearing sunglasses, I was able to stare at him once again, trying to establish where we'd previously met. He was about my height but weighed considerably more. He was nattily dressed in a white linen suit and carried a Panama hat. His demeanor looked shifty, even menacing. As we passed, he nodded to me. I returned the nod. I still couldn't place him. I continued window-shopping for another hour and found a silver pin with Aphrodite engraved on it. I knew it hadn't necessarily been made on Mykonos but the workmanship was first rate, had the maker's hallmark, and was stamped "sterling."

I wandered back to the hotel. Nikolas was behind the desk and Sophie was again talking to some tourists. She indicated she would be ready to go very shortly. I went to my room and put Aphrodite in my briefcase.

When I returned to the lobby, the linen-suited stranger was talking with Sophie. As I approached them, she said, "Philipp, I'm sure you remember Mr. Hargrave from your last visit. He was a guest when you and Dimmie were here."

"Why, of course. Mr. Hargrave and I have already run into each other twice today." We shook hands. "I thought I recognized you at the beach this morning, but wasn't sure since I hadn't seen you before without clothes."

Sophie giggled and Mr. Hargrave's face reddened slightly.

"Where do you come from, Mr. Hargrave?" I asked, attempting to establish some facts on why we were meeting here for the second time in two years.

"I live in Stockholm and come to Mykonos each year about this time to get away from my creditors," he said humorously. "Sophie and I have been friends for a long time, even before her husband was killed in that dreadful conflict. I write music and play the piano a bit."

Now I remembered where we'd previously met. I was in Stockholm on assignment three years ago, staying with my gourmet chef friend, Sven Christen. He had tickets for a performance of one of Mr. Hargrave's works. After the performance, Sven invited him to have a glass of champagne with us.

"Do you visit Stockholm often?" he asked.

"Only when I break a piece of Orrefors and need to replace it," I said. My reference to the Swedish glass manufacturer was one of the codes for "Identify yourself further."

"That is a very expensive reason for a visit," he said, "but any reason to come to Stockholm is a valid one."

Nothing, I thought. We've met in Stockholm once and twice here on Mykonos at the same hotel. He knows my Swedish chef friend and yet he didn't pick up on the Orrefors. Something was missing. Just then, Sophie indicated that she was ready to go.

"Pasta Nostra is not far away. We can walk there easily," she said as the two of us slowly sauntered around the corner and down a new-to-me lane. After about ten minutes we arrived at the restaurant, one Dimmie had recommended—a high compliment since you can't find bad food anywhere on the island.

Everyone in the place seemed to know Sophie: a lot of hugging and kissing, most of it quite genuine. We were seated in the extreme rear of the dining area where Sophie's favorite table was. No one could sneak up on me here, I thought. When the waiter approached our table, Sophie mentioned that she remembered I didn't like retsina. It may be the national drink of Greece but why anyone would enjoy wine that tasted like pine sap is beyond me. She asked if I preferred a red wine or a white. I didn't let on that one of my hobbies is the study of wines and that I was thoroughly familiar with Greek wines. Not everything need be told.

"I'll probably be having lamb so either would be fine. You choose."

She ordered a bottle of Biblia Chora Sauvignon Blanc, a white wine with a woody and fruity aftertaste. We sat and talked leisurely for about thirty minutes until the waiter reappeared ready to take our orders. We both chose tzatziki, (a yogurt, cucumber, and garlic dip) and the herb bread. For the main course, I chose moussaka. Sophie chose gemista (ripe tomatoes and peppers stuffed with eggplant, zucchini, rice and seasonings). I asked the waiter for another bottle of wine.

I asked Sophie to tell me all she knew about Mr. Hargrave. "He's been coming to Mykonos for about five years and always stays at my hotel. He travels alone but he loves to ogle the women at the nude beaches. So far as I know, he's never brought any female to his room. He is very polite to both Nikolas and me, and he leaves a very large tip for each of us."

"Did he ever say how he came to be staying at your hotel?"

"On his first visit, he referred to his acquaintance with the Greek Minister of Culture, a woman about my age, very lovely and widowed. She and I attended school together in Athens."

"Has he ever asked about me?"

"No, but you may want to ask Nikolas. He and Mr. Hargrave have gone 'out on the town' together."

As we finished our meal, the waiter brought each of us a piece of baklava without our having to ask. He also brought two small glasses of ouzo, compliments of the gentlemen eating alone at the front table. I looked in the direction the waiter indicated and found our benefactor lifting his glass. It was Mr. Hargrave.

When Sophie and I rose to leave the table, I said we should thank Mr. Hargrave. As we approached his table, Sophie said, "Mr. Hargrave, it was very thoughtful of you to send the after-dinner drinks. We appreciate your kind gesture."

"They topped off a most delicious meal," I added.

"I'm glad you enjoyed my little offering. May I invite both of you to join me at dinner tomorrow evening?"

Before Sophie could respond, I said, "Thank you but I already have plans for the evening."

He said he was disappointed.

"So am I," I said. I was glad not to be trapped at a table with him, for I began more and more to think something was awry.

We wished him a good evening and left.

As we walked back to the hotel, I told Sophie that I must catch the early ferry back to Athens in order to pin down some appointments I'd already agreed to.

"If you'll prepare my bill this evening, I'll settle up before I retire."

She agreed to do so and said she would bring the bill to my room when she'd completed it. I went to my room and retrieved sufficient dollars to cover the estimated tally. Within fifteen minutes there was a knock at my door. It was Nikolas with my bill.

"I'm sorry to see you leave so soon. I hoped we could go back to the beach and get more sun tomorrow."

I took the bill and counted out the exact amount. I offered an additional bill but Nikolas said personal friends are not expected to tip the management, but he took it anyway. I told him I'd miss the beach trip. He reiterated his regrets. I gave no more thought about my days' activities and decided to turn in.

I stripped, set my watch's silent alarm, and lay on the bed. Even though the room was designated a double, at more than six feet, sleeping diagonally is more comfortable.

Before I fell asleep, I re-thought about meeting Mr. Hargrave again. At first, I couldn't understand how he happened to be in the same restaurant Sophie had chosen for our dinner. Then I remembered that he probably overheard us talking just before we left the hotel.

My alarm vibrated. I awakened immediately. 7:30. I'd taken a shower before dinner last evening, so I decided to finesse one this morning. Also my stubble wasn't a full day old. Packing was easy, for I've learned to take out only what I need immediately and leave or replace everything else. Sometimes, a quick departure is the better part of valor—and value.

I'd just enough time to take a taxi to the pier or walk there, if necessary. A taxi stood a few feet from the hotel. I told the driver my destination and relaxed, comfortable in the thought that I was leaving Mr.

Hargrave behind. I needed to get more information on him before I did or said anything stupid.

When the driver stopped at the pier, I paid the fare, plus ten percent. With my luggage in one hand and my briefcase in the other, I stepped from the pier directly aboard the ferry. A steward stretched a chain across the entrance and the ferry departed immediately. Not too many passengers on board since it was the middle of the week and few tourists leave Mykonos until late Sunday evening.

I sat on one of the chairs portside. I re-played the last two days. No one except Z and Arlene knew I was coming to Mykonos. I hadn't alerted Sophie until two nights before my arrival. I first saw Mr. Hargrave on the nude beach and then, later in the afternoon, on the street. We'd met in the hotel lobby where Sophie reminded me of our previous meeting two years ago. I told only Sophie I was leaving. So only she and Nikolas knew of my departure.

After an hour or so, I realized I needed to alert Dimmie of my arrival and ask him to meet me at the pier. The ferry captain strolled by and I asked in Greek if he had a telephone I could use to call Athens.

"It's an extreme emergency," I said.

The captain handed me the ship-to-shore phone and offered a "glad-to-be-of-help" smile. I dialed Dimmie and apologized for not calling him sooner. I asked if he could meet me at the pier in Piraeus. I gave him the ETA. He assured me he'd be there. I handed the phone back to the captain.

The trip was interminable. I could hardly wait until I could check in with the London Office to ask for details about Mr. Hargrave.

I dropped off to sleep. When the ferry docked, I was the last to debark.

Dimmie got out of his Volvo and rushed over to greet me. We'd been friends for quite a few years. We hugged and kissed as Greek men are prone to do. After we settled in the Volvo, I told him that I'd received an urgent call from Munich and had to be there as soon as possible. Could he please take me to the Athens airport?

"Of course," he replied, but expressed great sorrow that I wasn't staying in Athens for a few days. His house was always open to me, he said, and his parents would love to see me again.

"Did you have a good time on Mykonos?" he asked. "How long were you there? Did you stay at Sophie's hotel? How is she?"

I answered each of his questions truthfully but made no mention of having met Mr. Hargrave. We made small talk on the way to the beautiful Athens airport, whitewashed and with marble floors. It's quite modern and everyone is very courteous. When we arrived at the Lufthansa post, I insisted that I'd be fine on my own. I thanked him for his courtesies and told him I hoped I hadn't disturbed his day's schedule.

We departed with a good strong handshake and another hug and kiss.

I went to the Lufthansa desk. I planned to take a circuitous trip back to London, as I often do, to throw off any would-be followers. Was I getting paranoid about Mr. Hargrave?

I purchased a one-way ticket to Munich using the British passport and the Barclay's Bank Credit Card issued by Z's Secretary. The flight was scheduled to leave in twenty minutes, so I went through the usual routine of being searched and x-rayed.

When we arrived in Munich, I went to the Lufthansa desk and requested a ticket to Rome, using my Italian passport and the Banco Italiano Credit Card also issued by Z's office. (They hadn't yet begun to be concerned about people buying one-way tickets.) I was able to get a flight within the hour so, having my boarding pass and still being within the secure area of the airport, I proceeded to my gate, grabbing a bite on the way. The airport is one of, if not the best I've ever been in—spotless, spacious, and bright with natural lighting from the many windows.

The touchdown in Rome was as smooth as a shuttle landing. I bought a one-way ticket to London at the British Airways desk. The flight didn't leave for two hours. I took a comfortable seat in a lounge and gathered my thoughts again concerning Hargrave. If he was following me, he wasn't being very discreet about it. I was reminded of my last trip to the Soviet Union when the KGB man assigned to track me wore the same suit and tie for three days. I reminded myself that Sophie said that he liked to visit the nude beaches so he could ogle the women, but she also said that he and Nikolas had spent several evenings together. Doing what? I asked myself. Were Sophie and Nikolas involved with Hargrave in something? I had no idea what it might be. And how does my friend Chef Christen fit into the picture? I must get to Z's office as soon as possible to clear my head.

When my flight touched down at Heathrow, I took the Underground to Sloane Square and walked the few blocks to the old Victorian Cadogan Hotel, where I always had a room, one of several reserved continually for Agency personnel.

On my first visit to the Cadogan several years ago, I was assigned the room in which Oscar Wilde was arrested and put in the "gaol." It had recently been redecorated and was light and cheery but the first night I didn't sleep well. The next morning I transferred to a nice corner room with a much larger bed, the size of which was my excuse for requesting the move.

After getting settled in, I dialed the special number and identified myself to the operator by the code of the day, a sliding scale no one could ever divine. When Z's Secretary answered, I re-identified myself to her and requested a meeting the following day to discuss a Mr. Hargrave and the events of the past three days. She immediately put me through to Z.

"Well, Philipp, what a pleasant surprise to hear from you so soon. How was Mykonos?"

I described my traveling alone because of Arlene's call to a luncheon in Paris.

"Yes, I know," he said, "a meeting was scheduled within hours of my leaving the flat. I regret I was unable to get to you before you and Arlene left for Charles de Gaulle, but the Ambassador called the meeting to discuss the capture of the mark at her residence. A possible problem arose concerning the manner of the cuff."

"I hope I didn't screw up the assignment."

"No, no. Just a legal technicality about where the mark *was* physically when he was Mirandized. I do believe it's been cleared up. My Secretary says you want to talk about a Mr. Hargrave."

"If I might see you sometime tomorrow, I would like to clarify some things I don't understand."

"Come about 11:30. We can have lunch together at the Club after our chat."

"11:30 it'll be, sir. Thank you."

When I put down the receiver, I realized I'd sensed nothing from the tone of Z's voice that would indicate he did or didn't know Hargrave. I thought about phoning Chef Christen in Stockholm but decided to wait until I'd talked with Z. Then I realized that I didn't know where Arlene was. It would be improper to call around trying to locate her. That would be another question to ask Z.

I walked to Harrods in Knightsbridge. I didn't have a shopping list, but I always enjoyed visiting that mammoth store. I'll bet you could buy anything from a grand piano to a box of toothpicks. At the first kiosk I came to, I purchased a copy of the *London Times*. There on the front page was a picture of Baba in Cannes, having a chat with Prince Albert of Monaco and other notables who often frequent the city. I remember well my first visit to the Riviera. It was four years ago, and I'd decided to stay on a few days after completing my assignment. I'd spent so many days in Europe that I almost forgot that my official residence was in Washington, D.C.

THREE

It's a good thing I don't have a pet or any potted plants. My pied-à-terre is on Capitol Hill, in an old house, which a Senator and his wife restored about ten years ago. They occupy the upper three floors with their housekeeper and I live in the basement. I really shouldn't call it a basement; it's decorated quite nicely and from the outside, it's just another pad of one of the workers on The Hill. I never, and I mean never, have guests, with the exception when others of my profession, females, are visiting in the City. The street entrance is down four steps from the sidewalk and four more steps after a left turn under the stairs to the 1st floor. Unless I'm being tailed, I can get in and out fairly easily without being seen. There are no windows on the street side and only one in the rear that looks out on a culvert half which is below the level of the back yard. There's a rear door but it hasn't been opened since I moved in. The curtains on the front and back doors and the rear window are opaque. So from the outside, one can't tell whether the basement is or isn't occupied. My telephone is unlisted and the only two persons who have my number are my boss in D.C. and Z in London. The telephone bill is taken care of by my D.C. boss. Whenever Arlene or Baba or anyone else wants to talk with me, they must call one of the two operators, give the appropriate codes, and then they're patched through.

Through the assistance of the owner of the *37*, who devised a very ingenious way to determine the code of the day, all I need do is look at the date on my watch and manipulate a few numbers in my head. Once the operator has been given that code, she'll ask for my personal code. I wanted 007 but that, of course, was already taken.

My apartment consists of one big room with two small rear ones. There's a Pullman kitchenette, complete with a refrigerator/freezer, a stove and a microwave. Near the kitchenette is the bath: a lavatory, a john and a shower. There's a small table and two straight chairs near the kitchenette. The remainder of the room is my bedroom/TV room, with a clothes closet in one corner, a dresser and a sofa, which makes into a double bed. I can watch TV sitting on the sofa or in bed. On the rare occasion when Arlene visits, the bed is quite comfortable for both. One advantage of living alone is that I don't have to wear clothes. I've always enjoyed being naked.

The housekeeper upstairs does my small laundry load. I don't jog on the streets but have a set of weights which keeps me well toned. When I awake each morning, I do my triples (legs straight above then to the left and then the right and back down almost to the bed) for my abs before getting out of bed, then push-ups and sit-ups and finally the Marine Corps aerobic exercises. Whenever I'm on assignment or just goofing off somewhere, I try to swim. In Paris, I work out at the Marine Corps Barracks next to the Army, Navy and Air Force Club. For a man of thirty-nine, I'm proud of the way I look, especially in a tux.

After returning to my hotel room following my "shopping tour", I finished reading the *London Times* and took a shower and shaved. I looked at my watch and decided it was about time for dinner. One of my favorite places to dine in London is Langan's near Green Park. Langan's is a spacious setting with heavy green velvet curtains suspended on brass rails. On any given day or evening, one might see a member of the Royal Family, a star of stage or screen, or some other famous or infamous person. I'm usually alone but on occasion have been taken as a guest. I was about to leave my room when the phone rang.

"Hello," I said. The voice on the other end of the line said, "Please wait for His Lordship."

"Philipp, I know we're meeting in the morning, but I thought you might like to go to the theatre this evening, if you're not already engaged. I have a ticket for 'The Mouse Trap' if you've not already seen it."

"I'd be pleased to accept your thoughtful gesture. I was about to leave for dinner at Langan's and, as you know, the theatre is just around the corner. What time is the performance?"

"It begins at eight sharp. There will be a ticket for you in the name of Philipp Devon at the Box Office. Enjoy the show and I'll see you in the morning. Cheerio."

Cheerio? I've never before heard Z use that farewell greeting. Perhaps he's trying to tell me something. I wonder whom I'll be sitting next to in the theatre?

I took the Underground to Green Park and walked the half block to the restaurant. As I entered the half-full restaurant, the maître d' asked if I was alone. When I said I was, he asked me to follow him to a very nicely located small table, one with a panoramic view of the entire restaurant. I ordered a glass of the house Chardonnay. Just after my wine arrived, a gentleman approached my table and introduced himself as Señor de Bollo from Madrid. I immediately recognized the name de Bollo for it was the name Baba used when introducing herself at the Embassy in Paris. I rose as we shook hands.

"You seem to be dining alone as am I. May I invite you to share my table?"

"I don't want to appear inhospitable, but I thought I'd have a quick and light fare since I must be at the theatre at eight. I wouldn't want to rush our meal together. I hope you understand."

"What play are you seeing?" he asked. When I told him, he said, "I've seen it several times. It's wonderful. I know you'll enjoy it. Well, Cheerio." He returned to his table.

That was the second "cheerio" in less than an hour. Should I have accepted his invitation? And I never responded to the de Bollo name. I must be slipping. Then I remembered I'd told Z that I was dining at Langan's and he'd signed off with "cheerio." Get with it, Devon. It may not be too late to repair any damage you might have caused.

I rose from my table and approached Señor de Bollo's table. He was a very distinguished looking man of about sixty, tall, white hair and with a military stature. I apologized profusely for my ungracious refusal of his offer to join him.

"If it's not too late, may I accept your kind invitation? My name is Philipp Devon."

"I would be delighted." He motioned to his waiter and said, "Paul, this gentleman will be moving from his table to join me."

"Very good, Count," said Paul. "I shall be prompt in my combining the two of you."

Count? And he knew his waiter by name and the waiter knew who he is.

I seated myself with the assistance of Paul who brought over the remains of my glass of Chardonnay. When I was seated, my new dinner partner asked, "Are you familiar with the Riojas of Spain?"

I didn't want to show off my knowledge of wines, so I simply said I'd tasted quite a few but I wasn't an authority on Spanish wines. I may not be an authority but I consider myself a connoisseur. I believe, as expressed by Galileo: "Il vino era luce impasse con humore. (Wine is light held together by water.)"

"May I take the liberty of ordering a bottle for our forthcoming meal?"

"I'd be pleased if you would."

"Paul, please bring us a bottle of Montebuena Rioja, the 1982 if you have any left."

"Straightaway, sir." Paul disappeared and returned in a flash with a 1982 Montebuena Rioja, which I knew to be one of the century's finest Spanish reds. A silver tastevan was suspended from a maroon and yellow striped ribbon around his neck, into which was poured a sip of the wine. A small amount was then poured into Señor de Bollo's goblet. He checked the color, the nose and the taste and pronounced it perfect. I already knew it would be, for Baba and I drank this wine every time we were together.

"This is one of the favorite wines of my family," he said. "We drink it often, and the 1982 is probably the finest of the last half of the twentieth century. Paul, will you please bring each of us the lamb?"

Now I was really intrigued. There was the name de Bollo and the wine of which Baba and I were so fond. I'd never met Baba's husband. I always assumed she made up the name, as we all do from time to time. Then he said he and his family always enjoyed this particular wine.

"Señor de Bollo, you mentioned your family. How much family do you have?"

"Unfortunately, we have no children. I have only my wife, Baba. She is an American. We have been married for ten years."

I hardly knew what to say or how to carry forward these stunning revelations. Should I admit knowing Baba? I can't say that we work together as business associates, for the Count may not know of Baba's undercover activities. Then I remembered her picture on the front page of the morning *Times* with the caption identifying her as the Countess de

Bollo.

Our food arrived. The lamb chops were covered with a dollop of mint jelly.

"I remember seeing the picture of a beautiful young lady on the cover of this morning's *Times* talking with Prince Albert. The lady was identified as the Countess de Bollo."

"Yes," said the Count. "That is she. Unfortunately, I couldn't be with her on this trip as I have business here in London; and had I been in Cannes, I would not have had the pleasure of meeting you."

Where do I go from here? Why did he ask me to join his table? We've never before met and yet I feel that Z has put us together, so to speak. Pursue it further, Devon; it was almost curtain time. I managed to eat a few bites of the magnificent entree.

"I'd really like to extend this conversation, Count, but I must get to the theatre. Could we meet for a drink after the performance?"

"That would be nice. Perhaps you would come to my flat on Davies Street, near the Connaught." He wrote down the address, the entry code and the flat number.

"I'll be pleased to do so and I look forward to seeing you there. Thank you very much and a pleasant good evening. A bientôt."

"A tu aussi."

The walk to the theatre was only a block and a half. It was now 7:55. I asked for the ticket. With it was a small envelope. Inside, the note read, "Accept his invitation."

After the theatre, I took a taxi to the Davies Street address, in one of the better parts of London.

"Come in, Philipp. I'm glad you could come. May I offer you some more of the Rioja or would you prefer something else?"

"Whatever you're having is fine with me."

"Then let's have a liqueur. Is a Grand Marnier Centenaire all right?"

"Grand Marnier is my favorite but my budget does not allow me to drink an 1827 liqueur very often," I said sheepishly, while showing off my knowledge. I hope he doesn't suspect that I'm lying. I keep a bottle in my apartment at all times.

"Yes, the liqueur was made in 1827 and was bottled in 1927. Liqueurs do not further age after being bottled, but I presume you already knew that."

Each of us took our first sip of this magnificent digestif after clicking our glasses and almost simultaneously saying "à vôtre santé."

"Philipp, you're probably wondering how I accidentally met you at

Langan's."

"The thought crossed my mind," I replied. Several times, I thought.

"We have a mutual friend whom I've known for many years. He's a poet and a musician, and a member of The Arts Club. He spoke very highly of you and said we should get to know each other better."

My mind was in a spin. Baba's husband knows Z? Does he know that his wife works for Z? Does he know that I sometimes work directly for Z? Could he know that Z, his wife, Arlene and I worked a sting in Paris just last week? Oh, God, give me the words I need at this moment! Tell me what to say but don't let me say too much.

"I'm having lunch with this mutual friend of whom you speak tomorrow at the Club," I said hesitantly.

"Yes, I know. He told me this afternoon and suggested I meet you tonight to get better acquainted."

"Did he say why?"

"He thought that since my wife and you have been friends for many years, and I've been Z's personal Aide-de-Camp for many, many years; it would be appropriate for us to meet. I know what you may be thinking at this moment. In our business, we were taught in our first lesson of indoctrination never acknowledge one knows another associate. However, by way of further identification, let me say that I know you've spent two days on Mykonos this past week and you're concerned about a certain Mr. Hargrave."

It was as if a ton of bricks had been lifted from my chest. He knows everything about me. He hasn't, however, answered the one question I still have.

"Does your wife know about your work with our mutual friend?"

"Yes, of course, my dear Philipp. Our marriage is a marriage of convenience that was suggested by Z to satisfy the need for Baba's being able to rub elbows with European royalty and the most powerful of the American elite. Baba and I'd been friends for several years before we were married and we both agreed each of us could be more effective in our work if the world knew us as husband and wife. I've come to love her very much and I believe she loves me.

"As for Mr. Hargrave, that is a different and complex situation. Our problem with him is that he is a double agent. He is charming, refined, cultured in the arts, dresses elegantly and has contacts all over the world on whom he can call at any time. Mr. Hargrave, however, has one major negative. He is bi-sexual. He has a list of females who can attest to his virility as well as a smaller list of males who can testify to his voracious appetite for men."

This information about Mr. Hargrave created as many questions as it answered. What is his relationship with my chef friend in Stockholm? What is his relationship with Sophie and with Nikolas? Why was he "stalking" me? Do Baba and Arlene know about Mr. Hargrave? I finished my liqueur and then stood up to leave.

"I suppose I should be going back to my hotel so I can digest everything you've told me. I really don't know that I can contribute any additional information you don't already know. I thank you for our time together this evening and I look forward to meeting you again soon."

"Thank you, Philipp. It was a pleasure meeting you. Z said I'd like you and I do. I regret that so much of what I've revealed to you this evening came as a shock. However, in our business, one plays everything close to the vest. Thank you for coming. Good night."

I left the apartment and walked to the Underground. When I exited at Sloan Square, I wanted to walk awhile and continue to mull over everything I'd learned this evening. I accepted all the "facts" that the Count told me, but there were several pieces of the puzzle that just didn't fit together. Being honest with your co-workers in this business is absolutely necessary. However, that doesn't mean one has to tell everything one knows particularly if it isn't pertinent to one's current assignment. And what benefit would I gain if I let Baba know that I'd met her husband? And I certainly can't ask my chef friend, or Sophie or Nikolas what they know about Mr. Hargrave.

When I got back to my room, there was a slip of paper under my door saying that my morning meeting had been pushed up to 11:00 instead of 11:30. No signature or name. I didn't sleep well. I wonder why? I couldn't get my mind to relax and push aside all the information I'd learned since my last good sleep on Mykonos. I conjured up some frightening things. I had vivid pictures in my mind of certain players being together. And the really big one that shook me the most was the thought of being stalked by Mr. Hargrave. I looked at my watch. 3:15. I got up and took a shower, then lay back across the bed. The next thing I realized was the sun peeking through the curtained windows. I looked at my watch again. 8:45.

I got up, shaved, dressed in a business suit and went to a small restaurant in Belgravia for a light breakfast of toast and coffee. I decided I needed to walk, so I began the rather long trek to Z's office. By the time I arrived, my watch read 10:50. As I entered the outer office, the receptionist recognized me and smiled. I gave her the morning's code as she opened the door to the inner sanctum. Z's Secretary greeted me with a hearty "Good morning" and said I should go right in.

Z's office is spacious yet cozy. Three walls are lined with volumes both old and current. The carpet is dark maroon and the furniture is sparse. Z was seated behind the rather large desk, which he'd told me was a gift from Prince Philip. There were two straight chairs in front of his desk. The Count sat in the one on the right. I was offered the other one.

"I hope you slept well, Philipp; however, knowing you, I rather doubt it," Z said. "The Count and I have been reviewing everything that has happened in the past week concerning you and Mr. Hargrave. I felt you needed to hear two sides of this situation, so that's why I asked the Count to brief you last evening."

I shifted ever-so-slightly in my chair anticipating the full explanation I was about to get.

"Mr. Hargrave is a complex individual, a man of many talents. He is also a multilingual, effete snob who was recruited while still at Oxford. After a few years working with us, we suspected he was rather rapacious in his sexual activities, and his social-climbing became known to too many people. I was about to call him in for a 'dressing down' when one of my associates in this office happened to be attending a soirée in Greenwich to which Mr. Hargrave was also invited. While looking for the water closet, my associate opened a door and found Mr. Hargrave in bed with both a man and a woman, a double *flagrante delicto*, if you will. There really was no way to explain away what he'd seen and Mr. Hargrave admitted to me he was bi-sexual. So I resorted to the only course of action open to me. I threatened either to expose him or to have him become a double agent. Understandably, he chose the latter."

This was the man who was so nice to Sophie and me at dinner? Now it became clear why Mr. Hargrave and Nikolas went out on the town together. I really shouldn't think that, for I've no proof. But I thought it just the same.

Z continued. "Because of his knowledge of and fluency in so many languages, I determined he'd be an ideal person for the enemy to lure away from our organization. So I began the process."

"Pardon me, but I need to interrupt in order to satisfy a burning question. Is this information about Mr. Hargrave known by the Countess, by Arlene or by the Stockholm chef?"

"Only by the chef," was the reply. "He'd been keeping tabs on Mr. Hargrave's operations in Stockholm, which appears to be his main city of contact. You see, Mr. Hargrave only moved to Stockholm after I recruited him to be a double agent. He originally was from Broadway in the

Cotswold and later, when he came on board with us, he moved to London."

"I feel better about having that information on the chef, since it was he who originally introduced me to Mr. Hargrave while I was on assignment in Stockholm and was a guest at his home."

"So he informed me. If I may continue," said Z.

"I apologize for the interruption."

"After Mr. Hargrave agreed to his new assignment, I contacted one of our plants in the enemy camp and told him of the arrangement with Mr. Hargrave. The plant 'casually' met him at a soirée in Stockholm, shortly after he'd moved there. We supplied Mr. Hargrave with accurate but stale information at first to pass on; and later, as his association with the enemy developed, we gave him snippets of relatively new data, some of which was already known by them but some was just being developed. As their confidence in him increased, he was asked by the enemy to take a 'vacation' to Mykonos, where he was to make contact with Sophie, who, incidentally knows nothing of his association with us or with the enemy. The contact with Sophie was to get her to put in a good word with her former schoolmate, the Greek Minister of Culture, his ultimate target.

"Fortunately for us, when he first arrived on Mykonos and was staying at Sophie's hotel, he became a 'good friend' of Sophie's brother, Nikolas,

who I feel certain doesn't dare tell his sister about his trysts with men as

well as women. On either his first or second visit to Mykonos, he met your

Greek Officer friend, who at that time was dating Sophie off and on. The

Greek Officer -- I believe you call him Dimmie -- is unaware of Mr.

Hargrave's job, his sexual orientation or his intent to make contact with

the Minister in Athens. There appears to be a plan afoot to replace the

Minister with one from the enemy camp. This, of course, I've assumed."

That clears up another of my concerns. I breathed a silent sigh of

relief. Dimmie and I had become good friends and I hoped he wasn't

involved in this twisted plot.

"The next point of discussion is whether or not you should tell the

Countess you've met her husband. What is your feeling about this,

Philipp?"

"Well, as you both know, the Countess and I have worked together on

several assignments. Also, I'm a great admirer of her as a friend. I don't

see that telling her of having met her husband would alter our relationship

in either a positive or a negative way."

"Both the Count and I agree. However, to clear the air, so to speak, the

Count has suggested you come to Madrid on a supposed assignment from this office and be the houseguest of them both. Of course, the invitation would be extended by the Countess."

The Count said, "You would be most welcome, Philipp."

"Thank you, sir. When should I expect to be invited?"

"The Countess will remain in Cannes until next Saturday, at which time she'll return to Spain. I'll be in touch with her and let her know of your assignment. I'll also suggest that it might be good for you to be a houseguest at the villa; and since you also are an old American friend, she might want to plan a dinner party for you. I'll also suggest to her a few people that I'd like for you to meet at the dinner. After you arrive in Spain and have been greeted at the villa, I'll be in contact with you immediately, to inform you your presence has been requested by your boss in Washington and you're to report as soon as possible."

It all sounded both reasonable and convincing. I was enthusiastic. "When should I expect a call from the Countess?"

"I'll telephone her on Saturday evening and ask her to call you immediately because you'll be leaving for Madrid next Monday. The time is now 11:55. My car will take us to the Club. The Count has other business, preventing him from joining us. Shall we go?"

We left the inner sanctum and Z and I continued to the garage. The

Count remained in Z's outer office and planned to leave by the front of the building. Z's chauffeur drove us to The Club.

FOUR

We entered the Club as the chauffeur drove away. I'd been in the Club with Z on several occasions so I knew what to expect. In the rear of the lobby and directly in front of the main entrance is a glass-enclosed arboretum filled with innumerable species of plants, mostly flowerless greenery, kept moist like a rain forest; a most pleasant greeting as one enters. We proceeded to the dining room, a large area with tables for two, four, six and eight, each place appointed with a napkin creased and standing on the plate. The crystal and silver gleamed.

When we were seated at Z's usual table, the waiter approached and welcomed His Lordship, acknowledging my presence. Without asking, the waiter placed a bottle of still water on the table. He proceeded to tell us the specials of the day. I knew Z preferred a Cobb Salad but I also knew he'd wait until the waiter finished his dissertation before ordering. He'd instructed me once before that it's impolite to cut short the presentation of the waiter. It's his duty to tell you about the specials and it's appropriate for you to listen, even if you've already decided on your meal.

After the waiter finished, Z said, "That is a splendid and diverse selection but I believe I'll have a Cobb Salad with bleu cheese dressing."

The waiter turned to me. "I'll have the same, please."

When the waiter left the table, Z said, "Philipp, I received a call from your boss in Washington, asking me if you'd completed the Embassy assignment satisfactorily. I assured him you had and The Ministry of Defense was most appreciative of the way the whole situation was brought to a successful conclusion. I told him of your proposed visit to Madrid and how that would take only a few days. He was in agreement with my assessment of the situation regarding the de Bollos and approved of your following through as I've previously outlined. He requested you report to him as soon as possible upon your return to Washington."

I acknowledged my understanding of the situation but didn't know how to approach the next topic tactfully, so I just dove in.

"Where is Arlene at this moment?"

"She is safe and awaiting her next assignment. After the Ambassador's luncheon on the day you left for Athens, she received permission from me to take some time off and relax undisturbed. I asked her where she'd like to go. Her first response troubled me. She said she needed to get away, to be by herself, and to think over her future work with the Agency. I asked her to explain. She said she wanted to settle down, lead a more normal life and not live in a constant state of not knowing where she might be tomorrow. At this moment, she's probably lounging on the shore of the Mediterranean in Marbella and is registered at the Andalusia Plaza under the name of Beatrice Devon."

I could hardly believe what I was hearing. Arlene was in Spain, on the Costa del Sol, registered in a resort hotel, using my name. I looked at Z quizzically.

He smiled and said, "If you catch the 3:00 P.M. flight from Heathrow, you can be in Madrid in time to catch the evening commuter plane to Marbella. You should arrive in time for a late dinner. I've informed her you were coming and to expect you later this evening. Here is your ticket to Madrid." Z handed me an envelope containing the ticket and 2,000 dollars. "Remember, when the Countess calls, you're to accept her invitation and tell her you'll be in Madrid on Monday evening. This will give you a few days on the beach, or wherever, with your Arlene. I'll telephone you on Monday evening, or at the latest Tuesday morning, with the urgent message from your boss, strongly requesting your presence in Washington as soon as possible."

Even though we'd not yet been served, I excused myself and took a taxi to the hotel. I gathered my bag and my briefcase and ran to the Underground which would be the shortest time span to Heathrow. I could hardly believe, before the evening was over, I'd be in the arms of my darling Arlene.

The flight to Madrid was the slowest flight I'd ever taken. However, we arrived at the designated ETA. I took a connecting bus to the Commuter Terminal and purchased a round-trip ticket to Marbella. The flight to Marbella seemed interminable; I was uncomfortably anxious the entire trip. When we landed at Marbella, I started toward the terminal when I recognized her running to meet me. We embraced as our lips met. We just looked at each other. We were both teary, but they were tears of extreme joy. We took a taxi to the hotel; I didn't bother to check in but went immediately to her room. In just a few minutes, we were entwined in each other's embrace and lost in ecstasy. I've never before been so thrilled to be with someone as I was at that moment being with my Arlene. The night seemed to go on forever, which was fine with me. When the rays of the morning sun lit the room, I realized that we'd been making love for almost five hours. I was thoroughly exhausted. I decided to get up, shave and shower; but as I began to slip away, she wouldn't let me go.

At 8:10, I awoke again. This time I managed to slip out of bed without waking her. After my shower, I came back in the room. She was still asleep so I put on a shirt, a pair of trousers over my pouch and sandals and went downstairs to get a paper and to order breakfast in the room after registering at the desk.

As I let myself in quietly, I heard the shower running and again the strains of "O, What a Beautiful Morning" wafted through the air. When she stepped out of the shower and entered the bedroom, I was overcome by her beauty – the silkiness of her skin, the shape of her breasts, the seductiveness of her movements. Within seconds I had my shirt off and had begun to undo my belt when there was a knock at the door. Knowing that it was our breakfast waiter, I approached the door as Arlene hurried back into the bathroom. The waiter entered our room and placed the tray on the table near the window. Seeing a half-dressed man and smelling the soap and perfume of a woman and eyeing the rumpled bed, he smiled with a broad smile and gave me a knowing wink. I signed the tab and gave him a few dollars and opened the door for his departure. He asked, in perfect Castilian, should I need anything he would be honored to oblige me.

"Gracias, señor. Muchas gracias."

"De nada."

When I closed the door and turned around, Arlene was already seated at the table, completely nude. I finished disrobing and sat down opposite her so we both had a great view, not only of the ocean but also of each other. Even though I was ravenous from the lack of food, I couldn't take my eyes off this gorgeous woman. We ate in silence the toast, butter and jam and slowly sipped the dark roasted Spanish coffee. Hardly a word was spoken.

Finally, she said, "Philipp, I love you and I'm so glad we're here together."

"I love you too, Arlene, and I'm thrilled to be with you also."

We finished our coffee and by a silent, mutual agreement, went back to bed after I had placed the DO NOT DISTURB sign on the door.

We made love again and neither of us seemed tired. I hadn't realized, until that very moment, how much I really loved Arlene and how much I wanted to spend the rest of my life with her. I sensed she felt the same about me. Before I fully realized what I was saying, I just blurted it out.

"Will you please marry me?"

She looked me in the eye and with a kiss on the lips, she began what I was afraid would be a turndown.

"My dearest Philipp, you know I love you very much and I'm the happiest when I'm in your arms. We both are living in the same world of deception and extreme risk and I fear for your life the most whenever I'm not with you. I've been giving a lot of thought to my future in this business. I've discussed it with Z but haven't decided what my best course of action should be. I would love to be Mrs. Philipp Devon or Mrs. Whatever-Your-Real-Name-Is but I cannot accept your proposal until I've decided on my future.

"I love you very much, dear Philipp, and I'm overwhelmingly happy when we're together. You are a great lover, so tender and yet so forceful, so masculine, yet your feminine traits show through when you're with me, and I love that. Each time we're apart, I can't wait until we're together again. You are handsome, intelligent, caring, attentive and sweet. Yes, I want to be your wife, but you must give me some time to sort out my future. Can you understand what I'm trying to say?"

Although I understood too well, I didn't want to hear it or deal with it. I loved this woman more than I've ever loved any other woman. She's everything I could want in a life companion. But I also must respect her position in the Agency and the dilemma she faced. I had to choose my words very carefully.

"Arlene, I understand everything you've said and I respect the decisions you're now wrestling with. I'll be as patient as I'm physically able to be. When I'm not with you, I'm a wreck. You fill my every waking moment with thoughts of our intimacy and my dreams are the same each night, dreams of our lovemaking. Arlene, I love you so much."

"Oh, Philipp, what shall I do? I like my job. I like working with you and Baba. But I also want to be with you more. What shall I do?"

"Perhaps we should continue as we are now, co-workers for Z, and lovers when we can be together. If that arrangement is acceptable to you, I'll be as patient as is humanly possible until you tell me you've made your decision."

"Philipp, my dearest one, you are the kindest, most thoughtful man I've ever known, and I love you more than you can ever know." We kissed again, long and passionately. However, I realized that she needed some time to herself so I put on my swimsuit, took a large beach towel from the bathroom and said I'd go lie on the beach for a while, to cool off!

I took the elevator to the basement and entered the corridor which extended underground from the hotel to the beach, which was crowded with both men and women, some of whom had disposed of their bras and were sunning on their blankets *au naturel*. I spread my towel out on the sand not very near anyone else. I dropped off to sleep from exhaustion but was awakened by a voice, which informed me I had an urgent telephone call. As I stood up and looked at my watch, I realized I'd been on the beach for more than an hour. I retraced my steps through the corridor, used my room key to enter the elevator and went to our room. Letting myself in quietly, I saw Arlene asleep. She was not wearing anything. I went into the bathroom and called the desk and asked that my call be put through. It was Baba.

"My dear Philipp, I am so happy to have found you. I understand that Arlene is with you. How wonderful. I also understand that you have an assignment in Madrid in a few days. I would like to invite you to stay with the Count and me here at our villa. It will be so nice to see you again and to have you know my husband." Her tone of voice was the usual sincere one.

"It's so nice of you to call and extend the invitation. I heartily accept. I propose to arrive in Madrid on Monday on the afternoon flight from Marbella; I believe it arrives about five. Oh, by the way, I've just seen in *OHLA!* your visit to Cannes. It was a very positive article and the photographs of you were magnificent, as they always are."

"Thank you, dear Philipp. You always know how to make a girl feel young and important. I shall have our chauffeur waiting for you at the airport when you arrive. His name is Philip also, but with only one p at the end. Will Arlene be coming with you or will she stay in Marbella?"

"I believe she is officially on vacation for a few more days. After that, I really don't know what her schedule is."

"Please give her my best regards and I look forward to seeing you on Monday. Ta ta."

When I finished the conversation, I opened the door to the bedroom. Arlene was still sleeping. I re-closed the door and stepped into the shower. After getting all the sand out of my body hair, I dried off and re-opened the door. She was still asleep. I slipped in the bed beside her and lay quietly on my back. I soon fell asleep.

When I awakened, I lay there thinking about the many pleasures I'd enjoyed in the past twenty-four hours with the one I love the most. The bathroom door opened. Arlene stepped into the bedroom eyeing my torso. She came over to the bed and took each of my hands, placing them on the headboard. She put her right index finger to her lips and quietly said "shhh." Then it began. Arlene was quite adept at massaging. She began with my hairy toes, then the feet, then the ankles and on up until every part of me had been kneaded and properly taken care of, including my scalp. I was jelly in her hands. And then to complete the massage, her still wet tresses were draped over my entire body, starting with my face, my chest and so on down to my toes. I was tingling all over. I knew from previous experiences I wasn't to move my hands until given permission to do so. The suspense was killing me. Finally, she took my left hand and placed it on my chest. Then the right hand was similarly placed. She leaned over and kissed my stomach as I gently grabbed her head and brought it up to mine. I kissed her on the lips and then whispered, as gently and as quietly as I knew how, "Thank you." We embraced for a long while and then we both fell asleep in each other's arms.

At 8:30, my wrist alarm began to vibrate. I rolled over on my side and realized that Arlene wasn't in the bed, neither was she in the shower. However, the balcony doors were open and the breeze was coming in briskly. I stepped onto the balcony in my usual state of undress and there was Arlene, equally undressed, staring out over the ocean. I sat down in the nearby chair and took her hand. It was then I noticed the tears. She'd been crying; her cheeks were wet and her eyes were red. I said nothing but squeezed her hand gently.

"Oh, my dear Philipp, I love you so much and I want to be with you all the time, but I feel that I need to have another talk with Z before I make a decision about my future."

I thought her decision was the right one and I told her so. I told her of

Baba's call and why Z wanted me to go to Madrid. I also told her my boss in Washington had requested my presence as soon as I could break away. I asked her how long she planned to be in Marbella and did she have enough money with her? She assured me she did and that she planned to return to London on either Tuesday or Wednesday. I suggested we dress for dinner, casually, of course, and have a drink at Dorothy's British Pub before dining at a restaurant of her choice. She liked the suggestions, so we both went back in the bedroom and watched each other get dressed. She laughed as she had often before when I put on my crotch pouch, saying that I really didn't need an enhancement in that area. I thanked her for the compliment and complimented her for not wearing a bra under her sheer embroidered blouse. When we'd finished dressing and descended to the lobby, I asked the Concierge for a taxi to Dorothy's. In a short time, we arrived at the Pub.

Inside was crowded and noisy as usual. Dorothy was from Cornwall and had come, with her teenage son, to Marbella after the death of her husband. That was about twenty-five years ago. Dorothy was now about sixty-five and Thomas, her son, about forty. The two of them had made this place the favorite watering hole for all expatriates in Marbella. The décor reminded one of old England. We each ordered a Guinness and found a table for two in the rear. When Thomas brought over the stouts, he said he thought he remembered me and asked wasn't I an American working in London? How he knew that bit of information I didn't learn until later. I complimented him on his super memory and introduced him to Arlene. He told her she was quite a looker. Arlene liked that. We'd almost finished our second round when Dorothy came over to say hello. I introduced her to Arlene. I asked her for a recommendation for dinner. She said the dining room at the Andalusia Plaza had recently been refurbished and a new chef engaged, about whom the locals were raving, not only about his cooking but also about his good looks. Dorothy winked at Arlene. I thanked her for her recommendation and told her how good it was to see her and Thomas again.

"Don't be such a stranger in these parts, my dear. Happy to meet you, ma'am."

I asked Arlene if dinner at the hotel was acceptable. She agreed and said she'd like to get a glimpse of this chef everyone seems to be raving about.

"I haven't seen a good-looking man in quite a while," she said as she grinned and blew me a kiss.

We hailed a taxi and went back to the hotel.

Arlene and I entered the dining room at about 10:15. There weren't many diners at that hour; it was too early for the Spanish. As we were seated, I asked our waiter if we might speak to the new chef.

"Si, Señor."

While we were looking over the menu and trying to decide what wine to order, Arlene said "Look coming out of the kitchen." As I looked up, I saw one of the most handsome young men I've ever seen. He was over six feet tall, blond and very muscular. He had the traditional toque set at a slightly jaunty angle. When he arrived at our table, I introduced us as Mr. and Mrs. Devon. He said his name was Sven Christen. I was visibly shaken, as was Arlene. "I come from Stockholm," he added.

"I have a friend in Stockholm who is also a chef, and his name is also Sven Christen."

"He's my father. It really is a small world, isn't it? How did you know I was the chef here?"

"We have friends here in Marbella who raved about the menu and the presentations by the new chef. I certainly didn't know that the son of my good friend in Stockholm was the new chef when I asked the waiter to ask you to come to our table. Will you sit with us a moment?"

He sat facing Arlene, who by this time was almost drooling.

He continued. "I'd been apprenticed to my father and had expected to join him at the Grand Hotel Dining Room permanently when this position opened up, and now I'm the Head Chef here. I believe one of my father's good friends knows the owner of this hotel, or something like that."

"Well, it's certainly a pleasure meeting you. Please give my best regards to your father when next you speak with him. I wish I were staying longer but I must leave soon. My wife, however, will be staying until Tuesday or perhaps even later. I'd appreciate it, if you have any spare time, you could spend some of it with her."

"Oh, I would like that very much, Mr. Devon. Mrs. Devon is a very lovely lady and I do love lovely ladies." Arlene lit up like a torch.

"We were trying to decide on the wine when you arrived. What entree would you recommend this evening and which wine should I order to accompany your recommendation?"

"I'd recommend the tournedos served with a clear broth and a simple garnish of mild herbs. For the wine, the best to accompany the tournedos would be a Rioja called Montebuena. If we have any of the 1982 left in our cellar, I'll retrieve a bottle for you. Will that be satisfactory to you both?"

"A splendid selection and the wine you suggest is an outstanding choice. Thank you, Sven. It was a pleasure meeting you, and don't forget to tell you father about our encounter."

"I'll remember. Thank you and bueno apetito," he said as he left our table.

I looked at Arlene in total amazement. "He is Sven's son and he recommends the wine which Baba and I always drink when we're on assignment together. There's more here than meets the eye. I believe I should check with Z. Will you please excuse me? Have the waiter pour your glass. I'll return shortly."

When I returned to our room, I reached Z almost immediately, even at that hour. I told him of our experiences beginning with a restaurant recommendation from Dorothy. Z then filled me in on quite a few facts. At the end of our conversation he asked to be remembered to both Dorothy and Thomas and, of course, to Arlene.

When I returned to the table, the wine, a 1982 Montebuena Rioja, had arrived and Arlene was sipping her first taste. "His Lordship sends his best regards to you," I said casually.

"Is that all he said?"

"He also said young Sven had been in training with his father for about two years. A situation arose in Stockholm when a man, known to the

Agency, and whose sexual proclivities ran to both men and women, began following young Sven."

"I can see why," chimed in Arlene.

"Z thought it best to get young Sven out of Stockholm and to continue his training, both as a chef and as a trainee, here in Marbella. When the opening occurred here, and Z had been so notified by Dorothy, Z discreetly inquired through Dorothy whether or not a highly trained chef with a superior recommendation could be interviewed for the job. When Sven arrived for his interview and prepared his first meal for the manager, he was hired on the spot. Concerning the wine, the 1982 Montebuena Rioja has become a signal among certain members of our organization. When Sven recommended it to you and me, it was his way of saying he was in on the game, assuming I'd recognize it since I was a friend of his father."

I stopped my briefing and tasted the wine. It was magnificent as always. When the entree arrived and we both had tasted it, we agreed that the chef's choice was a superb one and the wine complimented it to perfection. Our choice for dessert was a flan followed by Spanish coffee. There's enough caffeine in Spanish coffee to keep one awake all night, but I had no intention of sleeping that night.

After I signed the check and added a generous gratuity for both the waiter and the sommelier, Arlene and I proceeded to our room. She thanked me for a wonderful evening and again for last night and for asking Sven to look after her when I'm gone. This last "thank you" was done with tongue-in-cheek as we both were removing our cumbersome clothes. When I removed my crotch pouch, Arlene asked mischievously whether or not I thought Sven might have one also.

"Who cares?" I said.

The moon was streaming through the open windows and a slight breeze was just what I needed to cool me down. The excitement of learning the facts from Z, plus the wine, which I so much enjoy, and of course through it all, being with the one I love the most, had caused my ardor to be ignited almost beyond my control. However, Arlene had her techniques for doing just the right thing in bed, and so long as I took her lead, I was okay.

The Spanish coffee worked on us both as I'd anticipated. I was feeling at the peak of my emotions. Nothing could go wrong now. And then I remembered I must fly from Madrid to Washington on Monday and would be away from Arlene for I didn't know how long. She must be having the same anxious feelings, for our love making intensified.

Lying on my back with the cool breeze blowing gently over my body and Arlene sleeping soundly by my side, my mind was once again cluttered, planning the things I must do over the next few days. This morning, Arlene and I'll probably spend a few hours on the beach tanning. Then, in mid-afternoon, I'll take the commuter flight to Madrid where Philip, with only one final p, will meet me and drive me to the villa. I tried to get some sleep but was unable to do so.

I looked at my watch just after nine. The sun was going to be quite hot today. I must remember to take some lotion. I went into the bathroom and used the phone to order some breakfast. When I came back into the bedroom, Arlene was sitting up in the bed, watching my every move.

"You're so gorgeous," she said.

"Hey, that's my line."

She hopped out of bed, grabbed me for a big hug and one of the most passionate kisses I've ever experienced. We stood there for what seemed an eternity until there was a knock at the door. Breakfast had arrived.

After the tray was placed on the table and I'd disrobed, Arlene came out of the bathroom with her hair wrapped in a towel and nothing on. My first thought was to skip breakfast and go back to bed. But I knew we had to talk about her future before I left this afternoon. I poured us coffee as we walked out on the balcony *au naturel*. The footprint of the hotel is perpendicular to the beach and between each balcony is a floor-to-ceiling partition. No one can be seen from any other balcony or from the ground below because of the covered railing.

The coffee was hot and strong. I had a piece of bread with mine, but Arlene took hers straight.

"My dearest Arlene," I began, "when I leave this afternoon for Madrid and then shortly thereafter for America, I have no idea how long it'll be before we see each other again." I paused and looked her directly in the eye. She ran her hand over the hair on my chest and my stomach and then came and sat in my lap.

"You know I love you very much, my dear Philipp," she said in a whisper, "but I must sort out my personal conflicts before I take the big step of marriage. I want to be with you the rest of my life. You also know I like my job and I'm damn good at what I do. Also, I'm British and you're American and where we'll make our home is another of the conflicts I have.

"As you also know, my mother is only sixty-eight but has Alzheimer's, about which I can do nothing. That preys on my mind daily. When I visit her, she doesn't know who I am. Since my father passed away, I've felt the sole responsibility of looking after her needs, even though she is being completely taken care of in the nursing home. I have a little money stashed away but it's not a lot. If we get married, you'd be away on assignment, the same as now. You're about to leave for an indeterminate period. Oh, my dearest Philipp, please help me, please." Her tears began to flow.

I got up slowly from the chair, lifting her in my arms and carrying her to our bed. I gently placed her on the bed and lay down beside her. I was stroking her hair and tearing up at the same time.

"My dearest Arlene, the decision is yours and whatever it is, I'll look forward to being with you as often and as long as I can. The only reason I proposed marriage was I wanted to seal our relationship permanently. Now that you know my feelings on that matter, we both know we can still be together, married or not. So please, don't cry. The decision is quite simple. We can postpone the formality of a wedding until some later date when either you or I or both of us have decided to terminate our current jobs and go live together on some remote island not owned by either Britain or America." She laughed and wiped her eyes.

"Oh, my dearest Philipp, you always know exactly what to say to make me feel comfortable and completely at your command," she said, smiling at my growing erection. We decided not to go to the beach after all. I was more than eager to be "commanded."

When it was time for me to get dressed, I asked Arlene if she'd like to come with me to the airport. She said she would, so we both got dressed and took a taxi. We held hands the entire trip. When we arrived at the terminal, I paid the driver the fare both ways and instructed him to take "my wife" back to the hotel. Arlene didn't get out of the taxi. I leaned over and kissed her tenderly as she began to cry.

"Thank you, my dearest Philipp, for being so understanding."

I waved to her as the taxi pulled away, and went inside.

FIVE

The short flight to Madrid was uneventful as I'd expected. I didn't try to read. Instead I thought about the wonderful days I'd spent with my beloved Arlene. As we landed, I noticed a large black Mercedes parked near the outer gate. With my luggage in one hand and my briefcase in the other, I approached the driver.

"Señor Devon?"

"Si."

And in perfect English, he introduced himself as Philip. I told him my name was also Philipp but with a double p at the end. He laughed. When my luggage was stowed and I was seated in the rear seat with my briefcase at my side, we left the airport and headed south.

"How far is it to the villa?"

"It'll take us about one hour. The roads are quite good."

He closed the glass between us, which allowed me to review my orders and to be sure of the words I'd speak. Philip seemed to be about thirty and looked quite fit is his black chauffeur's uniform. He was clean shaven with a heavy shadow. He might be a bodyguard, I thought, for either the Count or Baba when they are somewhere dangerous. He wore dark glasses of the style seen on the Riviera. I assumed they were a gift from Baba.

The countryside was beautiful. We passed several walled villas but didn't pass any car or see any people on the road.

"This appears to be a rather out-of-the-way area of Spain," I said after tapping on the glass, which Philip opened. "How far is the villa from Madrid?"

"About two hours," was his reply. I remarked that every trip in Spain appears to be measured in hours rather than in distances. He laughed, but made no further comment. I sat back as he closed the glass.

In the haze of the evening, I could see up ahead what appeared to be a small village. As we neared the collection of buildings, I realized it was the homes and work places of the people who were employed by the de Bollos. The Mercedes turned into a nicely manicured allée of beautifully trimmed trees leading to the villa, which I saw in the distance. About fifty yards along the road, a pair of gates automatically opened and as quickly, closed behind us in a pincer-like movement. The car stopped in front of the villa. There stood Baba and the Count both dressed in the typical attire of wealthy Spaniards: he with riding trousers and boots and a leather sleeveless jacket over a long-sleeved shirt and she in a similar attire: long-sleeved shirt and skirt over boots. Philip opened the door and retrieved my bag.

"My dear Philipp," said Baba. "It is such a pleasure to welcome you to our home." I took her hand and kissed it, actually touching my lips to her skin. "I have the pleasure of introducing you to my dear husband, the Count de Bollo."

"The pleasure is all mine, sir," I said with the formality of meeting royalty for the first time.

"Please call me Francisco, if I may call you Philipp, with a double p at the end," he said with a smile.

"Thank you, Francisco. You and Baba are so gracious to welcome me to your home," I said as we entered the foyer. "This is magnificent," I commented, looking around to either side and up the staircase which spread before me.

"Your bags will be taken to your suite," said Francisco as we entered the library to the left of the entry hall. "Would you care for a cocktail or do you prefer wine?"

Baba spoke up. "Philipp loves the Montebuena Rioja as we do, my dear. He and I have enjoyed a bottle together in Stockholm, oh, so many years ago." She continued. "Isn't he just as I'd described him to you: tall, fit, handsome and almost as good at what he does as I," she said with a slight smile on her lips.

"Baba tells me you are on assignment here in Spain," said Francisco. "She also said that since you'll be meeting some very important people on this assignment, she wants to give a dinner party this week in your honor, to which several of them will be invited. She received a small list from Z."

I was feeling better all the time. Francisco was aware of my and Baba's associations in the past, and from his last comment, he also indicated that we all knew Z. So everyone seemed to be on the same page. And now that I'd been "introduced" to the Count, we could all talk freely.

About the time the maître d' announced dinner would be served at nine, the telephone rang. Answering it promptly, he said to Baba, "It is for you, Señora."

"I shall take it in my office," she said as she left the room. After she'd gone, Francisco said to me, "That went rather well, don't you think?" I told him I now felt I had all the players in the right positions and everyone knew the whole team.

Baba re-entered the room, crestfallen. "That was Z," she said. "He is taking you away from us, just as you've arrived. He wants to speak with you now. Frederico will show you the way," nodding to the attendant standing nearby.

I excused myself and went to the phone.

"I thought it best to tell Baba first and then you, so she'd know it was really official. I told her you must leave tomorrow morning. There is a ticket waiting for you at the airport desk for your ten o'clock flight to Dulles. Have a nice trip. Cheerio."

I hung up the phone and returned to the library looking as crestfallen as Baba looked when she'd received the news.

"What about your assignment in Madrid and the dinner party I wanted to give?" she asked.

"What can I say? This isn't the first assignment I've had that never got off the ground. Z said my boss in Washington wants me there pronto, for a meeting scheduled in the Pentagon at eight on Wednesday morning. I regret this early departure, for I was looking forward to your dinner party. Francisco, I feel we've met like two ships passing in the night. We must meet again soon and talk about baseball." Baba looked puzzled. Francisco assured her it was just an inside joke between us men.

Dinner was to be casual, just the three of us. Frederico showed me to my suite. The bedroom had a real double bed, one in which I could sleep straight. The bathroom had all the amenities of a five-star hotel in America. The sitting area had several comfortable-looking chairs. I quickly shucked my clothes and took a long and most satisfying shower. I lay down on the bed and looked at my watch. 8:10. I set the alarm for 8:45 and closed my eyes.

When the alarm rang, I put on my "uniform": my white, drip-dry trousers, but left my pouch in my briefcase; the white embroidered shirt I'd bought on Mykonos, even though Arlene said my chest hair showed through; and my brown Zelli loafers. I went downstairs and entered the dining room where Baba and Francisco were being seated by two servants.

The dining room, also enormous, had a long table that could comfortably seat sixteen. Over the fireplace was a carved wooden coat-of-arms colored in faded shades of blue, green, red and gold. The high-backed chairs were cushioned in antique tapestry.

After we were seated, the wine was poured. It was Montebuena. The light repast was an absolute treat. When the entree dishes had been cleared, in front of each of us was placed a flan with lightly toasted almonds and an almond syrup glaze. The cheese was a goat cheese with which I wasn't familiar but later learned had been made at the villa. Baba announced that coffee and liqueurs would be served in the library.

When we were seated, Francisco asked what liqueur would I like. I said I preferred Grand Marnier.

"Will a Grand Marnier Centenaire be acceptable?" he asked with a twinkle in his eye. I readily accepted his offer.

"What time is your flight?" asked Francisco.

"Ten o'clock."

"You should rise about six," he said, "giving yourself an hour to shower, shave and pack. Come down to breakfast at seven and Philip will be ready to take you to the airport at seven-thirty. Baba, we really should let Philipp get to bed, don't you think?"

Good nights were said all around. When I was alone in my bedroom, I stripped and crawled on top of the big double, having set my alarm for 6:00.

The night passed quickly. I arose, showered and shaved and, since I was already packed, I had a few minutes to meditate on the state of my life. I assured myself I was doing the right thing concerning Arlene, but I couldn't get it out of my mind that I should quit this crazy business and marry her and live happily ever after, wherever she chose. I went downstairs. As I entered the dining room, Francisco was seated at the head of the table. Baba was nowhere in sight. Anticipating my question he replied, "She's sleeping in." As my coffee was poured and the pan tostados (toasted breads) were served, Francisco handed me an envelope. "This is from Z." It contained ten 100-dollar bills. I put them in my trousers pocket and asked for a second cup of coffee.

"I'm very pleased you were able to come to my home," said Francisco. "You must come again."

"Thank you for your help but most of all for your friendship," I said as we rose and shook hands. He accompanied me to the car where Philip was waiting.

The flight was not crowded. A direct flight had been arranged as opposed to the circuitous route I usually took.

"No, thank you," I said to the stewardess when offered something to drink. I looked in my briefcase and counted the ten bills again. What I hadn't previously seen was a very small folded note, which read, "Thank you, my new friend." It was signed "Francisco."

Eight hours later, we touched down at Dulles International outside D.C. I took a cab to a corner two blocks from my house. This was my usual procedure whenever I arrived from overseas. One can never be too careful. I walked the two blocks, and after checking to see there apparently was no one watching, I entered my apartment.

It was so good to be home again. Everything was as I'd left it, even the shim I'd placed in the front door. The refrigerator was almost empty, as usual. After hanging up a few clothes, stripping and making a pile of dirty laundry, I telephoned the boss.

"Welcome home, traveler." His greeting was always the same. "I hope you had a pleasant vacation. We really should get together and have lunch, tomorrow at noon at the 1789?"

"That sounds good to me. I'll see you there."

The 1789 is a fashionable restaurant in Georgetown. However, the mention of it was the code for me to get to his office as soon after 8:00 as possible.

I put the pile of dirty laundry in a plastic bag along with a twenty dollar bill. I converted the sofa to my bed, showered and fell asleep immediately.

My wrist alarm woke me at 6:00. I did my exercises, shaved and noticed in the mirror that I looked tired. I must get more sleep. I dressed in a light blue, button down shirt and put on a conservative rep tie. My suit was a small pin stripe gray and my shoes, my standard black Zelli loafers. I picked up the plastic bag and let myself out. I ascended the steps to the apartment upstairs, hung the plastic bag on the doorknob and pushed the bell. I went to the Metro a few blocks away. The weather was clear.

After exiting the Metro, I walked to the building which housed the office on the 10th floor.

"You don't look so bad after that harrowing experience in Paris," said my boss as we shook hands and I sat down. The office was standard, no frills government-issue.

Charles Tufts was a man about fifty, over six feet tall, no facial hair but a heavy shadow of a beard, a weight lifter by hobby. He also was a Marine.

"Z tells me all went well with one slight misunderstanding about where the mark was actually arrested and Mirandized. It was cleared up rather quickly, I understand."

"Correct. Working with the Countess and with Arlene is always a pleasure."

"And how is Arlene?" he asked sheepishly. "As pretty as ever, I imagine. When are you two going to tie the knot?"

"We're still in the discussion phase," I replied, knowing that he'd been kept informed of her every movement over the past two years since she'd begun working for both him and Z.

"Please give her my fondest regards next time you talk to her."

"I know she'll be pleased you remembered her in such a nice way." I was laying it on rather thickly, but the boss and I had worked together so long that we understood when either of us was playing with the other's mind. He liked to pretend he didn't remember the details of my education or most everything about me.

"Remind me, Philipp, when you finished your language training, were you first or second in your class?"

He knew my class standing, but here again he was in the mind game.

"I stood first in Russian and French but only second in Spanish."

"How is your Spanish now?"

"It was quite good when I was in Spain yesterday." The game went on.

He continued. "Your college roommate was elected President of his country three weeks ago, wasn't he?"

"I believe you're correct, as always," I said, continuing the game.

"The United States will be sending an Official Delegation to his Inaugural and you have been invited to join the group, since you've been such close friends for so many years."

Was I about to be asked to spy on my roommate? How low can one go in this organization?

"The Delegation will be composed of twelve people, five representatives from both the House and the Senate, plus a personal representative of the President, and one other person, you."

"I'm certain this isn't just a renewal of old school ties. What am I expected to do?" I asked with a slight hint of pique.

"You'll have no duties at the Inaugural. Just sit on the dais and look pretty which you do so well." He was still at it. The knife was now in pretty deep. "But after the activities have been completed in the Capital, you'll be taking a vacation on the coast, observing an individual who's been rather conspicuous of late doing business with the enemy."

"What kind of business?" I asked.

"He's been lavishly entertaining one of the known enemy agents in the country. We know this because we have a mole in the enemy's camp."

"And what's my specific assignment?"

"You'll be invited to a final big bash, being given by someone you know, after the Inaugural activities in the Capital have been completed. At each event, you're to observe and listen, pick up anything that might tell you what kind of information is being given to the enemy. Under no circumstances are you to stand out in the crowd, which I know will be difficult for you."

The knife had finally been turned. Okay, my dear friend, here it comes right back at you. "Suppose there are ladies present who seem to be closely associated with the target. What am I to do? You know I'm much more effective horizontal than vertical."

"You're not to become intimate with any of the ladies present. Find some other way to accomplish your mission."

"Will the President be informed that my name is now Philipp Devon?"

"Yes and he understands you're in deep cover with one of the United States Security Organizations."

"Roger, Chief. And when do I leave on this mission?"

"There's a briefing tomorrow morning at 9:00 in the Conference Room of the Senate Foreign Relations Committee. Your attendance is requested. After the briefing, all present will be told the exact time to be at Dulles tomorrow evening."

"You don't give a guy much time to party, do you?"

"I can only imagine that you've partied many times over the past month. Be in touch before you leave Dulles and I'll give you some final instructions. Good luck and much success, my friend, and you know I mean that sincerely." He smiled as we shook hands.

I did know he meant what he said. I don't have a higher opinion of anyone with whom I've ever worked. He's not only my boss, he's my friend.

As I left the building, I decided to get an early lunch and then go home for a nap. I needed the sleep. There'd be plenty of time to pack tomorrow afternoon. I set my alarm for 7:30 A.M., closed my eyes and dropped off.

When I awoke, I showered and shaved and dressed quickly. I knew that usually, at these early morning meetings on The Hill, there'd be coffee and some pastries so I didn't plan to eat before the meeting.

As I entered the Conference Room, I looked for the coffee and those other things. There was nothing. Bad mistake, Mr. Devon, I thought.

The Conference Room was huge. This one had hosted many important functions and was well-known to the television audience. The red leather chairs were lined up on either side of the two tables arranged in a V formation so each of us could see the others. As the last of the eleven arrived and took a seat, the man running the show spoke up.

"Gentlemen, you'll form the Official Delegation to the Inaugural. Please identify yourselves at this time."

The five Senators were well known to me but the five Representatives were only names in the news except the Speaker of the House. I identified myself as Philipp Devon, the former college roommate of the newly elected President. The moderator/instructor for this meeting said the Vice President would also be in our Delegation. I tried not to look impressed or astounded, having met, dined with and protected many Heads of State.

Each of us was given an envelope containing a list of the United States Delegation, our Official Badges, our hotel assignments, the Program for the two-day activities in the Capital, the seating chart for the dais at the Inauguration Ceremony, admission tickets for the Reception and the Inaugural Ball and an invitation to a party being given by "a friend of both the President of the United States and the new President we were here to honor." The Host' name was not stated. The invitation didn't specify where or when that party would take place. Transportation to all these events was being handled by the Secret Service. The recommended dress for each of these events was clearly laid out by our State Department's Protocol Division. There was another smaller envelope in my packet, but since no one else asked about it or its contents I thought it better to open it later. We were instructed to be at the front entrance of the Department of State at exactly 2:00 that afternoon. Transportation to Dulles would be provided for the eleven of us. A business suit was recommended for the flight down. The Vice President would join us at Dulles and Air Force

Two would depart promptly at 4:00. There were no questions.

When I got back to the apartment, I opened the small envelope. It read, "My dear Philipp, I'm giving a small party at my place in the evening after the Ball. If you decide you've had too many cocktails, you're welcome to stay over. Several others have accepted my invitation to do so. I hope you can come." It was signed "37."

SIX

Air Force Two departed Dulles at exactly 4:00. The eleven of us, plus the Vice President and his bevy of Secret Service personnel, comprised the entire group of passengers. Of course there were six stewardesses to cater to our every need. Well, *most* of our needs. The Veep made a point of visiting with each of us. He saved me for last.

"Well, Mr. Devon, how long has it been since you've seen the new President?"

"Sir, I've only seen him twice since we left college and that was at reunions."

"He knows you're coming and has been completely briefed on your current name and somewhat briefed on your employer. He really has no need to know the specifics of what you do. I just want you to know how pleased I am you're with our Delegation."

"Thank you, Mr. Vice President. It's an honor to be included in your party."

Air Force Two touched down at exactly 9:31. We were instructed to remain seated until the Vice President and his party left the aircraft and departed the airstrip which they did in two limousines with tinted glass all around but no flags on the fenders. As soon as they pulled away, the eleven of us filed down the stairs. I was last. There were two more limousines awaiting us, and a small van for our luggage. The trip to the Capital took less than fifteen minutes. As my limousine pulled up to the curb at The Hotel Valencia, I was the only one who debarked. My luggage was placed beside me on the sidewalk. I'd brought a larger traveling bag on this trip because of the many "uniforms" I'd been instructed to wear. I carried my briefcase.

I entered a lobby full of foreigners. Several of the Official Delegations of other countries were also staying at this hotel. At the front desk I identified myself and signed the registration card. A bellman took my luggage and led me to the elevator. When the bellman stopped in front of and opened the door to room number 237, I was somewhat taken aback. The room was quite spacious and had most of the amenities I was accustomed to finding at the two- or three-star hotels in Europe. I gave the bellman a tip in the currency of his country, each of us having been furnished with the equivalence of $100 on the plane.

237, I said to myself. This is more than a coincidence. I recalled the spelling of the number 2 is a homophone for "too." Too, 37. And then it came to me. The yacht *37* is here "too" for the Inauguration. I remembered the invitation I'd received which had invited me "to my place." Now I knew for sure that the yacht was anchored off shore. I hoped that my mark would be one of the guests aboard tomorrow evening. I also hoped Sven Christen, Senior, would be aboard. Since he's dating the owner, I was sure he would be.

I opened my luggage and hung up my uniforms. I'd shined my formal shoes before leaving home, as well as my black loafers. My tuxedo had a few wrinkles but they would fall out before tomorrow night. My two suits and my shirts made the trip well. I looked at our schedule again.

Tomorrow: Breakfast in the room and then lunch in the Vice President's suite at his hotel at noon. Each person is to travel there by cab. Free in the afternoon until 6:30, at which time each of us will be picked up in front of our respective hotels for transportation to the Reception. Upon arrival of the Vice President and his party, we'll be ushered to the front of the receiving line, in which will be The President and his wife (whom I've never met) and several other dignitaries of lesser rank.

I looked forward to seeing my former roommate and how he might have changed. I know he's been briefed on my current name and job, but I hope our meeting won't be awkward for either of us. Having unpacked, it was time for bed. The room was adequate and the view overlooked a courtyard. Fortunately, the bed was king-sized. I stripped and fell asleep almost immediately.

My alarm went off at 9:00. When I checked in yesterday I asked that breakfast be served in my room at 9:30. I did my triples, push-ups and squats. Then I shaved and showered and was toweling dry, enjoying some intensely erotic memories of my nights with Arlene when there was a knock at the door. I wrapped the large towel around my waist and opened the door. To my surprise, it wasn't my breakfast; it was the chambermaid asking if I needed anything. She looked me over and quickly averted her eyes from my towel.

"Thank you but I have everything I need," I said in my best Spanish. Obviously, that wasn't exactly true, but it'd have to suffice for now. I had just closed the door and walked back to the bathroom when there was another knock at the door. This time it was a waiter delivering my breakfast. Fortunately, my towel was back to normal. He set the tray on the table near the window and I gave him a tip. He left the room and I dropped the towel.

I had a few hours until I was due in the Vice President's suite, to have brunch with a bunch of people about whom I couldn't have cared less. I was reminded of William Faulkner's response to the invitation from President Kennedy to have dinner in the White House with the other American Nobel Laureates. Faulkner declined and sent the following message: "It's a long way to travel to eat with people I don't know." But I had no such choice. I was going to the brunch anyway.

Having just finished a hearty breakfast, I thought of my dearest Arlene. I couldn't resist. I picked up the phone and dialed Z.

"Where is she?" I asked. "I can't stand being away from her this long."

"Calm down, my dear fellow. She is safe. I gave her a few days off to go and visit her mother."

"Can I talk with her?"

"That would be unwise. She's trying to decide what to do about her future, and since it concerns you, you shouldn't put in an appearance at this time."

"I miss her so much."

"I know you do and I truly believe the two of you were destined for each other. Therefore, you'll be united; I don't know when or where, but it's going to happen. Pull yourself together, Philipp."

That was good advice. It always is when Z speaks. I put down the phone and went into the bathroom and took a cold shower.

I lay on my bed without having set my alarm. I slept, deeply. When I awoke, my watch read 11:30. Panic! I hastily dressed and grabbed a cab at the front door. When I walked into the Vice President's suite, I was the last to arrive. The Vice President spoke directly to me.

"Mr. Devon, I do like your sense of timing. It is now eleven fifty-nine. Gentlemen, please be seated."

The brunch was undistinguished. When coffee was served, the Vice President looked at me and said, "Mr. Devon, I understand you know our hostess who's giving the party after the Ball."

"That's correct, Mr. Vice President. I've had the pleasure of sailing on her yacht several times."

"Tell us a little about her, if you will. Also what to expect when we get to her place," he said emphasizing "place."

"She's a difficult person to describe, Mr. Vice President. Her yacht is one of the largest in the world. Her main residence is Stockholm, but she's an American by birth and by allegiance. She's a mathematical genius. Her knowledge of most cultural subjects is vast and she has a coterie of friends worldwide. She has everything that money can buy except true love. She's been married and divorced five times but doesn't seem to be able to pick the right companion. She loves to entertain and I'm certain the Vice

President and his party will have a fantastic time at her 'place', as she calls

her yacht. Incidentally, Mr. Vice President, she prefers to be addressed as

'Madam Thirty-Seven', which is the name of her yacht."

"Thank you, Mr. Devon, for that insightful description. I'm sure we all

shall be anticipating the evening with her and her friends aboard the *37*."

The other ten looked at me with disdain. To them it appeared I lead a

very happy-go-lucky life with some of the world's most fascinating

people. And they were right. The fumes of jealousy filled the air.

When the brunch was finished, the Vice President and his party left the

room. Since the afternoon was our free time, I was the first of the

remaining to leave. I took the elevator to the lobby and pulled out of my

coat pocket a map of the city. The museum I wanted to visit was about

twelve blocks from this hotel. The walk would do me good. I needed the

exercise, so I just strolled through the streets of the city.

I arrived at my hotel at 3:55. I was to be picked up for the Reception at

6:30. Another nap was in order. I remembered to set my alarm for 5:00,

just to make sure I had plenty of time to get ready.

I awoke at 4:50. Since I'd missed my shave this morning, I was about

to step into the bathroom when I noticed a small envelope under my door addressed "Mr. Philipp Devon, Hotel Valencia, 237." I opened the envelope and read the card.

. "I'm looking forward to our meeting at my place tomorrow night. Please plan to stay over." The note was not signed.

I was standing on the sidewalk when the limo arrived. I was the first to be picked up. When the other five were seated, one of the Senators asked if I was having a good time. What an odd question, I thought. "Yes, Senator, I always enjoy a good time wherever I go. I remember my father telling me that whether you were working or playing, if you weren't having a good time, you weren't doing it right." No response from anyone.

The two limos arrived at the front of the Reception Hall. As we stood there, the Vice President's limo arrived with him and the Speaker. The Secret Service party surrounded our entire group as we entered the Hall. The Chief of Protocol, who was handling all visitors, both foreign and domestic, spoke to the Vice President and asked him to follow her to the head of the receiving line. We eleven followed like a column of ducks. The noise in the Hall was cacophonous so I couldn't hear what the President was saying to those ahead of me in line. When I got in front of the President, he put his arms around me and gave me a hug.

"Oh, Philipp," he said. "It's so good to see you again and thank you for coming to my party. May I introduce you to my wife? Carlotta, this is Philipp Devon, my college roommate, about whom you have heard me speak so many times."

"Carlotta, I'm so pleased to meet you." Looking at the President I said, "Well, you certainly married the most beautiful woman in this country." (I didn't learn until the next night that she was American.) They both laughed. As I was preparing to move on, the President said, "Philipp, I hope to see more of you during these festivities."

"And so do I Mr. President." We hugged again.

The President and I were about the same size and height. His black hair and black eyes defined him as definitely being of Castilian descent. Carlotta, by contrast, was diminutive and very pretty. The gown she wore complimented her gorgeous figure. It was a Dior; I could tell. Her skin was flawless and she wore very little make-up or jewelry.

The Hall was huge and beautifully decorated with baskets of flowers everywhere. As I mingled with the others, I noticed several people looking my way and asking the person next to them, "Who is he?" For someone who constantly tries to appear unnoticed and in the background at every event, I was having a ball.

At each end of the Hall were tables of finger food. On each side of the room were lengthy bars offering everything one could want.

After about fifteen minutes, a Secret Service man approached each of us and said the Vice President and the Speaker would be leaving shortly, but the Vice President wanted each of us to stay as long as we liked. Now perhaps I could attend to my assigned task.

The remaining ten of us separated and mingled with the crowd, speaking to a few old acquaintances and being introduced to some new ones. I'd wandered around the Hall for almost an hour before I spotted my mark, as the Boss had described him. He was talking with a very recognizable member of a foreign delegation, which I knew was on our enemies list. I staggered in his direction, pretending to be a bit drunk. He moved away from the gentleman with whom he was speaking and went to one of the buffet tables. Approaching him I said, "This is quite a party, don't you agree?"

"It certainly is. May I please ask your name? I saw you hugging the President."

"The President and I were college roommates many years ago. My name is Philipp Devon."

"Hello. My name is (he was definitely my mark)."

"Where do you come from?" I asked.

"I have homes in Washington, D.C., in Paris and here in the Capital. I'm an American but I spend most of my time out of the country."

"May I ask about your business?"

"I'm in the Import-Export business."

"What do you import and export?" I pushed hard.

"Anything that pays me good money," he said with a slightly whimsical tone in his reply.

"I'm in the Import-Export business, too," I lied. "I import a bottle or two of Grand Marnier from the Caribbean on each trip and I export lies to cover it up." I laughed heartily. He didn't.

"I apologize if I've offended you by inferring that your business is not a legitimate one," I replied sincerely.

"No offense taken. I think I'll get another drink."

"I think I will, too. May I follow you to the bar?"

"By all means," he said curtly and implied by his tone that he'd spent enough time with this inebriate.

As we approached the bar and placed our orders, I asked, "May I have one of your cards? You can never tell when I might have some business to throw your way." My voice was clear and my gaze sincere. He hesitated for a brief moment, then took out a card case, extracted one and handed it to me.

"Thank you. It's been a pleasure meeting you and I feel sure we'll be talking again soon."

I took my glass from the bartender and walked away. When I'd gone about fifty feet, I turned and saw him staring at me, so I saluted him politely and continued to walk away. After I'd mingled with the crowd again and was sure he couldn't see me, I watched as he returned to the gentleman with whom he had previously been speaking. I've always wanted to be able to read lips and this was one time I could've used that talent. The two of them continued to talk for a while. I decided to go back to the bar near where they were talking and give my mark a chance to speak with me again. As I approached them, they separated, walking away in opposite directions.

Although I hadn't discovered what he was selling, I found out the person who I believe was his buyer. To pursue the conversation further would've been too obvious, so I prepared to leave the Reception. I left by the front entrance where I found a line of waiting taxis. I arrived at my hotel shortly before 11:00. Although my mission wasn't completed, I hoped there might be an opportunity to talk with this gentleman again tomorrow night.

I awoke at 7:00, performed my daily exercises and again enjoyed breakfast in my room. The United States Delegation was to be on the dais no later than 10:00. Each of the lesser lights, like me, was to get there individually. After shaving and showering, I began dressing in my Inaugural uniform which consisted of my dark suit, a white shirt, a conservative maroon tie and my black oxfords, which I always hate to wear. Loafers are my shoes of choice if I'm not barefooted.

The taxi deposited me at the Dignitary Entrance to the Stadium at 9:35. The line for frisking wasn't very long so my wait was shorter than I'd expected. I arrived at my seat at 9:55. Plenty of time to spare, I joked to myself. Nine remaining members of our Delegation were already seated when I arrived. The looks I received from several said "You act like a PC, always showing up last." Ho-hum, I thought. I *am* a privileged character.

Shortly, the Vice President, followed by the Speaker, arrived on the dais and took their seats. I checked my watch. 10:20. The Ceremony was scheduled to begin at 10:30 and end with the speech of the President, who was to be sworn in exactly at noon by the Chief Judge of the country's highest court. The National Band continued to play martial music until it stopped at exactly 10:30. Everyone in the Stadium stood as the Band began playing the Country's National Anthem, after which the warm-up speeches began. There were a lot of them but each was relatively short. The last speaker finished at 11:55. I loved the precision. The Band began to play a march I knew was the President's favorite because we played it in our dorm room. During this march, the President and his wife and the Chief Judge approached the podium. While Carlotta held the Bible and the President placed his left hand on it, he raised his right hand and the Chief Judge administered the oath of office. At the conclusion of the oath, the Stadium erupted in cheers, which lasted a full two minutes. When the cheers died down, the President began his Inaugural Address.

I knew he didn't like to speak at great length, but I also knew he had many constituents who needed to be acknowledged and many representative groups who needed to hear his proposed programs outlined. The speech lasted only twelve minutes and was followed by tremendous applause. After the President and his wife and the Chief Judge left the dais, the remaining dignitaries were free to leave. After the Vice President and the Speaker departed, we remaining ten dispersed individually.

The Inaugural Ball was scheduled to begin at 8:00 after which the rest of us and the Vice President's party were going to the yacht for as long as the Veep wanted to stay. His plane was to be ready to take off whenever the crew was alerted by the Secret Service. All of us were to have our luggage packed and loaded in the van when we were picked up at our hotels.

When the Vice President decided to leave the Ball, we'd only been there about thirty minutes. I didn't get a chance to say my good-byes to the President and Carlotta, but I'm sure he understood.

When our limousines and the van arrived at the dock, we all stood around waiting for the Vice President and his party to board first. I asked the driver of the van to take my luggage and place it on deck after our party had boarded. As I, the last of the twelve, stepped on board, I asked a steward, whom I knew from my other trips, to retrieve my two pieces of luggage from the driver and have them placed in my stateroom.

Madam Thirty-Seven and Sven Christen, Senior, stood at the head of the gangplank. Our hostess was gowned in pale green chiffon which I knew to be a Dior, her personal designer. She warmly greeted each of us in her usual sincere, welcoming style. I noticed that the eyes of several members of our party were glazed over by the expanse and elegance of the yacht. After our party arrived on board, several others began to arrive. Soon there were approximately one hundred and fifty guests on board. The two bars were quite busy. The buffet tables on either side of the pool hadn't yet been attacked.

I stepped over to talk with our hostess. "I didn't realize I'd see you again so soon. Why did you decide to come to the Inaugural?"

"My dear, I thought you knew that Carlotta is my daughter."

"I'm sorry to have forgotten," I lied. I didn't know.

Our conversation was interrupted by the arrival of a few more guests. As I stepped back from the receiving line, I saw my mark coming up the gangplank alone. After he went through the line, I approached him and said, "May I show you to the bar?"

As we walked toward the bar, he asked, "How do you know our hostess?"

"I manage her investments," I said. This, of course, wasn't true but it was a ruse that had been worked out to lend credibility to my association with her.

"How do you know her?" I pushed.

"I never met her until I went through the receiving line a moment ago. I've been invited to remain on board overnight and travel to Miami where the boat will dock tomorrow afternoon. I was told, in my invitation, that everyone staying over and going to Miami would be American."

"Our hostess has a wonderful G-2 system for keeping informed." I used the military term for an Intelligence Officer, trying to learn more about my mark, if possible. Since he didn't comment on hearing the term, I pushed even further.

"Have you ever served in the military?"

"Unfortunately, I was rejected for poor eyesight and for chronic back pain," he replied.

"Do you wear corrective contacts? I notice you don't wear glasses."

"No. My eyesight has improved over the past few years but I still have the back pains," he said.

"I've found good wine helps me overcome pain", I said with a smile. No reaction.

Our hostess approached the bar. "I'll have my usual, Jason."

As the bartender poured a glass of red wine and handed it to her with a napkin (cloth, of course) she continued, speaking directly to us.

"The Vice President and his party will be leaving shortly and after about another fifteen minutes, the remaining guests who aren't staying overnight will also be departing. Oh, I do love to party." She looked genuinely pleased and particularly well dressed and coiffed for this event, although I didn't recall seeing her at the Ball.

As she walked toward the Vice President, he took her hand and they began to move toward the gangplank, followed by his party. The remainder of our Delegation, except me, also departed at that time. Not one of them seemed to notice I was remaining on board.

I didn't speak to my mark again until all the passengers who were going ashore had done so. Our hostess spoke to us as a group, all thirty-six of us. (I'd counted everyone a few minutes ago.)

"I'll be retiring shortly but you may talk, eat and drink as long as you care to. Breakfast will be served casually on deck at nine-thirty, weather permitting. Captain Andersen has informed me we may have showers in the early morning. If that be the case, then breakfast will be served in the dining room. I hope each of you has enjoyed the Ball and my little party. We'll be debarking at about noon or shortly thereafter. If you'll have your luggage ready in the morning by eleven, it will be collected from your staterooms and placed on deck ready for unloading. I bid you all good night."

A round of applause followed as Madam Thirty-Seven departed. After she'd left, my mark walked toward me and asked if we might talk some more. I looked at my watch and then replied that I was rather tired but I supposed a few minutes would be okay.

"Shall we walk toward the stern?" I asked.

"Yes, that would be fine," he replied.

When we were completely out of earshot from everyone else, he began.

"I know you saw me talking to a gentleman at the Ball this evening. He was the Minister of Foreign Affairs in the Administration of the former President," he lied. "He and all the Cabinet have been asked to tender their resignations as the new President wants to staff his Administration with people of his choice. The Minister was my main contact for doing business with the country. I need to establish my *bona fides* with the new Administration; and I know you have important contacts, not only with the President himself, but also with the mother of the President's wife. It would be most helpful to me if you could put in a good word for me."

"I say once again, I don't know what you're buying and/or selling that requires your association with the Ministry of Foreign Affairs. It would be highly presumptuous for me to ask a favor of the President without knowing why the favor is being asked."

"Unfortunately, Mr. Devon, I'm not able at this time to provide you with any further details."

"Well, in that case, I suggest, when you can tell me more, you contact the President of The International Bank in Washington, D.C. It's through him I conduct all the financial affairs of our hostess. He knows how to reach me at all times. Now if you'll excuse me, I need to retire." We shook hands.

When I was stretched out on my bed, I reminded myself that I didn't know much more about my mark than I did after our initial meeting. I did think that he might possibly be involved with the disclosure of State secrets to a foreign power, the details of which were yet to be discovered.

I slept well.

When I awoke, I noticed through my porthole the sky was overcast. I looked at my watch. 9:00. I don't remember sleeping so long and so well since I left the company of my darling Arlene. I did my exercises, shaved and took a long, hot shower. As I was toweling dry, there was a knock at the door. When I opened it, there stood Madam Thirty-Seven.

"May I come in?" she asked.

"Of course, if you'll excuse the state of my undress."

"My dear Philipp, I've seen you at the pool wearing less than you have on now," she said with a twinkle in her eye.

"Please sit down."

"I can only stay a minute," she whispered. "How did your meeting with your mark go last evening?" she inquired. "I purposely invited him to travel with us to Miami so you'd have an opportunity to speak with him."

How did she know about my mission? I know from past experiences she is knowledgeable of our business, but I'll be damned if I can figure this one out.

"Carlotta told me that the President knows that there's something foul afoot and he suspects the former Minister of Foreign Affairs and your mark. They have been seen together on many occasions in the Capital."

"We had a brief chat on the stern before I retired."

"Carlotta has promised to keep her eyes open for any further details and will pass them on to me. I'll pass them on to your boss."

I'm never shocked but sometimes surprised to learn who knows what about my business. This definitely was one of those times.

My visitor left without saying another word, only a knowing wink. I got dressed in my civilian traveling uniform and went to the dining room, since there was a fine mist in the air. I was one of the last guests to arrive. My mark was standing alone with a cup of coffee in his hand. As I was filling my cup, he approached and offered his hand and a cheery good morning.

"And a good morning to you," I responded. Neither of us said anything more. I wandered to the eggs and ham at the far end of the buffet. Having filled my plate, I took a seat at an empty table.

When I finished my coffee, Captain Andersen announced over the speaker that we would be debarking at 12:15. He reminded all of us to have our luggage ready for pickup in our staterooms at 11:00. I looked at my watch again. 10:40. I casually strolled to the port windows and saw the skyline of Miami nearby. I returned to my stateroom to check that everything was in order, after which I returned to the main deck with my briefcase and umbrella in hand. My raincoat was thrown over my arm. I purposely arrived on deck early so my mark, if he cared to, could say something more. He was nowhere in sight.

I watched the yacht approach the wharf and admired the dexterity with which the Captain maneuvered this big boat. Shortly thereafter, the chain was removed and we walked down the gangplank. Still there was no sign of my mark. Arriving on the wharf, I spotted my luggage and then a taxi. As I walked toward the cab, I looked around to see if my mark was anywhere in sight and if he might be seeking my attention. Nada.

I told the driver my destination, Miami International Airport. We arrived shortly. Before entering the terminal, I stopped to purchase a copy of the *Miami Herald.* The headline shocked me.

Greek Minister Assassinated

"The Greek Minister of Culture, Ms. Alexandra Stavros, was assassinated on Saturday afternoon as she was attending the opening of a new Cultural Exhibition in Athens. The assailant, who was shot and killed on the spot by an Exposition guard, has not yet been identified. Mr. Ian Hargrave, of Stockholm, Sweden, was also shot and killed. No further details were available at this time."

SEVEN

When the flight touched down at Dulles International outside Washington, I telephoned the office from the airport.

"Welcome home, Philipp. I trust you had a pleasant journey," said the boss. "Do you plan to be in town long?"

"So far as I now know," I replied.

"We must get together for lunch. How about meeting tomorrow at noon at our usual restaurant?"

"I'll be there, and thanks."

I hailed a cab to the coffee shop near my apartment, then home. Everything was as I left it. I went through my usual routine then took a nap. When I awoke and looked at my watch, it was already 6:00. I searched my cupboard for something to eat. I didn't want to go out, the weather had turned nasty and a steady downpour was filling the drain at my front entrance. I found a can of pork and beans and a can of sliced peaches. I turned on the TV news. There was nothing of world-shaking importance on the tube so I turned it off. I set my alarm for 6:30 AM and propped my head up with two pillows. My mind was on my sweet Arlene. Was she thinking of me? I was certainly thinking of her. I turned out the light, turned over on my stomach and went to sleep.

My alarm rang. I went through my morning routine and left my apartment. As I entered my office building, I performed the usual ritual and handed my raincoat and umbrella to the guard.

Leaving the elevator, I opened the door to the office, identified myself and was ushered into the inner sanctum. My boss was seated in his chair.

"Come in, Philipp. Have a seat. The White House reported that the Inauguration and all its attendant festivities went off as planned. The Vice President seemed genuinely pleased to have had you in his party. I'm sure your roommate was glad to see you again."

"He seemed so. I also learned the President's wife is Madam Thirty-Seven's daughter. I hadn't known that."

"I didn't pass that info on to you; I wanted to know from whom you would learn that fact."

"Her mother told me after all festivities were complete and I'd gone through the receiving line on the boat."

"Good," the boss continued. "Tell me about meeting your mark and what transpired."

I told him everything in detail about our meetings at the Reception and again on the yacht. I described our conversation on the stern and, although I saw him talking to a member of the other side, I regretted that I didn't find out what he was buying and/or selling.

When I finished, the boss said, "You did well, Philipp. You confirmed many things we already suspected. When the yacht landed in Miami, one of my men tailed him to his hotel where he registered under the name of Alex di Marchi from Rome, Italy. Later last night, he was visited, at the hotel bar, by an agent of the enemy you encountered at the Reception. My man overheard his conversation about meeting you and what a great and influential contact you could be in the new government. You made quite an impression on him."

"I didn't tell him anything of importance except how he could get in touch with me through the Bank here in D.C."

"You did well," said the boss.

I didn't bring up the assassinations of the Greek Minister and Mr. Hargrave. These were of more interest to Z.

"Thanks, but I have one question. How did Madam Thirty-Seven know about my mission regarding the mark?"

"Madam Thirty-Seven and Z have been buddies since Hector was a pup." The boss' use of that old Southern colloquialism surprised me; he was from Delaware. "It was Z who asked her to take her yacht to the Inaugural and assist you in any way she could in carrying out your mission, which he explained to her. She's been associated with us for many years and the beauty of that association is she knows and is known by almost everyone in the world of any importance. And another thing, my good man, she thinks you're gorgeous, especially in a bathing suit."

"I don't know whether to say thank you or blush."

"You just did both. Z called late last night and has requested your presence in his office as soon as you can get there. He has reserved a room for you at the Lowndes Hotel in Belgravia, registered in the name of Mr. and Mrs. Philipp Devon."

"Mr. and Mrs. Devon? Arlene's in London?"

"Yes, and she wants to see you as soon as possible. Z also said her mother died last Friday. Here's your ticket for tonight's flight, leaving at 7:05, and some spending money to tide you over until you return to D.C."

The boss handed me an envelope with twenty 100-dollar bills. I thanked him again and asked to use his bathroom. Inside, I put ten bills in my crotch pouch and the rest in my briefcase.

I thanked him again and left his office. When I got to the lobby, I used the pay phone to alert my laundress. Putting on my rain gear, I left the building and started toward the Metro. I was dancing on air at the thought of being with my dearest Arlene tomorrow morning.

When I approached the apartment, the plastic bag of laundry was hanging in the usual place. I retrieved the bag and entered my apartment. After taking off my rain gear, I stripped and hung up my laundry.

My watch said 10:30. I didn't want to go out for lunch so I checked my larder. In the freezer I found a frozen dinner of chicken with vegetables and cherry cobbler, and only 150 calories. It had been there quite a while. Fits my regimen, I thought. I set the timer on the microwave, poured myself a diet soda and waited. The food was okay but it was a far cry from the meals I enjoyed with my dearest Arlene.

I began to think about tomorrow — what I'd say when we met. Of course, I'd first offer my condolences on the death of her mother. Whether or not to mention a wedding?

The taxi ride from my apartment to the airport would be about fifty minutes this time of day. I got out of bed, converted it, got my big bag out of the closet and began to pack.

I left the apartment and walked to the nearest corner with my bag in one hand and my briefcase in the other and hailed a taxi to Dulles.

"You have a telephone call, Mr. Devon. You may take it over there," the desk clerk said indicating a phone at the end of the counter.

The boss said, "Philipp, I just wanted you to know if you decide to get married, we are all pulling for you. Give Arlene my best regards with a kiss." The boss was sincere.

I returned to the clerk, got my boarding pass and had both bag and briefcase tagged for carry-on. I proceeded to the food bar nearest the gate. I stopped at the nearby newsstand and bought a *New York Times* and settled in my seat. On the second page, I found the item I was looking for.

Greek Minister Assassinated

The report was the same as yesterday's except there was more.

"The man also assassinated at the Exhibition, Mr. Ian Hargrave, a resident of Stockholm, Sweden, was known to have accompanied the Minister to the Exhibition and appears to have been the target of the assassination rather than Minister Stavros, who apparently stepped into the line of fire at the critical moment. The Greek Government is continuing to investigate. The assassin's body has not yet been identified."

This news posed an interesting question: Since Hargrave was a double agent, which side rubbed him out?

I tried to sleep on the plane but was only able to cat nap. I didn't watch the movie; I'd seen it twice in the past six weeks. When the plane landed at Heathrow, I quickly exited and hastily walked to the Underground. The Lowndes was a few blocks east of Sloane Square.

I checked in. The bellman took my bag, stopping at Room 222. A flashback reminded me when Arlene and I'd first rendezvoused in Paris she was staying at a small hotel in room 222. Was this a foretelling of what was to come or was it just a coincidence? The bellman knocked and opened the door.

Arlene was seated in an overstuffed chair next to a round table on which sat a large vase of red roses. She was wearing a light pink dressing gown with pink slippers. Her hair was perfectly coiffed. I tipped the bellman as he left the room. Cautiously, I approached my love and gave her a kiss on the forehead, on the cheek and on the lips. I couldn't tell by her demeanor whether or not we were to continue to be an item, so I controlled my raging desire. I took her by both hands and held her close and whispered in her ear my condolences on the loss of her mother. I could feel her tensing and I thought I detected the beginning of a tear. I finally let go my tight hold and again took her by both hands.

"I've missed being with you so very much." I looked into her eyes and smiled, as she began to tear up again.

"Oh, my dear Philipp, I've missed you so much and wanted you to be with me so many times. I know you promised to wait until I'd made my decision about our future. These past weeks have been almost unbearable, trying to sort out by myself where I want to go with my life, and with you. You were so thoughtful to offer a simple solution that we could continue to be lovers even though our paths would continue to be diverse at times. I had a talk with Z, who listened intently as I bared my soul and my feelings for you, but also for my work with him. His advice shocked me at first, but as I pondered it, it made a lot of sense."

We moved to the two chairs at the table with the roses. I drew my chair close to hers so I could continue to hold her hand. She continued.

"Z explained that Baba and Francisco had a similar situation in their lives several years ago. They care very much for each other and wanted to spend more time together. They came up with the perfect solution. They got married and live together in their villa, even though each of them is sometimes on an independent mission." She paused. "Z also said he didn't believe our work would be enhanced by our getting married unless we could live together as husband and wife. He pointed out that I'm British and you're American, but that can be an enhancement to our work. Not being married and being away from each other makes our individual lives more believable and also gives the paparazzi one helluva good time trying to figure us out!"

Arlene paused for a lengthier time than before. She squeezed my hand. "Now that mother has passed on, I no longer have to look after her. So, my dearest Philipp, I have come to the following decision: I'd like to continue being lovers with the sweetest man I know, getting together whenever we can, for as long as we can; and somewhere down the road, we can officially become man and wife and live together at a location currently not known. So, if you'll accept my proposal, I accept your proposal of marriage, my dear Philipp, at a time and place to be announced later."

I got on one knee in front of her, took her right hand and said, "My dearest Arlene, will you marry me?" We repeated the traditional marriage vows to each other. We both stood and looked into each other's teary eyes. We kissed. I slipped off my jacket and tie and helped her remove her negligee. She took off my shirt and unbuckled my belt. I removed my shoes and socks. As my trousers fell to the floor, she said, "I've never taken off your pouch but I'd like to do so now." She gently removed it and slipped out of her slippers. I stepped out of my trousers and picked her up and carried her to our bed.

We embraced and hugged and kissed. As she lay on her back, I moved above her and began to kiss her face, her neck, her shoulders, her breasts and her stomach. She then pushed me away and, as I fell back beside her, she reversed positions and got on top of me. She kissed my face and licked my ears. She kissed my neck and then embedded her face in my chest hair. She then licked the hair on my stomach and put her tongue in my navel. Our passions were inflamed before we began our caressing. We were both breathing very hard. As I gently entered her, she whispered, "Oh, Philipp, I do love you so very much, and I want to be your wife." I replied softly, "I love you too, Arlene, and I believe we are already married in spirit."

Our making love was intense, passionate and prolonged. We'd cuddle, kissing and talking softly and then we'd begin again. I lost all sense of time and really didn't care if I never got out of that bed.

There was a knock at the door.

"Room service. I have a bottle of Champagne already iced and ready to be opened."

Arlene fled into the bathroom as I threw on a robe. When I opened the door, the waiter put the tray on the small table. On the tray was a bottle of

Laurent-Perrier Brut in an ice bucket and two crystal goblets. There was also a note in a small envelope, which read, "Congratulations." It was signed "Z." I tipped the waiter handsomely as he left.

Arlene came out of the bathroom as I shed my robe. She read the card and smiled. "He really is clairvoyant."

I filled both glasses half full. We clinked them as we both said, almost simultaneously, "To us."

The remainder of the afternoon was spent in soft conversation and making love, interspersed with sips of Champagne. When I finally looked at my watch, it read 6:30. I was famished. I asked Arlene if she'd like to have dinner at Langan's. Her smile told me I'd chosen the right place. I kissed her again and said I'd like to have a shower before she soaked in the bubbles. As we finished the last of the Champagne, she put on her negligee and I went to shower. When I got under the water, I did something I seldom do: I began to sing. My voice isn't suitable for a choir or even alone on a desert island, but I couldn't refrain from singing at the top of my lungs, "O, What a Beautiful Morning." The water felt warm and soft. I don't know how long I was in there but I finally turned off the water, dried off and re-entered the bedroom. Arlene was asleep in her negligee.

I decided to let her sleep. I sat down in one of the big chairs and retrieved a magazine from under the table. It was the latest edition of *POINT DE VIEW*. I casually thumbed through the pages and was surprised I didn't recognize one single soul. I must get out more, I thought.

Arlene stirred, opened her eyes and sat up in bed.

"You smell good," she said, "and I've never heard you sing before."

"I've never been this happy before."

I walked over to the bed, took her hand and helped her to her feet as she walked into the bathroom. Shortly, I heard the water running in the tub and a soft voice singing our song. It had been a beautiful morning and a beautiful afternoon.

The telephone rang. The operator said, "Mr. Devon, you have a call, may I put it through?"

"Philipp, I hope the Champagne was acceptable and also the roses."

"You sentimentalist," I responded. "You always know exactly what to do and say."

"Perhaps not what you expect this time," he continued. "I'd like for you and your lady to join me in my office for coffee, say about nine. Would that be acceptable?"

"Of course," I replied. "Should we bring our luggage?"

"No, but don't unpack."

"We'll see you at nine."

I walked to the bathroom door and knocked. "Come in." Even though she was covered in bubbles, she looked wonderful.

"A call from Z has requested the two of us be in his office tomorrow morning at 9:00."

"No rest for the weary," Arlene said with a twinkle in her eye. "I'll be ready in just a moment."

As I was tying my tie, Arlene appeared wrapped in a large bath towel. "May I go like this?"

"No," I said, "but I can come out of this suit very quickly and we can order room service."

"You are always thinking of me. I like that." I sat back down in the big chair and watched her get dressed. What a lucky man I am.

When she finished, we descended to the lobby and got a taxi waiting curbside.

"Langan's at Green Park," I said.

"Righto, Guv'nor."

As we entered the restaurant, I recognized Paul, the waiter who'd attended Francisco and me.

"Good evening, Ma'am and Sir. Will you be expecting anyone else or shall I prepare a table for two?"

"We'll be dining alone, Paul." He gave the slightest smile of appreciation that I'd remembered his name. "May we have a table in the rear?"

"Certainly, sir," he said as we followed him to a secluded spot. We passed a table of four men, one of whom I thought I knew. After the events at the Inauguration and then the assassination in Greece, I was beginning to feel a little paranoid. When we were seated, Paul said, "I shall be bringing a bottle of Champagne, compliments of the house, or would you prefer some wine, say, a Montebuena Rioja?"

Is Paul one of us, also? I thought. I'll ask Z tomorrow.

"Champagne will be perfect, Paul, and thank you for the courtesy of the house. To what do we owe this treat?"

"When you both entered the restaurant, I could see a glow of extreme happiness on the face of the lady, so I assumed this evening must be a special occasion." Paul then added, "I also remember, sir, that on your last visit to the restaurant, you had to leave rather abruptly, without finishing your meal; so I thought the house owed you some make-up time."

"You're most observant, Paul, and we both appreciate your gesture.

We look forward to the Champagne."

After Paul left the table, Arlene asked, "Isn't Montebuena Rioja the favorite wine of both Francisco and Baba?"

"It is, and I'm speculating on the possibility that Paul is also one of us."

After the Champagne arrived and we'd toasted each other and our renewed time together and our plans for the future, we both chose to have only a light meal. I decided when we returned to the room, we should open another bottle to celebrate *us*.

The meal was delicious as was the coffee that followed. When the bill arrived, there was a note attached: "A bottle of Montebuena Rioja will be awaiting you as you leave. Paul." I placed the correct amount on the tray and added an extra large bill. As we departed the restaurant, the coat-check girl handed me a package.

"Thank you, my dear," I said and gave her a small tip.

There was a taxi outside the restaurant. "The Lowndes in Belgravia, please."

On the way to the hotel, Arlene and I held hands and smiled at each other, but said nothing. As we entered the lobby, I spoke with the bellman and ordered more Champagne.

As I opened the door to our room, I smelled a new fragrance. The vase of roses had been removed and a vase of fresh lilacs was sitting in its place. I opened the card attached and we both read, "Have a happy reunion. Z."

The Champagne arrived. Arlene went into the bathroom. As I began to undress, she emerged wearing a Champagne-colored negligee. Before I poured each of us a glass of the bubbly, I quickly shed the rest of my clothes. Still wearing my crotch pouch, I turned to Arlene. Without a word, she removed it for me, slowly, teasingly. We hugged and kissed and then I poured two glasses. We sat down in the big chairs and held hands. Words didn't seem necessary. We just sipped and held hands. Then Arlene stood up and removed her negligee. I put down my glass and stood before her, our bodies lightly touching. We looked into each other's eyes and kissed. I embraced her warmly. She responded to my caresses. Even though our bed was only a few feet away, I picked her up in my arms and lay her gently on the satin coverlet on her back. I looked at her intently, my eyes devouring every inch of her magnificent body. I knelt at the foot of the bed and took one of her feet in my hands and began to kiss her toes. She sighed sweetly. After I'd kissed my way up to her knee, I began on the other foot. When I reached her other knee, I continued to kiss her body, alternating sides until I reached her stomach. I began to lick her soft, warm flesh and caress and kiss her beautiful breasts. Her neck and chin preceded my kissing her lips, which were moist and full.

With a slight twisting of her body and a little pressure on my chest, she shifted me onto my back and began to return the favors. Beginning with my toes and working her way up my legs, my hirsuteness presented no problem to her as she kissed and licked my stomach and chest. She kissed my chin, my cheeks, my forehead and my nose before repeating the intense kissing we'd so recently enjoyed together. Our mutual fondling and kissing continued for quite a while until we both agreed that the preliminaries were over and it was now time for the main event.

In our past love makings, we'd assumed every position described in the Kama Sutra, the ancient Hindu text on mystical erotica. We were quite adept at pleasing each other. Tonight, it seemed appropriate to simplify our making love and just devote our energies to what pleased the other the most. We continued like that until I went to the table and brought each of us another cold glass of the bubbly. Then we began all over again. We continued for several hours, alternating with a glass of Champagne until all had been consumed. In our eyes, we were newly married and this was our wedding night.

As we lay quietly on our backs, Arlene dropped off to sleep. I eased out of bed and went to take a shower. The water was very soothing and made me feel rejuvenated. After drying off, I re-entered the bedroom. Arlene was still sleeping; I quietly slipped in beside her. We both slept until the sunlight began to shine through the glass curtains. I awakened first and kissed her on her stomach. She stirred, sleepily, but didn't open her eyes. I waited a few minutes and then kissed her again in the same place. Again she stirred but didn't fully awake. I got out of bed and took another cold shower. I began to sing, "O, What a Beautiful Morning." The water was exhilarating. I realized I was ravenously hungry. I stepped out of the shower and dried off. When I entered the bedroom, Arlene was sitting in one of the big chairs wearing her negligee. As I said good morning, I leaned over and kissed her on the forehead. She smiled and drew my lips to hers. She stood up and we embraced. She kissed me again and then went into the bathroom. I could hear "our song" as she showered. When she re-entered the bedroom, I was sitting on the bed naked and erect.

"Don't you ever get enough?" she asked with a smirk.

"Never," I said. "But I could use some breakfast and coffee."

"So could I," she responded. We got dressed.

After we'd finished breakfast in the hotel dining room, we took our briefcases and walked outside into a glorious sunshiny day. A taxi was available. I directed the driver to Z's office building. We entered the inner sanctum. Z was seated in his usual chair behind his large desk.

"And how are the two love birds this morning?"

Arlene spoke first. "We're fine and I want to thank you for both the roses and the lilacs. You're most thoughtful and I might say, more than a little sentimental." Z smiled but said nothing.

"I appreciate your getting here so fast from the States, Philipp. I have a very important and most urgent assignment for you both." As usual, Z got right to the point. "One of our most loyal and trusted agents has died of natural causes. He'd worked on many assignments for me and for my predecessor. He was one of only a few agents who carried with him a special book containing code words. He was a distant relative of the Royal Family and his work with us was above suspicion. In all his years of service, he was never compromised. His cover was his former service in the military and being a cousin of the Queen. Now that he has passed, it's imperative that we recover that code book."

He paused briefly. "His widow lives in the village of Moretonhampstead in Devonshire. She was aware that he'd served the

Crown in some secret capacity but she's not aware that he was working for me or that he had the codebook. I've asked Scotland Yard to inform his widow you two are coming to her village and you're working in the same part of the Crown's work as her husband had been. She's also been told that you'll have a letter from the Crown identifying yourselves and asking for something from her husband's effects. I've made reservations at The White Horse Inn in Moretonhampstead for Mr. and Mrs. Devon who will be honeymooning there for several days. Here are your tickets for the 2:35 train for Exeter. There'll be a rental car in your name at the station when you arrive this evening. The drive to Moretonhampstead will take about thirty minutes."

"How will we identify the code book and how shall we go about getting it from his widow?" I asked.

"When you arrive at The Inn, you'll make a telephone call to the widow, (He identified her by name.), identifying yourselves as fellow workers with her husband and ask to be invited for tea tomorrow afternoon." Z paused as he handed me a sealed envelope with the embossed Coat of the Crown on the flap. "Your letter of introduction is enclosed, as well as a description of the book. It's small, about four inches by six inches and approximately one inch in thickness. The cover is dark gray leather and has no markings. Our deceased agent had been instructed to keep the book in his vault in his bedroom closet whenever it wasn't on his person."

"Is there any possibility that the widow will hesitate to surrender the book?"

"The letter of introduction specifically states that it's the wish of the Queen you be given the book. I don't anticipate any hesitancy on her part." Z rose.

"I have one question not pertaining to this matter. Last evening at Langan's, our waiter, Paul, who'd served Francisco and me, gave me a bottle of Montebuena Rioja as we left the restaurant. May I ask about his association with us?"

"Paul is my eyes and ears at Langan's. Since so much international mingling is done there, I decided that his presence would be most advantageous in keeping me informed of the activities. Paul has been with us for about twelve years. He also informed me after your meeting with Francisco that everything had gone as I'd planned. The gift of the wine was his way of saying 'I'll watch out for you whenever you're in the restaurant.'"

"You are not only most thoughtful and gracious but also very protective", Arlene said. "We appreciate your concern for our welfare." I sensed that she wanted to give him a kiss but hesitated.

We departed the office and returned to the hotel. My watch read 9:55. Since our train didn't leave for another four-plus hours, I suggested to Arlene that we might take another nap.

"My darling lover," she said, "I really need to do a little shopping before we depart. May I suggest while I'm out, you take another cold shower?" She kissed me gently on the lips. "I'll be back in the room by twelve. We can have lunch here in the hotel or in Belgravia."

I walked her to the front entrance of the hotel as she headed for her favorite store, Harrod's. I returned to the room and decided I needed that nap. Shucking my clothes, I lay across the comforter and thought of our new assignment. When I dropped off to sleep, my mind conjured up many of my past assignments, some of which were very grueling, some life-threatening and some most pleasant.

I recalled the time in Moscow when I was shot at and missed while pursuing a man known to be counterfeiting British pounds. As I chased him across several roofs, he fell to his death when his foot slipped on a loose tile. He had the engraved plates on his person.

I also remembered being captured in Kiev, being hung naked by my ankles with my hands tied to two iron rings on the floor. After many hours of hanging there, I was able to escape by twisting and then loosening the straps around my hands and, because of my hardened abs, I worked my hands down my legs to my feet and loosened those straps. I slipped out a basement window without any clothes. I "borrowed" pants and a shirt from a homeless man and got to the railroad station where I caught the next train out after explaining I'd been robbed of both clothing and money.

I recalled my visits with the rich and famous as well as the poor and indigent. Reviewing each previous event, I was convinced I not only enjoyed them, with some few exceptions, but also that I'd done a good job on each assignment. My service with both Agencies was interesting and meaningful and I really liked what I was doing. I've aged but I haven't slowed down one bit; my assignments have changed.

My thoughts turned to Arlene. I dreamed about our first meeting and about the missions we've had together, just the two of us, or with Baba. We three had become very good friends, but Arlene and I found that we not only liked working together but also loved each other very much. Our time together is pleasant and our sexual relationship is perfection. She is everything I could ever want in a mate and I believe the feeling is mutual.

Of course we have our arguments but they're few and far between, and making up is so much fun. She kids me about being a perfectionist, one who cannot tolerate in others the lack of total dedication to a task. I chide her about always looking so perfect. I told her I wished she'd sometimes wear jeans and a ragged shirt.

I was awakened by a warm kiss on my stomach and one slightly lower. The scent of lilacs was hovering over my body and my desire was rapidly welling up. As I attempted to pull her down on me, she resisted saying "The time is 11:30." As she got off the bed and walked toward the packages she had acquired, I went to the bathroom and took that cold shower she'd previously suggested. When I re-entered the bedroom, she had taken off her dress and was standing in her underwear. I immediately fell to my knees and surrounded her with my arms. She turned slightly and patted me on the head. "Later, my darling; later."

As we packed, I noticed the bottle of Montebuena Rioja sitting on the table. I dropped it into one of my shoe bags. We left the room and checked out, deciding to have lunch in Belgravia. We left the hotel, I carrying both suitcases and Arlene carrying our briefcases.

The sandwich shop was near the Underground. We ate quietly, exchanging fond looks at being in each other's company. Afterwards, we took the Underground to Paddington Station. I purchased a *London Times*

and thumbed through the international section to see if there were any

further details on the assassinations in Greece. There was nothing.

EIGHT

The trip to Exeter was not a long one. When we arrived, we walked across the narrow street to the car rental agency. Arlene asked for a map of the area. We began our drive westward to Moretonhampstead, arriving about 7:00 P.M. After checking in and before dining, I telephoned the widow of our former associate. She was happy to know we'd worked with her husband and were newlyweds staying at The Inn. We were invited for tea at four "on the morrow."

The White Horse Inn is a quaint 15th Century establishment. Exposed beams were visible everywhere, even in our room. We descended the one flight to the lobby and the dining room where the host greeted us. He was the same person who'd checked us in and was also the owner, Mr. Cyril Newberry. The dining room was small with six tables for four. Each had a freshly starched cloth and a small vase of fresh flowers. After we were seated, the host appeared with a bottle of Champagne, which had been suggested "by your secretary who informed me that you were on your honeymoon." After each of us had been served a glass, including the host,

Arlene and I toasted and expressed our eternal love for each other. The dining room, filled with diners who obviously had been informed of our arrival, rang with a loud shouting of "Long live the happy newlyweds." We'd established our raison d'être.

Our room was smallish but had a double bed, a table with a lamp, a chiffonier with a mirror and an overstuffed chair. The small bath was near the rear wall. There was no closet. Our room was on the back of the Inn, "away from traffic", which, I learned at breakfast, hardly existed in this village. I'd parked our car around the corner near a building which stood only a few feet from the roadway, as the sign on the front of the Inn had instructed me to do. Since this Inn was the only public accommodation in the village, it was the focal point for village activity, especially the pub, which was open twenty-four hours every day.

When I'd closed and locked the door, I looked at Arlene and we both began to laugh. Who would have thought that our honeymoon would be spent in a small Devonshire village on the edge of The Dartmoor, in a 15th Century establishment, where the bedroom ceiling beams were exposed as was the light hanging in the center of the room? Laughing, we were able to come out of our clothes and jump into bed. As we slowly regained our composure, we snuggled without any cover. The two windows were closed, as were the curtains. The room was quite warm. We began to fondle each other and touch our most intimate places. We took turns kissing and licking each other's body.

Our making love began slowly but in a very short time was fast-paced and torrid. I thought about the noise we were making. What would our neighbors think? Then I remembered that we're on our honeymoon and doing only what might be expected of us. Throwing our concerns to the winds, we continued pleasuring each other for several hours until both Arlene and I agreed we needed a rest. Since we were quite sweaty and the bath had no shower, I toweled myself and then Arlene. When I lay back, I pulled the sheet over us so we wouldn't be cold before dawn. Shortly, we were both asleep.

I awoke first and entered the bath stepping into the small tub. My six foot plus frame could hardly manage to get all of me in. I managed to wash almost every part of my body and then stood up to finish. I then remembered I hadn't washed my hair. I got on my hands and knees and proceeded to do so. I began to act silly, thinking of the primitive facilities we had "chosen" for our honeymoon. I began to laugh aloud as I opened the bathroom door. Arlene was sitting in bed with a smile on her face.

"You took so long I was beginning to think you were playing with yourself," she said, jokingly. I walked around the bed to her side and leaned over to kiss her on the forehead and the lips. She responded warmly but then quickly jumped out of bed and rushed to the bathroom, saying "I can hardly wait to try it myself." When she'd filled the tub and gotten in, she began to sing our song. After a rather long time, she emerged with just a towel wrapped around her head. I was still sitting upright in bed, naked, and of course, erect. She approached me with a mischievous look in her eyes and began to twist the hair on my chest around her fingers. I purposely didn't respond, although I wanted to take her then and there. She moved around my side and began to massage my back and shoulders. I couldn't resist anymore. I grabbed her and pulled her down on my body. I kissed her passionately. We clung to each other as our temperatures rose precipitously. As I entered her very gently, she smiled and whispered in my ear, "You are my one and only, my dearest man, my most passionate lover. Don't ever let me go. Keep me near you forever. I love you so much."

When we finished making love, we lay side by side. After several kisses, I rose and went into the bathroom to dry off again. When I returned, Arlene had put on her negligee, the Champagne-colored one, and was sitting in the overstuffed chair.

"Let me dress you," she said quietly. I retrieved my crotch pouch from the table and handed it to her. She put it on and adjusted its position. "Is that all right?" she asked. "Perfect." I replied. She put on my shirt with the buttoned-down collar and tied my tie. She helped me step into my trousers, fastened my belt and zipped me up. As I sat down on the bed, Arlene put on my socks and shoes. When I stood up, she helped me with my suit coat. "You look wonderful," she said. "Now if you'll go downstairs and look around the village, I'll be down in thirty minutes for breakfast. I'll meet you in the dining room." I kissed her tenderly and left the room.

There was nobody in the lobby except the manager who greeted me with a hearty smile and asked if we found everything we needed. I assured him the accommodations were quite nice and we were happy to be staying at his Inn. I excused myself and walked into the street.

I returned to the Inn just as Arlene was descending the stairs. We entered the dining room and were seated by the owner. My watch read 8:35. Since our appointment for tea was at four, I wondered what we could do for the next seven-plus hours. Arlene saw in my eyes the quizzical look of "what now?" The manager brought us a small, hand-written menu for today's meals. I chose scrambled eggs with a rasher of bacon, dry toast and, of course, a pot of tea. Arlene's appetite was also huge; she ordered the same. The servings were large and tasty. The tea was Earl Grey. When I requested a second pot, the manager said, "You must be from London. I can spot a Londoner straight away. The local citizens never order a second pot of tea. They always come back at four for tea and scones."

When we finished breakfast, we left the Inn and walked around the village for about an hour. There were a few shops, an appliance store, another pub and an establishment where hand-made articles and locally preserved foods were sold. There was also a garage for automobile repairs and one service station. The local grocery store had a pharmacy and a flower shop. While walking around the village, I was looking for the street on which our afternoon hostess lived. It was about four blocks from the Inn and only two blocks long. Finding the right house shouldn't be difficult.

Our motor tour of the area took us northward to the town of Chagford, one of the five original stannary towns, where tin coins were first minted for use throughout England. We found a nice café for lunch.

We arrived back at the Inn at 3:15, "freshened up" and left for the short walk to our appointment. The house sat very near the street, almost on the curb. I knocked twice using the antique iron knocker on the door.

We were greeted by a lady of about seventy years, attired in a plain blue dress, a gold bracelet and tiny gold earrings. I introduced us as Mr. and Mrs. Devon. She smiled and said, "Please come in." The house was small, really a cottage. We entered the living room and sat on two straight chairs. Our hostess sat on the sofa, in front of which stood a small, low table. A polished silver tray held a teapot, a cream pitcher, and a glass plate of lemon slices. Three ironed linen napkins were nearby.

While pouring tea, she said, "I'm so pleased to meet you and to wish you both a pleasant stay in our little village. It's nice to meet someone who actually knew my husband and worked with him." I handed her the envelope which I'd taken from my inside breast pocket. "Oh my," she said, "I've never before received a letter with the crest of the Queen on it." She looked quite impressed. "When I received the call that you were coming and would have something for me, I never expected a letter from the Queen." She read the letter slowly. Her smile changed into a most quizzical expression. "A book my husband kept in his safe?" she said questioningly. "I don't recall ever seeing him with such a book. Of course, we never talked about his work. I knew it was important, but I never suspected he was working for the Crown." She paused. "Would you like more tea?"

"No thank you," we said in unison as I waited for her further comments. They didn't seem to be forthcoming.

"Have you opened the safe recently?" I asked.

"After my husband died, I wanted to open it to see if our wills and the deed to this house were still there, but I couldn't remember the combination."

My heart sank. What now? "Did you keep it written down some place within the house?" I asked

"No, my husband thought that would be unwise."

"Do you remember any of the numbers in the combination?"

"Yes. The first number was the last two digits of the year in which he was born, and the second number was the last two digits of the year in which I was born. But I can't for the life of me remember the third number. I do remember it had no significance to my life or to anything we did together. He did say one time that the combination was of prime importance and I should always remember it."

Prime importance. That struck a familiar chord.

"Would you mind if I tried to open the safe? Perhaps I can be successful since your husband and I worked for the same organization and we did occasionally discuss several events which might have some bearing on the combination he chose." I was making this up as I went along.

"That would be fine, Mr. Devon. Come with me to my bedroom. You can come too, Mrs. Devon. I'm not accustomed to being alone with a young man in my bedroom," she said cheerily.

We accompanied her. She opened the closet door and pointed to a small safe on the floor, behind some boxes, which she removed. I knelt down and looked at the dial. It was the standard safe which each of us in the Agency had been issued; but we'd been instructed that the usual right-left-right procedure had been reversed.

"May I please have the first number and then the second one? I rarely ask for the birth date of a lady but I'm sure you understand the significance of my request." She gave me both numbers. My mind was running rapidly through all the one and two digit prime numbers I thought would have been of interest to her husband. And then it struck me. Everyone in the Agency knew of the *37*. With an air of complete confidence, I turned the dial to the left stopping on 37. I took the handle in my hand, prayed to Heaven and turned it. The door opened.

"My goodness," she said with tears in her eyes. "You've convinced me that you really are who you said you were and this letter from the Queen is authentic." She reached into the safe and took out a small, dark gray plain leather-bound book. "Could this be what you're looking for?"

I took the book and opened it. In it were columns of five-digit numbers in the first half and random length numbers in the second. I stood up and looked her in the eye. I wanted to hug this sweet lady, but decorum prevailed.

"Thank you, so much. You have contributed immensely to the memory of your husband. For all of us who worked with him, my deepest appreciation. I shall be most pleased to inform the Crown of your invaluable help in this most important operation." She was beaming through her tears.

At the front door, our hostess said, "I don't believe you'll tell me what this is all about, but meeting you both and knowing that I've done the right thing for my country is sufficient for my memories. Thank you, my dear new friends."

I did then what I'd previously not done. I took her hands in mine and bent forward, kissing her on the forehead. She smiled.

We walked back to the Inn, holding hands, not saying a word. We arrived in our room and closed the door. I lay the book on the bed and took my dearest Arlene in my arms. I was truly overcome with emotion, knowing that we'd successfully completed another mission. We both were ecstatic and agreed that we should rest for now and savor the moment. I looked at my watch. 5:15. I then remembered I hadn't informed the proprietor of the time we'd like dinner. Arlene said "Perhaps at six." Putting the book in my briefcase, I descended the stairs.

The proprietor wasn't behind the desk and neither was he in the dining room. I saw the door to the kitchen and wondered if I dare enter someone's kitchen without an invitation. I gently rapped on the door and was greeted with a hearty "Come in." The proprietor-cum-chef, attired in a long white apron, was busy at the stove preparing what I was certain would be shepherd's pie. He turned and smiled and said, "I knew you couldn't stay away after smelling the aromas coming from my kitchen. Are you pleased?"

"It's certainly a compelling aroma," I said. Then I asked, "At what time would you like us to arrive for dinner?"

"Others in the village will be here about 6:30. Some will stop at the bar for a pint or two before dining. A few have asked if they could be introduced to "that happy honeymoon couple." He paused. "If I'm not being too presumptive, Mr. Devon, would you and Mrs. Devon spend a few minutes before dinner in the pub greeting a few of my regulars?"

"We'd be honored, Mr. Newberry. Thank you for telling me of their wishes. Should we arrive about 6:15?"

"That'll be splendid. I'll alert my regulars."

When I got to our room, I informed Arlene of my conversation with Mr. Newberry. I informed her that we're well known in the village and were expected in the pub about 6:15, and that it might be appropriate for us to buy a round of drinks since we'll be meeting the "regulars." She thought that sounded "peachy."

We quickly changed clothes, brushed our teeth, combed our hair and left the room. As we entered the pub, there were approximately twenty people awaiting our arrival. We were greeted with loud cheers and applause. I thanked everyone for being so kind to the "unknown newly-weds" and announced: "My wife and I would like to buy a round for the whole lot of you." Another round of applause with "oohs" ensued. The chef then entered the pub and informed me he'd coordinate our meeting each of the regulars and, as an aside, he would introduce them "in the order of their importance in the village." There is a hierarchy of rank everywhere, I thought, even in a small village like Moretonhampstead. Arlene and I were ushered by the chef to a place at the end of the bar. When everyone had been served, the chef approached us, accompanied by a man of about sixty.

"Mr. and Mrs. Devon, may I present the Mayor of our village, Mr. Edward Farnsworth?"

The introductions continued until every one of the regulars, from the mayor and the doctor and his wife to the mail carrier had shaken our hands. Then, almost on cue, we all sat down to dinner. The shepherd's pie was nothing less than magnificent: encrusted aged beef with fresh asparagus and hot, freshly baked rolls. I asked if I could bring a bottle of our favorite wine. I went to our room and got the Montebuena I had in my shoe bag. For dessert, we chose boysenberry pie. It was very tasty with a pot of tea. Oh, how I wanted a cup of coffee.

We were the last to leave. I stopped at the front desk while Arlene went on to our room. The chef had now reverted to being the manager and was standing behind the desk.

"If you'll prepare our bill, I'll pay it now since we'll be leaving rather early."

"Certainly, sir. Give me a few seconds and it'll be ready." He added a few figures on the already-prepared statement and handed it to me.

I looked it over quickly and offered him cash, since I hadn't seen any sign of credit card use anywhere in the village. I added a generous gratuity. We both smiled, shook hands and I went up to our room.

Arlene was already undressed, wearing her Champagne-colored negligee and seated in the overstuffed chair. I closed the door, locked it and began to undress. Wearing only my pouch, I faced Arlene and stood there motionless, waiting for her to make the first move.

"I'll say again, you are absolutely gorgeous." I walked closer to her. She remained seated, removed my pouch and began to caress my legs and my buttocks. She slowly got up, licking my stomach and my chest. I remained as motionless as I could. She turned me around and kissed my back in several spots and then both shoulders. It was I who now turned around and kissed her gently on the lips. I picked her up and walked slowly to our bed, placing her on top of the comforter.

The phone rang. "Damn! Damn! Damn!" I said as I picked up the receiver. The voice on the other end asked me to identify myself, which I did using the appropriate codes, and then heard Z's voice.

"I truly hate to intrude on your honeymoon, but I have some urgent things to say." Z then began a coded message. At the completion of his conversation, I said, "Arlene and I will be leaving here about 6:00, driving to Exeter to board the 8:05. We can be in your office shortly after noon." Z closed our conversation with "cheerio."

The coded message hadn't mentioned any names, but the "cheerio" gave me a clue that it had something to do with either Francisco or Baba. When I hung up, I told Arlene everything Z had said. We discussed the message and agreed that we'd understood it correctly. My mind was in a spin. I was startled to hear the information Z had conveyed, even though I didn't know for sure about whom he was speaking.

Arlene and I talked for quite a while. Neither of us seemed in the mood to continue what we'd begun. I looked at my watch. 11:30. I lay back on the bed, staring at the bare light bulb. With it firmly fixed in my mind, I switched off the light. Arlene and I said nothing. We were both thinking about our meeting with Z and the revelations that would be forthcoming. Finally, I pulled up the sheet, kissed her on the lips and turned over on my stomach. I drifted off to sleep. It was a fitful sleep, in which I imagined all kinds of scenarios. I awoke shortly and looked at my watch. 2:20. I was wide awake. Arlene was asleep. I might as well get up, I thought. I eased out of bed and sat in the overstuffed chair in the dark. I went over again everything Z had said. I knew from the coded message that a death had occurred and one of our friends was involved.

Arlene awoke at 5:00. We packed and departed. We were silent as we drove toward Exeter.

After a brief breakfast, we walked to the station, after turning in the rental car, arriving at 7:55. The train pulled in; we boarded and took our assigned seats. I asked the conductor if I had time to step off the train to get a paper from the box just a few feet away. He agreed and I dashed to the box, put in the exact change, took a paper and rushed back as the conductor closed the door.

There was nothing in the *Times* about anyone's unusual death, not even a friend of a friend. I re-read the paper from cover to cover. Nothing. Arlene and I looked at each other often but words didn't seem appropriate.

The trip to London was long and boring. When we arrived at Paddington Station, I hailed a taxi. As we walked into the office, the secretary asked for our codes and ushered us into the inner sanctum. Z was seated behind his desk. He looked very depressed, and I noticed that his eyes were red.

"My dear friends and colleagues," he began slowly and hesitantly. "I regret to inform you that yesterday evening Francisco was involved in a tragic automobile accident in which both he and his driver, Philip, were killed instantly."

The news hit me hard. I looked at both Z and Arlene in total disbelief.

He continued. "Yesterday morning, he left my office and caught a plane to Madrid. Philip picked him up at the airport. On the way to his villa, several men jumped in front of the car. As Philip swerved the car trying to miss them, he ran into a culvert and the car flipped over in the ditch. The attackers ran, taking nothing from the wreckage, which was discovered about an hour later by an anonymous caller to the police in that area."

"How is Baba and where is she?" I asked.

"The police notified her about two hours after the accident. They made arrangements to have the bodies taken to a funeral parlor in a town near the villa. Baba is at the villa under the care of her doctor."

"May I ask how you found out about this tragic event?"

"I received an anonymous telephone call informing me there'd been an accident and both the driver and the passenger were killed. I traced the call. It came from a pay phone in Madrid."

I was in shock. Arlene held my hand.

"Why would anyone want to kill Francisco?" I asked.

"Francisco was working on an assignment concerning an international cartel involving drugs. He told me before he left he knew the name of the drug lord and would have sufficient proof to give me in a few days. I warned him to be careful and to take no chances. I offered him backup but he declined, saying he felt sure his identity hadn't been compromised."

"Could we see or talk to Baba?" I asked.

"She is safe in her villa. I have posted three of my men to stay in the villa under the guise of working for Francisco, but chiefly they are there to see that all necessary arrangements are being carried out correctly and to protect Baba."

"Where do we go from here?" I asked.

"Arlene, my dear, you need to take some time and settle your mother's estate. I have arranged for you to be housed with a friend near your mother's home. She has a car and is at your disposal until the estate is settled. She will pick you up in front of the Lowndes Hotel this afternoon at 4:00. Her name is Margit Schmidt and she is about thirty-five, a five foot six-inch blond with blue eyes. She's been on my payroll for about seven years and is quite adept at looking after individuals who need such care.

"As for you, Philipp, you are booked on a six o'clock flight to Madrid. I also have arranged for young Sven Christen to take his vacation at this time. Sven is not only in superb physical condition, he also holds a black belt in Judo. He too has been trained to look after people who need looking after.

"I want you, Philipp, to mentor Sven, as I trained you. He'll meet you at the airport in Madrid with a company car and will serve as your driver

for the next few weeks, or as long as it takes to find out what's going on.

You both are booked at the Hotel Madrid in adjoining rooms, the reason

being Sven will plant hearing devices in your room and on your telephone

to overhear and record any conversations you may have with whomever

you may invite to your room or talk to on the phone. He'll also install a

hidden camera. Are there any questions?"

"Sir, I have no idea what I'm looking for or whom I expect to contact

or be contacted by."

"You are registered as Mr. Philipp Devon and driver. You're in the

international trading business and have spent quite a bit of time in both

Columbia and Venezuela. The concierge has been furnished this

information with the request he assist you in making "business contacts",

if possible. Just keep your eyes and ears open and report to me at least

once each week."

Arlene and I rose from our chairs as Z stood up. I asked him to keep

me informed of the funeral arrangements and requested his permission to

attend. He agreed. We shook hands as he wished each of us "Godspeed."

We left the building and decided to have a leisurely lunch in Hyde

Park near the Serpentine, so we could watch the ducks and ease our tensions. We entered the Park at Albert Gate, found a semi-secluded spot near the water and sat down on the grass. We purchased a few lunch items at a nearby kiosk.

Neither of us was very talkative, being quite despondent over Francisco's death. My newest assignment in Madrid had all the trappings of a witch hunt. But the thing that disturbed me the most was the realization that I'd be separated from Arlene for God knows how long. Seated on the grass and watching the ducks gliding over the water, I looked at Arlene. She was smiling. I took her hand and leaned over to kiss her. As our lips touched, the tears began to flow from our eyes as we held hands.

"My dearest Arlene, this is certainly not what I had in mind to do when we returned to London. We both know, however, we can never plan on anything with the expectation it'll come to pass. I'll miss you terribly. I love you, Arlene, more than life itself."

With tears in her eyes, she said "Oh, my dearest Philipp. Being without you at my side will be painful. But I'll look forward to the day we'll be together again. We both knew when we said our vows this kind of life would be constant until we both decide to leave it permanently. I shan't call you in Madrid for I know you'll be extremely busy." She smiled as she wiped away her tears. "I'll pray for your safety each night before I sleep, and I'll think of you lying beside me as I cuddle my pillow."

I leaned over and took her in my arms. We hugged and kissed.

"I'm not very hungry right now, so you have the lunch with Ms. Schmidt."

We gathered the lunch and walked out of the Park, arriving shortly at the hotel. I checked my watch. It was 3:50. There was a sedan parked in front. The driver got out and approached us. Margit Schmidt was exactly as Z had described her. We three introduced ourselves and Arlene got in the sedan as Margit put the luggage in the trunk. I waved as they pulled away from the curb, until they were out of sight.

"My dearest Arlene," I said to myself, "when will I see you again?"

NINE

I took the Underground to Heathrow and boarded my flight to Madrid. I tried to recall every possible person who could be involved in Francisco's death. I didn't omit anyone. I've learned never to discard out-of-hand any information.

My thoughts turned to Mykonos. There was Mr. Hargrave who got himself killed. Why and by whom? Why had he made such an effort to hook up with the Greek Minister? I thought of Nikolas; is he somehow involved in this tangled mess or was his relationship with Hargrave purely sexual?

I'd no idea who or what I'd be looking for. Z seemed to think that the answers to these questions might be found in Madrid. However, he didn't specifically say that but said I should stay on the case wherever it took me.

Having Sven with me was probably wise but of course in no way could his companionship compensate for my not being with Arlene.

We touched down three minutes early. As I deplaned, I saw Sven standing in the door of the terminal. Carrying my briefcase and one piece of luggage, I approached him as a businessman greeting his driver. I never know who might be watching.

Sven said, with "professional driver" written all over his face, "Good evening, Mr. Devon. May I take your luggage?" He was dressed in a black uniform with a black, billed cap. I handed him my bag but kept my briefcase. We went directly to the car and left the terminal grounds. Sven opened the glass between us and said, "It's good to see you again, Mr. Devon."

"Thank you, Sven. It's good to see you also. When we're together in public, you'll please address me as you just did: Mr. Devon. But when we're in hotel rooms or by ourselves with no one around, please call me Philipp."

"You got it, Philipp."

As we drove into the city, he asked about our mission.

"To be quite honest, my friend, I don't know." I described all the details of the accident that I knew.

"I'm truly sorry to hear that. Will we be going to the funeral?"

"I believe we will, but as yet I don't know the time or the place. I should hear from Z sometime tonight or early tomorrow morning."

We pulled into the parking garage of the Hotel Madrid and I asked the attendant, in Spanish, if we might park the car ourselves.

"Si, Señor." He directed Sven to a parking spot. I gave Sven a few coins for a tip.

We each took our luggage from the trunk and with my briefcase in hand, went to the lobby's Registration Desk, Sven carrying both pieces of luggage. I spoke in Spanish.

"My name is Señor Philipp Devon and this is my driver. I have a reservation for a suite registered in my name for the both of us."

"Si, Señor Devon. We were expecting you. You have a telephone call from London. She said it was urgent," handing me a slip of paper.

The bellman took our bags. Our rooms were on the 5th floor. Mine was a corner room and Sven's adjoined mine. When the bellman had been tipped and departed, Sven opened his bag and began to pull out the equipment necessary for his tasks. I went to the telephone in my room and called the number given me. Z's secretary answered and, after the proper identifications, rang Z.

"How was your flight, Philipp?" Z asked as soon as he picked up the phone.

"Uneventful."

"The funeral is tomorrow at four at the Church near the villa. Ask the concierge to give you a map and directions to Ciudad Real. My men at the villa are expecting you. Baba is also expecting you. She is much better and has recovered from the initial shock."

"The only suit I have with me is the dark one I took on my honeymoon. I don't know what Sven brought with him, but in the event I'm invited to a formal function, in the line of duty, of course, what am I authorized to buy and how should it be paid for?"

"Purchase whatever you and Sven need and use your London bank card. As you know, the charges will come directly to my desk, so be prudent in your selections."

"I'm always prudent, sir; you know that."

He laughed. "When I have more information, I'll send it by coded message or through one of my men at the villa."

I looked at my watch. 8:55. I was extremely hungry. I thought we should order dinner in the room. We looked at the menu in the Hotel Services book and I decided to order tournedos. I looked at Sven to see if he remembered that was what he'd recommended to Arlene and me. He smiled his assent. I ordered dinner for two. I also ordered a bottle of Montebuena Rioja, just to see if it might stir up any interest.

Sven was in his room putting together the elements of our bugging systems. I walked into his room to see if he needed any help. He didn't. We talked about his physical training for about fifteen minutes. A knock on my door signified the arrival of our dinners. The waiter placed the tray on the center table in my room and opened the bottle of wine. I signed the check, adding a generous tip. The waiter exited the room with a most sincere "gracias", carrying my bag of laundry.

When I laid out the dinners on the table and poured two glasses of wine, I called Sven to dinner. As he entered my room, I said, "I always like to be naked when I'm in my apartment in Washington, and I'm always naked when I'm with my dearest Arlene. I propose to be naked while I'm in this room and if you have any problems with that, let me know now."

"I'm always naked too, when I'm alone", he answered.

With that having been said, I removed my remaining clothes but Sven kept on his briefs. He didn't comment on my crotch pouch for he was wearing one also.

The tournedos were good but not so good as the ones Sven had prepared for Arlene and me. I told him so. He nodded in agreement. The wine wasn't a 1982, but a 1984.

We chatted as we ate. I told him about the plan to drive to Francisco's funeral tomorrow and the visit with Baba at her villa beforehand. He'd never met either Francisco or Baba, so I briefed him on my past relationships with both. He asked several pertinent questions. He's a bright young man who grasps each situation rapidly.

When we'd finished dinner, Sven completed his installations on my telephone and a camera in the air vent. I looked at my watch again. 10:35.

"I'm going to turn in," I said. "If you have no objection, I'd like to leave the door open between our rooms in the event I get a phone call and we need to coordinate the picking up of the receivers." He agreed. As I spoke, the telephone in my room rang. Sven went to my bathroom and picked up that receiver. A man spoke.

"Philipp, this is John. Welcome to Madrid. Mother would like to take you shopping tomorrow afternoon. She has a short list but wanted me to remind you that you should remember to pick up some things for your family and friends back home."

"Thank you, John. I'll be delighted to accompany your mother shopping. Shall I pick her up at your house or will you come to the hotel?"

"She'd like for you to pick her up here at 4:00, if that's alright with you."

"My driver and I will arrive a few minutes before 4:00. It's good talking with you; I'll see you both tomorrow." We replaced the receivers and I looked at Sven. "Did you get all that on tape?"

"All of it, but you need to explain it to me."

"That was one of Z's men at Baba's villa confirming that you and I should arrive at 3:30. I've been instructed to use my lapel mike and record the names of everyone I can recognize at the funeral. Z's three men will record the tag numbers of all the cars present for the funeral. They'll do that by speaking into their lapel mikes so they won't be noticed writing. You're to engage some of the other drivers in conversation during the service in the Church and learn as much as you can about their passengers."

"You got all that from your short conversation?"

"It was all in the code I've been using for several years. Z modified the standard code for more personal conversations."

"Wow! I sure do have a lot to learn."

"That's why you and I are on this assignment. I'm to teach you as much as you can absorb while we pursue our targets. It may take one week, two weeks or a month or more, particularly since I've no idea who we're looking for. Now let's call it a day." We both went to bed.

I awoke at 6:30 and heard huffing and puffing in the next room. When I walked to the door, I saw a naked Sven doing one-arm pushups on the carpet. I watched in amazement. How can a man of his size do that many one-arm push-ups? I heard him counting quietly: …seventy-three, seventy-four, seventy-five. He stopped and got up. When he saw me at the door, he said, "You work out too, don't you?"

I was flattered that he'd noticed, since there are at least fifteen years between us. I try to keep in shape with my daily exercises and an occasional visit to a gym.

"I do triples before I get out of bed. You're familiar with triples where you lie flat on your back with your palms by your side, extend the legs upward and then lower them to the left, then to the right, then down straight keeping your feet off the bed. Then I do sit-ups and other exercises on the floor. I also have a small set of weights in my room just for toning."

"I know you aren't old, but I'd like to know how old you are," he asked.

"Thirty-nine last April," I said. "May I ask your age?"

"Twenty-five last week."

"How long have you been a black belt?

"I started Judo when I was sixteen and I've had a black belt for five years."

With that conversation ended, I suggested we order breakfast in the room. He let me order for the two of us — "so long as it's healthful and huge." I ordered bacon and scrambled eggs, dry toast, jam, skimmed milk and coffee. He overheard me ordering and commented, "You don't eat as much as I do."

I shaved and showered first, while Sven manned the phone, so that I'd be robed when breakfast arrived. Just as I was stepping out of the shower, a knock at the door was followed by "Room Service." The same waiter as last night smiled as he said "Good morning" in perfect English, and then put the tray on the table. I signed the check including a nice tip, causing him to smile and say "Muchas gracias, Señor."

After the waiter left, I shucked my robe and called Sven for breakfast. He came in naked and seemed at ease since we both had done our exercises in the nude.

"Do you think we'll find someone at the funeral that might be our mark?"

"I'm hoping so, although I don't even know what he or she looks like."

"When we get to the villa, will I have a chance to meet the Countess?"

"How'd you know she was a Countess?"

"Z told me when he called me in Marbella. He also said she was one of the most beautiful women in the world, or had been at one time."

"I don't know if you have a girl friend back in Stockholm, or even a new one in Marbella, but it wouldn't be appropriate to hit on the Countess at this time." We looked at each other and laughed.

After he'd finished breakfast, he shaved and showered. I checked my watch. 8:20.

"Have you checked out the camera? I asked.

"I have your clear picture permanently recorded."

"I hope I had clothes on."

"I am ever vigilant. Don't worry."

I called the concierge and asked him to send up the *Herald Tribune*. In the *Tribune*, there was a write-up of the accident and the death of the Count. There was no mention of the funeral arrangements. That probably helps my pursuit, for anyone who attends the funeral from outside the immediate family will stand out.

I decided Sven and I would remain in our rooms until after lunch, waiting for any calls that might come in before we left. I remember

Francisco's driver telling me it was a two-hour drive from the villa to Madrid. We should leave the hotel no later than 1:00. I checked my watch again. 9:50.

I decided to take a nap. I told Sven, who said he'd remain alert. I dozed off and dreamed of my dearest Arlene on our trip to Moretonhampstead and how much fun we had on our honeymoon. I relived the wonderful times we had making love. I remembered every curve of her body. I remembered the scent of roses and of lilacs.

I awoke suddenly and went to my bathroom and took a cold shower. Oh, how I miss Arlene.

When I stepped out of the shower and was toweling dry, Sven came into the room and asked if I was all right.

"You were talking incoherently, but occasionally mentioned Arlene. I know you miss her, Philipp, but I'm sure she's all right and the two of you will be reunited soon."

"Thank you for your concern and your understanding. Arlene and I recited our marriage vows and, as far as we're concerned, we're married. She's the only woman I've ever loved this much, this intensely. She's not only gorgeous but also sweet and tender and deeply passionate. I can't bear it when I'm not with her, nor can I bear the pain of thinking I might never see her again."

"Why would you say that? Arlene is doing what she must do. Z told me this when he told me I'd be working with you. I know how difficult it is to be away from the one you love. I've a girl friend in Stockholm who I plan to marry as soon as I can get back there. I miss her terribly and have taken so many cold showers to deal with my sexual frustration I'm afraid I'll shrivel up and be all wrinkly. You've got to concentrate on our current assignment. I believe you're the best agent in Z's group and I've admired you since I first heard from Z and my father about your past accomplishments. Cheer up, Philipp. We'll both attain our destinies in due time." I looked at him. How could a man so young know so much about the really important things in life? How could this giant of a man be so understanding and caring about the tender moments of life? If we both hadn't been naked, I would've given him a hug.

"You're a fine man, Sven, and I'm proud, not only to be working with you, but also to call you my friend."

"Thank you", he said as he turned and went into his room.

The phone rang. I looked at Sven as he rushed to my bathroom phone.

"Señor, Devon, there was a gentleman on the telephone who said he would like to make an appointment with you for this afternoon."

"Did he give his name?"

"No, Señor."

"Did he say why he wanted the appointment?"

"No, Señor. He only left a telephone number. Would you like it now?"

"Yes, please."

Sven came into the room. "What do you think that was all about?"

"I've no idea but I think I'll wait until we return this evening to call

him, although I'm very curious about how he knew I was here."

TEN

We had lunch in the room as we discussed a number of possibilities for the call.

"When I do call him back, I'll ask, first, how he knew me and that I was staying at this hotel; and second, the nature of his business and the purpose of our proposed meeting?"

We both got dressed and Sven went to the car. He was to tip the attendant and tell him we'd return later that evening. He was to bring the car up to the attendant's cage and I'd meet him there. We exited the hotel ramp and continued in the direction of Ciudad Real. Sven kept the glass open. We chatted about different things. I liked his approach to our assignment and the more I was with him, the better I liked him. He's smart and dedicated and I'm pleased that Z has made me his mentor.

We arrived at the villa at 3:20. As we pulled into the courtyard, we saw three young men, one of whom I knew from a previous assignment.

"Good afternoon, Mr. Devon."

"Good afternoon, Bryan. It's good to see you again."

"This is Felix and this is James, Mr. Devon."

"Gentlemen, I'd be pleased if you'd call me Philipp, with a double p on the end." We all laughed. "This is Sven, my driver, and a trainee under my tutelage." We all shook hands as Baba came into the courtyard and ran toward me, putting her arms around me, giving me a big hug and a tearful "Welcome." I kissed her on the cheek.

"Countess, may I introduce Sven Christen from Stockholm?"

"It is so nice to meet you, Sven. I know your father well."
We were all ushered into the library and seated around the center table. Baba spoke.

"Philipp, I'm devastated by Francisco's death. I don't know what I shall do without him. We loved each other so very much." She began to tear up and dabbed her eyes with a silk handkerchief. "As you already know, he was very fond of you; as am I. You have been a wonderful friend and a superior co-worker. Have you any idea how this all happened?"

"No, Countess, I do not; but Sven and I have been charged with finding out and I can assure you we'll not stop until those responsible have been captured."

"Oh, my dear Philipp, you are such a comfort. Thank you both for being with me on this sad day."

Baba rose as did we. We followed her to the entry hall where she put on her black hat with veil and her black gloves and carried a Missal bound in black leather. Even though she was in mourning attire, she looked magnificent.

"Philipp, will you please ride with me to the Church?"

"Certainly, Countess. Bryan, you, Felix and James will ride with Sven."

Before we got in our cars, I took Bryan aside and discussed his call to me regarding the compiling of the lists of attendees and cars. He'd already briefed Felix and James and I told him Sven would be keeping an eye on anyone looking around, winking, nodding or doing anything suspicious.

The ride to the Church took less than five minutes. When we arrived, there were several cars parked nearby and ten people standing on the steps awaiting Baba's arrival. I assisted Baba in getting out of the Rolls and offered her my arm as we approached those already gathered. After she'd greeted them, I was assured that she knew each of them and mentally crossed them off my list of suspects.

The Church was more of a Chapel as one would expect on an estate. It was small, of granite, with five rows of pews on either side of a center aisle. There were a few people inside but none were known by Baba. I assumed them to be from the nearby village. The Priest greeted Baba and me as we entered. Francisco's casket was positioned in front of the altar and was covered with a spray of white lilies and greenery. We sat in the first pew on the right.

The service was brief and so was the interment in the Church cemetery, which I later discovered contained the remains of only Francisco's family. When we left the cemetery and re-approached our cars, Bryan told me three additional cars arrived after we went in. Since Baba and I left the Church through the side door, I wasn't able to see the additional people.

When we arrived at the villa, I escorted Baba inside and went back to talk with my associates. As I stepped into the courtyard, my four friends gathered around to report their findings. Each of the ten people standing at the door to the Church awaiting Baba's arrival had signed the Funeral Register as had the other six who were already in the Church. None of the other five late arrivals had done so. All the cars had been "tagged" and Bryan had already called in the numbers to the Vehicle Registration Bureau in Madrid, with whom Z had made arrangements for Bryan to be furnished the names and addresses of the owners of each car. Bryan, Felix and James had written all their data on note cards. I looked at the registrants of the three other cars but didn't recognize any name. However, one of the cars carried not only a Spanish licensing permit but also a registration in the country of my former college roommate.

The five of us went back inside the villa and joined Baba in the library for sherry. We took our glasses from the silver tray held by the maître d' and sat down. Baba spoke.

"Gentlemen, I cannot adequately express my sincere thanks for your services in this time of grief. I have had prepared a light supper to which I invite all of you to join me. And to Bryan, Felix and James, I would be pleased if you would stay one more night before you return to your homes. I know you, Philipp and Sven, will be driving back to Madrid tonight but you must join the rest of us for a small repast." We all nodded in agreement as we sipped our sherry. Baba continued.

"Philip's body was cremated according to the wishes of his family. A private service was held yesterday in Madrid."

Baba rose and led the five of us into the dining room. Having eaten "a small repast" here before, I knew what to expect. The main course was a rack of lamb. For this course, the sommelier opened two bottles of 1982 Montebuena Rioja. Baba said "This wine has been a favorite of ours for over twenty years. It has also become a badge of recognition among some members of our profession. I would like to drink a toast to each of you men, in appreciation for what you have meant, not only to me during these past few days, but also for the fine service you render to the Agency and to all we serve."

She rose and raising her glass to each, continued. "To Philipp, my dear, dear friend, I love you." She then turned to each of the other four and said, "To you Bryan, Felix, James, and to you, Sven, my heartfelt thanks for your service. God bless each of you." She sipped her wine and sat down. We each rose and silently toasted her and then sat. It was an emotional time for each of us, especially the younger men who were relatively new to this group and who were noticeably impressed and slightly awed. As we finished dessert and coffee, I spoke.

"Countess, it is always a pleasure to be in your company, and in times like this, to offer our admiration of your service and your dedication to your country. I sincerely hope each of us will have the pleasure of seeing and being with you from time to time. Thank you. And now Sven and I must leave." I nodded to her.

We five left the room and walked into the courtyard where we shook hands and I thanked each of them and said goodnight. Sven and I departed and returned to Madrid.

As we entered our rooms, I checked my watch. 9:16. I picked up the phone after alerting Sven and dialed the number.

"Hello," said the voice on the other end of the line.

"This is Philipp Devon. You called me?"

"Yes, Philipp. How nice it is to talk with you again. We met at the Inauguration of your former college roommate and again on the ship to Miami. My name is Alexandro Marchidi."

I did a quick mental search and remembered that he was an American and when he arrived in Miami, he'd registered at a hotel under the name Alex di Marchi which is an anagram of Marchidi.

"Mr. Marchidi, I recognize your voice but the name on the card you gave me was a different one."

"I must have given you a business card which I use in the Caribbean and in Spain. How are you?"

"I'm fine. How did you know I was registered at this hotel?"

"I have left instructions, for which I pay handsomely, with the Senior Desk Clerk at each of the more upscale hotels, to inform me if any gentleman registers who is in the Import Export Trading Business. Quite often I find that we're able to do some business. I was surprised, however, when I was alerted to your being here in Madrid."

"And?"

"You told me at the Inaugural Ball that you also were in the Import Export Business and said perhaps we would meet again soon and might be of service to each other."

I don't remember having said those words but I wanted to determine what he was doing in Madrid at this particular time.

"What is the specific purpose of your request for an appointment?"

"You sound a little annoyed by my call, Philipp."

"You will please excuse me but I've buried a dear friend this afternoon. That was my purpose in coming to Madrid. I hadn't planned to do any business on this trip."

"I offer you my sincere condolences. I do hope I haven't called at an unfortunate time."

"Thank you for your condolences. I'd planned to leave Madrid and go back to Washington tomorrow but I suppose I could delay my trip by one day."

"Good. Can we have lunch tomorrow say at 1:00, at the Cantina del Toro? I can pick you up at about 12:20, if that's acceptable to you."

"I have my own car, thank you. I'll meet you at the Cantina at 1:00."

"One it is. Until then, adios, Philipp."

"Good bye, Mr. Marchidi."

Sven and I hung up the receivers. I brought Sven up-to-date. "I saw Marchidi or di Marchi, or whoever he really is, at the Inaugural Ball talking to a known agent of the other side. When I tried to approach them, they split and each went in a different direction. I followed Marchidi to the bar and it was there we talked and I asked him for his card. He'd also been invited to board the *37* and travel back to Miami. He's an American." I paused. "Do you know about the *37*?" I asked.

"My father and the Madam have been seeing each other since the death of my mother. He's told me all about her and how she fits into the scheme of things."

"Of course, Sven, I'd forgotten. She also knew my mark was an American. How? I don't know. Perhaps Z told her, or it might have been your father."

Sven looked puzzled. "I don't believe my father knows Mr. Marchidi, but shall I ask him?"

"Will you? When you call him, don't use the name Marchidi or di Marchi? You tapped our phones. Someone else may have done so."

"I'll call him right now." He picked up the phone in my room and got his father in Stockholm fairly quickly. I picked up the one in my bath.

"Hello, Dad. I'm calling from Madrid where I'm working with a good friend of yours from Washington, D.C. Do you happen to remember the American who was invited to board the *37* for the trip from the Inaugural back to Miami? He's just telephoned my friend and asked for an appointment for lunch tomorrow."

"Hello, Sven. You sound just like a seasoned businessman. You don't even ask about the health of your father, but jump right into the purpose of your call."

"I'm sorry about that, Dad. Please forgive me; how are you?"

"I miss you greatly ever since you left to be a chef somewhere far away. Yes, I do know the man you're talking about. Our hostess had inquired from her daughter about the rumor that something was rotten in Denmark. He'd been seen on several occasions talking with a high official and was suspected of being in nefarious businesses, possibly the worst kind. You be sure to watch your step, my son, and tell my friend to be extremely careful in dealing with this man. He'll cheat you on every transaction."

"Thanks, Dad. I knew I could count on you to be in on every little trade secret." Sven, Junior, laughed. "I love you, Dad."

"I love you too, my son. Goodbye."

"Bye, Dad."

"Well," said Sven as I re-entered my room, "now you have your answer."

Sven sat on the edge of my bed.

"What are the plans for tomorrow?" he asked. "What shall I do while you're inside?

"You'll find a parking place on the street so you can see the front of the restaurant. When I come out, pick me up promptly. Now, I want to alert Z about our findings and ask some assistance from him in this matter. Get me the tape of my conversation with Marchidi and the one with your father." As he retrieved the two tapes, I got the coder/transmitter out of my briefcase. I put the two tapes in and pushed "DIAL."

I explained to Sven: "This machine dials a similar machine in Z's office and, as soon as Z's machine answers, this machine encodes the voice data from these tapes and sends it to Z's machine where it's decoded. His machine creates a tape in the normal voice just like the ones we're now sending. As soon as these two tapes have been sent, I'll use the machine to create a new tape of the information which Bryan, Felix and James furnished me regarding the cars at the funeral and the information we received from the Vehicle Bureau. I should hear back from Z, either by telephone or more probably via this machine as soon as he's listened to the tapes."

"When might that be?"

"It could be within the hour or early tomorrow morning."

I was emotionally spent, having buried Francisco and consoled Baba as best I could. Then there was the intrigue of tomorrow's lunch with Marchidi.

"I need sleep," I said. I lay across the bed as Sven left the room. I was asleep soon. In my dream I plotted my route of attack for tomorrow. I'd find out who Marchidi was and his connection to the other side — and then the image of Arlene surfaced and I was unable to plan anything further. Her face was so vivid before me. I could almost smell lilacs in the air. I was now fully awake. I grabbed a pillow, caressed it, turned over on my stomach and fortunately went back to sleep.

The telephone rang. I jumped like a startled rabbit. Almost immediately, Sven was in my bathroom, ready to pick up.

"Philipp, I got your messages. They are quite interesting." Z began to speak in code. "I have just finished talking to the Chief of Police in Madrid as well as the head of the Interpol Bureau there. The information which you and Sven furnished from the three different sources, presents a very clear pattern of what's going on. The owner of the car which was at the funeral is the immediate boss of the man you're having lunch with today. He also heads up a drug cartel doing business in Spain as well as throughout the Caribbean and was the mark our deceased friend was about to finger." Z paused briefly.

"While you're at lunch, two Policemen from the Traffic Division of the Madrid Police Force will enter the restaurant and come to your table. They'll ask your host to come outside. If he protests, he'll be handcuffed for resisting arrest. If he claims diplomatic immunity, his goose is cooked for he has none. His boss does, but he won't be told that we know that bit of information. He'll be encouraged to telephone his 'immediate supervisor' to come down and pay all the traffic fines and violations which your luncheon host has incurred in Madrid over the past two years. If his boss doesn't show, your luncheon host will be jailed. If he does show, Interpol will be on the spot to confront him about arranging the murders of Francisco and Philip."

Z paused for Sven and me to absorb all this. "Interpol's had a tail on him for some time. They know the location of his residence and will have it under surveillance tomorrow. If he tries to leave the country, they'll intercept him."

"It sounds so cut and dried. I fear we're overlooking something important," I said.

Sven spoke up. "Sir, I'll be in my car parked with a clear view of the front door of the restaurant. Can I help in some way?"

"As a matter of fact you can, young man. You can assist our luncheon guest in putting on his wire so he can tape the entire conversation at the table."

"Yes, sir, I can do that, but I was hoping to do something else, something more physical."

"Be patient, my young friend. There'll be sufficient muscle on the site as I've just explained. I want you to reserve your strength for your mentor. He'll probably need it where you both are going. As soon as this day is over and you two are back in the room, give me a call. I have a new and most interesting assignment for you both. Au revoir, mes amis."

When we'd put down the receivers, Sven came into my room looking quite puzzled.

"This isn't the way I thought this assignment would end," he said.

"It's not over yet." I looked at my watch. 5:35. "I'm going back to sleep," I said as Sven left the room.

When I awoke at 7:15, not hearing any huffing or puffing this morning, I looked into Sven's room. He was conked out on his back, snoring like a windstorm. He hadn't bothered to cover himself since all the covers were on the floor where he'd thrown them when we were awakened earlier. Once again I marveled at the strength and power of his body and hoped that someday, "when I grow up", I might look like that. I wish.

I got in the shower after shaving. The water was warm and soothing on my tired body. Yesterday was quite a day. It appeared that my promise to Baba might be fulfilled sooner than I'd thought.

Sven dropped me off in front of the Cantina at 12:55. There were two parking places within eyesight of the restaurant door. He pulled into the nearer one.

I entered the restaurant and saw my mark seated at a table in the rear. The other tables were fully occupied. He rose as I approached.

"It's so good to see you again, Philipp," he said as we shook hands.

"Thank you," I said with little warmth in my voice. I didn't return his compliment.

"You're looking well." He paused. "I was sorry to learn of the death of your friend. He must have been very close, to bring you all the way to

Madrid for his funeral."

"I have many acquaintances but very few real friends," I said. "To lose one so close was a real blow."

"May I order you a drink? I'm having campari and soda."

"No, thank you. I'll just have water." He seemed pissed.

"I'm very pleased that you could make this time available for us to talk."

"I still don't know what you want to talk about. Please be more specific?"

Two uniformed Policemen approached our table.

"Which one of you is Mr. Marchidi?" asked the taller one.

"I'm Mr. Marchidi."

"Sir, your presence has been requested by the Chief of the Traffic Division down at Headquarters. Will you please come with us?"

"What's this all about?" Marchidi shouted vehemently.

"Sir, I do not know. I was instructed to invite you to come with us to Traffic Division Headquarters."

"Well, I certainly don't intend to go with you for whatever purpose."

The taller of the two Officers physically grabbed Marchidi, causing him to stand up. The other Officer placed a handcuff on Marchidi's right arm, turned him around and placed the other handcuff on his left arm behind his back. Marchidi was visibly confused and mad as hell. The other patrons of the restaurant seemed equally confused.

"Why are you doing this to me? I have diplomatic immunity," he shouted as he was being led out of the restaurant. When they got outside, they forced Marchidi to get in the back of the squad car, handcuffed to the shorter of the two Officers. The taller one drove away.

The other patrons of the restaurant were staring at me. I shrugged my shoulders in a gesture which implied "Search me." I walked out the door. Sven pulled up immediately.

As we entered the room, I listened for the phone. We both sat for a few minutes in silence. I suggested that we order lunch.

"What's your pleasure today, my friend?" I asked.

"Whatever you decide is fine with me, just lots of it."

I ordered a light repast for me and a double portion for Sven. We sat in my room and made small talk for about twenty minutes. There was a knock on the door. Sven went into his room and I threw on a robe. It was our same waiter.

"Señor, you lunch ready," he said in broken English and grinning broadly. After he set the tray down and received a tip in cash, he grinned again, more broadly. "Gracias, Señor Devon. Muchas gracias."

When he left the room, Sven came back in. Before we finished our coffee, the telephone rang. Sven went to his station.

"Well, my friends," said Z, "you've done it again." Z now began speaking in code. "Your luncheon host pulled his 'diplomatic immunity' stunt. When the Officers arrived at Police Headquarters, he was confronted with over five thousand pesetas in traffic and parking violations. Refusing to pay, he was afforded one telephone call. He, of course, dialed his immediate boss and explained what was going on.

"The man on the other end of the line refused to help him, called him 'estupido culo'(a stupid asshole), and told him that he was fired. All of this conversation was being taped. Totally frustrated and not in control of his emotions, Marchidi said he couldn't be fired because he knew too much. Later Interpol got him to describe how his supervisor was running drugs to the Caribbean and had ordered the murder of de Bollo who was about to finger the whole racket.

"The Agents watching his boss' house immediately stormed it and arrested him without one shot being fired. Now he's in the custody of the Madrid Police and will probably be arraigned immediately on several counts, among them trafficking in drugs internationally and being accessory to two murders. I feel certain that Interpol can come up with some additional charges without much effort." Z paused for a second. "Interpol decided to release Marchidi after he paid his traffic fines. They felt he might lead them to others involved in the same business."

"I'm very pleased this has turned out the way it has," I said. "Would it be okay for me to ask you to speak with the widow of our late friend and tell her of the denouement?"

"Of course, I shall, probably tonight or tomorrow morning at the latest."

"One thing more," I said. "I want you to know how pleased I am with the participation and contributions of my protégé. He's a quick learner and I'm pleased to have him on board."

"That's always nice to hear. Thank you both for your positive reports. I'll be back to you sometime tomorrow. I have a new assignment for you both. I've one final detail to confirm and then I'll explain it to you. Merci beaucoup. Au revoir, mes amis."

"One more point, sir, if I may." asked Sven.

"Certainly, what is it?"

"I'm on a two week vacation from my chef's job. If this new assignment takes more than nine days, what do I do or say?"

"This assignment will probably take no more than two or three days. If it should run over, I'll be in touch with your boss and explain the delay. My best regards to you both." Z hung up.

"What do you think this new assignment might be and where?" Sven asked.

"I haven't the foggiest idea, but I can assure you if Z says it's important, you can bank on it. Since we both have been through some rather grueling experiences over the past two days, I suggest we take a nap."

Sven agreed and went to his room. When I lay down, I began to think again of my dearest Arlene, wondering what she might be doing at this very moment and how she was progressing. Oh, how I miss her! I can't seem to get her out of my mind. I rolled over on my stomach and tried to sleep, but sleep would not come. After lying there for about twenty minutes, I got up and walked around the room.

I heard Sven snoring. I sat in one of the big chairs and remembered the times I'd spent with Arlene. I became anxious our plans for the future would never come to pass, that I'd never see her again. I worried about this feeling until tears began to trickle down my cheeks. Normally, I never have such feelings about the future, but these were so vivid. I got back in bed and tried once again to sleep. This time, I made it.

When I awoke, I saw Sven sitting in the same chair I'd just vacated. He was staring at me with a very serious look.

"Philipp, something is really bothering you. Is it something I've said or done?"

After I got up and sat on the edge of the bed, I told him I had a premonition that I'd never see Arlene again.

"My friend, you cannot concentrate on our assignments if Arlene still is the focus of your attention. She'll be all right. She is busily occupied I'm sure. Please don't worry."

I looked at my watch. 6:15. "Would you like to order a bottle of wine while we wait for Z's call? It may not come until tomorrow."

"Sure. Why not? What's your pleasure?"

"I think I'm in the mood for a hearty Rhône, something with big body and gusto." I looked in the Hotel Information Packet but I found nothing about the wine selections. I picked up the phone and asked Room Service if the wine list included a 1979 Rhône."

"Yes, sir. We have a 1979 Hermitage La Chapelle."

"Señor, please bring us a bottle."

"Si, Señor. Pronto."

We sat on either side of the table, in the overstuffed chairs. Within ten minutes, our waiter arrived with a tray having the wine and two goblets, the right shape for a Rhône. He opened the wine. I got up and went to my briefcase and retrieved a handsome tip.

"Gracias, Señor Devon, muchos gracias."

After he left, Sven asked, "What's the appropriate tip on such an occasion?"

"He's been our waiter since we arrived and has done a fine job above that of a normal service person. I thought a little extra above the normal fifteen percent would be about right."

I poured the wine. We lifted our glasses, clinked them as I said, "To us, a great team and a very compatible and budding friendship." Sven watched me as I held the glass to the light, took the nose first and then inhaled the aroma by putting my nose in the glass. Only after that instructive ritual, which he imitated precisely, did we take a sip. The wine was perfection, as I knew it would be.

"How do you like this wine?" I asked.

"Not only is the wine excellent, but the instruction was equally as good." He smiled.

We sat and sipped from our glasses, refilled them, and sipped some more. I looked at my watch again. 7:30. No rush for dinner and there remained about a half glass for each. My next thought was to order another bottle but decided against it. If Z called tonight, I didn't want my tongue to be heavy and coated or my speech to be muddled. We sat silently meditating. Sven spoke first.

"Philipp, I've never before had a friend like you, someone a little older who respected my talents and my abilities and was willing to take me on for more training. I'm deeply indebted. Thank you."

I didn't reply immediately but was deeply moved. I remembered so vividly how I was taken on by Z when I was about Sven's age. Z guided me in a similar manner, the way I was trying to teach Sven the ropes.

Finally, I said, "Thank you, Sven, my new friend, for being so quick to learn and so easy and receptive to instruct." We shook hands and then returned to our meditative thoughts.

I was about to pick up the phone to order our dinner when it rang. Sven ran to my bathroom.

"Philipp, I had a telephone call last Thursday morning," Z paused and then continued in code, "from Monaco, asking if I could send Baba and you on another mission. It was explained to me. I said I'd like to check the availability of you and Baba and would call back as soon as possible. The

221

unfortunate accident occurred and Baba is in no shape to do anything right now. I telephoned Monaco after lunch today and asked if I could send another agent in her place. After assuring them that the substitute would be most capable, they agreed." Z paused.

"It appears that there is a problem at the Casino with one of the daily habitués. The Casino personnel have been unable to prove it, but they believe he's cheating. They've asked for our assistance because this individual is frequently seen in the company of known undesirables. After the assassination of Minister Stavros, the new Minister has been at the tables almost every night." He paused again.

"I'd like for you and Sven to fly to Monaco this evening. You'll be picked up at the airport and taken to the Palace."

Sven looked at me with a questioning demeanor.

"Sven, I've seen you at the tables in Stockholm and was convinced that your talents in that department could be put to good use. You'll be partnered with one of the world's greatest card sharks. He always wins." Z paused again.

"Sir, I appreciate the confidence you've expressed in my abilities, but to tell the truth, I don't believe I'm ready for this assignment. And furthermore, sir, I only have two driver's uniforms with me. I don't even own a tux."

I spoke up. "I own one, but it's old and well used. We both will need the appropriate clothes for this assignment."

"I've made arrangements for you both to be fitted in the Palace tomorrow morning with the necessary clothes and accessories, to include shoes, so you may be admitted to the Casino properly attired. Your tailors will be in your suite at ten o'clock."

Sven looked at me again with a "I can't believe this is happening to me" look.

"Your plane leaves tonight at 10:15. Leave your car at the airport and give the keys and the parking ticket to the desk clerk. Your tickets will be at the desk in your name, Philipp. You'll have dinner during the flight. I'll telephone you at the Palace tomorrow evening at six, local time. Good night."

Sven came back into my room, jumping up and down shouting "yes, yes, yes." I grabbed him by one arm and said, "Settle down." He was so excited he couldn't easily do so. I let him give off a little more steam.

"We need to wind up things here quickly and get on our way. Remove the camera and I'll remove the two phone taps. Get dressed and check your room thoroughly."

We took the lift to the basement. I tipped the attendant in cash while Sven went for the car, the parking charge having been added to our bill.

When we arrived at the airport, I stayed in the car until it was parked. We got the ticket and proceeded to the terminal. Z hadn't told us on which airline we were flying. I looked at the Departing Flights and found there was only one flight to Monaco leaving at 10:15. It was Air France. We walked to that desk, picked up our tickets, left the keys and parking ticket and walked to the gate. When we boarded, we were again seated in First Class, both aisle seats across from each other. As the plane took off, I looked at Sven. He looked at me and grinned.

The plane landed smoothly. We debarked and entered the terminal. We were approached by a driver in a uniform similar to the one Sven was wearing. He identified himself as a palace driver. We followed him to his limousine. As we approached the Palace, we noted the surrounding lights were sparkling and the view of the Mediterranean was awesome.

We got out and were met by a gentleman dressed in white tie and tails. He introduced himself as the Major Domo, calling each of us by name. Another attendant retrieved our luggage and preceded us into the entry hall. The Palace is only four stories high but extends quite a distance in both directions from the entrance.

"Please follow me, gentlemen," said our formally attired leader.

We entered the elevator and rose to the 4th floor. We followed him and soon came to a door which the attendant opened and asked us to precede him.

We gathered in the drawing room as the other attendant arrived with our bags. As we identified each, it was placed on the luggage racks in our bedrooms. The formally attired attendant said our breakfast would be served here in the drawing room at 9:00. I was just about to ask him what we should wear when the tailors arrive, when he said, "There is a robe and slippers in each of your closets. Your tailors will come to your suite at exactly 10:00 to measure you for your new wardrobe. If you should need anything during the night, dial 6. If you have no further questions, I bid you a good night."

We both said good night and went to our bedrooms. I thought what a novel experience for Sven. I've been here once before with Baba.

After I'd showered, I crawled into the biggest bed I ever saw. I thought about tomorrow in the Casino. How would I recognize the mark? How would I challenge him? What physical encounter might ensue? Could Sven and I handle both the mark and the Greek Minister? How to do all of this with the minimum amount of fanfare? I spent some time planning our operation before I fell asleep.

ELEVEN

I awoke at 7:30, went to my bathroom and splashed cold water on my face. The wine last night was really good. I didn't have a headache. Walking into the drawing room, I found Sven looking out the window at the blue Mediterranean. He was obviously overwhelmed with not only the view but also the fact of our being where we were.

"Good morning, pardner," I said in my best John Wayne imitation.

"Good morning to you, Philipp. I hope you slept as well as I did."

"Like a baby. Let's talk a bit before our breakfast arrives about what we're supposed to do."

We sat in the comfortable-looking overstuffed chairs near the windows after we'd retrieved our robes and slippers and put them on the nearby sofa.

"We have an interesting situation on our plates. The alleged cheater is hobnobbing with the newly appointed Greek Minister of Culture, or vice versa. Why do you think the Minister is in the Casino gambling almost every night in close proximity to our alleged cheater?"

"The obvious answer is both are on the other side and probably find the Casino a good neutral spot where they can exchange information without attracting much attention," said Sven.

"A good analysis, but why is the alleged cheater cheating?"

"Probably because he's a good shark and finds it fascinating to make some extra cash easily."

"An excellent observation," I said. "We don't know how he's gambling, whether at Vingt-et-un, as the French call Blackjack, at craps or at Baccarat. What do you consider your specialty?"

"I'm pretty good at Baccarat. What's yours?"

"I usually win at Blackjack."

"What if his specialty is craps?"

"Then we both must become specialists fast."

There was a knock on the door. "Breakfast is served."

"Just a minute," I said as we put on our robes and slippers.

Two young men in identical green, black and white uniforms entered, each carrying a silver tray which was placed on the long table between the two sofas. The domes on each tray were removed, revealing scrambled eggs and Canadian bacon and toast without crusts.

"If you would care for anything else, including more coffee, please lift the receiver and state your request to the person who answers," said one of the men.

"Thank you. It all looks delicious and we probably will want more coffee. Would you please ask someone to bring two more pots?"

"Certainly, sir. Enjoy your breakfasts. As a reminder, your tailors will be here at 10:00," said one of the waiters. "Good morning," said both as they left the room.

"They certainly feed you well in this place," Sven joked. "How did they know what I wanted to eat?"

"When one is a guest and isn't asked for a preference, good manners dictate that one eats whatever is placed before one," I said with deliberate snobbery.

As we were finishing our meal and our second cup of coffee, there was a knock at the door. One of the earlier waiters entered with two pots of coffee, putting them on our trays after removing the first pots.

"Thank you," we both said as he left the room.

I looked at my watch. 9:25. "Just time enough for a quick shower and flossing," I said. When I came back in the drawing room, I heard Sven's shower running. Within the minute he came in toweling dry.

"It would be appropriate for us to appear in our robes and slippers and take our guidance from them." I said as we both re-robed.

There was a knock at the door. Two smartly dressed middle-aged men entered with two additional younger men pulling a clothes rack and carrying several boxes. Each was attired in formal wear.

"Come in, gentlemen," I said.

"Thank you and a pleasant good morning to you."

When the rack of clothes and the boxes had been placed near and on the large table, one of the tailors said, "Mr. Devon, if you and Mr. Christen will kindly take these two pairs of drawers and return here, we shall begin. You may leave your robe and slippers in your bedrooms."

Sven and I looked at each other and smiled. We did as we were told. When we re-entered the drawing room clad only in our new drawers, one of the tailors said, "You gentlemen obviously take good care of your bodies. It is so much easier to fit someone like yourselves than some of the older men we meet."

The process began with black hose and black patent leather shoes. A perfect fit for each of us, as was every garment in our new wardrobe.

"How did you gentlemen know what our sizes were?" I asked.

"We had been informed of your approximate weights, heights, waist sizes and your ages. We have had much experience in fitting guests here at the Palace."

"Who gave you that information?" I asked.

"These facts were given to me by the maître d'hôtel. I assume that your employer furnished them."

Z had done it again.

Finally, the cummerbund arrived. Sven looked at me as I pointed to the pleats, indicating that they were to be facing upward.

"I have always thought the cummerbund to be a most practical accessory, especially when one is going to the opera or to a play. It is a serviceable item which very easily holds tickets or their stubs," noted the chief tailor.

Having finished our tailoring episode, the four of them began re-assembling their boxes and straightening the rack of remaining clothes.

"Gentlemen, to whom will the bill for our new clothes be sent?"

"Guests are never charged for alterations or complete ensembles. It is our pleasure to be of service to you. Good morning, Mr. Devon, Mr. Christen." The four of them left the room.

"I suppose that's their way of paying us for our services," said Sven.

"Let's get out of these suits." We each went into our bedrooms and stripped. I took a deck of cards from my briefcase. "Let's play a little

Blackjack."

"I'll deal. I want to see a real shark in action," said Sven.

We began a two-hour session of my favorite card game. Not surprising to me, I won all but four of the deals.

"You're good," said Sven as we paused for a rest. "What's your secret?"

"Do you play bridge?" I asked.

"I'm learning but I consider myself fairly accomplished so far."

"In bridge, success comes if you can remember each card that's been played. Not only do you count trumps, but you must also count the other three suits, especially which cards of which suit have been played. You'll want to know if there are any more outstanding, un-played cards in that suit and if so, which. Occasionally, that knowledge will allow you to slough a loser instead of trumping the trick."

"All fifty-two cards?" asked Sven.

"All fifty-two. In Blackjack, it's important to remember when the last face card or ten was dealt and work out the odds of another one showing up after 'x' number of twos-through-nines have appeared. My overall win rate is about ninety-seven per cent."

"Holy cow!"

"In Baccarat, as you may already know, there are from two to twenty 'punters' or players against the dealer, whereas in Blackjack, there only may be from two to twelve. I try to find a table early in the evening where the dealer and I are the only ones. Occasionally, such a table will be in the back, away from the crowds."

"I always thought Baccarat and Blackjack were the same, but didn't want to show my ignorance when you mentioned them previously."

"I wonder what we'll have for lunch. I also need to find out what time we should arrive at the Casino." I dialed 6 and began, as instructed, to "speak to the person who answers."

"This is Mr. Devon. May we have lunch here in our suite and at what time will it be ready?"

"Your lunch will be ready whenever you would like, Mr. Devon."

"Thank you. Mr. Christen and I are ready now."

"Lunch is on its way. We should get our robes on again."

"Done", said Sven.

Within ten minutes, there was a knock at the door and two young men holding trays came in.

"Thank you, gentlemen," I said as they left the room.

The luncheon consisted of a Cobb Salad, plain crackers and coffee. I could really use a filet mignon and a small salad. But, as I told Sven, you must eat what is put in front of you. Sven was chowing down on his big salad and enjoying every bite.

"Do you think that'll hold us 'til dinner?" I asked.

"Probably not. This is my kind of lunch, but I bet you'd rather have a plain salad and a small steak. Right?" commented Sven.

"Do you read minds too?" We both laughed.

When our lunch was over, I picked up the telephone. "Would you ask the maître d'hôtel if he would come to our suite when he is free?"

"Right away, Mr. Devon."

The maître d' arrived in about ten minutes.

"It's good to see you again, Mr. Devon. It's been a while since you were last here. How have you been?"

"Very well, Alberto. May I introduce Mr. Sven Christen?" They shook hands.

"Alberto, what time should we plan to arrive at the Casino this evening?"

"About 9:00. All the serious players will have arrived by that time. Your car will be here at 8:45. I shall have dinner prepared and served in your suite at 7:30. Would that be acceptable?"

"Would it be possible for the two of us to have a small filet mignon, medium rare, with a baked potato and some butter and sour cream at 7:00?" I asked.

"Certainly, and perhaps gelato for dessert?"

"An excellent choice. One more question please, Alberto. I believe the tailors said you gave them the details of our measurements. May I please ask who gave them to you?"

"It was your secretary in London who informed me of your arrival and that you both would need tuxedos for your stay. Are you satisfied with your ensembles?"

"Perfect, Alberto. Did my secretary say anything else regarding our visit?"

"Only that you and Mr. Christen would be here two or perhaps three nights and that your work would be concerned with one of the patrons in the Casino who is suspected of card-switching. I know of your reputation, Mr. Devon. I am certain you will again be successful."

"Thank you, Alberto. Mr. Christen and I are looking forward to an evening of fun. If we happen to meet someone who isn't being honest, we'll tell the proper authorities. Would you please bring me two new decks of cards exactly like the ones used for both Vingt-et-un and

Baccarat?"

"Certainly." Alberto left the room.

"He remembered you from your visit with the Countess. I'm impressed. You must have made quite an impression on him."

"Alberto isn't a member of our group, but he has the complete trust of Z. All the members of his family were assassinated by the Germans in Rome during the Second World War. He was a baby at that time and was in Naples with his mother's sister. Alberto is about forty years old or perhaps slightly older but looks much younger. He's worked his way up from a kitchen servant to his present position because he's honest, trustworthy, tight-lipped and very observant. He was of great help to the Countess and me when we needed it most."

Alberto returned with the cards. I thanked him, closed the door and looked at my watch. 3:10.

"I'm taking a nap," I said as I went to my bedroom, stripped and fell across my bed. I left Sven standing in the drawing room, looking at the sea.

I awoke at 4:30 and walked into the drawing room. I could hear Sven snoring. I sat at the table by the window, opened one of the decks and removed the ace of spades. I replaced the remaining cards in the box, took the ace to my room and stepped into the shower. As I was toweling dry, I walked back into the drawing room. Sven had returned to the windows, staring out over the Med.

"You should come back here on your honeymoon. I'm certain your bride would like it," I said, sitting down at the table. He'd already showered.

"May I join you?" he asked.

"My pleasure. Let's try a few hands of Vingt-et-un. You deal."

I gave him the other pack; he shuffled and asked me to cut. He dealt two cards to each of us, one face up and one hidden, alternating the recipient. I looked at my face-up card: the ten of hearts. The two of clubs was hidden. The three of diamonds was on the board in front of Sven. While he was looking at his hidden card, I took the ace of spades which I had palmed as I came into the room and switched the two of clubs. This exchange was done quickly and, with much practice over many years, quite deftly. Sven turned up his blind card: the ace of spades. I couldn't believe that my instruction period had come to an abrupt end.

"You can't have the ace of spades. I have it," I said as I turned over my ace. He was flushed and didn't know what to say, so I said it for him.

"I'd planned to play with you for several legitimate deals, but when your ace of spades turned up, my instruction period was finished."

I showed him how I'd palmed the ace and substituted it.

"This is the situation I'll cause to happen after I've played Baccarat with our mark and several other people for awhile. It's easier to substitute a card when there're several people at the table. Everyone is concentrating on either his own holdings or the cards of the dealer."

"What will you do after accusing the mark of cheating?"

"I'll call for the floor manager and explain to him what's happened. The procedure is, when such an incident occurs, both parties involved are asked to leave the table with the floor manager. They're taken to a private office and questioned. They're also searched. It wouldn't surprise me to find our mark with several other aces on his person. If he has no other cards on him, then I'll ask the floor manager for a record of his earnings over the past few weeks. I believe the record will show a series of wins inconsistent with the odds of the game. Z has already had his past winnings checked out, and the people at the Palace have alerted the Casino personnel of their suspicions."

"What about the Greek Minister?" Sven asked.

"If he's at the same table and observes the incident, watch his reaction and, if he leaves, follow him. If, however, he's engaged at either Vingt-et-un or craps, stand next to him and watch his movements. In any event, keep a close tab on his actions."

I looked at my watch again. 6:10.

"We should practice getting dressed. I have no idea how long it'll take us to tie the other's tie." After I went into my bedroom, the telephone rang.

"Philipp, I'm just checking in to see if you and your protégé have things under control," said Z.

"I believe we do. We both have been outfitted for this evening's party from stem to stern. I do have one question. What do we do if our friend from Greece is not present this evening?"

"Interpol told me that he arrived last evening and most probably will be in attendance at your party. Another bit of information for you. The man who had our friend put away has been identified as a co-worker of the man from Greece. You should have plenty of backup this evening."

"Thank you. We both appreciate your assistance and your concern. Alberto sends his best regards." Z hung up.

"So, Mr. Hargrave was probably shot by a member of the opposition. The Greek who will be with us this evening may have a similar plan in mind for our mark. This evening could be quite exciting. Are you ready for some action?"

"You bet I am."

"Then let's finish dressing." We swiftly and expertly tied each other's ties. I looked at my watch again. 6:45.

"I suggest we take off these clothes and have dinner."

"Alberto said our meal would be served at 7:00, but we would like it now, if that's possible," I said to room service. I paused. "Thank you."

After we shed our formal attire and put on our robes, we sat in the drawing room. When the two trays were placed on the center table and the two silver domes removed, there was a small steak, a baked potato, sautéed mushrooms, some peas and a croissant. The coffee pots completed the presentation.

During the meal, we discussed the procedure I'd designed to catch our target. I always have qualms about trying this in the Casino where there'll be several world-famous patrons, as well as a few lesser-known lights. But I was quite good at this maneuver and had used it several times, causing a minimum of disturbance.

After we'd finished the meal and before we got dressed for the evening, we got out the cards and refreshed our techniques. Sven dealt as before and I was the patron. But in the many deals we tried, the ace of spades never came up. I practiced palming any card.

At 8:40, we arrived in the vestibule. As we headed toward the Casino, our driver said "Tonight will be a big night. Several American movie stars are here for the Film Festival. There are also some international dignitaries in town and are expected to be present."

I looked at Sven who looked a little uneasy.

"Don't worry, my friend. If I see someone I know I'll introduce you as my cousin from Stockholm who is touring the Continent with me." He looked a little calmer.

We arrived at the Casino. There were assorted expensive sports cars and limousines parked in front, each with a livered driver guarding it. Entering the Big Room, I saw an old friend coming towards me.

"Philipp, you charming man, why do you never call me? You know I love your company and our conversations", she said licking her lips.

"My dear Lucy you know I travel all the time. I would love to spend some time with you while I'm here, if that's possible. May I introduce my cousin from Stockholm, Sven Christen?"

"You never told me you had such a handsome cousin. Sven, I'm Lucy Baldwin", she said as she extended her hand. Sven took it and performed the Continental kiss in his most gracious manner. She continued to eye him from head to toe, clearly undressing him. "Stay in touch, my dear Philipp."

When she left, we walked toward the Baccarat table where there were several ladies and gentlemen playing. I didn't know what my mark looked like. I only knew that he looked foreign. Almost everyone in the Casino looked foreign. Z said he looked sort of mousy and Eurasian. I centered my attention on one such individual and watched his performance. It appeared he was winning almost every time. However, to avert suspicion, he'd lose whenever there wasn't much riding on the bet. I watched him for about thirty minutes before taking a spot directly across from him. I watched his actions and counted the number of times he substituted the ace of spades to win the deal. I was certain I'd located my mark.

I noticed that the newly appointed Greek Minister, whose picture Z had shown me, approached our table and stood directly behind the target. In no time, my mark wavered and appeared to be fainting, as the Greek Minister left his position and wandered into the crowd. My mark slumped over the table as several ladies screamed. I headed for the fleeing Minister and tackled him as two large men grabbed him and ushered him through a door marked PRIVATE. I went back to the Baccarat table and my mark. He appeared to be dead. Several other Casino personnel cleared the area and carried him through the same door. I signaled Sven that we should leave. When we walked outside, our driver pulled up. A few minutes later were back in our suite.

We looked at each other as if to say, "What the hell happened?" I reviewed the events of the last hour. Nothing appeared out of the ordinary until the Greek arrived at the table; then almost immediately, he departed and my mark slumped. He couldn't have been shot for no shot was heard. He must have been stuck with a needle. Sven said nothing; he just looked at me in stunned silence. I started to say something as the phone rang.

"Philipp. When the Greek stood behind the mark, he probably injected him with the contents of a vial of something yet to be determined. I received a call from Interpol immediately after they had him in custody. I should have a more complete report for you in an hour or so." Z hung up.

"I think I'd like a drink", said Sven.

I picked up the phone. Alberto answered. "Alberto, we'd like a bottle of Montebuena Rioja, the 1982 if you can find one. If not, any year will be fine."

Sven and I took off our tux jackets and cummerbunds. We loosed our ties and shucked our shoes. Within a few minutes, there was a knock at the door. Alberto had a silver tray on which were a bottle of 1982 Montebuena

Rioja, an opener and two crystal goblets. He poured our glasses and said, "I understand you gentlemen had a most interesting evening. I hope you enjoy the wine. Good night." He left the room.

The wine tasted great. My protégé and I had trained and practiced for what was supposed to be a difficult evening, one of intrigue and legerdemain. However, the other side took out my mark for me. I didn't get to show how good I was at Baccarat. I didn't get to impress my protégé with my talents under fire. I want to be more a part of the action like I used to be, getting more involved, risking my life. I seem to be a "has been."

I refilled our glasses and we sat in silence.

"I've been gypped!" I said. "Tonight, I felt as useless as tits on a bull. I might as well not have been present at all."

"Don't beat yourself up, Philipp. You taught me some wonderful examples of card-sharking. You also introduced me to a beautiful woman. Fantasizing about her will help me get through my work until I see my girl again."

His remarks triggered my thoughts of Arlene. I'd been able to sublimate my thoughts fairly well until he said "beautiful woman." Now I was as horny as a toad. Where is she at this moment? Where is my

Arlene?

The phone rang. Sven picked up the phone in the drawing room while I got the one in my room.

"Philipp and Sven, I have some additional information from Interpol. Your mark was injected with a syringe filled with a concentrated amount of digitalis which caused his heart to speed up and brought about his death. The syringe was found in the pocket of the Greek. In the pockets of your mark were found several aces of spades. Interpol has taken the killer to their headquarters and shall be charging him with the murder of your mark and possibly with the murder of his predecessor." Z paused, giving me an opening.

"Where is Arlene?" I asked.

"She's still wrestling with her mother's estate. There have arisen some complications regarding the ownership of certain properties. She should be finished in about another ten days."

"I'm not sure I can wait that long."

"You can wait as long as you have to, my friend. Arlene is very busy and doesn't need to be distracted." Z paused for his last statement to sink in. "Sven, you have a reservation for tomorrow morning at 11:30, to return to your kitchen. And you, Philipp, your flight is at 11:15 for London.

Don't forget to pack your formal wear. Alberto will furnish you with clothing bags. Good night, my friends. I'm proud of you both, even if you didn't get to show your expertise, Philipp."

We put down the receivers. I immediately picked up the phone and said, "Alberto, may we please have two garment bags for our formal wear? And may we please have another bottle of wine?"

I looked at Sven, who said nothing, but only smiled.

After the garment bags and wine arrived, I began to lose the remaining pieces of my penguin outfit. Sven followed my lead. As we started on the second bottle, we became more verbal and were feeling quite lonesome for our loves. A little glazing began to show in Sven's eyes. I couldn't control my tearing up like a kid. How do two naked, slightly inebriated men console each other? Crying seemed to be the best remedy, so we both did. We daubed our eyes between sips of wine. I finally spoke.

"Sven, my friend, I'm gonna miss you a lot. You've been a good traveling partner and a super protégé. I wish it could last longer but that's not to be right now. When you get back to Stockholm and you and your lady set a date for the wedding, I'll await an invitation, but I plan to come anyway."

"And to you, my friend, I drink a toast. You're a super guy, a wonderful mentor and the best, damned thing that's happened to me in my career. You can expect me to show up at your and Arlene's wedding, whether or not I get an invitation." We clinked our almost empty glasses. I poured the remainder in each glass. We just sat there.

I got up first and headed toward my bedroom. Stopping at the door, I turned around and saw Sven lying on his sofa with his head buried in a pillow, sobbing.

I entered my room and closed the door.

I set my alarm for 9:30. As I opened my bedroom door, I saw Sven still lying on the sofa face down with his head in a pillow, sound asleep. I stepped into the shower and tried to wash away the cobwebs. My sleep last night was difficult and intermittent. I couldn't get Arlene out of my mind. When I stepped out of the shower, Sven was still asleep. Using the phone in my room, I ordered the usual food and hot coffee — lots of it — for the two of us, with a double portion of eggs for Sven. I spread his robe over him and let him sleep. When the breakfast arrived and was put on the table, the aroma of the coffee awakened him.

"Good morning, sunshine," I joked. "You certainly are a sound sleeper. Are you ready for breakfast or would you prefer calisthenics?"

"Coffee, and lots of it." He got up, sat on the sofa and poured himself a cup. Before I'd finished my first cup, he was on his second. We just sat there, silently, drinking our coffee and occasionally looking at each other. When we finished, Sven went to shower. When he re-entered the room, toweling dry and smiling, he said, "I really am going to miss working with you, Philipp, I hope it won't be too long until we pair up again."

"Ditto," I replied. We finished off the remainder of the coffee. I looked at my watch. 10:15.

"Let's get dressed," I said. I dressed in my traveling gear and Sven in his driver's uniform, each of us carrying luggage, plus my briefcase. We went to the vestibule, said goodbye to Alberto and pulled away from the Palace. Perhaps, I thought, I'll get to be more physical on my next assignment. I really miss the good old days when the risk of being roughed up a bit was part of the job. Now it seems I'm being put out to pasture. I may be thirty-nine but I'm as sharp and strong as a twenty-nine year old. And when I was making love to Arlene, I had the stamina of a nineteen year old. I'm definitely going to talk to Z about being given more dangerous, more physically demanding assignments.

TWELVE

We arrived at the airport with time to spare. I bought copies of the
Herald Tribune and *POINT DE VUE.* After getting our boarding passes,
we left the counter, shook hands and went our separate ways.

The flight to London left on time and arrived three minutes ahead of
schedule. I took the Underground to Sloane Square and walked to the
Cadogan. The desk clerk gave me a message: "Come to the Office
immediately." I left my luggage and the garment bag at the Hotel, carried
my briefcase with me and took a taxi to the Office. After the proper
identification, I entered Z's office. He rose from his chair and came
around his desk to meet me. I sensed something terrible had happened.

"Please sit down, Philipp." I did. Z pulled up the other chair near mine.
"I have some tragic news. Last evening, Arlene was run down by a lorry in
the village. She was carried to the local hospital in an ambulance, but died
on the way."

I sat there, numb. What Z said didn't register. I waited for him to
correct his last sentence, but it never came. I stared at the telephone. I

couldn't feel my body, which seemed to be floating in space. I waited for the telephone to ring, to say there'd been a mistake in the identification of the victim. Z put his arm around my shoulders and said, "I'm so sorry, Philipp."

"Where is she now?" I finally asked.

"I have a car waiting. We'll drive to the village."

I rose and turned to face him. I looked right through him. He picked up my briefcase and his and we left his office in his private elevator. His car was waiting. The driver headed toward the village.

I couldn't find my voice. I tried to speak but nothing came out. We continued in silence for almost two hours until we reached the hospital. The car pulled up to the Emergency Entrance. As we entered, Z guided me to the elevator. We descended to the basement and turned into a small corridor. Near the end of the corridor, Z opened a door. There were two men in white smocks and a woman standing nearby. I recognized Margit Schmidt. On a gurney in the center of the room was a body draped with a sheet. One of the men approached the gurney and pulled back the sheet from the top of the body. The body was badly mangled about the face but was still recognizable. I reached under the sheet and took her cold hand. I leaned over and tried to kiss her lips, but her face was so severely cut that her lips weren't really lips anymore. It was at that moment that reality returned. I fell on my knees and began to sob. Z approached me and tried to assist me in standing up. I couldn't. My tears flowed uncontrollably. I shouted her name over and over, but there was no relief. Grief consumed my entire being. The last thing I remember was falling to the floor.

When I awakened, I was in a chair in one corner of the room. The gurney with Arlene's body had been removed from the room. Z was holding my hand and saying, "Philipp, Philipp." I looked up and saw in his eyes the same big tears that had been streaming down my face. I'd obviously been given something. It was only at that moment that I realized what had happened and that I'd never again see my dearest Arlene.

"Philipp, I think it best for you to remain here in the hospital overnight. My driver will take me back to my office and return tomorrow morning for you. The Doctor has given you something to help you sleep. I know this is a tragic shock. The Doctor and I think it best for you to remain overnight."

Z and the Doctor assisted me in getting to my feet and into a wheelchair. We took the elevator to the 1st floor. They assisted me out of the wheelchair and into a straight chair. A nurse began to undress me. There was no opposition from me. In a few moments, I was flat on my back in the bed; the room was dark.

When I awoke, the early morning light was streaming into the room. I looked under the sheet; I was totally naked. I looked for my briefcase and then for my crotch pouch. Neither was anywhere.

A nurse entered the room and spoke.

"Good morning, Mr. Devon," she said. "How are you feeling this morning?"

"Where are my briefcase and money pouch?"

"The gentlemen who came with you last evening took both of them with him. Would you like some breakfast?"

"Just coffee."

The nurse went to the window and opened the blinds. The sunlight hit me directly in the face. She adjusted the blinds. "I'll have your coffee in a few minutes." The room was stark white with no accessories to brighten it.

After she left, I went into the bathroom and splashed cold water on my face. I looked in the mirror and recognized a rather gaunt Philipp Devon, unshaven, dark bags under both eyes and uncombed black hair. When the nurse returned with the coffee, I asked, from the bathroom, for a razor and shaving cream and a comb. After she'd left the room, I poured a cup of coffee and then another one. I stepped back into the bathroom as the nurse arrived with the requested articles.

I shaved and then stepped into the shower. The water felt good but I was exhausted and sad. I began to cry again.

When I'd toweled dry, I combed my hair and walked back into the room as the Doctor arrived.

"Good morning, Mr. Devon, I'm Doctor Craine," he said as I pulled on my trousers. He mercifully didn't ask how I was feeling. I sat down on the bed and poured another cup of coffee. He approached me and took my pulse. "You've had quite a shock. Your friend who brought you in last night said that as soon as I felt you were ready to leave, he would send his driver back to bring you to his house." He paused and looked me in the eye.

"Mr. Devon, I'm aware of how important she was in your life. Your friend told me all about your relationship. He also said she had no brothers or sisters and both parents were deceased. I regret having to ask you this question, but you're the person who was the closest to her. Had she ever spoken about where she would like to be buried in the event of her death?"

"Her death." The words shook me. Although I knew Arlene was gone forever, I hadn't allowed myself to think of that word.

"No, Doctor, we never spoke of it. We believed that our lives together would go on forever."

"You must make that decision soon for funeral arrangements have to be made."

"I'd like to call my friend and ask him the same question. You see, she was like a daughter to him."

"Certainly. I'll go and sign the release papers now," he said leaving the room.

I dialed Z.

"Good morning, Philipp. Shall I send my driver now?"

"The Doctor has just released me. He asked me where Arlene's body would be buried. We never spoke about this. Did she ever say anything to you?"

"Only one time; we were talking about Francisco's death. She said she wanted to be buried beside you, but didn't specify a place."

"Since she was English and I'm American, will that present any problems?"

"I don't see that it will. She loved her country, as I know you love yours. Since you have no siblings and your parents are deceased, you two can be buried side by side, or if her body be cremated, her ashes can be inurned or strewn anywhere. It's your call."

"I don't know what to do right now. The Doctor told me that funeral arrangements had to be made shortly. I can't think straight."

"Philipp, I'll speak with the Doctor and ask if your decision can be delayed for twenty-four hours."

Doctor Craine walked in.

"The Doctor just came in. Would you like to speak with him?"

"Yes, please." I handed over the receiver.

"Good morning. This is Doctor Craine."

I finished dressing while the two of them spoke.

"Thank you, sir. I'll repeat your requests to Mr. Devon and tell him I've agreed with them. He's now released from the hospital if you'd care to send your driver. Good morning."

"Your friend said he will assume all responsibilities for the disposition of the body and I'm to tell the undertaker he'll receive his instructions tomorrow morning. His car and driver should be arriving shortly."

"Thank you, Doctor Craine. I do appreciate your help. I'm just not prepared to make any decisions right now."

"I understand, Mr. Devon. If you'll remain here in the room, I'll let you know when the car arrives."

"Thank you, Doctor." In a short time, he was back and accompanied me to the hospital exit. I got in the car. I tried to put all this together, but my mind was thinking of only one thing — my dearest Arlene. Oh, how I miss her and shall continue to miss her for the rest of my life.

We arrived at Z's office.

"Philipp, I've had some time to think about the current decision you have to make, and I'd like to offer the following suggestion for your consideration. You told me you'd agreed to be married. I believe that Arlene's body should be cremated and her ashes strewn over some body of water that had particular meaning to you both." He paused. "I realize you wouldn't be able to visit her grave, but you know she'll always be with you wherever you are."

On the way in, I gave some thought to cremation, but hadn't decided where Arlene's ashes should be strewn. Now that Z made the suggestion, I knew it would be the right thing to do.

"Could we have a memorial service for her somewhere that was meaningful to us both?"

"Where did you have in mind?"

"In Marbella or at Baba's or aboard the *37* perhaps."

"When I talked with Madam Thirty-Seven last night, and with Sven,

Senior and Junior, each offered to have you with them for a while. Madam Thirty-Seven said her yacht was currently in Stockholm and would be there for a few weeks. She is flying today to Dubai. She also said you could stay aboard for a week or so, and there would be only the crew aboard. She also suggested that I invite both Svens to join you on board. If that meets with your approval, you could then have a memorial ceremony on board with me and two or three of your closest friends. I could also invite the Countess if you'd like for me to do so."

"I'd like that."

"I'll notify the funeral director to proceed with the cremation and I'll have one of my men pick up the urn and bring it here to my office. You and I can fly to Stockholm with the ashes. I'll notify both Svens of your desires and call the Countess to see if she could join us. If all this meets with your approval, we can have the memorial service on board on Saturday, three days from now. Is that too soon?"

"No, that'll be alright. I'll return to the Cadogan and await your call. I really should have a dark suit, but mine is back in Washington. I have the tux shoes but I don't have a suit."

"I'll arrange for you to be properly outfitted at Austin Reed this afternoon at two, including shoes. You can pick up everything tomorrow.

If you'd like to do so, please join me this evening for dinner at Langan's."

"I'd like that. Thank you. Now I'd like to rest a bit before I go for my fitting. Will you please excuse me?"

Again, Z put his arm around my shoulders and said, "Philipp, I know this is a traumatic time for you and for all of us. But we'll make it through the next few days, with God's help." He handed me my briefcase and said my pouch was inside.

I looked directly at Z and noticed a tear. I left his office and took a taxi to the Cadogan. I looked at my watch. 11:00. I shucked everything, set my alarm and lay down. Sleep came quickly.

When I awoke, I shaved and took a hot shower. As I was toweling dry, my thoughts came back to Arlene and what we'd meant to each other. I relived the honeymoon in Moretonhampstead, our visit to Marbella and aboard the *37*. I tried to picture her as I remembered her at the Lowndes. I remembered the Champagne-colored negligee. I remembered the smell of roses and of lilacs. I remembered the massages we gave each other. I could see every curve of her beautiful body, taste the smoothness of her skin and feel the warm embraces we enjoyed. I began to shake. I sat on the bed and cried. I buried my face in my pillow. The pain of my grief was unbearable.

I lay there for a few minutes, then got up and dressed and left the hotel with my briefcase containing my pouch and walked to Austin Reed. There is a sandwich shop nearby. I looked at my watch again. 1:30. I finished my brief lunch and entered the store, introducing myself to the greeter who took me to the fitting room.

The fitter handed me a pair of boxer shorts. "Please go in this room and undress, Mr. Devon." When I came out wearing only the boxers, the tailor and his assistant began a process very much like the one I'd experienced at the Palace. This time I wasn't amazed they had my measurements. I knew Z had furnished them again.

In less than thirty minutes, they were finished. I was instructed to return tomorrow at 12:30 for the final fitting. I could then carry everything with me. When I'd redressed in my old clothes, and they did feel old by this time, I left the shop and returned to the hotel. I decided I needed another nap, so I took it.

I awoke at 5:00. I took another shower, dressed and took a taxi to Langan's. As I entered, Paul approached and greeted me by name. I also called him by his name and was ushered to Z's table.

I'd been seated less than five minutes when Z joined me. We shook hands. Paul arrived with a bottle of our wine and two goblets.

"I asked Interpol to check out the driver of the lorry and to determine if there's any connection to anyone or anything else", Z said. "I got their report before I left the office. The driver and the lorry have disappeared. It appears that this was a hit-and-run, possibly deliberate. Arlene had been working on a drug-smuggling operation, similar to the one on which Francisco was working. There might be a connection."

I was stunned. Of course, there's a connection. I was sure Arlene had been killed by the same group that killed Francisco. Now it was up to me to find out who had ordered her death. Z had no further details.

"I also spoke with the Countess. She will meet us in Stockholm on Saturday morning. Both Svens will join us on the yacht, and Madam Thirty-Seven confirmed her earlier statement that you can stay aboard as long as you like. She also indicated, if you wished to do so, you could travel with her to Leningrad in about ten days for a wedding. You already know some of the guests. So, I would suggest you take your tuxedo and all accessories to Stockholm. I also notified your boss in Washington, who sends his condolences and said you could take as long as you needed before returning to D.C."

"I believe you've covered everything and the arrangements sound like they're the right things to do. Thank you."

We talked about several things during the dinner — my state of mind and why rest was important; a possible assignment in Leningrad, if I chose to go there; and when and who should go through Arlene's personal effects. Z suggested when I get back from Stockholm or perhaps Leningrad, I should take a day or two and sort through Arlene's household. I'm not looking forward to this and I'll put it off as long as possible. I'm in no shape to do it now. All I could think about was why Arlene had been killed and what was the connection with Francisco's death?

When we finished, I informed Z that I was to pickup my new clothes at 12:30 tomorrow. He said he'd call me this afternoon to let me know the time of the trip to Stockholm. We parted with a strong and sincere handshake.

I needed to walk so I headed for the hotel. I had nothing in mind to do, but I thought Z's suggestion of further rest sounded like good advice. When I got to my room, I shucked everything and lay across the bed, intending to relax and sleep, if possible. I soon realized that I might not have a good night's sleep for quite a while. I wished I had a sleeping pill but since I'd never taken one, the thought soon vanished. I got up and washed my face in cold water. I tried to sleep again. Nothing seemed to work. I lay on my back staring at nothing. I looked at my watch. 12:10. I took another shower and tried again to sleep. It was no use.

I got out of bed and knelt at my bedside. I've never considered myself to be a practicing Christian, but I felt the only one I could turn to now would be God. I began talking. I asked God to help me through this terrible time. I confessed I needed help and didn't feel I could cope by myself. I really didn't know how to pray, but I did the best I could. I expressed my love for Arlene and told Him how much I was missing her. I asked if He would please help me through this and tell me how I was going to live without her at my side. I was crying but I continued to pray. There were long pauses between each of my requests. Finally exhausted, I rose and got into bed.

I awoke at 7:00 as light filled my room. A feeling of calm had come over me and it was at that moment I realized I could make it without Arlene at my side, because I knew she would always be with me, no matter where I went. I looked at the window where sunlight was piercing the curtains. It was shining directly on me. I felt refreshed and rejuvenated. I got up, shaved and showered, redressed in casual clothes and went to the lobby. The night clerk, just going off duty, said, "Well, sir, I see you got that sleep you were looking for last evening."

I walked down Sloane Street to the place in Belgravia where Arlene and I had breakfast the last time we were together in London. There were flowers on each table, which I hadn't remembered. "Just coffee," I said. Then I realized how hungry I was and asked for the full breakfast.

The coffee tasted good and reminded me of the coffee that Arlene and I enjoyed in our room at the Lowndes between our love-making. It was a pleasant but sad reminiscence. The realization of my loss of Arlene kept recurring.

After breakfast, I went back to my room, stripped and put on boxer shorts. I put my pouch in my briefcase, left the hotel and took a taxi to Austin Reed.

I looked at my watch. 12:28. I like to be punctual. I was welcomed and escorted to the dressing room. As I entered the designated cubicle, I took off everything except the drawers and stepped outside. The two fitters were ready with my new ensemble. There was also a tailor standing by. The entire ensemble fit superbly. I undressed in my cubicle, handed each piece back to the fitter, then redressed in my old clothes. I took the garment bag and the shopping bag of accessories, and thanked everyone. I took a cab to the hotel, hung up my acquisitions, striped off my old clothes and lay across the bed. In a short while, I was asleep.

I slept more soundly than I had in quite a while. Z said he would call this afternoon, so I'd set my alarm for 3:00. When I awoke, I splashed cold water on my face and sat in a chair and waited for Z's call. I'd sat there for more than two hours when the telephone rang.

"Philipp," Z said, "please come to my office tomorrow morning at eight. The urn is being flown down and it will be here at that time. We'll then go to the airfield and take off for Stockholm. Have you all your clothes?"

"Yes", I replied. "Sir, I have one further request. Ever since her death, I have been thinking that it was tied to Francisco's death. In my mind, I am convinced that the same people responsible for the one are responsible for the other. I would like to be assigned to the task of proving it."

"The people at Interpol are working on this same theory. I'm sure they would welcome your input. I'll make a call."

THIRTEEN

Saturday dawned. I looked at my watch. 7:00 on the dot. I got up, shaved and showered. I realized I was completely relaxed, no longer tired. I dressed in my traveling clothes. Gathering my luggage and briefcase, plus the two garment bags, I went to the lobby, said goodbye to the desk clerk and hailed a taxi.

After giving the passwords, I entered the inner sanctum. Z was seated behind his desk and there, in the center of his desk, stood a plain bronze urn about twelve inches high with a cover topped with a beautiful twisted finial. I stopped my forward motion, put down my luggage, lay the two garment bags over one of the chairs and approached the desk. I picked up the urn and brought it to my lips. I kissed the top, put the urn back on Z's desk and sat.

"The urn is beautiful," I said.

"I thought you would be pleased with its simplicity. How're you feeling this morning?"

"Like a new man. I had a talk with God last night and was assured that

all will be well." Z said nothing. I continued to look at the urn. "I'm
ready."

He pushed a buzzer. His driver entered the room and took my luggage
and the two garment bags. Z picked up my briefcase along with his. I
carried the urn. We descended to the garage. When the luggage and the
bags had been placed in the trunk, Z and I got in with the urn in my arms.

Z's jet seats eight but he and I and Arlene's ashes were the only
occupants. Z asked if I wanted to put the urn in the compartment between
our seats. I preferred to hold it.

When we arrived, we taxied to an area near the hangars where his car
awaited. After our luggage was transferred, we got in, I still holding the
urn. We arrived shortly at the wharf where the *37* was moored. Captain
Andersen greeted us and escorted us to our staterooms. Z planned to stay
only one night. As we descended the private stairwell, we were led aft,
down the long corridor with a pair of double doors at the end. We entered
a huge drawing room, which had double doors ahead and two single doors
on either side. It was Madam Thirty-Seven's suite. After my luggage and
garment bags were placed in my stateroom, and I'd placed the urn on the
table, we re-assembled on the main deck. Sven, Senior, arrived and, after
handshakes all around, went to his quarters with an attendant. He soon re-

joined us. The Captain said lunch would be served on the main deck at 2:00. Within fifteen minutes, young Sven arrived. After giving his father a hug and a kiss and shaking hands with Z, he came over to me and put his arms around me and gave me a hug. His eyes were glazed over.

The Countess arrived. Her luggage was taken to her stateroom. We each greeted her, I with a kiss on her cheek. When young Sven addressed her as Countess, she said "I have been told that you are now a member of this close-knit family. Please call me Baba."

The attendants seated us around a circular table near the pool. The meal was a light fare since the Captain said we'd be dining after the ceremony. During the first course of boiled shrimp with a mild cocktail sauce, I told the others about my plans for the ceremony.

"Just before the sun sets, I'd like to ask His Lordship, Baba and Sven, Senior, to gather on the starboard side of the main deck. I'll ask Young Sven to join me in a small skiff. I'll be holding the urn. We'll pull away from the ship until we get into the channel. I'll then spread Arlene's ashes on the water. When Sven and I have returned to the yacht, we'll all gather on the main deck, on the starboard side, and toast the memory of my dearest Arlene."

Only Baba spoke. "My dear, Philipp, your dearest Arlene would approve of the arrangements you have just described. They are so beautiful." She dabbed her eyes. No one else spoke.

The Captain announced that sundown would be at 5:41. Sven and I should leave the ship at about 5:15. I looked at my watch. 4:10.

"If you'll excuse me, I'd like to spend some quiet time in my room," I said.

I went to my stateroom, closed the door, took off my coat, picked up the urn, and sat in the overstuffed chair. I looked at the urn. It was so beautiful. I assured myself Arlene would approve of what we were planning to do. At that very moment, the thought occurred to me that I should speak with God again. I knelt and picked up the urn, holding it close to my chest. I don't really know how to pray or talk to God, but I did my best. I thanked Him for the times that Arlene and I'd spent together. I thanked Him for the love that we'd exchanged. I asked Him to help me remember her in a happy way for the rest of my life. "Amen," I said as I re-placed the urn on the table. I looked at my watch. 5:00. I put on my coat and carried the urn to the main deck. The four of my closest friends were already there.

The Captain led Sven and me to the lower deck. The doors were open and I could see the waiting skiff. Sven was helped in. He sat down and took an oar in each hand. I was helped in holding the urn. We pulled away from the yacht and Sven rowed very slowly at first, then a little faster. When we were about two hundred yards from the yacht, I noticed a flowing current into which Sven maneuvered the skiff. The small eddies were rather calm and knowing as if welcoming a most important event. The sun was sinking in the western waters. I opened the urn and began to slowly pour out Arlene's ashes, watching them drift with the well-defined current. When the urn was empty, Sven rowed us back to the yacht.

We returned to the main deck and approached the others. A waiter brought a silver tray with five glasses of Champagne. We each took one and faced the current. "I would like to propose a silent toast to the memory of Arlene Fulghum," I said quietly. Each of us drank, in silence, and re-placed the glass on the silver tray. I also put the urn on the tray and requested it be placed in my room. We moved to the dining room. Everyone was waiting for me to speak.

"My dearest friends," I began, "we've just said goodbye to our Arlene. We've paid her memory our sincerest respects. I know you'll agree she'll always be with us in spirit as we each go our separate ways. I truly believe that Arlene would want us to be happy now. So, I would like to propose a toast "to friends." We all rose as our Champagne glasses were filled. In unison we said "To friends."

The dinner consisted of a duck pâté with the remainder of the Champagne, followed by Beef Wellington, accompanied by green beans. The wine was, of course, a 1982 Montebuena Rioja. After the cheeses, accompanied by a tawny Spanish Port and fresh walnuts, we enjoyed a Peach Melba, followed by coffee and petits-fours. "I know Arlene would've loved this dinner, for we did like to eat well," I said as we all laughed.

"Your Lordship, you must dine with us more often," said Baba.

"I know I lead such a drab life. No fun at all," he responded, smiling. "I suggest we five gather in the drawing room near our bedrooms for a nightcap. Then we won't have far to walk when we retire for the evening." We all smiled as we followed Z's lead.

A waiter arrived with a tray of liqueurs. The conversation was light. When the liqueurs had been consumed, Z said he needed to get to bed as he was leaving quite early. We said good night and went to our separate rooms.

When I got in my room, I stripped. I was about to sit down and read one of the magazines I found on the table when there was a knock at the door. I threw on my robe and opened the door. There stood young Sven.

"May I come in?" he asked. "Philipp, I couldn't go to sleep without expressing to you my deepest sympathy. When I got the call from Z, I couldn't believe what he was saying. I cried. You mean a lot to me and I know what Arlene meant to you, and the plans you had made, and the ….." He stopped talking and broke into tears. I put my arms around him to console him. His sorrow was genuine and that made it more difficult.

"Sven, your sympathy means a lot to me, and I appreciate your coming by to tell me so. I cherish your friendship and look forward to working with you often in the future. If you really want to, and Z will allow it, I'll ask him about pairing us up on some future assignments. Would you like that?"

"Oh, yes, Philipp, yes. You've been a great mentor and I'm just now realizing how much I have to learn to succeed in this business. It'd be a pleasure to work with you on any assignment."

I hugged him again. "Now get some sleep and I'll see you at breakfast."

"Good night," he said as he left the room.

I decided to go to bed also. I crawled under the sheets; satin, no less. Again, sleep came easily.

I don't know what awakened me. The yacht lay at anchor; it was not swaying. I looked at my watch. 2:35. I got up and put on my trousers and my slippers and went to the main deck. I walked around, feeling my way, since I knew the layout. On the far side of the pool, I saw somebody lying on one of the chaises. As I neared the figure, I recognized Baba, wrapped in a terry-cloth robe. When I was quite near, she spoke.

"Philipp, my dear, I see you too could not sleep."

I sat down on the chaise near her. "I've been asleep," I said, "but I was awakened by some strange feeling."

"I too have had that strange feeling ever since Francisco's death. I feel as though he is trying to tell me something, a clue as to why he was killed. I know he was about to expose the drug Mafia in Spain, but that doesn't seem to be the complete story. I am frightened, Philipp."

"Can you tell me any other details of your dream?"

"I can't put my finger on anything concrete but I'm certain that his death was associated with more than Spanish drugs. I feel there is someone else who knows more about this incident, perhaps an Arab."

"Has your suspicion led you to any individual?"

"Not yet," she said, "but I have a feeling that tells me to keep looking."

"My advice is for you to go back to bed and try to sleep. We can talk about this later."

"I must be leaving immediately after breakfast to be in Monaco this evening. I've been invited to be the guest of The Prince."

"Which Prince?" I inquired.

"Why Albert of course; who else?"

"I noticed in yesterday's *Tribune* that Prince Andar of Saudi Arabia will be in Monaco tonight. The Film Festival is still going on, isn't it?"

"Yes, it is, but Prince Andar is coming to Monaco to visit his sick mother. He's never before shown any interest in the Film Festival."

"I'll check with Z when he gets back to his office, to see if he's discovered any additional information on Francisco's death. Now you should go to bed." I didn't mention the information Z had given me about the possibility that Arlene's death might be linked to Francisco's. I needed to pursue that further.

"As you wish, my dear Philipp. Good night, again." She kissed me on the cheek, turned on a small flashlight and descended the stairwell.

I looked at the pool. I couldn't resist. I took off my trousers and slippers and dove into the water. What an exhilarating feeling it was to be swimming naked in a pool on one of the largest yachts in the world.

After ten minutes or so, I climbed out and looked for a towel. There were none on any of the chaises and the box at the end of the pool contained only life jackets. "What the hell," I thought. I descended the stairwell, trousers in hand, wet and naked, and made it to my room without meeting anyone. I dried off and climbed into bed, congratulating myself for having an experience that I haven't had since I was a teenager. It felt super.

I awoke again at 7:30, showered, dressed casually and headed toward the dining room. The steward informed me His Lordship left the yacht at 6:00; the Countess departed at 6:45; Mr. Christen, Senior, had already eaten and was lounging by the pool; and Sven, Junior, hadn't yet arrived.

I asked for a hearty breakfast, whatever the cook wanted to prepare. I was hungry, I told the steward, and would like some coffee as soon as possible. The coffee arrived. Oh, was it good! I was having my second cup when young Sven moped into the dining room wearing his robe and slippers.

"You look like you've been dragged through a keyhole backwards," I said, immediately recalling that I'd told Nikolas the same thing, although I knew Sven hadn't had a date after last night's dinner.

"I had a terrible dream and couldn't wake up to stop it," he said as he joined me.

"Do you remember what it was?"

"Yes. I was working with you in Spain at the time the Count was killed and we both got mixed up in a web of intrigue involving not only the Spanish but also the Arabs."

"Which Arabs?" I inquired.

"I believe they were from Saudi Arabia, or maybe it was Egypt. I'm not sure."

I was startled by Sven's revelation, particularly since it followed so closely the conversation with Baba earlier that morning.

"Tell me all you can remember, Sven."

"Why is my dream so important to you?"

"Don't question my motives or my inquiries, my friend. If you and I are to work together, we have to share all our thoughts and our dreams, no matter how absurd they may appear."

"What is your pleasure this morning, sir?" asked the waiter.

"Just coffee for now please."

"Now tell me about your dream," I repeated.

"We were in Spain, having arrived just after the accident. We went right to the Church where the funeral service had already begun. Seated in the rear of the Church were two Arabs wearing burnooses. The hoods were pulled up close so I couldn't see their faces." Sven stopped and took another swallow of coffee. "I was trying to get to them to find out who they were but I couldn't move my feet. That happens in dreams, you know. You can't get your legs to move faster."

"So you never saw their faces?"

"No. The next thing I remember I woke up and found myself sweating. I threw on my robe and slippers and came here to get some coffee. That's all I remember."

"That's a lot." I told him of my conversation with Baba at the pool earlier that morning and of her feeling that in some way Arabs might be involved in Francisco's death.

"Let's keep this information about your dream to ourselves for now. When I get a chance, I'll tell Z."

The waiter re-entered the room and Sven ordered breakfast.

"I'm going to get into my trunks and join your father at the pool," I said leaving the room.

"We haven't had much time to talk since we were together on that trip to Tangier," I said as Big Sven and I shook hands. I took a beach towel from the pile nearby, the pile that wasn't there earlier this morning, and spread it on the chaise next to him.

"Yes, Philipp, you're right. I want to thank you for being my son's tutor. He's raved about your association since he first met you in Marbella. You are somewhat of an idol."

"Your son is a fine man and I'm pleased that Z has allowed us to work together. He's a quick learner and very observant. Someday, he'll be a super agent."

"If he had his way, he'd tail you like a puppy dog for the remainder of his training period." We both laughed at the image.

"Sven, I believe you know the details of Mr. Hargrave's death. There is one thing I don't fully understand. If he was being used to get to the Minister, why was he gunned down in her presence?"

"It's my understanding from talking with Z, that the enemy had discovered his bi-sexuality and thought he might be too risky for their operations. Killing both Hargrave and the Minister at the same time would place doubt in the minds of the Greek authorities as to who was the target. A rather clever maneuver, I'd say. The enemy's plant, the new Minister who succeeded Madam Stavros, was put in place to assist them in implementing their proposed operation of running drugs into Greece from the Arab World."

Sven said the Arab World. Could this be the connection Baba

suspects? And how does young Sven's dream get him involved? I'm beginning to believe he might be clairvoyant.

"I don't have any knowledge of an Arab World drug operation", I said. "Could this be what Francisco had discovered and was about to expose?"

"I've thought about that too, but neither do I have any knowledge of it."

Young Sven walked up where we were lounging, wearing only a black Speedo — no robe, no slippers. He leaned over and kissed his father and then shook my hand.

"I figured since there're no ladies on board, I could relax my dress code." He dove into the pool.

"When I grow up, I hope to have a body like that," I said jokingly.

"He works on it daily and is proud of his accomplishments," Sven replied.

A waiter appeared and asked if we cared for more coffee, or something a little stronger. Sven and I requested more coffee. The waiter turned to young Sven.

"I'll have some mineral water, please."

While young Sven was still in the pool, Sven, Senior, and I continued our previous conversation.

"Do you have any knowledge of any Arab countries being involved in the drug trade?" I asked.

"Nothing specific, but I know, from previous contacts in the Arab World, that both the Saudis and the Egyptians have been engaged in it at one time or another."

"Have you ever mentioned or discussed this matter with your son?"

"No. Why do you ask?"

I told him about Baba's suspicions and Sven's dream. A slight frown came over his forehead. It was more of a revelation than a shock.

"My son hadn't been informed about any of my past operations and relationships with Z. When he was hired, it was strictly on his abilities and potential. I was allowed to tell him of my associations with the Agency, but didn't think it appropriate to go into too much detail until he had further training and exposure. I was thrilled when Z got him the chef's position in Marbella, and I was doubly pleased when you became his mentor."

The waiter arrived with the coffee and the mineral water. Young Sven hopped out of the pool and sat on a nearby chaise as he toweled dry.

"What were you two plotting? I hope it was about my future in this business."

"We were discussing the possibility of getting you a side job as a fortune teller," I said jokingly.

"As long as I can work with you, that'd be okay."

We three talked about our business in general, about some of the experiences we'd had and about some of the people we'd met, nothing too specific or revealing. Young Sven took in everything that was said. I could almost see his brain working.

"I think I'll have a swim," I said, jumping into the pool. Young Sven remained with his father. While I swam, I noticed the two of them talking intently. Young Sven was shaking his head "no." When their conversation had apparently ended, I got out of the pool and returned to my chaise.

"My father thinks I should get back to my chef's job, but I'd prefer to stay here."

I spoke up first. "Z thought your being in Marbella was important. I believe he still does. After hearing your dream, which I've relayed to him, I'm certain he thinks there may have been more to Francisco's death. So you see my young friend, part of your continuing education is to listen to your elders, take their suggestions seriously and report your findings to me. Any questions?"

"Only one. When do I have to leave?"

"I believe sometime tomorrow would be appropriate." I paused and then said quite seriously, "Sven, you'll never know how important you've been, being by my side during this most traumatic experience. You're not only my protégé and my confidant but also my friend. I'll be thrilled when Z decides that you and I can work together again. Until that time, your place is in Marbella."

Young Sven stood up, pulled me up by both hands and gave me a hug. He turned and walked rapidly to the stairwell.

I wanted to say something but words failed me. I looked at Sven, Senior. He smiled and blinked.

"Ever since his mother died, I've tried to be both father and mother. He's a serious young man who hasn't quite found his niche. When Z put you two together, it was a great event in both our lives. He admires you greatly; he's told me so. I'm pleased that he's in your care, for I know you'll train him as you were trained by Z.

"My life was very empty until Doris and I found each other. She's a fine lady and needs love and affection as much as I do. Sven has told me he fully approves of our relationship. He has a girlfriend here in Stockholm, a charming young lady of whom he's very fond. He wants to get married and raise a family, but he also wants to be successful in our business. He is currently wrestling with that dilemma. He admired the relationship you and Arlene had and hoped that he and his young lady would have a similar one. Arlene's death was devastating to him, as it was to all of us. Now he feels even closer to you. Philipp, I'm so proud to have Sven as my son, and I'm pleased to have you as his mentor."

I wanted to say something but words wouldn't come. I offered my hand. He took it.

"I've never before heard anyone call Madam Thirty-Seven by her real name," I said. "Doris is such a pretty name. When do you expect her to arrive?"

"Day after tomorrow. We leave for Leningrad the following day. The wedding is scheduled for Saturday afternoon in the Cathedral. You're coming with us I hope."

"Doris, if I may call her that when she's not present, has invited me and Z encouraged me to bring my formal gear with me. I don't know any of the details of the wedding."

"Doris has invited the entire wedding party and a few extra friends to spend Saturday evening on board," said Sven. "She plans to give the couple their wedding feast here. You've already been counted as one of the thirty-seven. I believe you know the groom. His mother was a friend of mine and my wife. She was French and her late husband was Russian, titled I believe. The groom and Sven are the same age and have sailed together here in the Baltic."

"I believe I do know the groom. He was a college roommate of Senator What's-His-Name's son. Refresh my memory."

"Boris is a fine young man with a good head for business. He's marrying the daughter of Duke Maltzov, whose grandfather was Aide to the Czar. The ceremony is being held in the Cathedral in Leningrad with all the pomp and ceremony of a Russian Orthodox wedding. Since you speak Russian, Doris thought you might like to attend, especially since you already know Boris."

"I'm pleased to be included." I paused and looked around the deck. "Have you any plans for lunch?" I asked.

"I was about to ask you to join Sven and me at my Club, if you'd like that."

"I'd be delighted. What's the uniform?"

"I usually wear a business suit. If you'd asked Sven, he would've said 'clothes.' He's a practicing nudist."

"So I was told. At what time should we leave?"

"About 11:45. I'll call my driver."

I looked at my watch. It was 10:00.

"I'd like one more hour of sun. Shall I meet you both in the drawing room?"

"Yes. I'll notify Sven, or if you see him first, please tell him of our plans." He left the main deck as young Sven appeared, still in his Speedo.

"Can you please tell me about your conversation with my father?"

"In what respect?" I asked.

"Did he say anything about me and my girlfriend getting married?"

"He said that you and she were very much in love. He also told me that you were having butterflies, not being able to make up your mind between getting married and furthering your career with the Agency."

"I really do like her, Philipp, but I also love my job."

That sounded just like Arlene's statement when I asked her to marry me.

"You said you liked your girl friend but you loved your job. Do you really love her or are you just a horny young man who needs constant sex?"

"Wow. You certainly do get right to the heart of the matter. I like her very much and sexually, we're very compatible. I'm very happy when I'm with her and I miss her a lot when we're apart."

"Do you miss her, that particular 'her', or do you just miss the sex part?"

Sven paused and thought about my question. He started to say something but stopped before the words came. Finally he said, "This is the first time I've thought about her in the way you've just described. When I think about it, I mean seriously think about it, it's probably the sex I miss the most." I thought I saw a little blushing in his cheeks.

"Sven, my young friend, you're a healthy twenty-five year old, who obviously needs more sex than you're getting. Until you feel that you love her for more than her body, my advice is to wait a while before getting married. What's her name?"

"Helga. She is a former Miss Scandinavia."

My heart skipped a beat. I didn't want to pursue that. I'll ask Sven, Senior, privately, I decided.

"Your father has asked me to join you and him at his Club for lunch."

Sven joined me in the pool. We swam a few more minutes, got out, toweled dry and headed to our rooms. I went into the bathroom, shaved and showered, got dressed and went to the drawing room. Sven, Senior, was already there.

"I really enjoyed our talk," he said.

"So did I."

Young Sven came in looking like a model for *Gentlemen's Quarterly*.

The Club was near the Grand Hotel. I'd never before been in this Club. It reminded me a lot of the Cosmos Club in Washington, D.C., where I'd been a guest on several occasions --- formal and sedate with a hushed atmosphere. As we entered the dining room, I looked around, checking out the other diners. No one looked familiar. The waiter brought the menus and greeted Sven, Senior, cordially. Young Sven and I were introduced as his guests. I ordered a seafood salad. Both Svens ordered the bouillabaisse. We had mineral water and declined the waiter's suggestions for dessert.

"I'm looking forward to some more sun, this afternoon," I said as we got in the car.

"Me too," said young Sven.

"I think I'll just read in the drawing room. The waiter will be asking about our evening meal. What would you two like?" asked Big Sven. We gave him our orders.

After lunch I changed and headed for the pool. Young Sven was already there.

"This may be the last time we get to see each other for quite a while," he said. "I have to go back to being a chef when I really want to be a spy."

"Our business is not really spying though many would call it that. We are observers. We keep our eyes and ears open and learn as much as we can about the affairs of others. Whenever we think we may have discovered something of importance, we report it up the chain of command. With you as the chief chef in your dining room, I feel certain you'll be exposed to quite a few international celebrities as well as some lesser lights. When you think you have some tidbit that might be important, you know to call Z's headquarters and ask to be put through to me. I'm your mentor. You report only to me and to no one else. Is that clear?"

"Yes, sir." he said sheepishly. "I don't expect to find much as a chef in Marbella."

"Sven," I began, "when Z brought me into his training course, I was an American who had to learn the ways and mannerisms of a Brit. I was assigned to an agent who was working in the Emirates. I was in Abu Dhabi; he was in Dubai. I spoke a little Arabic but couldn't read it. There were no women. They were all kept captive in their homes. I soon became a raving, horny bachelor who would do anything to get laid. But I kept busy at my assignment, which was to watch for non-Arabic visitors to foreign facilities in Abu Dhabi.

"I spotted someone who made a weekly visit at the same hour on the same day to the same facility. I reported that fact to my mentor in Dubai. He'd had similar information about a visitor who did the same thing in Dubai, but on a different day. We compared notes and discovered that it was the same man. He reported our information to Z and before we could say jack rabbit, we'd uncovered a money-laundering ring tied to a black slave trade. Interpol was called in and the culprits were watched for a few days and then all were arrested. It was a big thing. I got to bust a few chops myself. I even got knocked down."

"How long did that take, from the time you arrived in Abu Dhabi?"

"Five weeks."

"Wow!" said Sven. "I suppose I'm too impatient, but I do fit your description of your life in Abu Dhabi. I'm observant, a good fact-gatherer, and horny."

"My advice to you is to take more cold showers."

"Sometimes it seems that I spend a majority of my waking hours in the shower."

"Concentrate, my friend, on your assignment. You'll find you'll get so involved in what you're doing your libido will subside."

"I hope so."

He and I stayed at the pool sunning and swimming. As the sun was slowly sinking into the sea, I said I wanted a nap before dinner. Sven remained on his chaise.

When I'd returned to my room, I took a hot shower. I lay across my bed, staring at the ceiling. Before long, I was gone. I awoke at the knock on the door.

"Dinner will be served in the dining room at 6:30." It was Big Sven. I looked at my watch. 6:10. I decided to go all out in my pursuit of leisure. I took out the white lace shirt that I'd bought in Mykonos. It was a little wrinkled, but what the hell. There'll only be three men at the table. I put on a pair of light tan slacks and ditched my shoes. I thought I looked like a Caucasian Don Ho.

As I entered the drawing room, Big Sven was reading a magazine. When he looked up, he said, "You look like James Bond in 'Casino Royale', replete with the open shirt revealing his hairy chest." We both laughed.

Young Sven joined us. "James Bond," he said. "You could pass for his double, and I suppose you have on occasion." We all laughed and went to the dining room.

The meal was just as we'd ordered. Big Sven had also agreed to our suggested menu. So here the three of us sat in this enormous dining room on this magnificent yacht, dining like kings and drinking the finest wine imaginable. We were having a ball. But the celebratory atmosphere was quashed when young Sven spoke during coffee.

"Dad, I'm going to miss you a lot. And I hope you and Doris have a wonderful trip to Leningrad. I don't know when I'll get back to Stockholm, but I'll be thinking of you every day and wishing for your happiness and safety."

I could feel the moment coming. I hoped I could handle it correctly.

"And Philipp, I'll miss you too. I'll miss the good times we've shared, our talks and the instructions you've given me. I'll do my very best in Marbella to make you proud of me. I'll ponder your words regarding married life and I'll concentrate on my assignment first before anything else. When things seem to be unbearable, I'll remember your advice and try to think pleasant and happy thoughts while taking a cold shower." He smiled. "I'll look forward to working with you again and I hope that day won't be too far off. I really am going to miss you, Philipp. I thank God we've become friends as well as co-workers."

I was afraid to look at him for fear I would tear up. I hung my head and looked at the tablecloth. Finally, I couldn't hold back any longer. I got up, walked around the table and pulled him up to me. We embraced in a great display of manly affection. While we were still embraced, Big Sven came around the table and embraced the two of us. Tears were in all our eyes. We continued to hug, and to cry. It's okay for men to cry when they have something special to celebrate or when they're expressing a deep emotion. It's also okay to cry when you want to tell someone how much you care about them and the words just won't come. I remembered I'd had the same feeling when I said goodbye to my dearest Arlene for the last time. I didn't want to think about that, but I wondered if young Sven and I would ever see each other again. I hugged more tightly. We three couldn't let go.

Finally, by mutual agreement, we untangled ourselves and sat down. I took the bottle of wine and went around to both Svens and emptied it in our three glasses. When I sat down, I lifted my glass and said, "To us." Both Svens responded, "To us."

We went to the drawing room, sat in three chairs facing each other and quickly fell asleep.

FOURTEEN

Big Sven and I awoke at about the same time. Young Sven was still asleep. The two of us quietly went into our bedrooms. I splashed cold water on my face and ran my fingers through my hair. I headed for the dining room. Big Sven was right behind me.

When we were seated, the waiter was there with coffee.

"Good morning, gentlemen."

"Good morning to you," we both replied.

"The young man will be along shortly," I said.

"May I suggest a Spanish omelet with hash brown potatoes?" said the waiter.

"Excellent," I said.

"Make it two", Sven added.

We sat in silence as we drank our coffee.

"Philipp, last evening at this table I had one of the most wonderful experiences in my entire life. I witnessed and participated in a true love feast. I was deeply touched by your actions."

At that moment, I realized how much I'd loved my father. He and Big Sven were about the same age; and when he died, I knew I'd miss him but didn't know how much.

"You remind me so much of my father. When I first met you several years ago, I knew I liked you, but I only realized last night just how much affection I have for you. And, Sven, if *I'm* not being too presumptuous, I'd like to consider young Sven as my younger brother."

Just then, he came into the room, barefooted with no shirt. He went directly to his father and hugged and kissed him on the lips. Then he came around the table and put his arms around me. Without a word, he took his place at the table. The waiter brought coffee and the omelets. We sat in silence until Big Sven spoke.

"Sven, my son, Philipp and I have had a wonderful conversation this morning, and we have mutually decided I can be his father and you can be his younger brother, if that's all right with you."

Young Sven looked at me and smiled. We both looked at Big Sven, who nodded. We talked as we ate. We sipped our coffee as we talked. We talked about our future assignments and where they might take us. Nothing was said about our parting later today. It was a joyous meal.

When breakfast was over, young Sven said, "Dad, why don't you join

Philipp and me for a swim?"

"I don't have my bathing suit with me," he said.

"That's okay. There's just the three of us on board. We can swim bare-assed."

Big Sven looked at me.

"Why not," I said.

We got up from the table, went to our rooms and shucked our clothes. I grabbed a towel, wrapped it around my middle and proceeded to the pool. As each of us arrived on deck, we jumped into the water. We splashed and frolicked like school kids.

After a few minutes, we got out and lay on the chaises. Big Sven draped his towel across his body, but young Sven and I remained undraped. We three sunned for about an hour. The waiter brought us mineral water and coffee. "Would you gentlemen care for a sandwich?" he asked. We each declined his offer with thanks.

The waiter returned an hour later and announced that lunch would be served at noon by the pool. Not surprisingly, we each ordered a Cobb Salad and iced tea. "That's what Z always has at his Club," I said. The mention of Z's name changed the atmosphere noticeably and I regretted having brought it up. It reminded me of the seriousness of our work. We reverted to silence and continued our sunning. Young Sven jumped into the water one more time but Big Sven and I remained on our chaises.

When the waiter arrived with lunch, small tables were brought up alongside our chaises. The mood turned jovial again as we talked about the huge yacht we were on and how much fun we'd had together over the past few days.

"Since I should be at the airport by 1:30, I'd better go pack," said young Sven.

"I'll have my driver here when you're ready to leave," said Big Sven. When he'd left the pool, Big Sven asked me if I wanted to come with them.

"I think not," I replied. "You two should have some time to yourselves, and I'm not sure I want to go through another goodbye this afternoon."

Big Sven nodded his agreement. He and I left the pool and went to our rooms. When we three gathered in the drawing room, young Sven had dressed casually, using his driver's uniform trousers and a polo shirt without a logo.

"Where'd you get that shirt?" asked Big Sven. I don't believe I've ever seen it before."

"I borrowed it from Philipp, if he doesn't mind," he said with a smile.

"I really don't like to lend my clothes to others, so why don't you consider it a gift."

He blinked. We went to the main deck. As we stopped at the gangplank, I looked at young Sven and he looked at me. We smiled and shook hands as they left the yacht.

When Big Sven returned, his eyes were red.

"I think I'll get one more swim. Will you join me?"

"Thanks, Philipp, but I think I'll pass this time - - perhaps another time and another place."

He went to the stairwell. I shucked off my clothes and threw them on the chaise. Then I dove in the water. It felt cool and refreshing. I like the feeling of being naked in the water. It always reminded me of the times my father and I went skinny-dipping in the pond near our house. I was about eight years old the first time. The last time was the year before he died. I miss him so much.

I got out of the pool and lay on the chaise. After a while, Big Sven came to the pool in a new swim suit and sat on a nearby chaise. I waited for him to talk if he cared to do so.

"You know, Philipp, I'm now fully retired from the Agency. Oh, I make an occasional trip for Z if he feels I can be of assistance. When Z hired young Sven, I was thrilled. So was Sven. He'd always said he wanted to do what I did, even though he knew very little about my work. We discussed, in general terms, what an agent does and what perils he's likely to encounter. The more I told him, the more enthusiastic he seemed to be about someday becoming one of us." Sven paused briefly.

"Then when Hargrave started stalking Sven, I thought it best if he could be transferred away from Stockholm. At first, Sven had mixed emotions about leaving both his girl friend and me, but I convinced him that to be a good agent, he must do as his superiors ordered. When the job in Marbella opened up, or to be exact, when Z created it, both he and I thought that would be a super place for him. I even told him that he might find a Spanish girl that would take his mind off Helga." Sven paused again.

"Do you know if Helga has ever traveled to the Greek Isles? Specifically, has she been to Mykonos?" I asked.

"Yes, she was on Mykonos just this past spring. Why do you ask?"

"I met a young girl, a former Miss Scandinavia, on a nude beach on Mykonos. She was with an acquaintance of mine. We only spoke one time, but since we were all nude, I can tell you that young Sven has great taste for beauty."

"Too much, I suspect. I realize Sven is a handsome twenty-five year old with raging hormones, but there was something about Helga I didn't trust when he brought her home the first time. I'll say this to you, Philipp, but I'd never say it to Sven. In my opinion, Helga is a gold-digger, always asking for gifts, and possibly an oversexed one. Whenever they were together in our living room, she had her hands all over my boy's body. I came in unexpectedly one evening and found the two of them naked on the floor. They didn't know that I saw them; I went directly to my bedroom. Sven and I never talked about it, but it's worried me ever since."

I thought it best to let the matter ride hoping Sven would find someone else more worthy of him, but I did tell his father of the advice I gave Sven about postponing marriage until he had more experience in the business. I sincerely hoped he'd take my advice. "Perhaps it would be a good thing if I asked Z to pair us up as soon as possible on another assignment."

"That would be wonderful, Philipp. I know Sven would be pleased to be working with you again." After a brief moment, he said, "May I invite you to dine with me tonight at one of Stockholm's finest restaurants? It's called 'Pontus' and it's located in the Hotel Stureplan across from Stockholm's largest park, Humlegarden, and not far from my home."

"I'd love to," I replied. "I know the area well having once been your house guest. Shall I notify the waiter that we'll be going out for dinner?"

"If you will, thank you."

I wrapped a towel around my middle and went to the dining room. I knocked on the kitchen door. A waiter answered my knock and I informed him of our plans. Later, when I entered the drawing room, I found Sven sitting on a couch.

"What time would you like to leave?" I asked.

"I've telephoned my driver to be here at 6:20. It's now 5:55."

"I'll be ready at 6:15," I said as I went to my bedroom. This time I left the door open. In a few minutes, as I was putting on my socks and shoes, Sven came in.

"You look quite dapper in that suit," he said, "almost like a Secret Agent." We both laughed as I finished dressing.

The drive to the hotel was brief. As we entered, there was a young and shapely blond coming out of the elevator on the arm of an older man. When she saw Sven, she tried to avoid a confrontation, but the distance between us was too small.

"Hello, Helga," said Sven.

"Hello, Mr. Christen." Helga looked at me and immediately

recognized me.

"Helga, this is my friend from America, Mr. Philipp Devon. I believe you've met before."

"Have we? I don't remember. Please pardon me but my uncle and I are going out for dinner and we're already late," she said as she and the older man walked out the lobby door.

Sven looked at me and shrugged his shoulders. "Her uncle?"

I didn't want to say the wrong thing so I clammed up. I thought he looked old enough to be her uncle but he also was sweating and looked like he'd just had an extended session at a massage parlor. At dinner, I didn't bring up meeting Helga, but I mentally put it in my "to do" file. I must tell young Sven at my earliest opportunity everything I know about her.

The dinner was exceptional, as Sven had promised. The restaurant was quite crowded but neither he nor I recognized anyone we knew. The décor was most elegant, with draped walls and potted palms between Doric columns. When we completed our meal, we walked outside as Sven's driver appeared.

"What time do you expect Doris to arrive tomorrow?" I asked.

"Her plane lands at 2:40. My driver and I will pick her up at the airport."

"Then I'll have time for a swim and some sun in the morning."

"Certainly. You might as well take advantage of no one else being on board until she arrives."

We sat in our drawing room for about an hour, discussing the forthcoming trip to Leningrad and the wedding dinner on Saturday evening. I confirmed that the dress would be tuxedo for the men. We said good night about 10:00 and went to our rooms. I closed the door and began to reflect on meeting Helga again. How far young Sven has gotten involved with her and what promises he may have already made to her worried me. Has he asked her to marry him? What has she told him about herself?

I finished undressing, lay on my bed and once again stared intently at the ceiling for a few minutes and then fell into a deep sleep.

When I awoke, my watch said 8:30. I got up, went into the bathroom and picked up the phone.

"May I please have my breakfast at poolside in fifteen minutes? I'll have my usual and, of course, a pot of coffee. Thank you." When I'd replaced the receiver, I showered, toweled off, wrapped a towel around my middle and walked, bare-footed to the pool. The weather was beautiful;

not a cloud in the sky, as they say. It's going to be a hot day.

I chose one of the chaises, spread my towel and lay down on my stomach. The waiter arrived shortly, greeted me by name and placed the tray on the small table nearby. I sat up and poured a cup of coffee. I lifted the silver dome and found eggs and bacon the way I liked. When I'd finished eating and was on my second cup, I lay down again on my stomach. The sun was warm and soothing. I was about to drift off when Sven arrived. He had a towel around his middle, which he took off and joined me.

"Did you sleep well?" he asked.

"Like a newborn baby. How about you?"

"Not so well. After seeing Helga, I was worried about my son. I thought about their relationship all night. In fact, I even saw the sun come up this morning."

"Sven, you mustn't worry. I determined last night I'll call Sven when I get back to London and have a talk with him, explaining everything I know and suspect about her."

"Thank you, Philipp. I'm starting to feel better already."

The waiter arrived with a tray of food and placed it on the table near Sven. There was a stack of three pancakes, already buttered, with syrup dripping down the side. Sven poured a cup of coffee and dug in. While we ate, we talked about the forthcoming trip to Leningrad.

"Other than the sixteen members of the wedding party, do you know who the remaining eighteen guests might be?"

"Doris has invited some of her friends who know the young couple, but I don't know their names. The party on board should be a rousing success. Doris has engaged a small ensemble for the evening. The dinner, of course will be in the dining room. I'm really looking forward to it."

"So am I."

We finished our breakfast. I dove into the water; Sven followed my lead. Again, we splashed around like children. He tried to put on a calm face and a carefree attitude, but I could tell that he was still worried about young Sven.

"I wonder how far Sven's relationship with Helga has gotten," he said. Did he tell you anything about his plans for the future?"

"He and I talked about our respective lives, mine and Arlene's and his and his girlfriend. He did say he hoped to marry her when he could get back to Stockholm. I told him about the advice Z had given to Arlene and me, about the advantages of remaining unmarried and continuing our trysts whenever possible. I pointed out to him the long times away from home and the various assignments he might have. I believe I got him thinking more seriously about his job with the Agency than about a wedding."

"Oh, Philipp, my new son," he said as he paused and looked at me with a twinkle in his eye, "you are so re-assuring and so level-headed when it comes to matters of the heart. A father has difficulty being rational at times. Thank you for what you are, for what you mean to both young Sven and me; and as for your plans to talk with him, I am deeply appreciative. Thank you."

We both agreed that we'd had enough sun so we wrapped our towels around our waists and headed to our rooms.

"Let's have a light lunch here in our suite at about noon. You order for us, if you'll be so kind," said Sven. He went into his bedroom and closed the door. I went into my bedroom, closed the door and took a shower. I called and ordered one egg salad sandwich and one chicken salad sandwich for each of us, plus iced tea, to be served here at noon. I sat in my chaise and took a cat nap.

When the knock on my door woke me, the waiter said lunch had arrived. I threw on a pair of slacks but no shirt and walked bare-footed into the drawing room. Our lunches were laid out on the long table between the sofas. I'd just sat when Sven arrived. He looked a tad calmer than he had before. He was dressed for his trip to the airport. He sat and we both dug in. We were quiet during our meal except for a casual comment about some unimportant thing.

"What have Doris and you planned for this evening's meal?" I asked, always thinking about the next one.

"She'll be tired from her trip. It's a long way from Dubai. I suppose she might decide to have dinner in her room. You and I can eat wherever we want. Let's wait and see what she decides."

"Sounds like a good plan."

Sven rose and said, "I'll leave for the airport now. We should return in about two hours, if her plane's on time."

"Good. I promise not to be bare-assed when you get back." He laughed as he left the room.

After he'd gone, I went back into my room and called Z.

"Philipp, my friend, how are you?"

"I'm just fine. Young Sven flew back to Madrid and on to Marbella yesterday. Sven, Senior, and I have enjoyed each other's company, in and out of the pool, at the dinner table and just lounging here in the drawing room."

"That's nice to hear. Is there anything I should know?"

"I'm worried, and so is Sven, Senior, about young Sven and his relationship with his girlfriend. I discovered that she is the same Swedish model I met on Mykonos. Big Sven and I casually met her last evening as we were going to dinner. She was coming out of the hotel elevator with an older man, whom she said was her uncle, but who looked like a john who had just had his money's worth upstairs."

Z was silent for a moment. "Have you and Sven, Senior, discussed her probable occupation?"

"We have, but I've not mentioned any of this to young Sven. I'm calling to get your advice on whether I should tell him over the phone or wait until I see him again, wherever and whenever that might be."

"My advice to you is to say nothing to him until sometime later. I'll insure he does not return to Stockholm until you've had that talk. Give my regards to Sven, Senior." He hung up.

Rather than risk dropping off to sleep again and not being presentable for Doris's arrival, I dressed in my casual trousers, a polo shirt with no logo (one of my two remaining) and my black loafers and went up on deck.

The sun was still quite hot. The sky was clear. I really wanted to jump in the pool again. I sat on one of the chaises which I pulled under the canopy. A waiter brought me an iced tea.

In approximately two hours, Sven and Doris walked up the gangplank. I was somewhat startled for I had dropped off to sleep. I immediately walked toward them. Doris was smiling broadly.

"My dear Philipp," she said, "how wonderful it is to see you again."

"Thank you, Madam, it's always a pleasure to be in your company."

"Please call me Doris when we're alone and there are no strangers around."

"Thank you. I want to thank you for inviting me to travel to Leningrad with you. I'll look forward to seeing Boris again."

"You'll love his bride. She's adorable."

"I'm sure she is," I responded.

"Let me get settled in my room and then you and Sven and I can have a little chat in my drawing room. Come down in about ten minutes."

She went to the stairwell followed by one of her attendants carrying three pieces of Louis Vuitton.

After she left the main deck, Sven said, "She's a marvelous person and I'm so fortunate to have found her. Or to be exact, she found me. We were both at a reception in the Royal Palace and His Highness introduced her to me. My wife had passed away a few months before. She seemed to have known that fact, for she graciously offered her condolences. We shared some Champagne. She invited me to a soirée she was giving the next night aboard the yacht, which I accepted. We saw each other a few times while her yacht was moored here. Then she invited me to take a cruise with her and her other guests on the Baltic. The next cruise was the one on which you and Arlene were aboard.

"Doris and I have hit it off, so to speak, quite well. She's a lusty woman and I'm a virile man. We enjoy each other's company quite often and quite intensely, if you know what I mean."

I did and was happy to hear about it. I immediately thought about Arlene and me, and what fun we'd enjoyed in each other's arms on so many occasions. I must stop thinking that way, I told myself. It's not good for my health, physically or mentally.

"Let's go below," he said. We headed for the drawing room. The doors to Doris' bedroom opened and she came in, casually but elegantly dressed in an apple green pants suit with only one piece of jewelry: a diamond and gold eagle pin.

"My, what courtly gentlemen you are. You don't have to get up when I join your company."

"My mother would kill me if I didn't," I said.

"Your mother obviously raised you right, Philipp."

We sat and the waiter arrived with both coffee and hot tea. He poured tea for Doris and offered her the plate of sliced lemon and the canister of sugar cubes. Then he poured coffee for Sven. When he asked for my preference, I took coffee, black. He left the room.

"Philipp, as you already know, I'll be giving the wedding dinner aboard the 37 after the ceremony. I also have asked the entire wedding party and a few extra guests to stay overnight. The dress for the wedding is formal attire. I understand you have your ensemble with you."

"I'm always prepared for any occasion," I joked.

"Good. The wedding will be in the Cathedral on Saturday afternoon at four o'clock. There'll be a reception in the Hermitage shortly thereafter. The attendees at the ceremony and reception will be the wedding party, you and Sven and I, the Minister of Culture, The French Ambassador, The Chief of the Imperial Guards who is a cousin of Boris' late father, and The Head of the Russian Orthodox Church in Leningrad, who'll perform the marriage ceremony. I plan to wear comfortable shoes, for as you know, at a Russian wedding, everybody stands the entire time. There are no seats in the Church."

She sipped her tea again. "Before dinner, weather permitting, we'll have Champagne on the main deck, or, as an alternative, in the casino lounge. If, after dinner, anyone would like to visit the casino, they will certainly be welcome to do so, and please, Philipp, let the bride and groom win at least once," she said with a smile. "Do either of you have any questions?"

"Only one, Madam, I mean Doris. Am I supposed to watch for any unusual happenings at these functions?"

"Z has indicated that one of the friends of the groom may want to contact *you*. Make yourself available. Now, if there are no more questions, what shall we do about dinner?"

"If you aren't too tired from your trip, I'd like to take us out," said Sven.

"I'm never too tired to dine with two handsome gentlemen. What do you suggest?"

"There is a fine French Restaurant in the Grand Hotel in Saltsjobaden, only a short drive from here. The food is excellent and the ambience is most pleasant. It'd be my pleasure to have the two of you as my guests," he said.

"That sounds good to me," said Doris. "How about you, Philipp?"

"You know me. I was born to be a guest." I enjoy being surrounded with the luxuries of 5-star hotels, mixing with royalty and the world's beautiful people, and dining in the finest restaurants, but I know I'll never be a host in this incredible world of the super rich. I wasn't born into that glamorous world and shall always be an outsider, only a guest.

"Good. I shall call for a reservation and my driver. Shall we leave here about 7:45?"

"I'll be ready. You men will be in a suit, exactement?"

"Oui, Madam," said Sven.

"Certainment," I added.

We left the drawing room and agreed to re-assemble at 7:40. I shaved and took another shower. I put on my new Austin Reed suit which, I thought, is fast becoming old.

As we walked down the gangplank, I saw Sven's driver standing beside a charcoal Mercedes with the two rear doors open. He assisted Doris to her seat while Sven went around and got in next to her. I sat up front with the driver. The drive to the Hotel was about twenty minutes. As we entered the lobby, I saw the entrance to the restaurant off to the left. Sven led the way.

"Bonjour, Richard, comment allez-vous ce soir?" Sven said greeting the maître d'.

"Très bien, merci, Monsieur Christen. Et vous?"

"Très bien."

"Votre table est prés. Suivez-moi, s'il vous plaît.

We were seated at a circular table. The dining room was huge with a green and white color scheme throughout. There were fluted columns on three sides atop which were large arrangements of multicolored silk flowers. The white tablecloth and napkins, I surmised, were damask. The petite vase of flowers held some kind of small white lily. The silverware was sterling, not an import from China. The waiter also greeted Sven by name and acknowledged Doris and me with a slight nod.

"Philipp, will you please order the wine?" asked Sven as he handed me the list. "I always prefer a red and so does Doris."

"Let me see if my favorite Bordeaux is on the list." I said, looking at the list and then to the waiter who had remained standing by the table, "Je voudrais le 1982 Château de Pitray, s'il vous plaît."

"What's that wine?" asked Doris.

"It's from the Côte de Castillon."

"I wonder why a French restaurant in Sweden would have it on their wine list," said Doris. "I've never heard of it."

"Trust me." I said. "You'll like it."

The sommelier arrived with the correct wine and vintage. He poured a small amount in his tastevin, which he took from around his neck, then in my glass. I knew it would be excellent, but I went through the protocol, after which I pronounced it *parfait*. Together we lifted our glasses and said *Skoal*. Doris smacked her lips and took another small sip.

The waiter took our orders. Doris and I ordered vichyssoise while Sven ordered escargots. I was in the mood for a something simple so I ordered the coq au vin after Doris ordered trout. Sven could not decide between the trout and coquille St. Jacques. He finally settled on the scallops. I'd have preferred a Chablis with the fish, but Sven had said they both preferred red wine at all times. There's a Latin expression: *De gustibus non est disputandem*. (There can be no dispute about taste.)

The vichyssoise was excellent; light and very creamy. Sven raved about the snails.

"The trout," said Doris, "was cooked just right and the fresh horseradish was tangy but not biting."

I really liked the coq au vin. All the vegetables were perfectly blended. We agreed that our meals had been outstanding.

When the waiter approached the table again, he poured the remaining wine and placed before each of us a menu of desserts.

"Not for me," said Doris.

"Nor I," I repeated.

Sven said, "Je voudrais une tarte aux pommes (an apple tart), s'il vous plaît."

I really wanted a cup of coffee but decided I could get one back on the yacht, along with some Grand Marnier.

After each of us had thanked and said goodnight to the waiter, the sommelier and the maître d', we left the restaurant. Sven's driver was waiting; he'd probably been alerted by the maître d'.

When we'd reconvened in the drawing room, I said, to the waiter standing by, I'd like a coffee and a Grand Marnier. Doris said good night and went into her bedroom. Sven also said good night and departed. I kicked off my shoes, undid my tie, took off my suit jacket, opened my shirt buttons and lay back in the overstuffed chair. The coffee and liqueur arrived. I took them and my clothes to my bedroom, closed my door and sat down on the soft chair.

I've had a good day, I thought. I finished my drink and coffee, stripped and lay across the bed, again staring at the ceiling. In what seemed like only seconds, I was asleep.

FIFTEEN

After a night of pleasant sleep, I awoke thinking about the trip.
Doris said we'd leave mid-afternoon and arrive sometime during the night,
in which case, tomorrow morning I'd wake up in Leningrad. I looked at
my watch. 7:20. I got up, shaved and showered and dressed in light-
colored slacks, my white see-thru shirt, which I obviously prefer to all my
others, and my black Zelli loafers. When I entered the dining room, no one
else had arrived. There was a buffet on the sideboard. The waiter poured
my coffee while I served myself eggs, grilled sausages, hash browns and
toast. Sven came in. He had a smile on his face that clearly asked, "Guess
what I did last night?" For a sixty-two-year-old man, he was in remarkably
good shape, but I assumed he wasn't in a gym during the night.

"Good morning, Philipp," he said. "I trust you slept well."

"I did, thank you, and clearly you had a good evening also."

He looked at me and smiled. His coffee was poured as he served
himself and sat across from me.

"I understand we'll be departing mid-afternoon," I said. "That'll give me a few more hours of sunning."

"Doris told Captain Andersen we'd shove off about 3:00. She also said she'd like to get some sun this morning. The three of us shall have some time to chat."

We talked about the dinner last evening and how elegant and wonderfully presented it was.

"Your selection of the wine was outstanding," he said. "How did you come across that particular vineyard?"

"The owners of the vineyard have been friends for about twenty years. He's a retired member of our compatriots in France. We met at a party in Paris when Z was visiting. The wine has received many awards at wine Expos and the 1982 is currently rated by the wine gurus a 94 on the 1-to-100 scale."

"Well, it certainly was an excellent selection and I'm happy to be introduced to it."

While we were discussing the wine, Doris entered wearing a flowing pink negligee and pink slippers. Her hair was arranged softly about her face. We both rose.

"Good morning, Philipp," she said. "I hope you slept well after such a magnificent meal."

"I slept like a baby," I said.

She only nodded to Sven. I assumed they'd said good morning earlier.

"Philipp, your selection of wine last evening was wonderful. Perhaps I should acquire some for my guests." Her coffee was served.

"It would be my pleasure to have several cases delivered to you as my house gift." The wine isn't expensive and I knew I could telephone my bank in Switzerland and have the wine charged to my account. "Do you plan to be in Le Havre anytime soon?"

"Yes, I'm planning to be there in about a month. Z has asked me to host a party for several of his friends."

"How many cases of a newly tasted wine do you usually acquire?" I asked.

"Usually four or five, but since I've already tasted this wine, I'd like to purchase ten cases."

"It would be my pleasure to have ten cases ready at the dock in Le Havre for your arrival."

"I'll accept your offer of two and I'll pay for the remaining eight. Is it a deal?"

"It's a deal. I'll order them before we sail."

"I'd like to get some sun before lunch, if I may join you gentlemen."

"It would be our pleasure," I said.

"Jason, we shall have lunch by the pool at 11:30. I believe chicken salad sandwiches and iced tea would be fine."

When she finished her breakfast, we three left to change. I arrived on deck first and lay down on one of the three chaises already arranged with small tables near each. Sven and Doris came out together. When she removed her beach robe, I was reminded what a stunning woman she was at fifty-plus. Her legs were perfect, her waist, trim and her one-piece swimsuit showed off her tanned body very well. As she lay down next to my chaise, she patted me on my stomach and said, "Philipp, you are so gorgeous."

That comment triggered the thought of my dearest Arlene's words at the Lowndes. It was exactly what she'd said, but at that time I was naked. I thought maybe I should strip for Doris but decided not to. Sven lay down on her left. We made small talk for a while before I got up and dove into the pool. The water was warm. I swam a few laps and then returned to my chaise and lay on my stomach. Jason brought chilled mineral water.

We lay in the sun for about an hour when Doris asked, "Philipp, when was the last time you saw Boris?"

"It was in New York about eight months ago. We had a drink at The

Plaza Bar."

"Did you discuss his forthcoming wedding?"

"Yes we did, although at that time I didn't know I'd have the pleasure of attending."

"Did he mention one of his groomsmen, John Beecham?"

"No, I don't recall that he did."

"Z indicated that Mr. Beecham would like to talk with you privately after the wedding dinner. Can you make yourself available?"

"Yes I can. Have you any information concerning the subject?"

"None."

We continued to talk but Doris said nothing more about my forthcoming meeting with Mr. Beecham or, for that matter, anything about the wedding. I combined the information I had: Mr. Beecham is a friend of Boris; he must be about young Sven's age; he's been in touch with Z; and he probably knows about our business. He wants to talk with me. Should I let him come to me, or should I approach him? I just love intrigue.

I dove in the water one more time before lunch. While I was in the water, three waiters arrived with the three trays. I got out, toweled dry and sat down on my chaise. Sven had thrown a towel over his shoulders but Doris remained uncovered. I don't know if she was deliberately trying to entice me but it was working. I became aroused. She and I stared at each other, not at our eyes but at our bodies. Lunch proceeded as Jason brought three more iced teas. As we finished, Doris spoke.

"Philipp, I don't want to appear insensitive to your feelings or to infringe on your personal time of mourning your dearest Arlene. However, you're one of the most handsome men I've ever known. Many of my guests have asked me about your eligibility. When we get to the wedding, you'll be introduced to several beautiful young ladies, any one of whom I'm sure you would find attractive were it not for your recent loss and your period of mourning. I respect that and shall honor it." She paused.

"Having said all that, I want you to know that, as a woman who's had much experience with men, five of whom I've married, I understand that you need to be thinking about your future. I'm not pushing you or suggesting you go have a fling with one of these beauties; but I want you to know I'll do whatever you want me to do, to assist you in any way regarding your future life."

Doris paused again and looked me straight in the eye. I got up, leaned over her and kissed her on the forehead.

"You sweet dear man," she said as she wiped away a tear. I knew that Doris was sincere in her comments. I also knew that I missed and shall continue to miss my dearest Arlene for quite a while. One cannot be married in spirit to another person for any length of time and not be thoroughly shaken by a separation, particularly if it's permanent. I know I'm a young, well relatively young, virile man who needs to be loved and caressed often. I appreciated what Doris said about being of assistance when I'm ready.

"I think I'll swim again," I said. "Will either of you join me?"

"Here I come," said Sven, as he jumped in the water, pushing me in as he did. We splashed around like we'd done yesterday. I looked at Doris, smiling.

"You two boys have fun. I'm going to have a nap. Will either of you join me?" she said, looking over her shoulder and winking. Sven looked at me and also winked.

"Go ahead," I said. "I'll go take a cold shower." We both smiled knowingly.

He got out of the pool, toweled dry, took a sip of his iced tea, and went to the stairwell. I swam a little longer then lay on my chaise. I thought about my Arlene, but I also thought about Doris' words of assistance.

I must have fallen asleep. When I turned over and looked at my watch, it was 2:30. I wanted to be on deck to watch our departure. I went to my room, showered and put on my light slacks without a shirt or shoes and returned to the main deck. We soon began to move away from the dock, the side thrusters working all out. I pulled up a beach chair near the rail and watched Stockholm slowly recede into the horizon.

Doris and Sven came on deck.

"This calls for a celebration," said Doris, "a celebration of life and for the forthcoming wedding." Jason appeared with a silver tray, a crystal ice collar holding a bottle of Champagne, and three flutes, and of course, three linen napkins. He set the tray on the table nearby, deftly opened the Champagne and filled our glasses. Doris spoke.

"To friends," she said as we each sipped. "To life," she said as we sipped again. "To Philipp's happy future," she said as she and Sven sipped. Jason refilled our glasses and departed. Doris looked at me and said, "Philipp, my dear, I sincerely hope you have fun tomorrow, and I really mean that." I knew she did.

We sat at the rail and watched the Swedish coastline pass by. Then the Captain steered starboard as we headed for the Gulf of Finland. Soon, we could see the lights of Helsinki off the port side. The air became chilly so we all went inside. As we approached the stairwell, a waiter appeared.

"We shall dine at seven, informally in my drawing room," said Doris.

"Very good, madam."

"I'd like to lie down and read a while before dinner, if you gentlemen have no objection."

"None at all," I said, as she went into her bedroom and closed the door.

"I think I'll rest a bit, too," said Sven as he entered his bedroom.

I went into my bedroom, slipped out of my trousers and lay across the bed.

Promptly at 7:00, the waiter knocked.

"Dinner is served, Mr. Devon."

I put on a Polo shirt, trousers and my loafers and entered the drawing room. I was the first to arrive. A small round table replaced the long one between the sofas. Three places had been set and a straight chair was positioned at each. There was a small vase of white lilies with some greenery. There were Bordeaux wine glasses. As I stood admiring the elegance of the informal dinner, Sven came in at the same time Doris entered.

One of the waiters seated Doris. Three waiters removed the three covers. Behold! Quail with quail eggs and fresh asparagus. Jason brought a bottle of 1982 Montebuena Rioja and filled each glass. Doris spoke.

"The quail and eggs were flown in yesterday from the south of France and the asparagus came from Alsace. I hope this combination will suit your palates."

"A most tasty way to arrive in Leningrad," said Sven.

"After breakfast, perhaps you two would like to do some sight-seeing. I have a car and driver standing by if you would care to use it.

I spoke first. "If it's alright with you, I'd like to lounge about, swim and sun."

"And I think I'll just read and accompany Philipp at poolside", said Sven.

"As you wish", she said. "We can have lunch by the pool."

I went on deck. I continued to think about Doris' offer of assistance with my future, perhaps to introduce me to someone who might be attractive, sweet and in need of some sexy male companionship. I didn't punish myself for such thoughts. I knew I had to get on with my life no matter how much I missed and thought of Arlene.

I returned to my room, stripped, sat down on my chaise and dialed Z.

"Hello, Philipp. How is your life going at this point? Has Doris set you up with any one yet?"

"Not yet, but she has indicated a desire to assist me with my future life."

"Doris is a great person and a wonderful friend. She's also a valued part of our business. She'll never do anything that would make you uncomfortable, but, if you'll allow her to do so, she'll insure every possible opportunity for your future happiness and pleasant life will be steered your way."

"I thought you might like to know that she has indicated that a Mr. Beecham would like to make contact with me after the dinner tomorrow night."

"Right," said Z. "John Beecham is a member of our group who has infiltrated the enemy camp and has indicated he has something to say that might tie in with Francisco's death. I told him you'd be on board and he should convey that information to you. Mr. Beecham is a close personal friend of the groom, who knows nothing about his or your association with our group. John's introductory comment to you will be the daily code and your response to him will be your personal code, which I've told him. Have fun tomorrow." Z hung up abruptly as he always does. Even if the line is secure, brevity is the better part of any conversation.

As I put the receiver down, there was a knock at my door. "Philipp, may I come in?" asked Sven.

"Come in, please."

When he entered and saw me butt naked, he said, "I hope I've not come at a bad time."

"You are always welcome," I said. "Sit down, please."

As he sat on the side of the bed, he said, "I've been thinking a lot about my son and I wondered if you've had a chance to speak to Z about his situation?"

"I did and I told him everything I knew about Helga and how you and I'd met her in the hotel lobby. I asked Z if I should call Sven and talk with him or would it be better to wait until I could see him again. He indicated that I should wait. He also assured me that he'd insure Sven didn't return to Stockholm until after I'd spoken with him."

"Oh, I feel so much better knowing that."

"Don't you worry about Sven. I'm certain I can convince him not to pursue his relationship with her any further."

"You're such a fine man, my son," he said, smiling warmly at the mention of our new relationship. He got up to leave; I also. When he got to the door, he turned and said, "Philipp, I only wish you'd come into our lives earlier." We shook hands.

I went back to the chaise and thought about how and when Mr.

Beecham and I could get together. Knowing that Doris was in on the planning of this meeting, I knew she would steer us together in her inimitable way. I decided to call it a day. I turned out the lights and lay down. Tomorrow, I thought, should be a busy and interesting day. And then I slept.

I rose at 8:00, shaved and showered, put on my swimsuit and went to the pool. I swam several laps and was about to get out of the water when I noticed Jason's arrival.

"Good morning, Mr. Devon. I thought you might like to start your day with some coffee and bread." He put the tray on a table near a chaise.

"Good morning to you, Jason. You're a most welcome sight. Thank you for being so thoughtful."

I sat on the chaise and poured a cup from the silver pot. The croissants were warm and freshly buttered. Nearby was some orange marmalade. I thought: What a great life. Finishing my breakfast, on my back I felt the heat of the sun already high in the sky. We were docked at the wharves in Leningrad and the steeples of the churches and the taller buildings were visible from my horizontal position. We were actually in the Neva River not too far from the Hermitage. The Cathedral was nearby. I got up and walked to the rail to get a better look at the city. What a magnificent city.

It was Tsar Peter's "Window to the West." The canals were patterned after those in Venice.

I'd not been in Leningrad for several years. I maintained my fluency in the language by reading copies of *Pravda*. Occasionally, I'd pick up one of the books I'd studied. I re-read some of the works of Lermontov, Pushkin and Dostoevsky and concluded that the Russian language was the most difficult of all the languages I'd studied. Russian idioms are a challenge and Russian vulgarities take first prize among all the insults in the linguistic world.

I went back to my chaise after a few more laps. This time I lay on my back. The sun had gotten quite hot and I wanted to be sure that I didn't overdo this tanning bit. I set my wrist alarm for one hour. I got up, dove into the pool once more, swam a lap or two, got out, toweled dry and went to my room. The phone was ringing.

"Philipp, I'd like for you to fly back to London tomorrow morning. You have a reservation on the 9:30 flight. I've also asked our young friend in Marbella to be here. You two are going on a new assignment on Thursday. Have a good time at the wedding and at dinner." Z terminated the conversation as usual.

I thought about what and where this new assignment might be, and why was young Sven being involved. Was this some further training for him? Or does he possess a special talent about which I haven't been informed?

The phone rang again. "Mr. Devon, would you like lunch in your room or do you plan to return to the pool?"

"Here in my room, thank you, Jason. Surprise me with a selection of your choice."

When Jason arrived, I'd changed into my trousers. He put the tray on the table and removed the silver dome. I saw a hot Reuben sandwich, a dill pickle, some potato chips and iced tea.

"I couldn't have chosen a better meal. Thank you."

The Reuben was spectacular. I imagined being at one of the restaurants in New York's Times Square. When I finished, I picked up the phone and called Doris's room.

"Doris, this is Philipp. I've just talked to Z who's made a reservation for me on a morning flight which leaves at 9:30. May I please ask your driver to take me to the airport leaving here at 7:00?"

"Of course, Philipp. I'll have Jason serve you coffee and toast in your room at 6:30."

"Thank you, my dear. What time should we depart this afternoon for the wedding?"

"My car will be here at 3:00. Would you like for me to tie your tie?" I detected a bit of coquettishness in her voice. So I played along.

"I'd be pleased to have you do so. Shall I come to your room or shall we just meet in the drawing room?"

"The drawing room will be fine. I'm not accustomed to having such a handsome young man in my bedroom in mid-afternoon. Comprendez-vous?" she said, continuing her flirting.

"Merci beaucoup, Madam. J'arriverai à trois heures moins dix minutes, s'il vous plaît." (I'll arrive at ten of three.)

I looked at my watch. 1:15. I dare not lie down now having been heated by the morning sun. So I decided to exercise again. The triples, the push-ups and sit-ups always get me in the mood for a good day. But I felt that I might need a little more energy this afternoon and evening. When I finished with everything, I felt like an old-fashioned clock spring, tightly wound and ready to pounce.

Cooling down a few minutes, I shaved and showered. I laid out my tuxedo and all the accessories and dressed. I looked at my watch. 2:42. I checked myself in the mirror and went into the drawing room. At exactly 2:50, the door to Doris' bedroom opened and out stepped a magnificently attired woman in a robin's-egg blue Dior with the same color shoes. Her hair was beautifully coiffed. On her left shoulder, she wore a round diamond and blue sapphire pin about two inches in diameter. She looked stunning. She came over to where I was standing and said, "Close your mouth, you're drooling." Then she took the ends of my tie and very quickly tied a perfect bow. And she did it from the front.

"You look even more gorgeous than usual," she said.

Sven appeared on the scene. He also looked handsome in his formal attire. Doris tied his tie.

"I'm thrilled to be accompanied by two of the most charming men I know," she said. .

The trip to the Cathedral was relatively short. We walked toward the front of the Cathedral. As we entered the building, we were ushered to a spot near one of the magnificent windows. Doris stood between Sven and me. The Cathedral is a fine example of Romanesque Gothic with stained glass windows all around, through which the sun comes streaming onto the mosaic tile floor.

The ceremony began promptly at 4:00. The attendant ladies identically attired in aqua chiffon gowns stood in a semi-circle in front of the audience. The groomsmen stood strategically placed throughout the

Cathedral to assist anyone who might become faint from standing so long. The ceremony lasted almost ninety minutes. At the conclusion, everybody rushed to the waiting cars and limousines for the short trip to the Hermitage.

The Hermitage is rated by most art connoisseurs as one of the most important Art Galleries in the world. The reception was held in Malachite Hall, a gigantic, spectacular rectangular room with multiple towering three-foot diameter Doric malachite columns on each side. The bride and her attendants and the groom stood on one side and greeted the guests. The groomsmen stood around aimlessly, trying to look important. I tried to pick out John Beecham but they all looked alike. When I went through the receiving line and spoke with Boris, he didn't appear to recognize me.

"Boris, I'm Philipp Devon. I met you in Washington at a reception given for your father just after he was elected to the Senate. It was held at the home of the Vice President."

"Of course I remember you," he lied, but graciously followed protocol. "I'm so happy you could come to our wedding." He looked as if he wondered why I was there.

Even though this was 1984, the waiters were dressed in Tsarist-period costumes and, served the guests Champagne in crystal glasses from silver gallery trays. The room was filled with about eighty guests. After some forty-five minutes, the bride and groom waved goodbye and left the Hall. After another thirty minutes, the remaining guests departed.

I knew Doris arranged for the bride and groom to travel to the yacht in her limousine and then the driver would return for the three of us. After the bride and groom were aboard, Captain Andersen had orders that no one was allowed to board until Doris had done so and could greet each of her guests as they arrived.

When the last of the guests were aboard, stewards retrieved the gangplank, isolating the yacht from possible intruders. Each guest was ushered into the dining room where inside the door stood an easel on which was posted a seating chart. When all the ladies were seated and the gentlemen took their positions behind their chairs, Sven and I took our assigned places. No one spoke. Doris made her entrance. Before she was seated, she welcomed the bride and groom and all their attendants, and the remaining guests, and sat down. We all followed her lead. Before the conversation began, Doris lifted her glass of Champagne and proposed a toast "To Boris and Eva. We wish for them many years of happiness together." Everyone responded, "To Boris and Eva."

At the conclusion of the first course, the waiters stood behind each gentleman and, on a nod from Jason, simultaneously removed the soup plates from the ladies and then from the men. As they left the room, Doris spoke.

"It's a pleasure to welcome each of you to the *37*. For those of you who are staying over this evening, your luggage has been retrieved from the Cathedral close and placed in your staterooms. Under your chargers you'll find the number of your room. At the conclusion of our dinner, we'll all gather on the main deck before retiring. I sincerely hope each of you enjoys your dinner and that your visit on board will be a pleasant one."

The meal was magnificent. There was some pleasant small talk but everyone was so busy enjoying the meal and commenting on it to his or her partners that no one really felt like talking. As the dinner concluded, Doris said from her chair, "My two guests who have traveled with me from Stockholm will lead us to the main deck for liqueurs." She nodded to Sven and said, "Mr. Christen" and with a nod in my direction, "Mr. Devon." There you have it. Now John Beecham will have no trouble finding me.

When the guests arrived on deck and had been served his or her choice of liqueurs, a young man of about twenty-eight to thirty approached me and said, "Mr. Devon, my name is John Beecham. We have a mutual friend who told me you were interested in numbers as am I." We shook hands. "Does the number (he gave the code of the day) have any interest for you?"

"Yes it does, Mr. Beecham. I also like the number (I gave him my personal code). My name is Philipp Devon, that's Philipp with a double p at the end. Let's go to the stern and view the lights of the city." We walked aft. When we'd gotten away from everyone, he spoke again.

"My father was with Barclay's in London and was one of the personal bankers to the Emir of The United Arab Emirates. The Emir and he were considered close personal friends. My father died of cancer last year and I received a personal letter of condolence from the Emir, inviting me to be his honored guest at dinner on my next visit to Abu Dhabi. When I was hired by our friend in London two years ago and put in training with one of his seasoned men, knowing that I was fluent in both French and Arabic, he sent me to the Emirates, ostensibly to look for business for my father's bank. I showed our friend the letter of condolence from the Emir, and he thought it would be productive if I accepted his offer of a dinner and got to be better established with the Monarch and his coterie of friends."

John paused, took a sip of his liqueur and continued.

"When I arrived in Abu Dhabi two months ago, I sent a message to the Emir that I was staying at the Sheraton. A courier brought to my hotel an invitation to dine on a certain evening at the Palace. I accepted verbally. On the appointed evening, I arrived at the Palace and was immediately ushered into the Throne Room where His Majesty greeted me personally. His interpreter was nearby since the Emir ostensibly spoke no languages other than Arabic. When I told him I also spoke his language, he was most impressed. He rose, put his arm around my shoulders and we walked together to the State Dining Room where ten other men were already assembled. Each of them approached and the interpreter introduced me to them. I didn't indicate that I spoke Arabic."

John paused again and we both sipped our liqueurs.

"During the dinner, I was seated next to one of the Emir's sons who spoke very good English. We talked about his interests in both sports cars and postage stamps. There were two men seated directly across from me who talked constantly to each other, to the exclusion of everyone else. I couldn't hear or understand everything that was being said because they were speaking quietly and I was talking and listening to the Emir's son. However, I did hear the word 'pharmaceuticals', which as you know is the socially acceptable word for 'drugs'. I also heard a few phrases containing the words 'our Spanish Agent in Madrid' and a name that sounded like Macredy or perhaps it was Macrady. Would those names mean anything to you?"

"They certainly do. Would you happen to remember the names or anything else about the two men you've just described?"

"I don't remember their names because they weren't clearly spoken at our introduction. I estimate they were both about thirty to thirty-five and one of them had a deep scar across his right cheek. Each had a mustache."

"Nice work, John. You've given me quite a bit to work on. Have you reported this experience to our friend in London?"

"Yes, I have and he appeared to be quite interested in my report."

"I'm flying back tomorrow morning. I'm sure he and I will discuss a more thorough analysis of your facts. We should get back to the others. It's been a pleasure meeting you, John."

"And you also, Philipp."

We shook hands and walked separately back to poolside. Shortly, Doris bade her guests good night, informed everyone that breakfast would be served in the dining room at 9:00, and then retired. Soon, the bride and groom waved goodbye to everyone as they descended the stairwell. They were followed by almost all the bride's attendants, accompanied by many of the groomsmen. The only persons remaining on deck were Sven and I, one bride's attendant and three groomsmen. Previously, Sven and I agreed we would be the last to leave the party.

Within a short time, the remaining female and one of the groomsmen vanished down the stairwell. Sven and I and the two groomsmen remained on deck. The other two were more than inebriated. I noticed the two of them whispering in the shadows and before Sven and I realized what was happening, they'd stripped and jumped into the pool, butt naked. I looked at Sven. We both laughed and sat down to see how long it might be before one or both of us would have to rescue them. They shouted and splashed around like Sven and I had done. Soon, they got out of the pool, wet and shivering. I went to the cabinet nearby and got two beach towels. They thanked me, dried off, gathered up their clothes and disappeared down the stairwell.

After they left, I looked at Sven and asked, with humor in my voice, "Would you like to take a dip?"

"I think not," he said, "but you go ahead if you care to. I'm going to call it a day. Good night."

"Good night, father," I said. We both smiled.

I thought about shucking everything and jumping right in, but the better part of my upbringing prevented me from doing so. Instead, I went to my room and went right to bed.

I awoke as my alarm began to pulse and went through my usual routine. Toweling dry, I noticed a note under my door. When I opened the flap, there were two notes inside.

"I'm so pleased to have you aboard. Take care of yourself, you dear man, and please come to see me again soon." It was signed "Doris."

"I've enjoyed being with you these past few days. God bless you. Please look after my other son. He needs your guidance." It was signed, "Your father, Sven."

I'd just adjusted my pouch and put on my trousers when there was a knock at the door. It was John Beecham.

"I wanted to say how much I enjoyed meeting and talking with you last evening. I hope our paths will cross again soon."

"Thank you, John. I'm certain they will." We shook hands and, as he turned to leave, the waiter arrived with my breakfast tray. He put the tray on the table and said, "Mr. Devon, it's been a personal pleasure for me to have served you on this trip. You're a fine gentleman and I just wanted to wish you 'Godspeed' on your journey."

We shook hands after I thanked him for his service. I finished dressing, poured a cup of coffee, and ate two pieces of toast. I took my briefcase and garment bags in one hand and my luggage in the other. When I arrived at the gangplank, I saw Doris' car and chauffeur.

The ride to the Leningrad Airport wasn't very long and the roads were certainly not crowded at that hour. After I retrieved my luggage and said my thanks and goodbye to the driver, I went to the Aeroflot desk, got my boarding pass, checked in at customs and went to the gate. The waiting area also wasn't crowded and didn't receive many more passengers before we boarded. I was seated, as usual, in a First Class aisle seat. After takeoff, my tray was pulled down and covered with a white napkin. Breakfast was served and I was famished.

SIXTEEN

The plane touched down at Heathrow twelve minutes late. I took a taxi to the office and after the usual procedures entered Z's inner sanctum.

"Thank you, Philipp, for flying back so promptly. I hope your time on the boat was restful and your old energetic self is once again in good form."

"Thank you for giving me the past few days to say goodbye to Arlene. I believe I've regained the proper prospective on my life and my future, and I'm once again ready for a new assignment."

"Good." said Z. "Please tell me what you and John Beecham talked about."

I told him everything Beecham told me. He listened intently and said nothing during my recitation. When I finished, he said, "I'm very interested in two things: the first is the identity of the two men he heard talking at the dinner table and second, the identity of the Spanish Agent in Madrid. The reference to McCredy is probably your friend from the Inaugural whom we know as either di Marchi or Marchidi " He rifled through some papers on his desk and selected one sheet.

"I'm asking you to go to Abu Dhabi tomorrow. Young Sven will accompany you, first so you can have a back-up if needed; second, so you can continue to train him in the fine points of our business, and third, you can have that talk with him about the girl in Stockholm. He'll be arriving from Madrid in about two hours. You both will be at the Cadogan this evening. Your flight leaves Heathrow tomorrow morning at 10:00. Good hunting."

"At some time in the near future," I said, "I'd like to visit Arlene's mother's home to go through her personal effects. It has to be done and I believe I'm now prepared to tackle the job."

"When you return to London, I'll ask my driver to take you to the house."

He rose and offered his hand. The meeting was over and from here on out, I was on my own. I said good morning to his secretary who handed me an envelope containing two one-way tickets to Abu Dhabi and ten 1,000-dinar notes, the monetary unit of the Emirates, each dinar equal to about twenty-eight cents American. Sven and I ought to be able to live on 2,800 American dollars for quite a while even if we don't have return tickets.

I took a cab to the Cadogan and asked the desk clerk to have my tux shirt laundered and my complete formal attire held until I called for it later this month. Sven will be in the adjoining room. I put down my luggage, washed my face and went out to lunch. I returned to the small restaurant in Belgravia. I tried to plan my actions. How would I get into the Palace? Should I use John Beecham's name? How would I begin to locate two Arabs each having a mustache and one with a scarred face? Sven and I might be in the Emirates longer than expected.

When I finished lunch, I looked at my watch. 12:10. I walked back to the Cadogan. I stripped, put my pouch in my briefcase and lay across the bed.

I felt something pulling on my right big toe. I jumped up, startled, and found Sven at my bedside.

"Hello, Big Brother," he said happily. He pulled me to my feet and gave me a hug.

"People might begin to talk," I said, smirking. "How are you, Little Brother?"

"Couldn't be better now that I know I'll be working with you again."

He went to his room. I followed. He shucked his clothes and his pouch and sat down in an overstuffed chair to remove his shoes and socks. I sat on the edge of his bed.

"Are you completely briefed on our new assignment?" Sven asked.

"As well as I ever get briefed." I explained what I'd learned from John Beecham and the details of our current assignment.

"How do you plan to begin?"

"You mean 'we', don't you? You're in this as deep as I am."

"How do *we* plan to begin?" he corrected. I pulled from my briefcase the paper Z had retrieved from the stack on his desk.

"First of all," I said, "when we land in Abu Dhabi tomorrow afternoon, we'll take a taxi to the Hotel Sheraton. Z selected this hotel because it's very near the Corniche, the promenade that runs along the Gulf for about a half-mile. It's a place where much *business* is transacted. After that, we'll play it by ear. I've several ideas which I'll share with you as we go along." The paper contained other information such as the rules of protocol and manners in Arab countries.

"Have you been back to the Emirates since your initial training there?"

"Several times," I replied. "I do have a few contacts who I'll probably call on for guidance." I paused. "Have you had lunch?"

"I picked up a sandwich and a drink at Heathrow before getting on the Underground."

"I'd suggest we take a nap; it'll be my pleasure to have you as my guest at dinner."

"That'll be great. I can use a little sleep."

"I'll set my alarm for 6:00. Did you think to leave your tuxedo and accessories with the desk clerk?"

"I did, and I asked him to hold everything until I called. You see, I've learned a few things from you about planning ahead."

"Get some sleep."

We both retired. When my wrist alarm vibrated, I got up and checked on Sven. He was lying on his back, snoring as usual. I grabbed him by his big toe and pulled hard. He sat up.

"A dose of your own medicine," I teased.

We both showered and dressed and took a taxi to Langan's.

"Have you ever eaten here?" I asked.

"Never."

"I think you'll like it. You never know who you might see."

As we entered the restaurant, a waiter whom I'd not seen before greeted us. I inquired, "Is Paul on duty tonight?"

"This is his night off, sir."

"Could we please have Table 17?"

When we were seated, I said to Sven, "Tonight is like a reunion. You're my guest so order anything you want. Would you like some wine or do you prefer a cocktail?"

"I know you always drink red wine so that's what I'll have."

The waiter, who remained standing while this conversation was in progress, presented me with the wine list. I decided that we'd first try a Chardonnay to be different and then have a red with our meal.

"We'd like a bottle of 1982 Mâcon-Lugny, Les Charmes, if you have it."

"Certainly, sir."

When he left the table, I looked around to see if possibly I knew any of the other patrons. I didn't, but I recognized a few of the more prominent ones. Sven was agog at the ambience and the obvious distinction of several diners. When our wine arrived and the ice bucket was properly placed, the waiter showed me the label, opened the bottle and poured a little in my glass. When I pronounced it "fine", he poured. I raised my glass and said, "To us, for a successful venture." Sven raised his glass and repeated, "To us."

Before we ordered, I thought it might be the best time to bring up the subject of Helga.

"Sven, my friend, I want to talk to you about Helga."

"Why, is there something wrong?"

"There may be and I need to tell you what I know. When I was on the Island of Mykonos a few months ago, I went to a clothes optional beach with a male friend. After several hours, he asked if I'd like to take a walk to the other end of the beach. When I said I'd prefer to sit and sun, he took off down the beach alone. In about an hour, he returned. There was a beautiful young girl with him. He introduced her as Helga, a former Miss Scandinavia. After a few minutes of conversation, I began to feel like a third wheel on a bicycle so I excused myself and caught a cab back to my hotel. Later that evening, he and I met on the street as he was returning to the hotel. He looked like he'd had the most wonderful sexual experience of his life. He looked haggard but had a smile on his face. He told me that he and Miss Scandinavia had sex for several hours. I assumed he'd performed to her satisfaction for he said they had a date for the next afternoon."

The waiter appeared, brought each of us a menu and poured the remaining Chardonnay. I looked over the menu and asked Sven what suited his palate. He looked a little uncomfortable about what I was telling him. He said he'd like a small steak and a baked potato. I asked for the same, both medium rare, and some sour cream and butter for the potatoes. I also asked the waiter to bring us a bottle of 1982 Montebuena Rioja. When he left the table, I continued.

"When I was with your father in Stockholm the other night, we went out for dinner, and, as we entered the hotel where the restaurant was located, we met Helga coming out of the elevator with an older man. She tried to avoid us but your father called her by name. She said the man with her was her uncle and they were late for dinner. The man was in the same condition as my friend on Mykonos. He looked like he'd been worked over and enjoyed every minute of it."

All the time I was talking, I was looking him in the eye. He began to show signs of a tear appearing but remained in control. I continued.

"Sven, I don't know the extent of your relationship with Helga. I don't know if you have proposed to her and if so, did she accept? I don't know anymore about this situation, but I felt I needed to tell you my impression based on the facts I know."

He remained quiet. With his head bowed and looking at his wine glass, he said, "I haven't proposed marriage nor have we had any conversation about getting married. In all the times I've been with her, I admit the relationship was entirely sexual. She made me feel so masculine and so wonderful. She did things to my body that had never been done before. When I told you I wanted to get married when I got back to Stockholm, I was thinking about your relationship with Arlene and hoping I could have that same relationship with Helga. Now that you've told me these things, I must admit I've wondered what a beautiful and highly sexed girl like Helga was doing for sex while I was away."

The waiter brought the red wine, and, after I performed the ritual, filled our glasses. When he left, I continued.

"My little brother, I wrestled with whether or not to tell you. I certainly didn't want to hurt you in any way, but because of my feelings for you, I felt I couldn't shirk my duties. I'm now going to give you, in plain words, my impression of Helga. She is probably a prostitute. She probably didn't feel like telling you of her profession for one of possibly two reasons: she'd begun to like you or you were such a magnificent performer in bed that she didn't want to give you up. In either case, she wasn't being straight with you. She was using you. I'm truly sorry to bring you this information.

"I talked with your father and it was only after I told him what I suspected, that he told me he'd suspected the same thing. He loves you too much to plant a seed of doubt in your mind if he'd been wrong in his suspicions. After we'd compared our thoughts, he begged me to tell you everything he and I knew and had seen. He wants to protect you from any further damage she might cause."

"Philipp, this is so hard for me to hear and to swallow. I've been foolish in my relationship with her. I was guided by my dick instead of my brain. I'm afraid I've also let you down, that you've lowered your opinion of me and of my potential for being a super agent like you. That hurts more than finding out about Helga. I'm so ashamed."

"Let me assure you my opinion of you and of your potential in this business hasn't diminished one iota. You're a bright young man who learns quickly, listens intently and asks appropriate questions when you're not sure of something. Those are the attributes of a successful agent. In addition, you're handsome, in superb physical shape and you wow the women. Arlene said so. Don't let your hormones get in the way of your duties, even if you are a horny twenty-five year old. I can relate to your situation even if I'm a decrepit thirty-nine. Stay cool, you and I are a team. We work well together and I'm pleased that Z has the same opinion."

Our dinners arrived. We chowed down; we were ravenous. The atmosphere began to clear. Sven was relieved to put all this behind him. I felt he'd suspected what I told him and didn't quite know how to proceed in solving his dilemma.

When we came out of the restaurant, I asked him if he'd like to walk awhile and see a little of London at night. He agreed. The walk wasn't very long or very tiring but when we got back to our rooms, we agreed the fine meal, the wine and the walk made us both tired. We took showers and sat in the two chairs in my room. Sven looked as though he wanted to talk. I kept silent as he spoke.

"Philipp, you're the kindest man and the best friend I've ever known. You've shown me you have faith in my abilities; you're a great mentor. But more than those things, you've shown me you were genuinely concerned with not only my future but also my feelings. I very much appreciate what you did for me this evening." His eyes began to become moist. "All I can say is 'thank you'."

"You're welcome. Now let's get some sleep and prepare a plan for our assignment. Our plane leaves at 10:00. I'll set my alarm for 6:30. We can take the Underground and have breakfast out there. Goodnight, Sven."

"Goodnight, Philipp."

I awoke and checked on Sven. He was also awake. We shaved and showered, dressed in our traveling clothes and walked to the Underground. We checked in at British Airways for our boarding passes, and went to one of the eateries in the terminal and had coffee and pastry. The waiting room was not crowded. We sat down and read the paper I'd bought.

We were in First Class, across from each other. The flight to Abu Dhabi would be about ten hours. Sven watched some of the movie. I'd seen it twice. We talked about our mission to which he offered some very cogent comments about how to gain access to the various places we needed to penetrate. I told him everything I knew about the Emirates and particularly about Abu Dhabi. He listened intently. The stewardesses brought us lunch and tried to make us as comfortable as they could. They paid particular attention to Sven who turned on his charm full blast whenever they smiled at him.

We touched down at 7:15 P.M. local time. After going through customs, we took a taxi to the Sheraton. Our accommodation was one large room with two queen-sized beds, a sitting area with a view of the Gulf, a large bath with both tub and shower, and two large closets. After we unpacked and hung up our suits, we dressed in our casual attire—slacks and shirt and loafers. We agreed we could use some food.

The dining room was reasonably large and was nicely appointed as I'd remembered from my last trip. The tablecloth was white as were the cloth napkins. When the waiter came to our table, he was dressed in the traditional long white dishdasha with a red-checkered smagh headdress and a black rope agal around it. The menu was quite diversified, more than I remembered from my last visit, and the food was very well prepared and quite tasty. I signed the check with baksheesh, a tip of fifteen percent. Leaving the restaurant, I noticed that the lobby was full of non-Arabs in business suits. I suggested to Sven that we take a walk along the Corniche.

The Corniche is a cantilevered ledge extending over the water. It's about twenty-five feet wide and extends for approximately one-half mile from the Sheraton. About every twenty feet is a lamppost with a hanging basket of flowers, watered each night after sundown by utility trucks carrying distilled water. Between each lamppost is a metal seat for two or three persons. The many oleanders and palms lining almost every major street in Abu Dhabi are watered in the same manner every night.

The Corniche is very popular for strolling and for husbands and wives pushing baby carriages. The family promenades end about 9:00 or 9:30, and are replaced by businessmen, sometimes in pairs and sometimes solo, stretching their legs. It's not unusual to see two men holding hands as they walk along. In fact, it's quite common in many areas of the world, not including the United States or Britain, to see men holding hands and sometimes kissing on the lips.

Since the hour was now a few minutes after ten, all the families had left; only men were now parading. Sven and I walked from the beginning near the Sheraton to the other end and then back. Deciding that we'd had enough exercise, we returned to our room.

I decided to take a shower before I slept. When I'd finished and came out of the bathroom toweling dry, Sven had fallen across his bed without removing the counterpane and was snoring loudly. I hope that doesn't keep me awake, I thought, as I pulled back my counterpane and lay down on the top sheet. It didn't, and shortly, I was asleep. I hadn't set my alarm; we needed to adjust to the new time.

I awoke at 7:55. Sven was still on his back and snoring. After my usual morning routine, I came back in the bedroom, Sven was still snoring. I grabbed him by a big toe and shook vigorously. He sat up and smiled.

"Time to have some breakfast," I said.

"Uno momento," he said as he lay down on the floor. First came the crunches, then the push-ups, then the one whose name I can't remember. Three sets of ten. Then he sprang to his feet and went into the bathroom without saying a word. I could hear him singing as he showered. When he came out, I asked him the name of the tune he was singing.

"I was making it up as I went along."

"I didn't know you were musical."

"There're lots of things about me you don't know," he replied with a grin. "When I know you better, I'll tell you more." He laughed heartily.

We got dressed in our casual attire over our pouches and went to breakfast. The dining room was crowded and we had to wait a bit for a table. When we were seated, the waiter asked if we would like coffee.

"How did you know we were coffee drinkers?" asked Sven.

"All you Americans drink coffee like Arabs."

I chose some fresh fruit and a waffle with blueberry syrup. Sven skipped the fruit and ordered two waffles with the same syrup.

"Remember, I'm still a growing boy," he said, smiling again.

"When do you plan to stop growing?" I asked, looking around the dining room to see if I saw anyone I knew. Seated at a table in one corner of the room was a young man I'd met on my last trip. He was then a banker with the Iranian Bank Melli. I caught his eye and we both nodded our recognition. Shortly, he came over to our table and said, "I remember you from our meeting in the Bank. I am Jamil Shopaki."

Both Sven and I stood up.

"Hello, Jamil, I'm Philipp Devon. This is my brother, Sven. It's good to see you again."

"What brings you to Abu Dhabi, my friend?"

"Please be seated. I'm here on business and Sven is touring the world so I let him tag along."

"Remind me. What is your business?"

"I gather data for a Travel Agency in the States."

"Oh, yes, I remember. Will you be in Abu Dhabi long?"

"That depends. I have a message for the Emir from a friend who asked me to deliver it in person, but I have a problem. I've never met the Emir and haven't the slightest idea how to get an audience with him." I paused and then added, "My Travel Agency is promoting travel to the Emirates and business is booming."

"I'm sure that my boss at the Bank would be pleased to arrange a meeting with the Minister of State. You could talk with him and if he decides your message is meaningful and personal, he will take you in to the Emir. His Majesty is quite open to foreign visitors, especially those bringing in business."

"That would be wonderful, Jamil. You are most kind to offer. When might it be possible to see your boss?"

"He is returning to Abu Dhabi tomorrow evening and will be in the bank the next morning. If you stop by the Bank at about ten o'clock, I shall introduce you to him."

"Could Sven come along too? His plane doesn't leave for a few days and he'd like to meet as many people as possible before he leaves."

"I believe that would be all right. Shall I see you both the day after tomorrow at ten?"

"We'll be at your bank at five of ten. Thank you, Jamil, for your kind offer of assistance."

"Not at all. It was a pleasure to see you again, Philipp, and also to meet you, Sven."

He shook both our hands. We sat as he left the dining room.

"What is the message you have for His Majesty?" Sven asked.

"I bring him greetings from John Beecham who recently dined with the Emir and his guests, two of whom we're attempting to identify."

"You're making this up, aren't you?"

"In our business, my friend, it's sometimes necessary to deceive in order to accomplish our mission. It's important to find out as much information as possible while revealing very little of what you know."

Sven looked at me with a slight frown on his face, which conveyed that he'd taken in all I'd just explained. The frown then turned to a smile, but he made no comment.

"Today, we can walk around the main part of town which isn't very large, or we can take a taxi and travel to some of the outlying regions. What is your pleasure?"

"I'd like to walk around downtown to see how developed Abu Dhabi is. But first I'd like to get in a swim if that's okay with you."

"Sounds fine to me."

I signed the check and left baksheesh in cash. We went to our room and changed into our swimsuits. I told Sven his Speedo barely covered his equipment. He laughed and said, "Yes, it's a growing problem."

"It seems to have had no problem growing as far as I can see," I said with a smirk. We donned the terrycloth robes from the closets and slipped on the beach sandals. We stashed our briefcases in the closets and took the elevator to the 2nd floor where the pool and sun deck were located. I remembered the Hotel Security Office was adjacent to the pool area.

"On my last trip, I made friends with one of the security guards who'd traveled to America and wanted to know more about the country and the people." When we arrived at the pool, I went to the Security Office and asked for Mohammed.

"Today is his day off. He'll be here tomorrow."

"Thank you," I said as we targeted two chaises from the far corner of the pool. We brought them to the sunny part of the deck. We lay down on our beach towels. The pool area was not crowded. It was still late morning. Most businessmen did their business in the morning and then spent the rest of the afternoon at the pool. I stretched out and remarked to Sven how much hotter the sun was in Abu Dhabi than in Stockholm.

"We're a few degrees farther south than we were in the Arctic Circle," he said, stretching a point about the location of his hometown.

We'd been out about an hour and a half, jumping in the pool every fifteen minutes or so, when Sven said, "I'm hungry."

"Imagine that." I called one of the waiters standing under the awning.

"What is your pleasure, gentlemen?"

"We'd like two chicken salad sandwiches and a bag of potato chips each, with a big glass of iced tea," said Sven before I could speak. "I hope I didn't speak out of turn by ordering ahead of you."

"It's about time you pulled some weight in our operation," I responded with a smile. "If you'd like, when we get back to civilization, I'll teach you some points about wines."

"That would be great."

We jumped in the pool one more time before lunch arrived. Sitting beside the pool, I sensed Sven was becoming more comfortable working with me. I liked the way our friendship was developing and it reminded me so much of my own beginnings when Z chose me as his protégé. I could visualize Sven as a fully trained agent on his own and that pleased me.

Lunch arrived and was placed on the two small tables nearby. I signed the chit and added baksheesh. The chicken salad was delicious and I'm glad Sven ordered two for each of us. I was hungrier than I thought.

The pool area was filling up rapidly. The only women present were the wives or girlfriends of visitors. There were no Arab women for they're not allowed to uncover. Some of the visitors were very hairy; I could pick out Arab men instantly. Almost all had hair on their faces, shoulders, chests, backs, arms and legs. I fit in somewhat but Sven stood out like a freak. His massive body had little hair anywhere. I thought to myself he only shaved daily because I did. He certainly didn't need to.

I looked around the assembled group of Arab men and tried to decide, first, if I knew anybody; and second, did any of them have a deep scar on his face. Almost all had mustaches, so that was of no help.

We stayed at the pool until 1:30 when the sun became unbearable. I wanted to buy some bottled water. We returned to the room, showered and put on our casual attire including a cap with a visor. The hotel also provided walking sandals, the one-size-fits-all type, with a strap over the arch.

As we left the lobby, several taxi drivers beckoned for our attention and began quoting prices. There was a lot of competition. We walked on out to the street and began our sightseeing.

The Sheraton is a ten-story hotel on the Gulf. There's a hospital nearby, also on the water. Behind the hospital, there's a roadway, which extends out over the water until it makes a T. Along the arms of the T many boats were docked. We walked out to the T and looked back toward the hotel. We were approximately a mile from our room. I made a mental note to come here at night. Perhaps I might find a clue to our search.

We walked for about two hours. The sun was oppressive; we felt drained and decided to return to the room and rest before dinner. I suggested the possibility of going out for our evening meal but Sven said he'd rather eat at the hotel because we might see someone we knew or wanted to know.

We showered after our walk and lay down to relax. We talked a bit about what we might say to Jamil's boss and how he might assist us in getting an appointment with the Emir. If he refused our request or said that he wasn't able to assist us, my plan was to go to the Palace and start with the guards. That wasn't a very good plan but it was all I had at the time. We both drank some bottled water. It's amazing how much one can dehydrate in this climate. There was a knock at the door.

"It is Mohammed from Security."

I threw a beach towel around my middle, as did Sven. When I opened the door, here stood my friend, the Security Guard I'd met on my last visit. He was taller than I'd remembered.

"Good afternoon, Mr. Devon. I understand you asked for me at the pool."

"Good afternoon to you, Mohammed. It's great to see you again." We shook hands and sort of embraced at the same time. "This is my brother, Sven." They shook hands.

"I was happy you had returned to Abu Dhabi. I remember you from your last visit." I offered him a chair. Sven and I sat on the edge of our beds.

I repeated, "It's good to see you again, how have you been?"

"All right, I suppose. I was recently invited to interview for the job of Security Officer to His Highness but I was not chosen. They said I was too old."

"How old are you, Mohammed?" I asked.

"I am thirty-two. They wanted some younger punks who could be trained in the ways of the Palace. I have already had five years as Security Guard here and I know my job very well. I do not need any further training."

"I would agree, Mohammed. You're one of the most capable Security Guards I've ever met," I said, flattering him a bit. "And you certainly do have a way with the women. I saw you in action on my last visit."

"I do like women and they seem to like me, especially when I put on my swimsuit and walk around the pool. My suit is not very big where I *am* very big." He grinned and we smiled back.

Sven chimed in. "Mohammed, how do you keep in such great shape?"

"I work out at the gym before I come to work. You are in good shape to, Mr. Sven."

"Please drop the mister. I'm just Sven." Mohammed smiled.

"Mohammed, my friend, I'd like to ask your help. I'd like to locate a man who is a friend of His Majesty. One of my friends from London had dinner at the Palace a while back and this man sat across from my friend. They engaged in conversation and my friend wanted me to extend his best wishes to this gentleman. I don't know his name, but he has a very deep scar across his face and he wears a mustache."

"Every man in the Emirates wears a mustache," said Mohammed with a slight chuckle, "but I know the man you are talking about. He is the manager of Bank Melli and is a personal friend of His Majesty. He dines with the Emir often."

"Thank you, my friend. I can't begin to tell you how much this information means to me. Do you think I might get an appointment with this gentleman while I'm here? Do you happen to know his name?"

"Oh, yes. His name is Anwar al-Maldi. He is very well known and well connected here in The Emirates. I am sure that if you go to his Bank, he will be happy to see you."

"Mohammed," I said as I got up, "you are a great friend. Sven and I look forward to seeing you at the pool tomorrow afternoon."

"I look forward to it too, Mr. Devon."

"Please call me Philipp. My father was Mr. Devon." We all had a good laugh as I opened the door. After Mohammed left, Sven said, "You have a knack for laying on flattery so thick you can choke on it. I'm impressed with your tactics."

"All in the training, Sven; all in the training."

SEVENTEEN

I set my alarm for 6:00 P.M. I didn't want to oversleep. I'd caught up on the time change and adjusted to the heat fairly well. However, I couldn't get to sleep thinking about the current situation; first, seeing Jamil, and then having Mohammed identify Jamil's boss as one of the two men we're looking for. Although I couldn't sleep, Sven had no problem.

I continued to think about tomorrow morning. How was I going to ask Mr. al-Maldi to identify his cohort? Should I suggest Sven and I are interested in "pharmaceuticals"? How can I bring Spain into the conversation? Dare I mention the name "di Marchi"? That was it! I believe that di Marchi is negotiating the drug trade from Spain to Central America, and perhaps al-Maldi may be engaged in a similar activity for the Arabs here in the Emirates. That will be my tactic. But suppose that doesn't stir up anything. What else can I try? I wondered if the *37* had ever moored here.

I picked up the phone and dialed Z. I looked at my watch and noted the difference in time. Maybe he wasn't in yet.

"Hello, Philipp. How are you and the heat getting along?" Does the man ever sleep?

"Very well, thank you. My brother and I are drinking lots of water. We have an appointment tomorrow morning with one of the two gentlemen who were at the dinner John mentioned. Has the *37* ever moored here?"

"It was there about ten months ago and the Emir was given a dinner on board," he said in code.

"I could bring that dinner into the conversation. Can you tell me if a certain man was in attendance at that dinner?"

"Hold on a minute and I'll bring up that information. Spell his name for me, please."

I spelled al-Maldi in code.

"Yes he was and he was accompanied by his companion, whose name is spelled —" Z spelled Rashid Zanani also in code. "We know very little about these two gentlemen but the latter one is suspected of possibly trading in 'pharmaceuticals'."

"I believe that'll be my approach, to work into our conversation his companion and his business, and then I'll mention my friend in Spain." I spelled di Marchi.

"Be careful, my friend. You might try the approach of the Spaniard being a friend of your brother."

"Good idea. I'll keep you posted." I don't believe he heard my last statement; he'd hung up.

Sven woke up as I gave my codes to Z's Secretary.

"The boss said the *37* moored here about ten months ago and Doris gave a dinner on board for His Majesty. Our appointment tomorrow morning attended that dinner along with his companion. The boss believes his companion could possibly be in the 'pharmaceuticals' business," I briefed Sven.

"Companion? Do you think the companion could be gay?"

"Good question. I won't know that until our appointment. We'll explore it at that time, if it's appropriate. Are you hungry? It's dinner time."

"I thought you'd never ask."

We dressed casually. At 7:00 P.M., the only people eating were the foreign visitors, mostly Americans. I looked around the room and saw a couple of men I'd seen last evening, but no one of any note attracted my attention.

The meal was professionally prepared and delicious, quite a pleasant experience in Mid-East dining. When we'd finished dessert, we ordered coffee. Arabs like to drink Turkish coffee, which is quite strong, having been boiled at least three times and served in small cups, grounds and all. We drank it straight.

"I'd like a walk on the Corniche," I said.

"I'm with you," Sven said.

After I signed the check, with baksheesh added, we left the hotel and walked the short distance to the near end of the Corniche. The hour was still early. Mothers pushing strollers and fathers just walking along with the family inhabited almost the entire Corniche. It fact, it was so populated Sven and I sat on one of the seats and waited for the crowd to thin. After about an hour, there was room for us to walk without being run over by a stroller or a kid on roller skates.

We walked to the far end of the Corniche and turned around. As we approached the hotel end, we noticed Mohammed sitting alone on one of the seats.

"Good evening, Philipp, Sven. Would you like to join me while I wait for a date?"

"We wouldn't like to cramp your style or hinder your progress," I said.

"I don't have a date yet, but I'll have one before I go home. I almost never go home alone," he said proudly.

We thanked Mohammed for his invitation but we both declined, saying we were tired from all the sun we'd gotten today and we'd see him at the pool tomorrow.

As we walked away, Sven said, "Maybe we should've stayed. I haven't had a date in several weeks and for you, I believe, about the same."

"Thank you for your concern, but I'm still in mourning."

Sven looked like he'd just said the most awful thing possible.

"I'm sorry, Philipp. I didn't mean to minimize your grief and I certainly didn't mean to imply that either of us was on the prowl."

"You're a thoughtful little brother. I assure you I'm slowly getting over my dearest Arlene, but I'm not quite there yet."

We walked to our room. Sven said, "I really feel bad about what I said. Please forgive me."

"Not to worry," I said as we lay down.

We both awoke at 7:55. I did my triples in bed while he proceeded to do his floor work. I then joined him on the floor. We were not trying to compete or show-up one another but were giving it our all. I finished first and went to shave and shower. He then followed me for his morning ritual. We donned our pouches, got dressed in our business suits and carried our briefcases to the dining room. We ordered a hearty breakfast and lingered over coffee until 9:20. We left the dining room and asked the concierge for a taxi, arriving at Bank Melli in about ten minutes. We entered the lobby and took the elevator to the Executive Offices. As we stepped off the elevator, Jamil greeted us with a smile and a handshake.

"Good morning, Philipp, Sven. I trust you both are enjoying your stay in Abu Dhabi."

"So far, it's been quite pleasant. We met a friend I knew from my last visit and had a chat with him on two occasions. It seems that the Emirates are becoming more Americanized every day."

"We certainly have increased the tourist trade since you were last here. However, we still try to maintain our Arab customs and ways. Mister al-Maldi, will receive you now."

We followed Jamil into a very ornate corner room, appointed with marble tables and teakwood furniture. There was a plethora of Arab art on the walls and a magnificent multicolored Oriental rug covering the entire room.

"Mr. al-Maldi, may I present Mr. Philipp Devon and Mr. Sven Christen."

"Sabah 'il kher, Mr. Devon, sabah 'il kher, Mr. Christen. Please be seated."

"Good morning to you, Mr. al-Maldi," we both said almost in unison, in English.

We sat in the three chairs arranged in front of his massive desk. Mr. al-Maldi was about forty years old. He had a severely deep gash on his face, from the right eyebrow to the left cheek. It was hard not to notice and even harder not to comment. A male attendant arrived with a pot of coffee and four demitasses. We all declined both sugar and milk.

"Jamil tells me that you are brothers, but you have different last names. How is that?"

"We have the same mother but different fathers," I lied. Sven is Swedish and I am an American."

"Is this your first visit to Abu Dhabi, Mr. Devon?"

"No, Mr. al-Maldi. I was here about a year ago. This is Sven's first visit."

"I hope your accommodations at the Sheraton are to your liking."

"They are quite nice."

"Jamil also told me that you have a letter for His Highness."

"Not a letter, Mr. al-Maldi, just a verbal greeting from a friend who had the pleasure of dining with His Highness a few weeks ago. My friend said His Highness was so gracious and, rather than write a letter of thanks as we do in the Western world, he wanted to send an emissary who would deliver his thanks in person. We know the protocol of paying respect to such a person of His Highness' rank and position." I hoped that was enough sucking up for now.

"You are most correct, Mr. Devon. A person of His Highness' rank and position is most properly thanked, either in person or by someone of equal or slightly lower rank."

"Well, I assume one would classify Mr. Beecham and me of about equal rank, since neither of us has any."

"John Beecham?"

"Yes, Mr. al-Maldi, my good friend, John Beecham." His facial expression was visibly changed.

"Mr. Beecham's business is pharmaceuticals. His father was a personal friend of His Highness," I offered.

"And what is your business, Mr. Devon?"

"I gather data for a Travel Agency in the States."

"And you, Mr. Christen. What is your business?" Sven and I hadn't discussed this point. I hope Sven comes up with a convincing title.

"I'm a Master Chef, currently working in Marbella, Spain, at the

Andalusia Plaza. I'm on tour gathering information about my trade."

Beautifully done, little brother.

"When you were last in the Emirates, Mr. Devon, were you here on business or pleasure?"

"That trip was strictly pleasure. I had just debarked from a cruise on one of the largest private yachts in the world. It had moored here and I left the ship to continue my vacation travels elsewhere."

"What was the name of that yacht?"

"The *37*," I said, looking Mr. al-Maldi in the eye.

"The owner of that yacht gave a dinner aboard for His Highness, and I had the pleasure of being invited by His Highness to attend," said al-Maldi.

"I gather you enjoy the highest level of confidence with His Majesty."

"You are correct, Mr. Devon."

"May I also assume, Mr. al-Maldi, you have and can have an audience with His Majesty almost as you wish?"

"Almost."

"I am truly in the presence of a man of great trust, enjoyed by only a few, I am sure, in this country."

Al-Maldi liked my flattery and his demeanor, which had previously been rather cool, warmed.

"Would Mr. Christen also like to be presented to His Highness?"

"Yes, Mr. al-Maldi. That would be great, an event about which I could one day describe to my children," said Sven effervescently. Al-Maldi smiled.

"Well, gentlemen, I shall be pleased to arrange an audience with His Majesty for tomorrow morning, say ten o'clock. If that is agreeable, be here in my office at nine thirty. We shall take my car to the Palace."

"You are most kind and gracious, Mr. al-Maldi, and I am certain that John Beecham will be most pleased to hear what you have done for him and for us." We rose and shook hands all around. We left the office and approached the elevator when Jamil spoke.

"You noticed I did not speak during your interview with Mr. al-Maldi. In the Arab world, it is correct protocol for one to make an introduction and then be quiet until spoken to."

"One thing I forgot to ask Mr. al-Maldi. Does he travel much and has he recently been to Spain or the Caribbean? I had the feeling that we'd met before but I couldn't place where the meeting might have taken place."

"Mr. al-Maldi was in the Caribbean just a few months ago, attending the Inauguration of Central America's newest President."

"Then that's where I probably saw him, at the Reception before or the Ball after the Inauguration. Would you please convey that information to Mr. al-Maldi for me?"

"Of course, Philipp, I shall be pleased to inform him."

"Jamil, you have been most kind in arranging this meeting. Both Sven and I are deeply indebted. May we please invite you to join us at the Sheraton dining room this evening as our guest?"

"Unfortunately, Philipp, I am dining with Mr. al-Maldi and his best friend this evening, but thank you anyway."

"Then may I ask you to ask Mr. al-Maldi if he, his friend and you would be our guest this evening, either at the Sheraton or at a restaurant of his choice?"

"You are most kind, Philipp. I shall ask him and will leave a message for you at your hotel." We all said our goodbyes as we arrived in the lobby and shook hands. A taxi was waiting for us at the door, courtesy of Mr. al-Maldi.

When we were back in our room, we discussed the meeting. Sven said the flattery of Mr. al-Maldi obviously worked. I complimented him on telling almost the whole truth about his work. After we'd exhausted our mutual critique, I picked up the phone and dialed Z. I told him every detail of the meeting and that I'd invited Mr. al-Maldi, his companion and Jamil to join us at dinner this evening.

"Good work," he said as he hung up.

Sven and I agreed we were famished and we'd like to eat by the pool. I called room service and ordered a Club sandwich, potato chips and iced tea for each of us. We changed into our swimsuits, took beach towels and went to the pool. We were early enough to get two chaises and place them where I could watch the Security Office. I'd be able to see Mohammed when he arrived.

We finished our lunch and lay back to absorb some rays. In about fifteen minutes, a waiter came over and said I had a telephone call and I could take it in the Security Office. If Z was calling, I'd prefer not. Reluctantly I picked up the receiver.

"Philipp, this is Jamil. Mr. al-Maldi asked me to call you and accept your invitation to dinner. His driver will pick up you and Sven at the hotel at 7:00. Dress will be very casual; no ties or jackets. Mr. al-Maldi's friend, Mr. Rashid Zanani, will also be joining us. Mr. al-Maldi asked me to thank you for your offer to host the dinner, but he would like for you and Sven to be his guests at his Club."

"Sven and I accept with pleasure his kind invitation. We shall be ready at 7:00 where you have indicated. Thank you."

As I hung up the receiver, Mohammed arrived.

"I hope your meeting this morning was a successful one. What did you think of Mr. al-Maldi?"

"He looked like a very successful businessman who obviously has the ear of His Majesty."

"That he does," said Mohammed, "but be cautious, my friend. He has spies everywhere who report back to him on everybody and everything."

"Sven and I've been invited to dine with him and his friend this evening. I didn't meet his friend this morning. Have you met him?"

"Oh, yes. He is well known here in the city. He is—how do you Americans say it? — light in his shoes."

"You're saying that his friend is gay?"

"Gay as a three-dollar bill."

"I was under the impression that sort of life-style was banned in the Arab world."

"It usually is, but Mr. al-Maldi, being an advisor to the Emir, has immunity for himself and his friend."

"Are you saying that Mr. al-Maldi is also gay?"

"Possibly."

This bit of information put another slant on our mission. Should I or shouldn't I use this in conversation with Mr. al-Maldi? I have only Mohammed's suspicions and no other proof. This should be a very interesting dinner, I thought as I headed back to my chaise. Sven was half-asleep but roused when I arrived.

"Mr. al-Maldi has invited you and me to be his guests at dinner this evening at his Club. Jamil will also be joining the group, as will al-Maldi's friend, Mr. Rashid Zanani."

"Wow! You work fast. Is this a formal affair or can I go nude?"

"We both can be casually attired, no ties or jackets. We're to be out front at 7:00."

"I'd better brush up on my Arabic," said Sven.

"I think it best that no one knows you speak the language. Jamil knows that I speak Arabic but you can take in anything that's said that I don't hear."

"As you wish. Now a little more sun is called for, don't you agree?"

"Definitely," I said as I lay down.

Mohammed appeared in his swimsuit, if one could call it that. It was really a thong and not a lot of it. He paraded around the pool and sat down to talk with one of the blonds who appeared to be unattached. She obviously liked what she saw, as she played with the hair on his chest. They talked for a while. She gave Mohammed a piece of paper. He left and returned to the Security Office.

"I think Mohammed just scored," said Sven.

"I think you're right."

We lay in the sun for another hour and a half, when we both agreed not to overdo it. As we passed the Security Office, I winked at Mohammed and said, "Have a good evening." He replied, "You too."

When we got to the room and had our showers, we lay down.

"I believe Mr. al-Maldi wants us to wear casual dress tonight so he can see we aren't wearing a wire."

"Do you think he suspects us?"

"I don't know, but if I had the positions he has, both in the Bank and with the Emir, I wouldn't trust even my roommate."

"Are he and Mr. Zanani roommates?"

"I don't know. They are said to be *very* close, according to Mohammed."

"Are you saying both are gay?"

"I honestly don't know anything about either of their personal lives. Perhaps, you can pick up something I may miss."

"I wasn't too good picking up on Mr. Hargrave."

"That's probably because he was bi."

I could almost hear the wheels in Sven's brain turning. I lay there in silence. Finally, he spoke.

"What is our purpose in dining with these guys? We already know their names as the two who were at the Emir's dinner."

"You'll recall that John said he heard them mention 'pharmaceuticals'. Z would like for us to find out what their connection might be with di Marchi and why al-Maldi was in the Caribbean. I would also like to know if al-Maldi had a hand in Francisco's death."

"Have you devised a plan for bringing those names into the conversation?

"That's where you come in. You recently were in Madrid where you met and dined with Count Francisco de Bollo, who explained to you the recipe for the delicious meal you were eating that evening. Your father, who is a Master Chef in Stockholm and a friend of the Count, introduced you to him. You hoped to try the recipe in your restaurant and report back to the Count how it was received by your clientele, but, unfortunately, you understand that the Count was killed in an automobile accident."

"You're good. I like that. Just cue me when I should bring up those facts."

"I'll also bring up the fact that I was at the Inauguration of the new President. 'Why?' al-Maldi will ask and I'll say I was his college roommate. I'd like to know by whom he was invited? So you see we have lots to cover and very little time to do so."

"Will you mention meeting di Marchi at the Inauguration and again in Spain?"

"If it seems helpful to our plan."

"Please set your alarm for 6:00. I'll try to nap," said Sven.

I set my alarm as Sven asked. My roommate, as usual, was snoring in just a few minutes. I did manage to sleep and began to dream of Arlene. I woke up suddenly and reached over to the other side of the bed. There was no one there. I wept silently.

EIGHTEEN

6:00 P.M. I put my feet on the floor between our beds. I shook Sven and said, "Rise and shine." He awoke and looked somewhat startled.

"I was having the strangest dream," he said. "I dreamed I was having sex with Helga when my father walked in on us and laughed."

"Do you think he was laughing at your technique or was it something else?" I teased.

"My technique is perfect," Sven bragged. "I can't imagine why he was laughing."

"Why don't you ask the next time you see him? Tell him about your dream and see what he says."

We got dressed. I decided to wear my see-thru shirt, which I'd rinsed out earlier, light slacks and loafers. Sven put on the tightest yellow polo shirt I'd ever seen, very tight-fitting slacks, and loafers.

"Are you planning to seduce al-Maldi's roommate?" I joked.

"No, but it may loosen up the conversation."

We went to the lobby. I looked at my watch. 6:57. Parked in front was a limousine. As we approached, the driver said, in perfect English, "Good evening, Mr. Devon, Mr. Christen." Sven got in first. I felt a bit naked not having my briefcase with me, but both were locked in the room. The glass between us and the driver was closed. Sven and I remained silent during the trip.

When we arrived, the driver informed us we should tell the Club Greeter we were guest of Mr. al-Maldi. "He will direct you to the elevator. The dining room is on the top floor."

As we stepped out of the elevator, Mr. al-Maldi greeted us. We followed him to a table where Jamil and another gentleman were seated. Mr. al-Maldi introduced me to his friend.

"How do you do, Mr. Zanani?" I said. "This is my brother, Sven Christen."

"How do you do?" Sven said.

Zanani was about, thirty-five, five feet eight with somewhat feminine features and a mousy appearance. I noted that his eyes almost popped out, looking at Sven in his tight yellow shirt and crotch-hugging slacks. We all sat.

"You are so kind to invite us, Mr. al-Maldi. It was my intent to host you. The Sheraton is not as elegant as this but it is all I have to offer on this trip." Everyone laughed.

"I am pleased to get to know you both better and to learn a little more about your travels and your businesses," al-Maldi said.

"We travel all over the world, me for my Travel Agency and Sven trying to pick up new recipes for his dining room in Marbella. On some occasions we're able to travel together. Has either of you been to Marbella?"

"No, we have not. We do travel quite a bit but the Costa del Sol has not been one of our stops." Al-Maldi led the conversations.

"I was in Madrid quite recently," said Sven, "and had the good fortune to dine with a friend of my father, Count Francisco de Bollo. The Count explained to me the ingredients and preparation of the delightful dish we were enjoying. I had hoped to try it in my own restaurant and report back to the Count the reaction of my patrons, but unfortunately, the Count was killed in an automobile accident just after that dinner." Sven paused. "Do you get to Madrid in you travels?"

"Rarely. I prefer other parts of Europe and the Caribbean."

"I was in the Caribbean recently for the Inauguration of the new President," I said.

"And how did you happen to be there at that time?" al-Maldi asked.

"The President was my college roommate." There was another pause in the conversation. "Were you at the Inauguration, Mr. al-Maldi?" I asked.

"No. I was not. I do not know the President or anyone else in his Administration." I knew he was lying and I sensed he knew I knew because he did not look me in the eye when he said it.

"You missed a fine show. The Reception was fantastic and the Ball that evening was quite nice. But the highlight of the whole trip was the party aboard the *37*."

"That is a nice ship. As you know I had the pleasure of being aboard here in Abu Dhabi at the dinner given for His Majesty."

"Do you also attend these great functions, Mr. Zanani?" I asked.

"I have only been to one, the one at The Palace a few weeks ago. It was quite nice."

Sven stared at Mr. Zanani before he asked his question.

"Have you lived here in Abu Dhabi very long, Mr. Zanani? Where was your home originally?"

"I was born in Saudi Arabia, but I have been here in the Emirates for several years, about ten, I believe."

"Now there's a country that really interest me. I have never been there but I have several friends in the pharmaceutical business who travel there often," I said, looking directly at al-Maldi. "Do you get back there very often, Mr. Zanani?"

"I have relatives in Riyadh. I try to see them at least once a year."

This conversation was going nowhere. I began to feel it was a dead end, when the first course arrived. We'd hardly finished the first course when the second arrived. All conversation seemed to stop while we ate. I decided to stir things up a bit.

"Sven," I said, "I believe you told me that the dish you and the Count had in Madrid was similar to what we just tasted; I remembered the spicy charcoal-grilled lamb chops. I believe the dish is called riyaesh. Did I pronounce that correctly, Mr. al-Maldi?"

"You did indeed, Mr. Devon. Your Arabic is good. Where did you study?"

"My roommate, the President, and I studied it in college. We thought it was the up-and-coming language to learn. I'm glad we did. Sven and I both speak Spanish, also."

Jamil had remained silent since we got to the table.

"Jamil, my friend, do you get to travel very much in your job at the Bank or does Mr. al-Maldi keep you busy at home?"

"I am occasionally invited to travel with Mr. al-Maldi, but my job at the Bank keeps me busy."

"Mr. Zanani, are you associated with the Bank also?"

"Oh, no. I don't work at all. My time is spent in leisure pursuits. I like the theatre and music and occasionally Anwar —" He caught his error immediately. "---Mr. al-Maldi and I travel to Dubai to hear the Symphony. Sometimes we even travel to Rome and Paris."

"It must be nice to be able to enjoy life to its fullest, as you undoubtedly do."

The third course arrived. The conversation stopped again. I was about to throw in the towel when al-Maldi spoke.

"I have made an appointment for you, Mr. Devon, and Mr. Christen and me to have an audience with His Majesty tomorrow morning at 10:00. My driver will pick you up at your hotel at 9:30."

"That is very kind of you. We of course will be in business suits, correct?"

"That is correct. The audience will last no longer than three minutes. You will say the greeting of your friend to His Majesty's interpreter, who will translate it for His Majesty, who will reply in Arabic, which will again be translated by his interpreter. Then we shall all be excused from his presence."

"I was expecting to speak to His Majesty in Arabic if that's acceptable."

"Is your Arabic that good, Mr. Devon?"

"Aesif lae aefhaem. Hael yugaed honae aehaed yaetaek aellaem inglizi?"

"That was excellent. You said you were sorry you did not understand. Was there anyone here who speaks English?"

"Did I pass the test?"

"You most certainly did. I apologize if I offended you in my instructions."

"No offense taken."

Things began to ease up a bit, I thought. Sven looked as though he wanted to say something but he knew the rule.

"Sven, is there anything you would like to say to our host?"

"I would like to say what a pleasure it is to be in your presence and to have been invited to your Club. Your hospitality is superb, Mr. al-Maldi."

"Thank you, Mr. Christen." He turned to me. "May I ask, Mr. Devon, for some additional information about your friends in the pharmaceutical business? I am very interested in bringing pharmaceuticals to our country."

"Of course you may. While I was at the Inauguration, I met a gentleman who said he was in the Import-Export business. We talked briefly at the Reception and again at the Ball. He gave me his card. His name was Alex di Marchi, which sounds Italian but he is really an American. I met him again in Madrid a few days thereafter when he explained that he really was in the pharmaceutical business. I gave him my contact number in Washington, D.C., but I have not heard from him since."

Al-Maldi did not react to the name of di Marchi but Zanani was visibly uncomfortable at the mention of his name. I had to pursue this.

"Do you know Mr. de Marchi, Mr. Zanani? Your facial expression seemed to say that you did."

"I may have heard his name somewhere, but I do not know him."

"He seemed very much interested in the contacts I have with the President and others whom he knew. Do you happen to know him, Mr. al-Maldi?"

"I do not." Coffee arrived. Conversation stopped again.

I'd almost all the information I was seeking. I confirmed that Zanani was with al-Maldi at the dinner in The Palace and I knew that al-Maldi had lied about not being at the Inauguration. I was certain that Zanani knew di Marchi and if he did, so probably did al-Maldi. The piece of information that was missing was al-Maldi's tie-in to Francisco's death.

As we finished our coffees, al-Maldi rose. We all stood.

"It has been a pleasure having you as my guests this evening and I look forward to meeting you again in the morning," said al-Maldi. "My driver will take you back to your hotel."

"We have been honored by your gracious courtesies and we thank you for the pleasure of your company. Shokran gaezilaen (Thank you very much.)."

"Aefwaen (That's all right; it was nothing.)."

We left the dining room and descended to the ground floor. No one accompanied us.

When we returned to our room, Sven and I discussed the dinner conversation and the nuances noted by both of us.

"Zanani is not too sophisticated to avoid making a faux pas," said Sven. "His slip-up gave me more insight into their relationship."

"Al-Maldi is a shrewd character who plays his hand close to his vest," I added. "I wish I could've gotten more info on Francisco's death." I dialed Z.

"How was your dinner?"

"Excellent." I reported everything and our conclusions.

"He didn't take the bait on Francisco?"

"Not even a nibble."

"Then perhaps he wasn't involved."

"I get the feeling he was, but he's one shrewd cookie."

"And tomorrow morning you have an audience with the Emir?"

"Correct. The audience will last no more than three minutes, we were told. Is there anything I should tell His Excellency other than how much John enjoyed his hospitality?"

"You might want to mention that you've also been a guest on the *37*." While I was considering this last suggestion, Z hung up.

"That was a tiring evening," said Sven. "I think I'll turn in." He was flat on his back before I could comment. Perhaps tomorrow will be better. I too stripped and put my naked body to bed.

My alarm sounded at 7:30. As I arose, Sven spoke.

"I dreamed that al-Maldi and di Marchi were having a conversation when Francisco walked up. They both knew him. Francisco asked di Marchi when his next shipment was to arrive in Madrid. 'I'll let you know when it's expected,' said di Marchi. Francisco asked al-Maldi if he wanted some to bring to the Emirates. Al-Maldi declined saying that he had his own source. Who? Francisco asked, but then I woke up."

"You certainly do have vivid dreams." I went into the bathroom. Sven spoke from his bed.

"What if al-Maldi is using his bank as the conduit to import drugs into the Emirates? What if Zanani is the only agent involved in the transactions? That way, al-Maldi can deny any knowledge of Zanani's actions. Al-Maldi has the ear and the protection of the Emir but I doubt that Zanani would be covered if he got his ass in a jam? Maybe al-Maldi isn't gay but he allows Zanani certain privileges so long as he remains the fall guy."

"That's certainly a possibility," I said. "Al-Maldi may not know di Marchi. Only Zanani knows him, although the two of them are doing the business, and al-Maldi is being shielded from any direct knowledge of what's going on. Why don't you go back to sleep and finish your dream? You may be onto something."

"Perhaps Francisco discovered the business between di Marchi and Zanani and was about to blow the whistle when word got back some way to Francisco's killers to rub him out," he said.

"That too makes sense," I responded from the shower. "Who do you think tipped off Francisco's killers?"

"It could've been any number of people: maybe, Zanani, 'though I don't see him as a take charge guy; maybe, di Marchi, and don't rule out your friend, Jamil."

"You're learning fast, my friend. I already had Jamil on my list of suspects. You remember on our first day here, Jamil was having breakfast alone in the hotel dining room; and do you remember Mohammed's warning that al-Maldi has spies everywhere reporting on anything of interest."

"How far do you trust Mohammed?" Sven asked.

"I've been informed by a reputable authority that Mohammed is with Interpol."

"Wow!" exclaimed Sven. "That hairy strongman is with Interpol? I'll bet he gets a lot of inside information during pillow talk."

"You're right, my friend. On my previous visit, Mohammed and I established our bona fides with the permission of Z. I didn't tell you that detail earlier because part of your training is to reason to a logical conclusion and come up with logical questions and possible answers." Sven smiled and with his eyes said "Thank you."

When I stepped out of the shower, Sven took my place. While

dressing, the phone rang.

"Philipp, this is Jamil. I am glad I caught you. When you see His Majesty this morning, you may want to mention that you have also been a guest on the yacht *37*. It might lengthen the time of your audience." He hung up.

Z had suggested the same thing. What could possibly be the link between these two people coming up with the same suggestion?

"That was Jamil," I said as Sven came out of the shower. "He suggested I mention I'd been a guest on the *37*. I wonder how he knew." Sven didn't comment but appeared deep in thought.

"What are you thinking now?" I asked.

"I was thinking that maybe Mohammed and I could double-date and see what information we could find out."

"Yeah, sure. I know why you want to tag along with Mohammed after seeing him pick up that blond at the pool yesterday. Your horns are showing." We both laughed.

As we continued dressing, Sven continued his analysis.

"Do you think Jamil is trying to tell us something about the subject of our previous conversation?"

"I really don't know, but since two people have suggested that I mention my stay on the yacht, I definitely should do it. Let's get some breakfast."

We stashed our briefcases and went to the dining room. We both ordered waffles with syrup and coffee.

I looked at my watch as we retrieved our brief cases. 9:26. Al-Maldi's car and driver were out front. When we got to al-Maldi's building, the driver took the ramp to the basement and telephoned his boss that we'd arrived. We sat still. The driver indicated that Sven should sit on one of the folders. I moved to the left as al-Maldi stepped out of the elevator.

"Good morning, gentlemen. I hope you had a pleasant evening."

We both nodded good morning and I said we were looking forward to our meeting with His Majesty, especially Sven, since he rarely gets a chance to meet Royalty.

"Then may I assume that you have had Royal audiences before?"

"Yes I have," I said. "In Washington, D.C., I've met two Presidents and in London, my boss took me with him when he met the Queen."

"Then you know the protocol of such a visit. For the benefit of Mr. Christen, I shall say that one does not extend his hand unless His Majesty does so first. One looks His Majesty in the eye at all times. If His Majesty should offer coffee, which is unlikely, one takes only one cup. In our society, one never takes a second cup of anything unless one is planning to take a third. Even numbers are not considered proper in social situations. And when we are leaving His Majesty's presence, we back out to the door before turning around. Under no circumstances does one ever show the soles of one's shoes or feet to anyone. That is the most terrible effrontery one can commit in our culture."

"You're most thoughtful to brief us in such detail, Mr. al-Maldi. We both want to be correct in all our actions and we certainly don't want to embarrass you who brought us to the Throne." Wow, I'm good. Al-Maldi's smile attested to that fact.

We arrived at the gates of the Palace, a magnificent group of marble structures with relatively plain façades. Al-Maldi's car was waved through. The driver stopped in front of the most ornate of the visible buildings. I assumed it to be the building housing the Throne Room. We walked up the marble steps. The huge brass doors were closed. As we approached, the right-hand door opened and we entered a gigantic and ornately decorated room. As we walked across the marble floor to the large doors directly in front of us, we saw two huge uniformed guards. Each must have been seven feet tall and looked as though he was capable of handling any situation. Both guards opened the large brass doors and indicated that we should enter. It was the Throne Room. His Majesty was seated on the Throne at the far side of the room, on an elevated platform. As we approached His Majesty, he stood up and said, in perfect English, "Welcome to my home."

The Emir was dressed in a flowing white robe embroidered with gold threads. The robe hung open revealing a white dishdashe. On his head he wore a white smagh and gold agal. His slippers were embroidered with gold threads. I assumed the man standing nearby to be the interpreter. Al-Maldi addressed the Emir in Arabic and introduced each of us by name to His Majesty. The Emir stepped down the two steps and extended his hand to both of us. We shook. "You are welcome in my home," he said in English. Then he stepped back up and sat. We remained standing.

The Emir then said in English, "Do you speak Arabic?"

"I do, Your Majesty." I addressed him in the most cordial yet flowery terms I could muster in his language.

His response was in Arabic. "You speak very well, Mr. Devon. I am impressed that you have mastered our most difficult language." He dismissed the interpreter.

I continued to speak in Arabic. "Your Majesty, I bring you greetings from Mr. John Beecham who had the pleasure of dining with you a few weeks ago. Mr. Beecham sends his sincere thanks for your courtesies to him and he extends his best wishes for Your Majesty's continuing good health." I paused.

"I remember Mr. Beecham well. I knew his father, a most gracious gentleman. I am very pleased to hear from the young Mr. Beecham and to have his good wishes brought to my attention by such a distinguished gentleman."

"You are most gracious, Majesty." I paused briefly. "I trust that Your Majesty enjoyed his visit on the yacht *37* when it visited Abu Dhabi several months ago. I've had the pleasure of being a guest myself on several occasions."

"Then you must be a good friend of the owner."

"I am, Your Majesty. In fact her daughter is married to the new President in Central America who was my roommate in college. I had the pleasure of attending his Inauguration."

"How very interesting. I believe Mr. al-Maldi also attended the Inauguration. Am I correct?" He looked directly at al-Maldi.

"You are correct, Majesty."

I'd just caught al-Maldi in a lie. I looked at him directly as if to say "Naughty, naughty."

The Emir waved his hand. Immediately, an attendant appeared bearing a silver tray with four cups and a pot of coffee. Simultaneously, three additional attendants brought three straight chairs and placed one behind each of us.

"Please be seated," said His Majesty.

The coffee was served. I estimated that we'd been here about four minutes. He spoke again.

"Mr. Devon and Mr. Christen, what brings you to our country?"

"I'm with a Travel Agency in America, Your Majesty. I travel all over the world gathering information for my clients." Since the Emir had addressed us both, I looked at Sven, translated the Emir's question, and indicated with a nod he should speak.

"And I, Your Majesty," said Sven in English, "am a Master Chef at the Hotel Andalusia in Marbella, Spain. I'm on vacation from my work and am trying to gather as many new ideas as possible, which I might try in my own kitchen."

I translated Sven's comments for the Emir.

"You both are fine looking young men and I am sure that you enjoy your work. Is each of you married?"

"I lost my fiancée by death a few weeks ago, and Mr. Christen is not yet married."

"I offer you my deepest condolences, Mr. Devon. Losing a loved one is always difficult, but losing a fiancée is quite depressing I am sure, for you were not able to become husband and wife as you had planned. May I offer you another cup of coffee?"

"No, thank you, Your Majesty," I said as the attendant appeared with the tray on which we placed our cups. The attendant stepped up the two steps and received the cup of the Emir.

"How long will you be in our country?" he asked.

"I shall be here a few more days, but unfortunately Mr. Christen leaves tomorrow."

"In that case, if you do not have plans for this evening, I would like to invite you both to dine with me here in my home."

"You are most gracious, Majesty. We would be pleased to accept your kind invitation."

"You are at the Hotel Sheraton, I believe. My driver will pick you up at 7:30 and we shall dine here at 8:00. Is that satisfactory?"

"As you wish, Majesty. We are honored to be your guests."

He rose as did we three. He stepped down the two steps and shook hands with Sven and me. He only said goodbye to al-Maldi. We three backed away from the Throne until we got to the brass doors, which had re-opened. We turned and departed the building.

When we were again in the limousine, al-Maldi said, "The reason I previously told you that I was not at the Inauguration is that I had not wanted to be seen there or to have certain people know that I was there. I am sure you understand my position as an advisor to His Majesty."

I didn't understand what that had to do with anything but I nodded my agreement with his statement. The driver took us back to the hotel where we thanked al-Maldi again for his graciousness in arranging our audience with His Majesty and again for his courtesies to us last evening at dinner.

When we returned to our room, Sven looked like he was about to explode.

"I've met the head of a country who invited me to eat at his table. Wait 'til I tell my father about this."

I picked up the phone and told Z every detail of our meeting. I also told him that I caught al-Maldi in a lie and that his explanation for lying made no sense at all. I told him we've been invited to dine with His Majesty this evening at the Palace.

"You did well, my friends."

I told him about Sven's deductive reasoning and how pleased I was with his development under my tutelage. Z asked to speak with Sven.

"Sir." He listened as Z spoke. Then he said, "Thank you, sir," and hung up.

I looked at Sven who was grinning from ear to ear. "He thinks I'm doing a good job under your guidance and thanked me for my service." Sven approached me as I stood in the center of the room and gave me a hug.

"I haven't hugged you in quite a while. I just want you to know how much I appreciate all you're doing for me, Big Brother."

"You are welcome. How about some lunch and sun?"

As I ordered our lunch, we both changed into our suits and went to the pool.

The crowd was beginning to swell. We got two chaises and pulled them into the sun, facing the Security Office. When he saw us, Mohammed came over. He was again wearing his thong.

"How was your meeting with His Highness?" Mohammed asked.

"Very interesting. I learned one thing I'd already suspected. The banker can lie. The Emir has invited us to dine with him this evening."

"I'm impressed," said Mohammed.

"And another thing. Sven wants to know if you can get him laid this evening. He's leaving tomorrow."

"You aren't trying to horn in on my territory, are you Sven?"

"No, not really. I'm just a guy who needs a lot of sex."

"When you get back from the dinner, put on some casual clothes and come to the Security Office. My shift ends at eleven. Would you like to join us, Philipp?"

"Thank you, but I'll pass."

Our lunch arrived and Mohammed went back to his Office. We talked casually while we ate. Sven kidded me about being afraid of women. Then he apologized again.

We stayed at the pool for about an hour. After showering, we lay across the beds and continued to talk about this morning's experience. Sven was still on cloud nine. He asked if he really did have to leave tomorrow.

"If you stay too long, you'll blow your cover. When you return to Madrid, you can try to contact di Marchi if he's still available. Interpol or the Emir may have him tied up. Here is his card. Find out as much as you can about his association with al-Maldi and Zanani, and perhaps with Jamil. Let him know that you had dinner last evening with the Ruler of the Emirates. Report anything you find to me. I plan to leave in a couple of days, perhaps even tomorrow afternoon, to return to London."

"I'll do the best I can."

"I know you will. You always do."

I thought again that I would like to know more details about the investigation of Arlene's death. What is being done and by whom? Could I perhaps be assigned to the investigation?

NINETEEN

I set my alarm for 6:00 but awoke early. As I lay there, sorting out all we'd learned from al-Maldi, from the Emir and from Mohammed, the pieces didn't fit together. Al-Maldi's relationship with the Emir appears to be too solid for him to take chances that might jeopardize it. His relationship with Zanani appears to be one of information gathering on the one hand and a non-sexual companionship on the other. However, his explanation for having lied to me made no sense whatsoever.

How did he get an invitation to the Inauguration? Was he representing the Emir? Could he have arranged with di Marchi at the Inauguration the game plan for Zanani to be the main contact in the Emirates? Could Bank Melli be financing the drug trade to the Emirates? Mohammed seems to be certain that Zanani is "light in his shoes" but is probably the driving force in the importation or planned importation of drugs. His recognition of the name di Marchi tends to substantiate Mohammed's last assumption, and he did say that he occasionally visits Spain. How did al-Maldi and Zanani meet originally? How does Jamil fit into this puzzle? Why would he suggest mentioning the *37* which Z also suggested? Are any of them connected with Francisco's death?

By the time I considered these apparently disjointed facts, it was 6:00. The sun had drained my energy and I didn't feel exactly at my peak for the dinner this evening. I had a thought: let Sven ask some of the questions. When I turned and faced him so we could discuss the plans for this evening's conversation, I laughed. This huge naked hunk, gave the impression he was just a habitué of the gym with little talents for the subtle profession of sleuthing. I knew I was profiling his physique, but it seemed humorous to me. I grabbed his big toe and pulled.

"I have a job for you," I said.

"A job for me? What is it?"

"I'd like you to ask the Emir some of the puzzling questions we don't have answers to." I repeated my list of questions.

"Is there one particular question you feel I should start with?"

"Start with inquiring how al-Maldi was invited to the Inauguration. Was he representing the Emir? How about asking the Emir if he's ever heard of Mr. di Marchi? If he asks why, you can say he'd approached me in Spain asking if I knew anyone who was importing pharmaceuticals into The Emirates? You might follow up subtly with the question, 'What is Mr.

Zanani's occupation?' You ask because Mr. Zanani appeared to recognize the name of Mr. di Marchi last night at dinner. And to substantiate your occupation as a Head Chef, you might ask His Highness if he'd asked the owner of the yacht to dine at his table here in the Palace? Be prepared to ask any of these questions if I've failed to insert them in my conversations."

"I think I can handle those. Can I ask him if he would allow me to send his Head Chef some of my favorite lamb recipes?"

"Yes, of course. You're smart enough to know how and to what extent one butters up someone you're trying to curry favor with."

"Are we trying to curry favor with the Emir? What do you plan to ask him?"

"I'm not certain. We'll have to wait and see how the evening goes."

We both splashed cold water on our faces and began to dress. We wore the same suits we'd worn last evening but I wished we had two different ties. I picked up the phone and called the Security Office. Mohammed answered.

"This is probably a dumb question but would you happen to have two neckties that Sven and I can borrow for this evening? We don't want to wear the same ones as last night."

"We have a collection of ties left in the rooms by our foreign guests. I'll bring up several."

Within five minutes, Mohammed arrived with eight ties. They ranged from bright purple to yellow and black stripes, from big green flowers to solid brown. The two we chose were relatively quiet. Mohammed told us that we looked "sharp." We thanked him and I said I'd return them tomorrow. He insisted we keep them.

"See you about eleven, Sven," said Mohammed as he left the room.

"Do you really plan to go with Mohammed looking for lust in the right places?" I asked.

"Yes. Why?"

"Do you have protection with you?"

"I always carry at least one with me but perhaps I should have another one, just in case. Do you suppose Mohammed has an extra one, or maybe two?"

"Call him and ask?"

He picked up the phone and asked for Mohammed.

"Mohammed, this is Sven. Would you happen to have an extra bit of protection for me to use?" He listened for the response and then said, "That's all right. I think I'll pass. Thanks anyway."

"Mohammed said he never uses them. I really don't want to get involved."

"Wise move, my friend. One night of pleasure might cost you your career or even your life." He said nothing further.

We finished dressing and arrived in the lobby at 7:25. A limousine was parked in front. The driver called us by name in fairly good English and opened the right rear door. Sven got in first, then I. All the windows were darkened and the glass partition was closed.

After entering the Palace complex, the driver pulled up in front of another building, different from the one containing the Throne Room. It was of nondescript architecture but also constructed of marble. When we got out and approached the double brass doors, the one on the right opened slowly. Standing in the vestibule were the same two guards I saw guarding the doors to the Throne Room. Coming toward us was a gentleman in white attire. He looked like he was somebody important.

"Good evening, Mr. Devon. Good evening, Mr. Christen. My name is Sahib Khalifa. I am the Major Domo of The Palace," he said in perfect English. "If you will please follow me, I shall take you to the dining room where His Majesty is awaiting your arrival." We followed him down a corridor and into an anteroom, a sort of Green Room for visitors awaiting an audience with the Emir. As we entered the dining room, at the head of the table, sat the Emir. The room was very long and wide. The ceiling was more than thirty feet tall. There were several large tapestries on the walls and many sculptures on fluted pedestals. There were twenty-four chairs around the table but only three places were set. The chairs appeared to be European antiques with tapestry cushions. As we approached, His Majesty rose and greeted us in Arabic, shaking both our hands. I responded in Arabic.

"Please sit down, my new young friends," he continued in his language. It wasn't necessary for me to translate those instructions as two attendants pulled two chairs, one on each side of the Emir, away from the table. I was seated on the right of His Majesty and Sven on his left.

"I am so pleased you could come to my table this evening."

"The pleasure is all ours, Your Majesty. You are most gracious to invite us."

At each of the three places were put a glass of water and a glass of orange juice. A pita bread pouch, piping hot, was put on each bread plate. A medium-sized bowl of hummus was placed in front of each brass charger. The Emir tore pieces of the pita bread and dipped them in the hummus. We followed his lead. The hummus, which is puréed chickpeas or garbanza, as the Italians call it, was flavored with sesame seeds, olive oil and fresh dill. Waiters were very attentive in seeing each of us had additional hot bread to finish the hummus. When we were done, the bowls and bread plates were whisked away and a beautiful bone china plate was put on the charger. Another waiter brought in a silver tray on which were three smaller plates of pâté de foie. I thought it was goose liver but it may have been duck. Up until this point in the dinner, there had been no conversation. When the pâté was served, the Emir said he hoped we liked pheasant liver. That was a first for me and I'm sure for Sven.

"Your Majesty, I never before had pheasant liver pâté but it's so delicate and so tasty," I said.

"I have the pheasants flown in from your State of Montana and we feed them until they are quite fat. I am extremely fond of the pâté but it is not good for my cholesterol." He smiled broadly as he patted his large stomach. Again, I translated for Sven.

When we finished the pâté, the charger with its two plates was removed and a new china plate was put before each of us. Two waiters entered carrying huge silver trays. On the first was sliced lamb filets which had been broiled in sesame seed sauce. The second tray contained a very large silver serving-dish with fresh green asparagus. I immediately looked at Sven and licked my lips. The waiter served the Emir five filets of lamb. The other waiter put eight spears of asparagus on his plate. My plate was filled similarly and then Sven's. It was at this point that the Emir appeared to be ready to converse. He began with a very simple question after all the attendants had left the room.

"Mr. Devon, how well do you know the owner of the yacht *37*?"

"Quite well, Majesty. She is a world-famous hostess and a superb gourmet. As you probably already know, she is an American citizen who was also a friend of my fiancée."

"She is a lovely person and a most gracious hostess, I agree." There appeared to be a "but" coming next; I was wrong.

"She has been most unfortunate in her choice of husbands," I continued, "having been married and divorced five times and is currently dating Sven's father."

The Emir turned his attention to Sven. "Have you been a guest on the yacht, also, Mr. Christen?" I translated the Emir's question.

"Yes, I have, Majesty. As a matter of fact, the owner made her yacht available for the burial at sea of the ashes of my brother's fiancée." I translated.

"What a magnificent gesture, Mr. Devon. You and your family must be quite close to her."

"We are like one family, Your Majesty." It was a first-class double entendre.

"I had not met her until her yacht moored here in Abu Dhabi and my Minister of State informed me of her kind gesture of proposing a dinner aboard in my honor."

"I know she is very particular about the people she invites as dinner guests. If I am not being intrusive, Majesty, may I please ask how many guests were invited to accompany Your Majesty aboard?"

"You are not being intrusive at all. I invited my Minister of State and my Personal Aide, Mr. al-Maldi, whom you know."

"Mr. al-Maldi was so gracious to Sven and me last evening at dinner at his Club. Your Majesty also informed me Mr. al-Maldi had attended the inauguration of my former college roommate when he was made President. Was Mr. al-Maldi representing you at the inauguration, Your Majesty?"

"No. I do not know the new President and did not receive an invitation to his Inaugural. I was told by Mr. al-Maldi that he was invited by a friend who lives in the country and who was a member of the Cabinet of the former President." *Aha*, I thought.

"Does Your Majesty know of any business relations between your country and that of the President?"

"I am not aware of any."

"Sven, I believe you wanted to ask His Majesty a question about giving his Head Chef some of your recipes."

"Yes, I do. Your Majesty, would it be permissible for me to send your Head Chef some of my recipes for the lamb dishes I have created?" I again translated.

"I would be pleased if you would, Mr. Christen, and I know my Chef would welcome such a gracious gesture on your part." Again I translated.

"May I please ask another question, Your Majesty, about Mr. al-Maldi?" I inquired.

"Certainly."

"Is Mr. al-Maldi a native of the Emirates and how long has he been Your Majesty's Personal Aide?"

"Mr. al-Maldi was born in Saudi Arabia but has lived here for about fourteen years. He moved here from Teheran when he was made Head of Bank Melli here. He has been my Personal Aide for about five years. He was recommended to me by a member of the Royal Family of Saudi Arabia." He paused. "May I ask why you are so interested in Mr. al-

Maldi?"

"Mr. al-Maldi's companion, Mr. Zanani, appears to know the gentleman I met at the Inaugural who asked if I knew anyone who was importing pharmaceuticals into the Emirates."

"And what did you tell him?"

"At that time, I had not met either Mr. al-Maldi or Mr. Zanani. My response to him was that I did not."

"Mr. Devon, may I ask you a rather personal question?"

"Certainly, Your Majesty."

"Do you suspect that Mr. al-Maldi or Mr. Zanani may be involved in some way with the importation of, as you say, 'pharmaceuticals' into The Emirates?"

"I would not want to accuse anyone falsely nor would I want to tarnish anyone's character with only a supposition on my part."

"Please speak freely."

"Since Mr. Zanani appears to know the man who inquired if I knew anyone in The Emirates who might be importing pharmaceuticals, my answer to your question, Your Majesty, is yes."

"You are an astute man, Mr. Devon, and also a very gracious gentleman who, I am now certain, does not repeat rumors or attempt to instigate them. May I confide in you, Mr. Devon?"

"Your Majesty, I would be honored to be trusted with any information Your Majesty would care to share. I can assure Your Majesty that the only reason I brought up the subject is that I wanted to inform Your Majesty of my suspicions so that Your Majesty could take any action Your Majesty deemed appropriate."

"It is only within the past two weeks that I have been informed of the same suspicion that you have shared with me. My informant is a distant cousin of mine who works in Bank Melli here in Abu Dhabi." I thought of Jamil. "I had asked him to report to me any suspicions he may have regarding the importation into The Emirates of any illegal substances, or 'pharmaceuticals', as you call them. You and he had met on your previous visit to The Emirates at which time he reported to me how much he liked you and thought you were an upstanding man who could be trusted with sensitive information. I thought it might be helpful for me to meet you.

"When I was informed that you were here in Abu Dhabi and had a message for me from Mr. Beecham, I thought it appropriate to grant your wish for an audience. When you and your brother appeared in my presence, I immediately liked you both and felt that you were someone I could trust to assist me with my suspicions." I did not look directly at

Sven but instinctively knew that he was bursting with pride hearing the

Emir's praise for his demeanor. Also I didn't want to give away the fact

that he had understood everything the Emir had said. The Emir continued.

"My informant feels that Mr. al-Maldi knows nothing about this matter

but that Mr. Zanani does. At first, I was not pleased to learn of Mr. al-

Maldi's association with Mr. Zanani, but came to realize that Mr. al-Maldi

might be a good source of information regarding anything that should

come to my attention. I have allowed their association to continue. I have

never spoken to Mr. al-Maldi about his personal life but am somewhat

disappointed when he and his companion appear together in public so

often. I know nothing about their relationship and would not want to judge

Mr. al-Maldi nor Mr. Zanani wrongly."

"Your Majesty, I appreciate the sharing of this information with me

and I am pleased to learn that my suspicions, as I related them to Your

Majesty, have been accepted in confidence. I can assure Your Majesty that

this conversation is in the strictest of confidence and that I shall not

discuss anything that I have heard tonight with anyone who is not

present."

The Emir signaled that the desserts and coffees should now be served.

As soon as the attendants arrived, all conversation ceased. The dessert was a magnificently prepared baklava and the coffee was Turkish. The Emir asked us if we cared for a second cup. We both declined. At the completion of the meal, the Emir rose as an attendant pulled back his chair. Our chairs were also moved. Without saying a word, the Emir walked toward the door leading into the Main Hall of the Palace. Sven and I followed. When we three approached the huge bronze doors, one of them opened. The Emir extended his hand to each of us and thanked us for coming to his home. I thanked him profusely in my most flowery Arabic for the courtesies extend to us. As we turned to leave the Hall, I noted the limousine parked at the front of the building. The right rear door was open.

When we were again in our room, Sven looked at me in amazement and said, "We not only dined in the Palace with the Emir, but you've become his confidant."

I picked up the phone and dialed Z. I reported everything that transpired and the entire conversation with the Emir. When I finished my dissertation, he said, "Gentlemen, you have accomplished more than you can possibly realize. I'll report your evening's activities and conversation to Interpol. I feel certain they'll want to have conversations with Zanani and di Marchi." Thank you for your excellent service on this assignment.

You certainly do work well together." Z paused for just a second. "Let me speak with Sven."

I handed him the phone.

"Yes, sir," said Sven and then listened intently to Z's instructions. "I shall be on the plane to Madrid tomorrow morning."

He handed me the phone. "Philipp, I received a call last evening from your boss in America. He asked that you return home as soon as possible. Your laundry is ready." Z hung up.

Sven and I sat on the edge of our beds. I told him I'd also be leaving tomorrow morning. I said I believed the Emir would take some action to remove Zanani from Abu Dhabi, that is, if Interpol doesn't get to him first. The Emir might ask Interpol to have a conversation with al-Maldi to determine how much he knows, keeping the name of the Emir out of the investigation. I expressed regret that I wouldn't have an opportunity to thank and say goodbye to Jamil, but then I decided I shouldn't say anything. The Emir never named his confidant in the Bank. I asked Sven if I'd missed any nuances in the conversations. He said he understood every word and didn't notice any frowns or gestures by the Emir. I complimented him on his astute listening ability and once again, thanked him for being my protégé.

"Well, Little Brother, once again we must say goodbye. I feel certain that Z will have a new assignment for us before too long."

"Well, Big Brother, once again it's been a pleasure working with you. I've learned so much from you these past several weeks."

We both started to pack for the morning's departures. When we were almost finished, we were standing in the middle of the room. With no hesitation, Sven walked over and embraced me. I reciprocated.

My alarm awoke me at 7:00. Sven was snoring. Our flights did not leave, Sven's for Madrid and mine for London, until 10:30 and 10:45, respectively. I did my triples. Hitting the floor, I continued with push-ups and sit-ups. While in the middle of the latter, Sven bounded out of bed and joined me on the floor with his one-armed push-ups. Watching him, I felt so inadequate. We both then started that exercise whose name I can't remember. I was quite good at this, but Sven had a little trouble because of his massive torso. I felt rather superior because I could do something athletic better than he. That was a rarity. I suggested that he shower first. Once under the water, he started singing. This was the first time I'd really listened to him. He had a marvelous baritone voice. When he finished, I stepped into the shower.

"You have a magnificent speaking voice, one with so much

resonance," Sven said. "I would've thought you sang also. I know both

you and Arlene sang in the shower when you were together." As I was

toweling dry, he continued. "I said her name purposely. I wanted you to

hear it from me one more time before we part. I feel you're making

progress, not in forgetting her, but in dealing with her death. She'll always

be a part of you and I feel sure she'll be with you wherever you go. You

must be able to hear her name and not regress in your progress. Arlene

wouldn't have wished that on you."

I looked him in the eye and fought back the emotion that was welling

up inside me. I smiled and said, "I say again, I'm amazed how such a

young man knows so much about human nature and the feelings of two

people who were so completely in love. You're just the tonic I've needed

to complete the transition. I realize that she'll always be with me wherever

I go, but I've now admitted to myself she would want me to get on with

my life without her. Sven, you helped me when I needed someone the

most. I'll forever be grateful to you for being here and saying what you've

just said. Thank you."

Sven put his arms around me and hugged me. And I hugged him back.

I don't know how I could've gotten through my grief without him.

We finished packing in silence. Then I said, "Can I interest you in some breakfast?"

"I thought you'd never ask."

We got dressed and went to the dining room. The waiter arrived with our usual bottle of mineral water and two orange juices. We ordered a hearty breakfast.

"I haven't eaten since last night and I need nourishment."

"And some lovin' more often," I added with a grin.

"There is a cute señorita in Marbella who comes into the restaurant with her parents. She's smiled at me but I didn't want to jeopardize my relationship with Helga. Now that that's over, I think I'll be a lot more attentive to her needs, and mine."

"Let me know how things develop. Who knows, I might learn a few things from you on how to improve my technique with women." We both laughed.

We finished breakfast, returned to the room, picked up our luggage and went to the lobby to check out.

"You have a message, Mr. Devon," said the young man as he handed me a sealed envelope. I opened the envelope and took out an embossed card with the seal of the Ruler of The Emirates at the top. The message was short. "Come again. You are always welcome in my home." It was not signed.

I asked for some note paper and a pen. I wrote a short note to Mohammed. "Take care of yourself. Watch your back as well as your front!" I signed it "Philipp, friend."

The cab ride to the airport was about one hour. I charged our tickets on the Barclay's card. When we cleared Security, Sven's gate was to the left; mine to the right. We each put down our bags and brief cases and just looked at each other. We said nothing. Finally, we shook hands and parted.

The flight to London was about ten hours. My layover was about one hour. We touched down at Dulles at 6:10 the next morning. I took a taxi to my usual corner near the apartment. As I approached the building I've called home for eight years, I noticed a FOR SALE sign in front. I entered the basement and called my boss.

"Welcome back, Stranger. I'm glad you got home safely. We should have lunch. Let's meet at our usual place at noon." He hung up.

I unpacked. It occurred to me that I hadn't checked the upstairs. I hastily got out of my clothes and put together the pile of dirty laundry, packaged it, dressed casually, and went upstairs and rang the bell. I went back to my basement door and waited. The upstairs door opened and closed. I reentered my apartment and took a shower.

I put on my business suit under my raincoat. As I left the apartment, a slight drizzle was beginning. When I got to the office and had disposed of my rain gear, I took the elevator, gave the codes and entered the boss' office.

"Welcome back to this side. You've spent quite a bit of time in the other hemisphere."

I wasn't into small talk this morning. I wanted to know what was so urgent for my return.

"The Senator and his wife are leaving town. He's retiring. The building is for sale and you have to move immediately."

My first impression was this was all a joke, including the sign in front.

"May I assume you've selected a new residence for me?"

"I have in fact selected three, any one of which would be perfect. You have your choice of the Dupont Circle area, Georgetown or Rhode Island Avenue."

I knew that Dupont Circle had a Metro stop whereas Georgetown didn't. Rhode Island Avenue covered a lot of territory, from Connecticut Avenue to Silver Spring, Maryland.

"Have you looked at all these choice homes?" I asked sarcastically.

"I have, and you will too. Here are the addresses and the keys." He handed me three index cards and a key to each place.

"Have you a preference for me?"

"I do but I want you to select your own. Then we can discuss whether it's the one I've chosen."

I didn't like being preempted, especially when it concerns where I'm going to lay my head each night.

"What is my schedule for relocation?"

"You'll move tomorrow morning. I've arranged for a van to be at your current address at 5:00. I want you out of the neighborhood before 6:00. You'll be in your new quarters, unpacked and settled by 9:00.

"You're so thoughtful to allow so much time to move myself and my belongings." I was really miffed.

"You should get started on your tour of the sites so you can get back home after our lunch and start packing. After this move is complete, I've a new assignment for you that I'm sure you'll enjoy. You enjoy the islands, don't you?"

"Are we talking about St. Pierre and Miquelon or Fiji?" I asked with barely concealed sarcasm.

"Neither. I'll tell you all about it at lunch. Now get moving."

Having been curtly dismissed, I left his office. After donning my rain gear, I left the building. A drizzle was still coming down, not heavy, just the annoying type.

The nearest of the three was in the Dupont Circle area. For several blocks around the Circle in all directions is known by some as Weirdo-land. Here one can find the largest assortment of different types of lifestyles, colors of hair, odors, and causes in the entire Washington Metropolitan area. I walked the few blocks from the office to the address. Surprisingly, the place was not bad. I liked what I saw.

I took a taxi to the address in Georgetown. The basement apartment opened directly onto the street, which was not a busy one. I didn't particularly like the entrance arrangement but I reserved my opinion until I'd seen the inside. When I switched on the lights, I was overwhelmed by the color scheme. The ceiling was black, the walls were hunter green and the floor was a combination of black-and-white tiles. I turned off the light and locked the door.

I hailed another taxi and went to the address on Rhode Island Avenue. The building was near Scott Circle, an area that has seen much renovation over the past few years. The building had two stories and the entrance door was right on the street. The first floor had a living space and a small dining space with a Pullman kitchen. There was a bath with only a shower. On the second floor, there was a bedroom on the front and a slightly larger one on the rear. The bath between contained a tub and a shower. The entire house had been recently repainted and the upstairs had been re-carpeted. The downstairs was all wood floors, recently sanded and varnished. I liked what I saw and the neighborhood wasn't bad. The only drawback was the windows had no bars. The main advantage I saw was the extra bedroom where I could have overnight guests or cohorts if they happened to be in town. I locked up and went back to the office.

"That was a quick tour. Did you see all three places in sufficient detail to make your choice?"

"I did. I like the two-story house on Rhode Island Avenue."

"Why didn't you like the other two?"

"The Dupont Circle place is almost exactly a duplicate of where I am now and I thought a change of scenery would be nice. The place in Georgetown was hideous. I couldn't live in such a place with the current decor. So I chose the Rhode Island Avenue house even though there will be some expense in the curtains, plus bars at the windows."

"I chose the same one, the main reason being the extra bedroom which will accommodate guests or co-workers."

"Then it's settled? I get the house?"

"You get the house. However, there is another very important reason you need the extra bedroom. Z and I have talked about your recent assignments in which you've acted as a mentor for Sven Christen. Z feels that he should continue training with you for a while longer since you have done such a superior job training him so far. So, Z is calling him tonight and telling him of his new assignment. Z is also sending a new chef to Marbella as a replacement. Sven will be here in D.C. the day after tomorrow. Does that arrangement meet with your approval?"

"How about the curtains and the bars?"

"The windows have been measured and the curtains have been made. They will be installed tomorrow in the late morning and the bars before noon."

"What color did you choose for the curtains?"

"I thought chartreuse and plaid would be nice. Those were Pogo's school colors."

"You jest."

"Actually they're a light green with an opaque backing that'll keep out all light from getting in or out."

"You seem to have thought of everything, just as you always do. I appreciate you being concerned about my surroundings and I gratefully endorse each of your decisions. Has a telephone been installed?"

"Yes and the arrangements for billing and calling are the same as now.

"How will I get my laundry done?"

"There's a Korean hand laundry around the corner. Here's their card. Mr. Rhee has been contacted by the State Department and informed that a new Ambassador is moving into the neighborhood, Ambassador Devon. Mr. Rhee has been instructed that whenever Ambassador Devon brings clothes in before 8:00 AM, everything is to be ready no later than 3:00 PM. Mr. Rhee's laundry does much work for the State Department personnel living in the vicinity. You'll pay cash for each laundry job. Now, let's go to lunch. My driver will take us over to Langley. There's someone there who'd like to speak to you."

We took the elevator to the basement where the boss' car was waiting. The trip to CIA Headquarters in Langley took about twenty minutes. We were cleared by the gate guards and continued to the main building where a young man was standing at the entrance. I recognized him, even at that distance. It was John Beecham.

TWENTY

"John, my friend, it's good to see you again."

"And you also, Philipp. Good morning."

"What brings you to D.C.?" I asked.

"I'll explain everything over lunch," said the boss. We proceeded to the private dining room of the Director. No one else was in the room. A waiter brought Cobb Salads and iced teas. After we were served, the boss began.

"Philipp, tell John about your visits to the Palace."

I told him everything that happened. I also conveyed the good wishes and the thanks of the Emir to him for sending me as his emissary.

"The Emir spoke so very highly of your father and thanked you through me for your father's service to him."

"My father, as you may know, was Head of the Foreign Bond Division of Barclay's Bank. He also was the personal Aide to the Emir for several years. It's good to see you again, Philipp."

"And the two of you will see more of each other in the near future,"

430

said the boss. "Z has loaned John to work on a very special project. Because of John's past experience in these matters and his fluency in French, he is the ideal one to be involved with you and Sven." He paused and waited for one of us to ask the question. Finally, I did.

"And what is this new assignment that we three are so talented and experienced in?"

"John is being sent to Monaco."

"I know that place. I just left there a few weeks ago," I said.

"He will be housed in the Palace, but the assignment is entirely different. Monaco is where our suspect moors his yacht when he arrives from the Caribbean. We don't know exactly when that will be, but arrangements have been made for you, John, to stay as long as necessary to complete your task. We believe he passes counterfeit U.S. 20-dollar bills at the Casino."

"Philipp, you and Sven will be in the Caribbean, on Saint Martin. That's where our suspect keeps his yacht most of the year. We believe he travels from Saint Martin to Guadeloupe, to the small island below the big one, called Terre de Haut, where he is suspected of operating a small counterfeiting plant producing the bills."

"This sounds complicated," I injected.

"It is complicated. You and Sven are to ingratiate yourself, gain his confidence by implying that you suspect what he's doing and you both have had experience in those matters. I doubt if he'd take you to Terre de Haut, but you may not have to go there to discover enough about his operation for us to inform Interpol."

"Tell us more about this shady character."

"His name is Pierre Le Boeuf, or Peter the Ox. He lives on his yacht, which he named Les Petite Pommes de Terre, or Small Potatoes. Rather cute, don't you agree? He moors in the marina at the Baie des Froussards, the Bay of Cowards, located on the northern end of Saint Martin. The marina is quite large and the ships are well protected from the winds and from sight by very steep cliffs. The French Navy last sighted him entering the waters off St. Martin. They are very alert to all ships coming and going, particularly in that marina. It's the one The President of France uses when he visits the island to do a little sailing.

"Philipp, you and Sven will be staying at the Westin Resort and Spa at Anse Marcel, the official address of the marina. It's the only hotel at Anse Marcel and is considered one of the most luxurious resorts in the Caribbean. You'll need tropical casual dress, some attire for boarding yachts and the usual accessories that go with resort dress. You'll also want

432

to take your tuxedos. The French on the upper half of the island are known for their swanky parties, given at some of the most luxurious villas in the entire Caribbean. I expect you two to get invited to some."

"How will we get around on the island?"

"I don't want you to use a rental car. When you want to go somewhere out of Anse Marcel, you'll telephone Arnauld, the taxi driver who has been used by American dignitaries for several years. When you call for him, identify yourself as Philipp Devon. You and your brother are both playboys. Your father is a member of the distinguished family that owns Devon Publications. He's Chairman of the Board. Sven's father is the Head Chef in the Palace in Stockholm and is also Head of the Swedish Gastronomic Society."

"How do you suggest that the two of us get to be pals with Peter the Ox?"

"You might try the ploy that you've learned quite a bit about the printing industry and particularly the frauds who print modern copies of ancient texts, even books of the Incunabula, and sometimes even rarer documents."

"And what is Sven's specialty?"

"Sven is very interested in old sailing charts and maps as well as steel engravings. Since he speaks Swedish and Spanish as well as Arabic, those might come in handy somewhere, sometime. And you, Philipp, are fluent in Russian, Arabic, Spanish and - - what's the other one?"

"French."

"Oh, yes; now I remember." Here he goes again, getting on my case. He loves this game of snide remarks and challenges.

"Well, gentlemen, have either of you any further questions?"

John spoke up. "What exactly am I looking for in Monaco?"

"Peter the Ox is known to visit casinos. He and one of his local associates have been known to slip a few counterfeit twenties into the game, never many, no more than three on any one night. You'll alert the Major Domo in the Palace, Alberto, of your suspicions and ask him to alert the Casino personnel. You can set up a signal whenever you're certain that either is passing counterfeit bills and they will assist you from there. Your past experience of nabbing the forgery expert in Brussels should stand you in good stead in the Casino. You also are very astute at reading body English. Remember the dowager in Paris who was stuffing silverware down her front in the dining room of the Senate? And don't forget the time you were posing as a bank cashier in Amsterdam and the counterfeit king of Europe tried to exchange some of his bills with you? I

434

know you're very creative, and both Z and I felt you would be ideal for this assignment. Use your imagination."

The boss stood up as did we. John asked for a ride to the City. He said he was staying with a cousin in Georgetown so the boss' driver let him out there. I was let out two blocks from my apartment.

When I got there, I saw my laundry bag. I retrieved it and entered my apartment and began packing. When I finished, I looked in the refrigerator and the freezer compartment. Nada. That meant I had to go out for dinner. There are no restaurants in this neighborhood and I like to eat somewhere with lots of people around. I put my raincoat on and left the apartment. I took the Metro to Union Station. It's always crowded and there are lots of restaurants. I got a small pizza and a diet soda. When I'd finished that gourmet's delight, I walked by the frozen yogurt place and bought a peach yogurt with real fruit. I returned home, stripped and looked at my watch. It was 6:54.

I hadn't read a book for entertainment in quite some time. I looked at my meager book collection and realized that they had to be packed too. The only receptacle I had was the wastebasket. It's a good thing I don't collect expensive editions. I was able to cram twelve paperbacks and one hardback in with two magazines. The book I saved to read tonight was

The Bible. It'd been some time since I last opened it. I decided to test the saying that whatever's bothering you, if you randomly open The Bible, you'll find solace and perhaps a solution to your problem. I held the book in both hands and slowly bent it like I was shuffling a deck of cards. When the book opened fully, I was at the page containing the Twenty-Third Psalm. I sat down on the bed and read it. Then I re-read it. I got down on my knees by the side of my bed and began talking to God.

"You know me, God. I'm Philipp Devon. I haven't talked to you since that night at the Cadogan. When I awakened, the sun was shining right on my head. I took that as a sign that you'd accepted my prayers and I'd be all right without my dearest Arlene. Well, God, I'm about to be involved in the three things I've always heard you shouldn't be involved in at the same time. I'll be moving my residence tomorrow. And the next day Sven will arrive and after I brief him, the two of us will head off on a new job assignment. The third thing is the loss of a spouse. While I'm making progress in getting on with my life without my dearest Arlene, I still feel I've just lost her. I'll be honest with you, God; all these years I've tried to go it alone. But you helped me so much the last time I prayed, I felt I needed to talk with you again.

"So here I am. I've just read the Twenty-Third Psalm twice, but of course you already know that. It says that you'll be with me forever, even until the end of the world. I'm not afraid, God; I just need some assurance that my future is going to be brighter than it is at this very moment. I still miss my dearest Arlene terribly, but I realize that I've got to get on with it. Can you help me? I know you can, but will you?"

I don't remember the rest of my prayer or even continuing to pray. But I must have.

There was a knock at my door. I got up from the kneeling position, put on my trousers and said "Just a minute." When I opened the door, there stood a huge black man in a mover's uniform. I looked at him and had no idea who he was or what he wanted until he spoke.

"Mr. Devon, I'm Charlie Bragg. I'm here to help you move. Can I come in?"

I looked at my watch. It said 5:00 on the dot. I must've prayed all night. I was still in a stupor but invited him in.

"I see the biggest piece is the sofa bed, but if you'll help me, I think we both can lift it on the truck. I can get the rest by myself." He folded the sheet and the pillow inside and folded up the bed into the sofa. With strength I never knew I had, we easily lifted the sofa and placed it on his truck. He then came back for the remaining items. I noticed the cardboard on the shelf.

"Would you possibly have any newspapers and some tape? I want to stuff one more box," I asked the driver.

"I got the morning *Post*. You can have the advertisements, the want ads and the Style section. I never look at them."

I took the papers, folded the box and taped one end. I filled the box with the wadded newspapers, took five old 20-dollar bills from my briefcase and lay them on top of the papers. I folded the other end, taped and sealed it. I finished dressing, took the box upstairs and rang the bell. The lady, whom I'd never seen, was small and old but had a sweet smile.

"I wanted to say thank you for all you've done for me. I'm moving today to another part of town. I have a new job. Thank you and goodbye."

She took the box inside. I waited. I could see through the curtains on the door that she had the five bills in one hand and the other one was rubbing her eyes. I went back downstairs.

"I think we got it all, Mr. Devon. You wanna ride up front with me?"

I got in the cab as we pulled away from the curb and shortly we were at the new place. I helped the driver unload. We put everything in the big downstairs room.

"I'll straighten up later," I said. "Thank you for your assistance in getting me moved."

He put his hand to the bill of his cap, smiled and said, "You're welcome." And he was gone.

I looked at my watch. It was 6:00 on the dot. I had a lot to do today, straightening up my new abode as best I can with the meager amount of furniture I own. I want to take the dirty linens to Mr. Rhee. I need to find somewhere for Sven to sleep when he arrives tomorrow. However, I can't go out for long until the curtain and bars people arrive and are finished. There was a small Mom and Pop store on the corner, already open. I saw a man and a woman whom I recognized as Korean. I greeted them in their language and bought a roll and coffee, speaking Korean.

I returned home and ate breakfast. Then I opened the sofa bed and took the sheet and pillowcase around the corner to the laundry. As I went into the shop, a very distinguished-looking young Korean man greeted me in perfect English.

"Good morning, sir. How may I help you?"

"My name is Devon. I've just moved into the neighborhood."

"I have been expecting you, Mr. Ambassador. Your laundry will be ready by three today."

"Thank you very much, Mr. Rhee." He smiled.

When I returned to my apartment, I unpacked.

After I put away everything, I made a list of the things I needed to complete the furnishing of the house. First, and the most important, would be a bed and a chest in the front bedroom. The list grew. The phone rang downstairs. Where was the phone? I found it on the floor under the stairs.

"Philipp, I called to see how you're settling in."

"I was just making a list of the items I must acquire before Sven arrives tomorrow."

"That's why I'm calling. I took the liberty of sorting through our warehouse of odds and ends, which come and go almost as often as we do. I found two king-sized beds, two chests of drawers, two straight chairs, an overstuffed lounge chair, a rug for each of the bedrooms and one for the living room. In addition, I found linens for the two beds and four pillows, towels for both bathrooms and a few gadgets and towels for the kitchen. Have I covered your list?"

I was impressed as well as pleased that he'd covered all my needs so thoroughly, but I dare not let him think he's completely taken charge of my new house.

"You forgot a small table for the telephone," I said proudly.

"Oh, I forgot to mention it."

Damn, damn, damn, I thought. He's good, really good.

"When will these items be delivered?" I asked casually.

"Right after noon today. The curtain and bar people will have finished and won't be in the way of the movers."

What was so uncanny about the list the boss mentioned was the fact that it was almost identical, and in the same order, as mine. He and I had worked together for so long, we even thought alike.

Not surprisingly, everything arrived, and at the time he promised, too. I called the boss as the movers left.

"I want to thank you for all you've done to make me comfortable: for the new house, for its condition and cleanliness, for the window bars and curtains, for the furniture and rugs, and most of all for just being my friend."

"Don't get mushy with me," said the boss with humor in his voice and hung up.

For the next two hours, I got the beds made, put towels in the two baths and the kitchen, put away the remaining linens, took the cardboard boxes out to the street but away from the front of the house, went to pick up the laundry from Mr. Rhee and then sat down on the sofa. It was only then that I realized how extremely tired and sleepy I was. I went upstairs, stripped and took a shower. Even the glass stall had been scrubbed. I toweled dry and lay down. I didn't even look at my watch.

I awoke at 9:10. I was quite hungry. I threw on my casual clothes and went for a walk and dinner. Within a radius of five blocks, I'd located four restaurants I thought I'd like to try. In no particular order, I started with the French one. The room was crowded but I was seated shortly. The menu was not extensive but adequate. Since I had no appointments tomorrow and Sven didn't arrive until after six, I decided to have some wine.

"I'd like a carafe of the Merlot, please."

I was delighted to see coq au vin on the menu, so I decided to try the local version. When the waiter brought the wine, I ordered the coq au vin and a tossed green salad after the meal."

"You said after the meal?"

"Yes, I want to enjoy the wine alone and with the coq au vin. If I add the vinegar from the salad, it'll kill the taste of the wine."

"Okay," acknowledged the waiter somewhat perplexed.

The Merlot was nice. I looked around the restaurant to see if I knew anyone. I didn't. Shortly, the waiter returned with my meal. It was very tasty. The meat was tender and the vegetables were simmered just right.

The bread was a baguette sliced at an angle. I was reminded of my meal in Paris several years ago with Arlene. We'd dined at a small café off the Boulevard St. Germain. This meal brought back pleasant thoughts of the previous one.

I finished the entrée and the wine about the same time. The salad was green but unexciting. I paid the check, left a tip and went outside. I felt quite good. My stomach was full and the wine gave my step a slight jauntiness. As I approached my house, I realized I wasn't as cautious about entering as I'd been at my former residence. This neighborhood was different, more upscale and more family oriented. I passed no one on the streets as I walked home.

I locked the front door, turned out the lamp in the living room, went upstairs, stripped and lay down on my new king-sized bed. I didn't set the alarm.

The phone woke me up in a dark room. I turned on the overhead light and went downstairs to answer it. I must get an upstairs extension.

"Philipp, as you know, Sven is arriving this evening. Since he doesn't know the address of your new quarters, I suggest you meet him at Dulles. Tomorrow morning at 10:00, my plane will leave from the remote hangar at Washington National with you two as the only passengers. When you get to Miami, your tickets will be waiting in your name at the American desk. I'll slip an envelope with some spending money under your door tonight. Call me when you both get settled in your suite. Arnauld will be waiting for you at the airport."

"We have a suite?"

"Wealthy playboys always have a suite. They never travel other than First Class." He hung up.

I looked at my watch. 7:35. I'd slept twelve hours. What shall I do today? I don't have a tropical sport coat. I'll walk over to Connecticut Avenue this morning and purchase one. I checked my two hiding places for my cash. I had four hundred in 20s with more coming this evening.

I noticed I'd put the Bible on top of the TV. I sat down on the sofa and held it like I did before, to see where it would flop open. This time it opened to the Book of Daniel, Chapter 6. My eyes focused on Verse 3.

"Then this Daniel was preferred above the presidents and princes, because an excellent spirit was in him; and the king sought to set him over the whole realm."

I don't know how to interpret Scripture, but this verse said to me that Daniel had been chosen by God above all the heads of State because he had the right spirit. Was I being too self-centered to infer that God's Spirit was in me? I really believed what I was doing was for the good of my country and I was well-suited for this profession. I know I've taken risks which sometimes resulted in being fired at, but never hit. I also, on occasion, got into situations that appeared to have no way of escape. But I always got out and my mission was never compromised.

"If my thinking isn't correct, God, please set me straight," I said out loud.

I dressed casually and walked to Connecticut Avenue, where I knew there were several men's stores. I looked in several windows before I saw a coat that caught my eye. I walked in and asked the clerk about the beige coat in the window.

"That's the last of our summer line. We'll be getting in our fall wardrobes next week." He went to the window and removed the coat I'd indicated. I put it on. It fit perfectly. And the price was right, after some negotiating.

I walked back home, took the jacket out of the bag and put it on. I don't know when I've enjoyed bargaining as much as I just did.

I went to the nearby food store and got a chicken salad sandwich and a diet coke. When I opened the door to my house, the phone was ringing. It was Z.

"Philipp, I was calling to determine if you're missing your family here. We certainly miss your presence. You are aware that your little brother is flying in tonight and that the two of you will be taking a vacation to the Islands tomorrow. Watch out for the hot sun and the women. Ta ta."

I went upstairs, shed my clothes and took a short nap. I awoke at 3:15. I should leave for Dulles about 4:30 since Sven's plane is scheduled to arrive shortly after 6:00. I reset my alarm for 4:15 and turned over for one more nap.

TWENTY-ONE

My alarm vibrated. I got up, took a shower, dressed in casual clothes and hailed a taxi to the airport. I bought a coffee, a copy of the *Washington Post* and sat in the gate's waiting area.

As Sven came through the door, he had a wide smile. He was carrying his briefcase and two garment bags. I walked toward him and stuck out my hand for a shake. He dropped his briefcase and gave me a hug. This appeared to be his m.o. with people he cared about. I hugged back. We headed for the baggage carousel.

"I have two bags; I brought everything I had in Marbella."

"Good. Now my apartment will be crammed full," I kidded him. "You know I just have the sofa that makes into the queen bed. Is that gonna be okay with you?"

He looked a little taken aback. "I dunno. Since both of us sleep naked, I dunno."

"Oh, well, I know brothers who've always slept in the same bed, up until they got married. One night shouldn't make that much difference." I continued to watch his facial expression. He wasn't pleased.

We got his luggage and hailed a taxi. We were silent during the ride to D.C.

"Philipp, I've never slept in the same bed with a man. Even though you're my Big Brother, I think I'd better sleep on the floor."

"Suit yourself."

When the taxi stopped at my new house, Sven looked puzzled. "Is this where you live? I thought you had a basement apartment on Capitol Hill."

I said nothing as I paid the cabbie. With luggage in hand, we walked toward the door. I unlocked it and turned on the living room light.

"There's the sofa, Sven."

"What's upstairs?"

"Go see for yourself," I said, as he climbed the steps. In less than five seconds, he shouted, "You had me going there," as he came back down. I received another hug.

"I love you, Big Brother, but I don't wanna sleep with you."

I told him about my change of residence, why I had to move and about the activity on the first day here.

We took his luggage upstairs. Since we were leaving tomorrow morning, he left his bags packed with the exception of his toilet articles and some casual clothes. We came back downstairs.

"I never knew you were such a joker. I like it."

"Thanks. I don't have any food in the house so we'll have to go out for dinner. Do you have a preference?"

"It's your call. You know Washington. This is my first visit to the Capital."

"Let's try the Italian place. It's one of the four restaurants on my list to try."

He changed into casual slacks and the polo shirt I gave him. We walked around the corner and up the block. The place was not crowded. It was still early.

"I think I'll have spaghetti and meatballs and a green salad," I said to the waiter.

"I'd like the lasagna, no salad."

"Would you care for some wine?" asked the waiter.

"We're going to pass this evening. We have an early flight tomorrow morning," I said. "It's good to see you again. I'm pleased that our bosses made it possible for this joint assignment. Have you ever been to the Caribbean?"

"Not once. I was in Bermuda once and the Bahamas twice, but never to the Antilles. I assume that's where we're going."

"St. Martin, the only place in the world shared by two countries where there's no visible dividing line and visas aren't required. The currency of choice is the dollar. We'll be staying on the French side where French is very much in use. However, almost everyone on the island speaks English."

I briefed him on the details of our assignment. I answered his few questions. I stressed the ruse that we were playboy brothers, both very rich and talented in several areas. I mentioned that on St. Martin there's Orient Beach, the longest nude beach in the world, about two miles of white sand and naked bodies from the age of about six months to the upper eighties, male and female. I could tell that I'd sparked his enthusiasm.

The meal was adequate. I paid in cash with a tip. We returned to the house, went upstairs and stripped. When we'd settled back on the sofa, I turned on the TV, which I rarely do when I'm alone. The news was routine.

"Do you mind if we talk instead of watching TV?" Sven asked.

"Not at all." I turned it off.

"You remember that you suggested I try to forget Helga and see if I could find another girl in Marbella? You remember me telling you about the young señorita who came in the restaurant several times with her parents? Well, I asked her, her name is Rosa, if she'd like to go out with me on my day off. She agreed. I asked her for a date on the day I got back to Marbella. We were going out the next night. Then Z called and told me about this assignment. We didn't get to have the date and now I'm hornier than I was in Abu Dhabi. I hope there are some women on St. Martin who will find me attractive, for I do need some lovin'."

"Sven, I can assure you that at the resort where we're staying, you'll see many young women who also will need some lovin'. We'll have a suite and your room is yours whenever you'd like to entertain. Consider me not even there, even if I'm in my own room. You never can tell. I might even find someone who needs a little of *my* lovin'."

Sven looked at me and smiled. He knew without asking that I'd come to realize I had to get on with my life. I truly believed I could. We shall see.

"I'm gonna take a shower," he said, "and then I'm gonna hit the hay. Do we still leave our doors open?"

"Of course, my friend, but when we get to St. Martin, a closed bedroom door will mean 'Keep out; man at work!'"

He came out of the shower and I stepped in. As I was toweling dry, he said, "Good night, Big Brother, and thank you for everything you do for me."

"Good night, Little Brother."

My alarm went off at 7:00. We finished packing. I shaved. We got dressed in our casual tropical traveling clothes. We each had two pieces of luggage plus our briefcases, plus two garment bags. When we went downstairs, there was an envelope on the floor at the front door. I found twenty-five 100-dollar bills. We closed the house and stood on the street waiting for a taxi, when a Virginia cab stopped and asked for our destination.

"The Commuter Terminal at National Airport, please." After we'd unloaded and I'd paid the fare with a tip, we each got a baggage trolley, loaded it and pushed it to the Dispatcher's Office. We identified ourselves and confirmed that our departure was set for 10:00 on the boss' plane. We left the trolleys and took our briefcases to the snack bar in the Main Terminal. We returned to the Dispatcher at 9:50. Our pilot identified himself as Mark Stith, a retired Air Force pilot, even though he looked quite young. Our luggage and garment bags were loaded. Sven and I carried our briefcases on board and sat in two of the twelve plush seats. Although we were across the aisle from each other, the roominess of the plane allowed each of us to have a window view.

The flight to Miami took almost four hours due to bad weather. When we landed and deplaned, baggage carts were at the plane and our luggage was loaded. We thanked our pilot and proceeded on the long walk to the Main Terminal. We checked in at the American desk and each of us checked our two bags. We carried the garment bags and briefcases.

"Mr. Devon, you have a telephone call. You may use the red phone at the end of this counter."

"Hello, Philipp. You and Sven have everything you'll need?" asked the boss.

"Sports gear, dressy casuals and a tuxedo."

"Have a nice trip. Check in with me when you arrive and at least every three days or when you have something to report." He hung up. I wondered if all bosses had the same phone protocol.

The flight was uneventful. We landed at the Queen Juliana Airport on the Dutch side. After retrieving our luggage and walking to the curb, a cab driver holding a sign which read DEVON approached us.

"I'm Mr. Devon," I said.

"I'm Arnauld. Welcome to the island."

"This is Mr. Christen." We all shook hands.

Arnauld looked to be about fifty or fifty-five. He put our luggage and garment bags in the trunk. Sven and I got in with our briefcases.

"I believe you gentlemen have reservations at Anse Marcel. That's on the opposite side of the island in the French Sector. The drive will take about one hour, depending on traffic."

I knew the island was only about thirty-seven square miles and the roads left a lot to be desired, but I wasn't prepared for the many potholes we encountered, both on the Dutch and the French side.

We entered Marigot, the French capital. The streets were narrow and traffic was heavy. Overlooking the dock area was a fort, which had been erected many centuries ago to protect the city from pirates and other unwelcome visitors. After leaving Marigot, we headed due north for several miles on a very straight road, up and down over the island's topography. Soon we came to the small town on the water called Grand Case. Arnauld pointed out that in this little village were some of the finest restaurants on the island. Continuing eastward, we passed Aéroport de l'Esperance, the airport which is mainly reserved for the more wealthy French residents.

After a very mountainous drive with many curves and rather frightening narrow passages, we turned at a sign that read ANSE

MARCEL Soon we passed the crest of the mountain and began our descent toward the sea. We could see the marina, and at the very last turn, the Westin Resort and Spa came into view. It was an expansive and expensive-looking arrangement of private villas as well as the main Hotel. Arnauld stopped in front of the Hotel. A bellman approached with a dolly, which Arnauld and he began loading. I gave Arnauld a 100-dollar bill and told him that we probably would be seeing a lot of each other. Sven and I entered the lobby and went to the Desk.

"Bonsoir, Mademoiselle. Je m'appelle Monsieur Devon. J'ai une réservation pour une suite, s'il vous plaît."

"Bonsoir, Monsieur Devon. Avez-vous une pièce d'identité, s'il vous plaît?"

"Oui," I gave her my ID card.

Turning to Sven, she asked, "Et vous, Monsieur?"

"My name is Christen. Unfortunately, I don't speak French." He gave her his ID card.

"That's all right, Mister Christen. Everyone here speaks English."

"Mister Devon, you and Mister Christen have suite number 606 on the 6th floor. Here are your keys. You may go up to your suite now. Your luggage will be there shortly. Have a nice stay with us."

"Merci beaucoup, Mademoiselle."

"Je vous en prie."

We took the elevator to our floor. As we entered the suite, the drawing room view of the sea was magnificent. The room contained two sofas facing each other with a long coffee table between. The bedroom on the right had a view of the marina. The left bedroom faced the sea.

"I'll take the view of the marina, okay?" I asked.

"Sure."

Our baggage arrived. As each item was brought in, we directed it to the appropriate bedroom. I tipped the bellman $50.00.

"If either of you gentlemen needs anything else, please ask for Bernard and I shall respond immediately." He left the room.

I looked at my watch. It said 6:35. "I suggest we get a bottle of wine, order some dinner and relax this evening. We can begin our assignment tomorrow."

"Sounds like a plan."

I looked in the thick, leather-bound book of services on the desk in the drawing room. I found a Carte des Vins and a Dining Room menu. I read the selection of entrées to Sven. We decided on the tournedos. "We might as well compare them to your cooking." The list of wines was voluminous. The prices were exorbitant, but, what the hell. We're two very wealthy playboys on vacation.

"Would you prefer Burgundy or perhaps Bordeaux? Maybe even a Rhône?"

"Let's try something different," said Sven.

I chose a Burgundy, a 1982 Nuit's-St. Georges.

"I'm gonna get comfortable, but I suggest we keep our pants on until we've been served." We took off everything but our trousers. Soon, there was a knock at the door.

Bernard entered carrying a silver tray, the wine, two crystal goblets, napkins and a corkscrew. He placed the tray on the long table between the sofas and uncorked the wine. I signed the check and added a nice gratuity.

When he'd left the room, Sven and I clinked our glasses and I said, "To a successful assignment." We sat in the chairs on either side of the round table and looked at the sea while we sipped the wine. It was a superb wine and a great year. I'd had it before in Washington at the French Embassy. Within fifteen minutes, there was another knock at the door.

Bernard and another man had two trays, which they set on the long coffee table. When the silver domes were removed, the aroma filled the room. Again I signed the check and added a tip.

We stripped and sat on the opposite sofas. The tournedos were medium rare as I'd specified. Sven looked at me and smiled. "These really are good. They compare quite favorably with mine, don't you agree?"

"Almost," I said and smiled.

The wine gave out before the meal was completed. I picked up the phone and ordered another bottle. We both put on terry-cloth robes. The second bottle arrived. We finished our meals and slowly sipped the wine. We talked about our assignment, the mark, our cover and women. The latter subject got the most conversation and we both agreed it was about time we both got laid. We finished off the second bottle about 11:30. I hung the DO NOT DISTURB sign on the doorknob and locked the door. I could hear Sven snoring by the time I'd brushed my teeth. I didn't set my alarm but turned down the counterpane, the light blanket and the sheet and lay on my back. The bed was quite wide. The ceiling was fascinating. There were little white spatula marks where it had been put on in a delicate and intricate pattern. It reminded me of something but I couldn't remember what it was. In a few minutes, I was asleep.

When the sun's rays began to light up my room, I hadn't moved from the position I was in when I lay down. I looked at my watch. 8:15. I followed my exercise routine. When I finished, I just lay there sweating. Sven walked in and said, "Always lying down on the job."

He joined me on the floor and began his one-arm push-ups. He knew that made me envious so he did a few extra. When he'd finished, I got up and went into the bathroom. I didn't shave; I wanted to look rugged for a few days. At least that was my excuse. When I re-entered the drawing room, he said, "You forgot to shave."

"I didn't forget. I decided to have a rugged and manly face for a few days." He grinned and went to shower.

"I'll order breakfast for us. What's your pleasure this morning?"

"Surprise me. Just be sure there's lots of it."

I had on my robe when Sven came out of the shower. He put on his and sat on the sofa opposite me.

I'd forgotten to unlock the door and take in the DO NOT DISTURB sign, so I did both just as the waiter arrived with a dolly carrying our trays. There was also the local newspaper.

"What is our plan for today?" Sven asked.

"I thought we'd start by putting on our swimsuits, robes and slippers and walk down to the marina to see if there were any young women already awake to admire us. We can look over all the boats and get to know any of the owners or captains who might be on deck. After a reconnaissance of the marina, we can head to the pool for some sun and another reconnaissance of the other guests. After we've had some sun and are thoroughly sweaty, we can leave our robes and slippers on the chaises and come back to the marina for a second look. We'll go back to the pool if there are no takers of our manly attributes." I said all this acting like a braggart.

"Sounds like a good plan. I like it."

We put on our swimsuits, robes and slippers and went to the lobby. There weren't many guests there at that hour so we went to the marina. I'd spotted Peter the Ox's boat from my bedroom window. It was a beautiful piece of shipbuilding and would require a lot of appraisal time. If the Ox happened to be on deck, I'd try to strike up a conversation and get to know him better, get the preliminaries over with as soon as possible. We slowly inspected each boat as we progressed to the far end where the Ox's yacht was moored. None of the lovelies had as yet arisen for the day. When we got to the Ox's boat, we saw three men on the deck; two appeared to be crew. The other might be the Ox. We stopped, stared intently and discussed the sleek hull and the many marine accessories on deck. We were greeted by the man I suspected to be the Ox.

"Good morning," he said.

"Good morning", we both replied. "That's a mighty fine yacht you have there. Are you the owner?" I inquired.

"I am. The name's Pierre le Boeuf," said the hulking man walking toward the gangplank.

"I'm Philipp Devon and this is my brother, Sven Christen."

"Your brother? You have different last names."

"But we have the same mother", I responded.

"Would you like to come aboard?"

"We sure would. Thank you." We walked up the gangplank and shook hands with the Ox.

"Where are you guys from?"

"I live in Washington, D.C., and Sven lives in Stockholm, Sweden. We get together a few times a year and decided to come to St. Martin this time."

"Do you have families, I mean are you married?"

"Not yet, but we keep looking and hoping. So far, I haven't seen even one woman", said Sven.

"It's early. Most people party until the wee hours and don't come out until noon or thereafter. When did you arrive?"

"We flew in from Miami last night. We thought we'd get a glimpse of the boats before heading to the pool."

"Would you like a tour of mine?"

"That would be great," I said as he led the way around the starboard side toward the bow. "How big is it?"

"The published length is one hundred twelve feet. It'll sleep twelve quite comfortably and has a crew of two. Those are the guys you saw as you came aboard. Sometimes when I have a party, they double as my waiters. They also cook. Come on, I'll take you below."

We followed the Ox down the stairwell to the drawing room. It was comfortably appointed and could seat ten or twelve. We continued into the hallway and saw three doors on one side, four on the other, and one in the far center.

"The first door on the left is where Bruno and Paul sleep when the rooms are all occupied. At other times, they each have a room. The remaining five are all double-deckers and at the far end is my bedroom."

We walked into his room which had a large bed and built-in cabinets on both sides and a mirrored ceiling. There was a large bath on each side fore of the master bedroom. The port side bath opened into the master bedroom and the starboard one opened into the hall. All guests and the crew used the same bathroom. We returned to the drawing room and then went under the stairwell leading to the main deck. The dining room table and twelve chairs were most impressive. Aft was the galley.

"You've got a floating palace here," I said.

"It's not much but it is home," he said jokingly.

We returned to the main deck. "Sven and I are headed to the pool. Would you like to join us?" I said.

"Perhaps a little later. Thank you. How long do you plan to stay?"

"As long as we're having fun. Neither of us has any pressing need to leave. We'll just see what develops, either at poolside or on someone's boat."

"I'm giving a small cocktail party on board tomorrow evening and I'd be pleased if you would join me and my other guests. I can promise you there will be several young women present who are unattached."

"We'd be pleased to accept. Thank you, Pierre."

"I'll see you at the pool in about an hour. The party starts at 6:00 tomorrow evening and is very casual."

"Thank you again," we both said as we left the yacht. When we were out of earshot of the Ox, Sven said, "That was too easy."

"It was sort of smoothly done. I'm pleased that I haven't lost my touch," I said smiling.

"Did you notice the expensive-looking engravings on the walls of the drawing room?" Sven asked.

"I did, and since that is supposed to be one of your areas of expertise, you should pursue their origin, and, if you can work it into a conversation, ask if they're originals. Your reason for asking is that one of them appears to be a copy." I was hatching a plan as I spoke.

"What if he admits it's a copy?"

"You can tell him discreetly that you've had quite a bit of experience checking out copies and forgeries."

"Do you think I should wear my yellow shirt tomorrow night?"

"Yes, if you want everybody on board, male and female, to look at you. I plan to wear my see-thru white one I bought on Mykonos, to show off my chest hair. I hope it will attract women who'll want to check me out further down, if you know what I mean."

"You've loosened up quite a bit, Philipp. I'm happy for you. I'd also like to find at least one woman who likes big men, if you know what *I* mean."

"Did you bring some protection this time?"

"I did but I could only get LARGE. They were out of EXTRA

LARGE." He smiled.

"Good thing you're not conceited?" I said with a smile in my voice.

We arrived at the pool. There were few people. Sven and I staked out two chaises and faced them toward the sun. We spread our robes, put our slippers underneath and lay down on our backs. Both of us had gotten a good base in Abu Dhabi so I wasn't worried about getting too much sun the first day. A waiter came by and took our orders for two iced teas.

We talked about the Ox's yacht and what our plan of attack might be. I pointed out we didn't want to appear too eager or too knowledgeable. We were supposed to be on vacation for an indefinite period of time and I wanted to find out some information about his trips to Guadeloupe and the timing of his trip back to the Côte d'Azur.

We lay there for a little over an hour when the Ox arrived. He was wearing a thong. What is it with these thongs? Maybe I should give some serious thought to getting one. I laughed at the idea. My trunks were just fine. They have a low rise with short legs, split on the sides. Of course, I've never before used them to pick up girls. I'll see how they do for the first few days and if I need to get a thong, I will.

"Hello again, gentlemen," said the Ox.

"Drag up a chaise," I said. He did and spread his towel and lay down on his stomach.

I realize I have hair on my back, but I'm damned happy I don't have as much as the Ox. He looked like the Arab men we saw in Abu Dhabi.

"May I ask how many guests are coming tomorrow night, if I'm not being too curious?" I inquired. "And will light slacks and a casual shirt be okay? I have flip-flops or I can get some deck shoes in the lobby boutique."

"There'll be eight or nine and slacks and polo or casual shirt will be fine; wear your flip-flops. They'll be coming off soon after you arrive. Everybody on my boat goes barefooted. Other things are sure to come off too in the course of the evening."

"Why don't we just come nude and get the preliminaries over with?" Sven asked. "Just joking," he added.

"Sometimes that happens too. Be cool and see what develops."

I guessed the Ox to be about thirty-five, maybe forty. He was about six feet tall and weighed approximately two hundred, twenty pounds. He was in great physical shape. His black hair was professionally styled and his nails freshly manicured. He gave every indication that he was a very rich man.

The waiter returned. We asked for a refill of the two teas. Ox declined anything.

"I insist you have something as my guest," I said.

"What I'd really like would be a Bombay gin and tonic."

"One Bombay gin and tonic for our guest," I said to the waiter.

"I usually start about this time in the morning and continue until the party is over in the early hours of the next morning. Fortunately, I don't have any problems with my liver or with anything else. My Doctor tells me I'm just fine," he said. Soon, the gin and tonic and the two iced teas arrived.

"To each good health and much success in our pursuits on this trip," I said, intentionally using a double entendre.

"And that includes women," added Sven.

"Are there any more yachts of comparable size like yours that moor here?" I asked.

"Not in the marina. There's one so large it has to drop anchor a ways out and use its skiffs or its rowboats to get to the dock."

"Do you know who owns it?" I asked.

"I believe the lady is an American who travels all over the world. She doesn't seem to have a home."

"Poor girl; I feel so sorry for her," indicating that she obviously has tons of money and I wished that I was in her coterie of friends. I didn't want to pursue this conversation any further.

"Do you have a steady girl?" Sven inquired.

"Not at the moment. I've had many so-called 'steadies' over the years but I can't seem to find one who'll put up with my eccentricities."

"They must be pretty unusual for a girl not to latch on to you," said Sven.

"I've concluded that I enjoy the bachelor life, sailing the world whenever I want, going anywhere I want and not having to report or answer to anyone."

"That basically is what Sven and I do. Our interests are varied and we enjoy going places and meeting new people and finding out what makes them tick. Right now we're probably the horniest two brothers in the Caribbean."

"I hope that might be remedied tomorrow night. If you two have the wanderlust like I do, and you sound as though you do, you might want to take a little trip with me this weekend. I have a place in Guadeloupe. I'll go down on Friday and come back on Sunday. You're welcome to join me if you'd care to do so. There'll be just me and the crew and you two if you care to come along."

"We'd be happy to join you, Pierre. Thanks so much for the invitation, especially since you know nothing about us."

"I read people well and I decided when you two came on board this morning that you're probably more like me than any two guys I've met in a long time. It'll be fun."

"What clothes do we need to bring?" asked Sven.

"What you have on now and what you wear to the party tomorrow night will be sufficient. We'll sleep on board and you can sun while I go to my place."

"You've twisted our arms sufficiently to make us eager to travel with you on this magnificent yacht," I said, laying it on rather thickly.

"Good. You'll have all day tomorrow to lounge around the pool. When you come to the party tomorrow evening, bring your toothbrush. You can stay on board. We'll get underway early on Friday morning."

"I'm hungry," said Sven.

"You're always hungry," I said.

"Pierre, will you join us as our guest here at the pool for lunch?"

"Thank you but I must check out the boat for provisions, beverages and everything we may need for the weekend. I'll see you guys later." He left.

"Can you believe what's happening?" Sven wondered.

"I can and we must do some planning. We must plot our expected conversations to include when it will be appropriate to bring up the bit on forgeries. I plan to tell him about my friend, John. We don't want to display too much knowledge and scare him away, but somehow we need to find out what he's retrieving from the island. There's a lot to be done before we sail."

TWENTY-TWO

We ordered our lunch poolside. There was a notable lack of beauties at the pool today. I didn't see a single girl or woman with whom I'd like to make love. We donned our robes and slippers and entered the lobby. No beauties there either. What's wrong with this place, I wondered.

When we entered our suite, we each took a shower and settled on the sofas for further conversation.

"I thought this place was hot!" Sven commented.

"Down, boy, your horns are showing again."

"I can't help it, Philipp. I'm getting desperate. It's been almost two months since I was with a woman. I've tried exercises and cold showers and neither works. I go to sleep with an erection and I wake up with one."

"Steady. Tomorrow night should be an exciting evening. I'm looking forward to meeting a really nice woman, one who likes me for my body and not for my mind; I need a woman too." I paused briefly. "I think I'd like a bottle of red wine and no dinner. How does that sound to you?" I asked.

"Great. Bring it on. Tonight, I'll drink myself into oblivion. Wake me at noon."

I ordered a couple of bottles of Bordeaux. We sat in silence until the wine arrived. We didn't even get up to greet the server. We'd thrown our robes over our legs and just sat on the sofa very casually. After I signed and tipped the waiter, and our glasses had been poured, we got up, walked to the window, opened the curtains and I said, "Here we are, lovely ladies. Come and get us!"

"When we get on board tomorrow afternoon, I'll wear my slacks and my skin-tight polo shirt with flip-flops," I said.

"I'll wear my tight shirt and the tight slacks I wore at the dinner with Zanani," said Sven."

"Don't forget to take some protection and let me have a couple now."

Sven went into his room and brought me two packets.

"I hope these don't cramp your style," he said with a smile. "As I told you, they didn't have any EXTRA LARGE." We both sort of laughed, but not really.

We discussed our plan of attack for the trip, what we planned to do and say and when. I felt certain Bruno and Paul were in on this caper, but it was probably too risky to ask them any questions.

"How can you work your family's publishing house into the conversation?"

"The same way you'll work in your expertise on forgeries — subtly."

We discussed a few more topics, details about the yacht, the Ox's ready acceptance of both of us for the voyage, what other topics we might discuss with him, and last but not least, could he be of assistance in getting us laid.

We finished off the first bottle and started on the second. I looked at my watch. 8:20. I asked Sven if there was anything on his mind that he wanted to talk about.

"Like what?"

"I don't know. We haven't had a serious conversation about your future in quite a while. Are you pleased with the way things are going? Would you rather be on your own rather than working with me? Is there anything that bugs you?

"Philipp, to be honest with you, I'm worried about my father. Ever since my mother died, he's been at sea most of the time, literally. And then Doris came along. She's been very good for him. Dad's almost as horny as I am and Doris has been able to satisfy his needs in that department. But I can't see that arrangement going much further. Doris has a history of keeping a man just so long and then she wants someone new. I don't want my Dad to be hurt but I don't know what I can do to prevent it. Also, I would like to spend more time with him, in Stockholm or on Doris' yacht. But I also don't know how to approach that subject. Now I'm the one who's at sea."

I refilled both our glasses.

"Sven, you sound like a normal son who loves his father very much and wants the absolute best for him at all times. Your father's health appears to be excellent. He certainly gets enough exercise keeping Doris happy. Our business, unfortunately, requires us to put our personal problems and feelings on the back burner. If I may say so, you remind me of myself when I was your age.

"Z had just selected me to be his protégé; in fact, I traveled with him on many assignments. He was a good instructor and apparently I was a good student, for after only two years of tagging along, I was given my walking papers so to speak and told to get my ass in motion and be ready to solo from that point forward. Of course I kept in close touch with him, but the assignments he gave me required me to be innovative, smart, cunning and sure of myself.

"I'm now in my fifteenth year with Z and seventeenth with Charles, my American boss. I couldn't be happier. I know I was well trained and well groomed for almost anything. I'm pleased to say that in those fifteen years, I haven't faced any situation that I couldn't handle, and handle well. I've been shot at, mauled, captured and escaped, but I've not screwed up even one time and have been patted on the back verbally many times. The only difference between you and me is the fact that I have no parents but you have your father.

"My life is as pleasant as I've ever known it to be. Your companionship means a lot to me. We seem to click on most things except sometimes when you act like the horny young man you are instead of the sophisticated young man you should be. If I treat you as a little brother rather than a protégé, it's because I'm very fond of you and want the very best for you. You've many hidden talents and can be aggressive when called for. But you must become more of yourself and less trying to emulate me."

I poured the remainder of the bottle into our glasses. When I looked up at Sven, his eyes were glazed. He didn't say a word; he didn't need to. I'd just opened up my heart to him and also politely chewed his ass. His silence told me he agreed with me. We sat for several minutes without a word. He finally got up, put his glass down, grabbed both my hands and pulled me to my feet. The hug was the strongest I'd ever received. It was a sincere expression of his thanks. When we disengaged ourselves, he turned and went toward his bedroom. At the door he turned and said, "Good night, Big Brother, and thanks."

We called it a night and went to bed.

I awoke at 9:45 and went through my morning routines. Last night was an emotional time for me and I'm sure for Sven. I believe I know exactly how he feels, for I've been there. He's such a competent young man and I'm certain he has a bright future in our business. I've got to find some way to get him and Big Sven together more often.

I stepped out of the shower and toweled dry as I returned to the drawing room. He was still snoring.

I was hungry and Sven said to wake him at noon. I went to my bedroom and called room service. I ordered my usual and asked that when the waiter arrived, he be very quiet — "My brother is still sleeping." I sat on the sofa and thought about last night. I don't believe I can do anything about Sven's lack of female companionship but I possibly can do something about getting him back to Stockholm for a few days.

I returned to my bedroom and called the boss. I brought him up-to-date on all that had transpired since we arrived. I told him about our forthcoming trip to Guadeloupe and asked him if he would put in a call to Z and explain Sven's concern for his father, and might it be possible for him to go to Stockholm for a short visit when we're finished with this assignment. He said he would inquire and get back to me.

As I hung up, there was a quiet knock at the door. I wrapped a towel around my middle and opened the door. It was Bernard with my breakfast. He put the tray on the long table and poured a cup of coffee. I signed the chit and added a tip and said my brother would be calling for breakfast later.

After Bernard left, I ate leisurely. As I was finishing my last cup, Sven walked in. He looked absolutely washed out.

"What's wrong?" I asked.

"I dreamed my Dad died and I didn't make it home in time. It was so real, Philipp, I woke up crying."

"Come here. Sit down by me." He came over. I put my arm around his shoulder. He put his head on my shoulder. He was shaking.

"It was so real it was frightening."

I told him to sit there and lay his head back and I would order some coffee and some breakfast.

"Just some coffee. I'm not hungry."

I ordered another pot of coffee and sat back down next to him.

"Philipp, I know I'm acting like a baby but usually my dreams are premonitions of things to come."

We sat still and silent until the coffee arrived. I took it from Bernard at the door.

"I know I shouldn't have so much wine at night because it puts me in a very reflective mood where I conjure up all sorts of situations. I'm not blaming the wine. I enjoyed having it with you. It's just that a somber mood always seems to come after a lot of wine and I end up with a feeling of foreboding."

"Sven, my friend, you've a lot on your mind. There's our forthcoming party tonight and then the trip tomorrow during which you're to appear as an expert on forgeries. On top of all of this, you're extremely horny. I can assuage your fears on the tasks ahead but as for women, you're man enough to take care of yourself. Trust me, you can do it all in due time." I patted him on the head, removed my arm from his shoulders and stood up. "It's time for your morning exercises, and I wanna see you sweat buckets. Get with it."

He took one more sip of coffee and got down on the floor and began his one-arm push-ups. I'm always impressed by this feat of strength but this morning, he seemed to be extra strong. He added some new, more difficult exercises. Finally, he stood up and stretched and began the sidewinder. When he'd finished, he looked at me as if to say "Is that enough for today?" I slapped him on the butt and told him to go take a shower. I sat back down and had another cup. When he returned toweling dry, he was smiling.

"Now I'm hungry," he announced.

"You order your own breakfast and add another pot of coffee for me."

While he was sitting on his sofa and finishing his breakfast, I was sipping my coffee. .

"You always know what to say and what to have me do to get me back on track. I'm not really dependent on you; I just like being in your company and have you give me instructions on how to be a better agent." He paused for a moment. "I apologize for being such a baby last night and again this morning. Please forgive me."

"Forgive you for what? You're just acting like a man who was concerned for his father's happiness and safety. You've seen me on several occasions when I was concerned for the one I loved and crying when I was really worrying about her. It's alright for a man to cry over concern for another person. And when he cries in the presence of another man, it's a compliment and lets the other one know that he not only wants to share his concern but he also trusts him with his most intimate thoughts and emotions. I'm highly honored you thought enough of our friendship to share with me the thoughts that were bothering you. There's nothing to forgive; in fact, you've made me realize once again how important you are to me."

We got in our swimsuits and robes and went to the pool. There were several people already stretched out on chaises but we managed to find two empty ones and drag them to our side of the pool. After spreading our robes, we lay down on our backs.

There were two young women, and I do mean young—about twenty or so—lying on their backs directly across the pool. One was a brunette and the other a redhead. Both were extremely cute and shapely. I told Sven to lie still; I would swim to the other side and see if either or both would like to have some company. I dove onto the pool and swam a couple of laps and ended up at their feet.

"Hello," I said. "My name is Philipp."

"Hello, Philip," said the brunette. "I'm Barbara and this is my sister, Eloise."

"Hello, Philip," said Eloise. "Who is the guy with you?"

"That's my brother, Sven."

"Well, you and your brother are two very attractive men. Eloise and I were just talking about both of you. Where do you hail from?"

"I'm from Washington, D.C., and Sven is from Stockholm."

"You both have great-looking bodies. You must work out a lot."

"Daily," I replied, "and thank you for the compliment. You two also have great-looking bodies, if you'll allow me to say so."

"You definitely may say so," said Barbara. "Why don't you and Sven bring your chaises over here?"

"We'll be back in a flash." I dove in and swam to the other side. As I got out of the water, Sven asked, "Does the brunette want my body?"

"The ladies have invited us to bring our chaises over and lie down next to them."

"I'll lie down next to them or even on top of them," Sven answered.

"We've just been invited to be near them. Don't blow it with your horniness."

We picked up our chaises and walked around the pool. As we approached, I introduced Sven to each of them. He smiled and asked where we should put them.

"Philip, you can put yours here by me," said Barbara.

"And you can put yours here by me", said Eloise. It appeared we'd already been spoken for.

When we were settled, a waiter arrived promptly and asked for our order.

"What will you young women have?" I asked.

Both asked for iced tea.

"Four iced teas," I said to the waiter. "What brings you to St. Martin?"

"We're celebrating Eloise's birthday. It's tomorrow."

Both Sven and I said simultaneously, "Happy Birthday."

"And where are you from, Eloise?" I asked.

"I live in London and Barbara lives in Paris. Since neither of us works, we spend most of our days traveling the world. Daddy wishes we both would get married but we're having so much fun being 'unattached', we're in no hurry to settle down.

"Sven and I were in London just a week ago and I go to Paris often," I said.

"Do you both travel a lot?" Eloise asked.

"Philipp is with a Travel Agency and I'm a chef."

"That sounds really interesting," said Barbara. "You must travel all over the world."

482

"Yes," I replied. "I go to most of the exotic places on the Continent, but this is our first time in St. Martin. Sven has just been promoted to Master Chef. We're celebrating his promotion."

"Congratulations, Sven," said Eloise. "Could we help you celebrate by buying a bottle of Champagne?"

"You're kind to offer. We'll take you up on it if you'll allow us to get a little more sun and then go and get showered and more properly dressed to be having Champagne with such beautiful women," said Sven. What a suave stud he was.

"You're on, my new friend," said Eloise.

"Would you like to have some lunch with the Champagne?" I asked. "We can have it in our suite, if you would care to do so."

"You have a suite? You must be very wealthy or you entertain a lot," said Barbara.

"Not enough," said Sven. "My father is treating us to this trip and we both like to entertain."

"Why don't I order lunch and then we four can get showered in our suite. Sven and I will take one bath and you young women may have the other one."

"We only have our robes and slippers," said Barbara.

"Then we'll have lunch and Champagne in our robes and slippers. Is that alright?" I asked.

Barbara looked at Eloise and then at Sven and me.

"We've only met you a few minutes ago and already you've invited us to your suite."

"Sven and I are very casual. Quite often, when we're in London, Paris or even Washington, we give cocktail parties that start out with nothing but swimsuits and shoes and then usually the shoes come off," I said feeling my way.

"You guys both know how to party," said Eloise. "Barbara and I would feel more comfortable if we brought along a sarong and sandals."

"That would be fine with us," I said. I motioned for the waiter to come over. "What is your pleasure?"

The waiter took our lunch orders and Eloise ordered the Champaign. I asked him to serve everything in suite 606 in about thirty minutes.

"That's a coincidence. We're in 610," said Eloise.

"Well, shall we go? You ladies can get showered and Sven and I'll do the same. When you've dressed, come on over."

We got up, took our towels and robes with us, and went to the elevator. On the 6th floor, we accompanied the women to their suite and then went to ours.

"I wanted to be sure they were in 610 and not just local visitors to the pool," I said as we entered our drawing room.

We took showers and put on a pair of slacks and a shirt but remained barefooted.

"They've already seen us in swimsuits; we don't want to get too dressed up," I joked.

Our lunches arrived and were put on the long table between the sofas. In a few minutes there was a knock at the door. When I opened it, there stood Barbara in a pale blue sarong. Eloise had on a light green one. Sven and Eloise sat on one sofa and Barbara and I opposite. I opened the Champagne and poured. We toasted each other, "To new friends."

The lunch conversation went slowly. The two indicated they were from an upscale family on the Philadelphia Mainline. The women were not the most intelligent ones we'd ever seen. However, both Sven and I accommodated their style and choice of words, trying not to appear overly-educated or snobbish. After the Champagne was finished and the lunch was devoured, the situation took on an air of "What do we do now?" Sven and I exchanged looks. We sensed that we may not have chosen the best dates and that we had rushed things too fast. I got the impression I may have picked up a hooker. In our condition of no sex, however, we were happy to see them. The conversation dragged again.

"How long will you be in St. Martin?" Barbara asked.

"We really don't know," I replied. "We'd planned to stay until we got an urgent phone call, saying that we had to come home." I then added, "Or until we ran out of money." Everyone laughed. It was a forced laugh and we all knew it.

"And how long do you ladies plan to stay?" Sven asked, looking at Eloise.

"We have no limit on our plans. Barbara and I go wherever we want and do whatever we want and then go back home and begin planning our next trip."

"You've been to St. Martin before?"

"Oh, yes. We come each year. It's our favorite place in the Caribbean, especially Orient Beach. Barbara and I are nudists."

"So are Philipp and I," said Sven enthusiastically. "Neither one of us wears any clothes when we're in our rooms. Would you ladies like to get naked?"

"I suppose that would be alright. What do you think, Barbara?"

"I always like to be nude whenever possible. Could we have some more Champagne?"

I went to the phone and ordered another bottle, while at the same time removing my clothes. As I came back toward the sofas, Sven had stripped. Both ladies dropped their sarongs.

"You certainly do have a beautiful body," said Eloise, eyeing Sven from head to toe, pausing at his crotch and liking what she saw. "You do too, Philip."

"And I can say the same about both of you," I said as I gave Barbara the once over. We sat on the sofas, Sven and Eloise on one and Barbara and I on the other, but this time a little closer. I deliberately didn't make any more aggressive moves until after the Champagne arrived. We four sat very close and made small talk. Sven was having a hard time suppressing his growing erection.

The Champagne arrived. I went to the door, opened it just a tad, signed for the bottle and returned to the sofa. When I popped the cork, I poured each of us another glass. The small talk was forced. Everybody felt uncomfortable. Sven and Eloise were holding hands and sitting closer and closer. With a meaningful nod to Sven, I indicated that he and Eloise needed to go to his bedroom before he became more embarrassingly aroused. He whispered in Eloise's ear. The two of them got up and went into his bedroom and closed the door.

Barbara and I sat sipping our Champagne. The silence was deafening. I'd already decided that although she was a beautiful woman with a gorgeous body, it just wasn't the time, the place, or the person for me to get involved with any further. I'm a perfectionist and having had sex with Arlene, I convinced myself that no one could compare. From the expression on Barbara's face, I could tell she was reading my thoughts.

When we finished the bottle, Barbara thanked me for a lovely lunch and Champagne. She again complimented me on my body as she ran her hand through the hair on my chest. She got up, put on her sarong and shoes and came back to where I was standing. She took both hands, pulled me up, embraced me and kissed me on the lips. It was a sincere kiss and I liked it very much. She then turned and went to the door. Without saying another word, she left. I turned around and went into my bedroom and closed the door.

I lay across my bed and rehashed the last two hours. Although I felt I was ready while at poolside, when I sat looking at Barbara, both of us nude, I realized that I wasn't prepared to make the move. She reminded me of Arlene, not so much in her looks, but in the situation of us both being nude. I just lay there staring at the ceiling. The sounds coming from across the drawing room were loud and frustrating. The lack of sex and my failure to accept it when it was staring me in the face was unbearable. I got up and took a shower. Then lay down again. After a little while, I looked at my watch. It was already 6:15. I must have dropped off. I got up, opened the door and went into the drawing room. Sven was sitting on his sofa.

"Well, Sven, you look happy and contented."

"It was very nice and just what I needed. The edge has been taken off my sexual hunger," he said smiling. "And how was your afternoon?"

"Not so good. Barbara left just after you and Eloise went into your bedroom. I gave her no encouragement, so we called it quits."

"Eloise left right after we'd finished satisfying each other. I'm really sorry. I wanted so much for you to have a good time, too."

"Thanks, but I'm just not ready. I loved looking at Barbara's gorgeous body and I believe she would have made me feel very happy if I'd just followed through. But I didn't and that was that."

"Perhaps, we'll see them again. You can try again."

"I'm not sure Barbara will give me another chance. We'll see. *Que sera sera.*"

"Well, we better get ready for Ox's party. We're already late."

We stashed our cash in our briefcases along with our pouches and put them under our beds. We left the suite hoping to have a good time tonight and a successful trip tomorrow. As we approached Ox's yacht, there were a few people already on the main deck. Sven and I both stopped short when we saw two very attractive women talking to the Ox. They were Barbara and Eloise.

TWENTY-THREE

As we walked up the gangplank, the Ox met us at the top and welcomed us aboard.

"Let me take you around and introduce you. My friends," he said rather loudly, "these are two of my newest friends, Philip Devon and Sven Christen. Madelaine Charmont, Veronique de Soissons and Jean-Pierre Gallienne." To each woman I said, "Enchanté." To Jean-Pierre, I said "Monsieur." Sven said "Hello" to each of the three. Sven and I shook hands with Jean-Pierre. We followed the Ox to the next group.

"This is Chuck Belmont, Frances Hardaway and Bill Geeton." Sven and I said "Hello" to each one and shook hands with Chuck and Bill.

"And this is my oldest friend in the Caribbean, Louis Breville. Louis lives in Guadeloupe and just arrived from France today."

"Bonsoir, Monsieur Breville." Sven said "Hello."

"Call me Louis, please."

"And I am Philipp, with a double p at the end."

"And I'm Sven." We all shook hands.

"And these lovely women I understand you already know from the pool. This is Barbara Manning and her sister, Eloise Manning."

"Yes, we've had the pleasure of their company earlier this afternoon, but I didn't know your last name until now." I offered my hand to Barbara who took it and smiled broadly. Sven looked at Eloise sheepishly as he took her hand.

"You two are the only ones without a drink. What'll you have?"

"I'd like some red wine, thank you," I said.

"The same," said Sven.

"You didn't tell me how to spell your name, Philipp. I think that's real special," said Barbara. "Is it a family name?"

"No, I just made it up, to amuse my friends," I lied.

I noticed that Eloise couldn't take her eyes off Sven's tight yellow shirt. She looked flushed, I supposed, remembering her afternoon's encounter. Barbara was looking at the hair sticking out at the neck of my shirt and licking her lips. I became aroused. The Ox walked up and said, "Mingle with the other guests. Some aren't staying very late."

I excused myself from Barbara and went to the port side where the three French were standing.

"Vous parlez Français?" Jean-Pierre asked.

"Oui. Je parle en peu Français."

"Votre accent est parfait," said Madelaine.

"Merci beaucoup. Vous habitez ici à St.-Martin?" I asked.

"J'habite ici," said Madelaine, "Veronique, à Paris, et Jean-Pierre, à Monaco."

"May I assume that each of you also speaks English?"

"Yes, Philipp, with a double p at the end; we all do. Doesn't everyone, nowadays?" asked Veronique.

"I love your language and go to Paris as often as I can afford it."

"Pierre tells me that you and Sven are brothers. You have the same mother but different fathers," said Veronique. What is your business, Philipp?"

"My main interest is in my family's publishing firm, Devon Publications."

"Aha," said Jean-Pierre. "I know of your firm, an old and well-respected establishment."

"Thank you. We like to think we're well respected; we certainly are old. However, my daily business is traveling worldwide for my Agency. We're always looking at hotels, ships, condominiums, rental cars, restaurants and the like. Sven and I get together whenever we can. He was recently made Head Chef at the Hotel Andalusia in Marbella."

"What do you do for fun? What are your hobbies?" Barbara inquired.

"My hobbies are languages and wines. Sven's hobby is tracking down forgeries — books, paintings, engravings and the like. He's quite good and is already highly-respected in the field." I was looking directly at Jean-Pierre as I outlined Sven's expertise. I thought I detected the slightest raised eyebrow.

I mingled with everyone on board, not zeroing in on any one. Barbara and I had a brief conversation but we were not alone, so nothing of importance occurred. Chuck, Frances and Bill were from the States and had just met the Ox earlier in the week. Chuck indicated that he must get back to his other friends in Grand Case and needed to depart shortly. Frances and Bill appeared to be an item or at least Bill wanted them to be. Bruno and Paul were busy attending to the guests, replenishing their drinks, bringing finger food and mini-hors d'oeuvres.

After about an hour, Chuck said his goodbye to the Ox and waved a general goodbye to the rest of us. With his departure, five couples remained on deck: Barbara and I, Sven and Eloise, Jean-Pierre and Veronique, Bill and Frances, and the Ox and Madelaine, Louis having said good night and retired below.

When the ten of us mingled as a group, the Ox announced that, according to the custom of the ship, everyone should get as comfortable as one desires. I looked at Sven. I could read him like a book. He was ready to strip, but I cautioned him with my eyes to be patient and let others take the lead. Every one of us immediately took off our shoes. After a reasonable pause, the Ox took off his shirt. Sven and I followed his lead, as did Bill; but Jean-Pierre refrained. Veronique took off her blouse. She wore no bra. The other four followed her lead. The nine of us, excluding Jean-Pierre, who seemed uncomfortable with the whole procedure, continued our cocktail hour as though nothing had happened. After about twenty minutes, Barbara approached me and unbuttoned the top button of my trousers, unzipped them and lowered them to the deck. I stepped out as she threw them over a nearby deck chair. Eloise performed the same maneuver on Sven. Frances couldn't get Bill's pants down quick enough to suit her. Madelaine walked over to the Ox and did the same thing while removing her skirt. Within minutes there were five women and four men nude on deck with a drink in hand, while Jean-Pierre stood there, fully dressed, looking very perplexed.

"This is just like Orient Beach with cocktails," said Barbara.

"Jean-Pierre, my friend, I hope you're not uncomfortable. You've been

495

on my boat many times and have often participated in our strip-for-action routine. What's the matter tonight?" asked the Ox.

"I apologize to each of you but I'm just not in the mood to play this evening. If you will please excuse me, I'll go below."

The Ox spoke first. "I do hope the rest of us won't be reticent about having fun this evening. Let's have another round of drinks."

Bruno and Paul appeared fully dressed in their usual attire, work shirts and shorts, although they were now both barefooted. Within minutes, each of us had a new glass. Barbara took me by the hand and led me down the stairwell to the drawing room. We were followed immediately by the Ox and Madelaine and shortly thereafter by Sven and Eloise and Bill and Frances. Veronique remained on the main deck. After a brief time, the Ox went up on deck and brought her down to be with the rest of us.

"You have your choice of playing games or just watching others play games," he said.

Some of us immediately felt uncomfortable. While I anticipated there might be nudity during cocktails, I wasn't prepared to be a part of a group, some of whom would be watching others doing whatever they were going to do. Barbara sensed my uneasiness. She stood up and said, "Ladies, please come with me to the main deck so we can plan the activities of the evening."

Here we sat —four naked men, waiting for our dates to return with our evening's instructions. It's quite difficult to be in a group of four nude men without someone joking about something. The Ox said he hoped to be up for whatever Madelaine had planned. A double entendre if I ever heard one. Bill and Sven were ready for the games to begin. Their erections showed *how* ready. I just sat there like a stick-in-the-mud. Once again, I wasn't ready to show off for the others or be a part of the voyeurs.

Soon the ladies returned. I don't know who'd suggested what, but the final plans for the evening surprised me. Frances said she was not feeling well and asked Bill to take her home. Veronique asked Bill and Frances if she could get a ride with them back to Madelaine's house. She said Jean-Pierre would stay. The three of them went back on deck to get dressed. The Ox walked them to the gangplank and said good night.

After they left, we remaining six had another round of drinks. Soon, Barbara asked if she and Eloise could be excused and would Sven and I walk them back to their suite. She gave no reason for her request but I assumed they wanted Sven and me for another go at it. As the four of us returned to the main deck to get dressed, I whispered to the Ox that Sven and I would be back later to spend the night on board.

When we arrived at the 6th floor, Eloise took Sven by the hand and led

him to suite 610. Barbara asked if she might come in my suite. I opened

the door.

She sat on the sofa. I asked if she would like some Champagne. She

declined and asked me to sit by her. She then told me she knew about

Arlene's death. Sven told Eloise and said I might have some reservations

about the evening's activities. She took my hand and leaned over and

kissed me on the lips. I kissed her back for a very long time. It was very

pleasant and I became aroused. She rose and took me by the hand as we

walked toward the door. She kissed me again and said good night and left.

I sat down on the sofa. I thought about my dearest Arlene. I was

missing her more as each day passed. I wondered if I was ever going to get

over her death. I sat in the same position for an eternity, so it seemed. The

door opened. It was Sven. I had dozed off. I looked at my watch.11:55. He

came and sat next to me. After a brief silence, he spoke.

"Philipp, I know what a terrible time you're having. I feel guilty

having so much fun while you're having so much pain. Eloise and I just

seemed to hit it off perfectly. She is a talented young lady and also a good

teacher. In fact, we taught each other some wildly exotic new techniques."

He stopped briefly and then said, "Oh, Big Brother, I wish I could make your life more pleasant than it is right now."

I put my arm around his shoulders and thanked him for his concern. I assured him I'd be all right in due time. The circumstances, I said, hadn't yet occurred when I could make love to another woman. I also realized that I'd asked God for help in getting over my grief, but it hadn't happened. I know He answers prayers but why not mine now?

"Let's go back to the boat," Sven said. We got up, but first I wanted to call the boss. I told him all that had happened, leaving out, of course, that part about me almost getting laid, twice. I also told him that tomorrow morning we'll be leaving St. Martin headed for Guadeloupe and should return in two days. We left the suite. As we approached the boat, I saw Bruno and Paul, sitting on deck at the head of the gangplank. As we approached them, they smiled, stood up and one of them said, "Welcome back, gentlemen. I hope your evening was to your satisfaction. I'll show you to your stateroom."

We went down the stairwell to the drawing room and then down the corridor. "One of you can sleep in here and the other in there," he said, pointing to the last two doors before the Ox's room. Sven and I made our choices and went in and closed the doors. Even though I was separated from the Ox's bedroom by his bath, I could hear almost everything that was said or being done. I stripped off my clothes, buried my head between two pillows, one at each ear, and tried to sleep. With every sound coming through the walls --- every grunt, every squeal, and every lewd demand --- I could visualize my last few hours with Arlene at the Lowndes in London. It was exciting but also very painful. I turned over on my stomach and again placed the two pillows to my ears. Sometime later, I finally slept.

TWENTY-FOUR

I was awakened by the smell of coffee. I slipped on my trousers and went to the bathroom across the corridor, then into the dining room. Louis and Jean-Pierre were already at the table. Each had on a shirt and trousers. We greeted each other. As I sat down, Paul (his name was on his polo shirt) brought me a cup and asked if I'd like some breakfast. I said I'd like whatever he was preparing. "Surprise me."

Sven walked in totally nude. When he saw the three of us wearing trousers he reversed his path and came back also wearing only trousers. He greeted us by name and sat down next to me. Paul brought him a cup of coffee and asked about his wishes for food. Sven said he'd have "whatever you're serving." Louis and Jean-Pierre were not eating. We made small talk but no one said anything about last evening. Sven and I were on our second cup when the Ox walked in, nude. He sat down at the head of the table. He greeted each of us by name and again, nothing was said about last night. Paul brought his coffee and then the Ox spoke.

"It's now a little after nine. We'll shove off in about an hour. Philipp and Sven, I assume you've concluded that we're giving Louis a ride back home. Jean-Pierre decided to come along for the ride. There'll be just the five of us, plus Paul and Bruno. The rules of the boat, as I'm sure you've already surmised, are everyone dresses or undresses as he pleases. No ill feelings are tolerated on my boat."

We finished our meals in silence, with the exception of a non sequitur now and then by Jean-Pierre whose facial expressions alternated between bland and worried. At the conclusion of breakfast, I'd formed an opinion. He was a scared crook, suspecting that he might be exposed by either Sven or me, and wishing that the current situation would hurry and be over.

"I noticed your collection of engravings in the drawing room last evening," commented Sven. "I don't want to embarrass myself, but are they originals?"

"Why would you ask such a question?" The Ox spoke with some pique in his voice.

"I remember seeing one very similar to the one over the sofa, in Amsterdam, in the Rijn Museum. Of course, my memory could be playing tricks on me and I apologize for even asking such a question?"

"You have a very astute eye, Sven. That one is a copy of the Rembrandt which you refer to. The others are genuine. I asked a friend to make it for me so I could put it among the originals to see if anyone would notice. I compliment you on your knowledge of engravings."

"Thank you. I've devoted many of my leisure hours to the study of the really important engravings found in museums around the world. I've also assisted our Swedish Police in detecting and capturing forgers, not only of engravings, but of oils also. I'm sure you must be aware of the fact there are huge fortunes to be made in forgeries."

While Sven was explaining his expertise, I alternated my line of sight from Louis' eyes to Jean-Pierre's. Each appeared to be a bit nervous at the path Sven's conversation was headed. I jumped in.

"Sven is also a respected expert in determining the authenticity of the world's currencies. He's identified fakes but hasn't yet been able to put the authorities onto their sources. He and I often talked about going into the business of counterfeiting. He is quite good and counterfeiters are quite adept at not being caught." I took another sip of coffee. "Jean-Pierre, I don't believe you told me last evening about your profession. What do you do?"

"I have no profession. I was provided for quite comfortably in my father's will for the remainder of my life. I live in Monaco and I hire Pierre and his yacht for my pleasures. I love the water and go with him every time he has a spare bunk for me. We've made quite a few crossings in the past few years."

"Do you travel to Pierre's yacht wherever it's moored, or does Pierre pick you up in Monaco?"

"I always pick up Jean-Pierre in Monaco. He's one of my best customers," said the Ox.

"And what do you do, Louis, if I may ask?"

"Philipp, you and Sven like to travel to exotic spots all around the world, and it's obvious that both of you are men of means and good breeding. I too like to travel but don't have the means to do so. Pierre has been very good to me since we first met in Guadeloupe several years ago. The copy of the Rembrandt you so astutely noticed is my work. There are very few people with your eye, Sven, or I might add, who've ever seen the original. I also paint but engraving is my forte."

The Ox interrupted. "There are a few things I need to do before we shove off. Please excuse me, gentlemen." We got up from the table and went to our respective staterooms. After I'd left my trousers on my bed, I went up on deck *au naturel*. Both Paul and Bruno had donned shorts but they were bare-chested and barefooted. Sven arrived nude, as I'd expected. The Ox joined us undressed as he was for breakfast. Louis, being about sixty years of age, didn't share our style of dress, although he certainly wasn't insulting in any way. He arrived on deck in a pair of shorts and a polo shirt. He was, however, also barefooted. Jean-Pierre remained in his stateroom.

As we pulled out of the marina, I got a good view of our hotel and the associated cottages. When we cleared the reefs, Les Petites Pommes de Terre picked up speed and began what was to be a rather short trip to Guadeloupe. We ended up, however, not in Guadeloupe, but on one of the two small islands below, called Terre de Haut. We pulled near and dropped anchor. The Ox, now dressed casually in slacks and shirt with sandals, and Louis, who was similarly dressed, got in a skiff with Bruno at the helm, and went to the dock. Sven and I lay on two chaises on the opposite side, away from the view of the islanders. Jean-Pierre hadn't yet shown so I asked Paul if anyone had checked on him.

"He's known for his peculiar ways. On some of these trips, he doesn't come out of his stateroom except for meals. He's fine; I just checked."

"Did Pierre say when they expect to return?" I asked.

"Oh, they won't be back until tomorrow about lunchtime," said Paul. "There'll be just the four of us aboard this evening for cocktails and dinner."

"I certainly don't want to violate any rules of the boat, and I certainly don't want to invade your space, but Sven and I were wondering if you'd like to join us here for some sun?" He was well-tanned and appeared to be about Sven's age.

"When Pierre and Bruno, the only other people on board, have left in the skiff, I usually strip and sun for several hours until I decide to have my own cocktail hour and then dinner. Thank you. I will join you," said Paul as he shucked his shorts and lay down on one of the other chaises.

This seemed like a good opportunity to press Paul for information. I must do this delicately, I thought, so he won't realize what I'm doing.

"Paul, how long have you and Bruno worked for Pierre?"

"Bruno and I came on board two years ago, just after Pierre got us out of trouble with the French Authorities. We'd been bad and we got caught."

"If I'm not being too personal, may I please ask what kind of trouble?"

"We'd been passing bad money at the Paris nightclubs. It worked well for a couple of years and then some smart-ass detective challenged me at the door of the Moulin Rouge. Luckily, I had only one bogus on me and my excuse was that I'd received it in change when I purchased some articles on the street. I always carried an extra watch and some costume jewelry to authenticate my claim. He bought my story and I was only jailed for two days until Bruno bailed me out. He'd been working the clubs in Dijon and couldn't be reached. No charge of passing bogus bills was ever put on my record. However, Pierre got information that I'd been arrested and for what reason. He contacted me and said he'd like to hire me as a steward for his yacht. I told him about Bruno, so he hired us both."

"Why would Pierre want to hire two men who had a record of passing bogus bills?" I asked.

"Both Bruno and I are bi-sexual and he thought we might perform at some of his parties, which we do quite often."

"Has Pierre ever referred to your former trade while on this boat?"

"Never. Bruno and I were told at the beginning he'd have the records expunged and we'd be paid handsomely so long as we didn't see or hear anything. Our duties were specifically outlined to us. We were to act as the crew, as servants, as cocktail waiters and sometimes as entertainers. The ship runs by itself and being a member of the crew means knowing how to push buttons. Please don't tell Pierre I got naked with you guys."

"You can rest assured, Paul, that I don't even remember you being on deck while we sunned," I said in an attempt to gain more of his favor. "Do you happen to know why Pierre and Louis will be on the island overnight?

Where will they stay? I don't mean to be nosey but this is a very small island to have much going on and I'm sure they're not there for a happy time. Pierre can get all the women he wants right here on this boat when it's in the marina or if he brings his dates on board for a trip."

"All I know is that Louis lives on the island and that he works for Pierre. Tomorrow morning, Pierre and Bruno will return with one or more packages. Louis will remain on the island. I have no knowledge of what's in the packages and I don't want to know. Bruno and I are paid very well to keep our eyes, ears and mouths shut," he repeated.

"Does Pierre keep those packages on board or are they delivered to someone else in St. Martin?"

"Each time we come back from a trip, we dock at the marina for one or at most two days and then we head for Monaco to drop off his high-paying customer, Jean-Pierre."

"Gosh, Paul, it all sounds so mysterious, but it's none of my business so I ask you please don't remember we've had this conversation. I'll protect your ass if you'll protect mine."

"It's a deal," Paul said as we shook hands. All this time Sven had pretended to be asleep. His snoring was the fake kind. I could tell for I've heard the genuine sound. When my conversation with Paul ended, Sven "woke up."

"What time are cocktails served," he asked.

"Anytime you want them. What'll you have?" Paul said.

"We both like red wine," said Sven.

"Do we need to get some clothes on in case Jean-Pierre should put in an appearance?"

"He never comes out of his stateroom when Pierre is on the island. Do you guys mind if I stay bare-assed and join you for cocktails?"

"That would be acceptable, my new young friend. If you'll go for the wine, I'll follow and bring back the glasses. Sven, you can push these chaises aside and find us three chairs."

Paul and I descended to the galley. He pulled a bottle of Bordeaux and showed me where the glasses were kept. We returned to the main deck where Sven had set up the chairs, each of us facing the other two. As Paul uncorked the Bordeaux, I asked to see the bottle. It was a 1979, a great year in St.-Emilion. Paul poured as I said "To our health and success in the future." We all clicked glasses.

The wine was good and I noticed that Paul drank his faster than either of us. Sven noticed this also and kept Paul's glass reasonably full.

"I believe we may need another bottle. Would that be possible?" I asked.

Without saying a word, Paul went to the galley and returned shortly with the same wine as before. I assisted Paul opening the second bottle for he was getting a little uncoordinated. We continued to drink and talk. I let the conversation be guided by Sven, for I knew what the subject would be.

"What time did Madelaine leave this morning? I didn't hear her leave but I certainly heard every word, moan, and squeal that came from Pierre's bedroom. He sounded as though he was having a whale of a good time."

"Pierre always has a good time. Sometimes he'll have two young ladies join him at the same time. Bruno and I've learned to retire to the deck when such goings-on are in progress. We've slept on deck many nights."

"Pierre sounds like a man who really enjoys sex," I said.

"If there's anything he likes more than sex, its money. He's got plenty of it and always seems to have a fresh supply at every stop we make."

"I like both of them too, but I don't have an endless supply of fresh money," I said.

"It s almost like he's printing it. Maybe that's what he does on the island. Or maybe Louis does the printing and Pierre just brings it back to the ship. I know he gives a batch to Jean-Pierre 'cause I've seen the exchange while I was pretending to be working at something else." He poured the remainder of the bottle into his glass. "Printing money; I never even thought about it before."

"I think it best to forget what we discussed here and just forget the whole conversation. The wine was excellent and that's all that counts in my book," I said.

"You're right, my friends," said Paul slurring his words. "I'd better get some dinner started. What do you guys want tonight?"

"Sex," said Sven, "but I'll settle for a small steak, medium rare."

"Count me in for the same, if that's not too much trouble. But I insist we help you. Sven is a Master Chef and I do several odd jobs very well."

"Okay, if you won't tell Pierre. He'd be angry."

We retired to the galley. Paul got out all the ingredients for the meal. Sven took over the steaks and I set three places at the dining table. Soon the steaks were ready, the peas and the rolls were heated and we sat down. After taking only a few bites, Paul began to drop his head. He was fast becoming a sack of potatoes. Sven and I picked him up, head and feet, and carried him to one of the staterooms that was unoccupied. I had earlier identified the vacant ones in case of such an emergency. After putting Paul to bed, Sven and I finished the meal and cleaned up the kitchen. I looked at the wine rack and then at Sven. Without hesitation, I pulled another bottle, uncorked it, grabbed two clean glasses and led the way to the main deck.

The stars were sparkling in a clear sky. We sat in the chairs and began to sip and talk. I was facing the stairwell in the event Jean-Pierre should emerge, looking for something to eat.

Sven and I went over all the details that Paul had provided. We concluded that this small island was the location of the press or presses, that the Ox was engaged in the transporting and distribution of counterfeit bills, that Jean-Pierre was the entry to Monaco for the bogus bills, and that Paul was innocent of any knowledge about the whole affair. I knew nothing about Bruno's possible involvement and Paul hadn't given any clue that he knew anything about Bruno's activities. We still had no proof that the counterfeit bills exist, and at that point, I was uncertain how we could uncover them. Perhaps if I slept on it, I'd come up with a plan.

I said goodnight to Sven and went to my stateroom. The thought occurred to me that if Jean-Pierre got up looking for Paul and some food, an embarrassing situation might unfold. I went to the galley, made two sliced turkey sandwiches and took a small bottle of soda and placed everything outside Jean-Pierre's door. I went back to bed.

I awoke at 8:10 and went to the bathroom. I went to the dining room, still nude. Paul was at the stove preparing hot oatmeal. He had on a pair of shorts, a shirt and wore deck shoes. When he saw me, he blushed a bit and then quietly spoke.

"I'm truly embarrassed, Philipp, for being so much trouble last night. I'm also embarrassed for getting drunk and having to be carried to bed and I'm indebted to you and Sven for cleaning up the kitchen."

"Paul, my friend, I have no idea what you're talking about. Of course, after Sven and I drank three bottles of Bordeaux, I don't remember much of anything. I regret that you weren't able to join us for cocktails. We really had a great time. You're quite a good steward and I deeply appreciate your services."

"You're one helluva good man. I felt sure I could trust you to set things straight. Thank you, my friend, if I may call you my friend."

"And why couldn't you call me your friend? We've been through quite a lot together and are unable to share those experiences with anybody else." I winked at him.

He quietly said "thank you" as Jean-Pierre walked into the dining room. He had on slacks and a shirt but was barefooted.

"Good morning, gentlemen," he said. "Thank you Paul for the plate of food and the soda. I appreciate your thoughtfulness." Paul looked at me as I gestured "Me?"

He smiled and said, "Thank you. May I serve you gentlemen hot oatmeal with your coffee or would you prefer something else?"

"Sounds good to me," I said.

We all agreed.

While Jean-Pierre and I were enjoying our coffee and oatmeal, Sven walked in, naked as usual. He sat down and Paul brought him a cup of coffee.

"Is oatmeal, all right, Sven?"

"Oatmeal will be fine with a few slices of toast and a sweet bun, if you have one."

"I have croissants."

"That'll do just fine."

"May I have a croissant also," I asked.

"Certainly. Would you like one also?" Paul asked as he looked at Jean-Pierre.

"No, thank you."

I thought I would break the icy chill hanging over the table. "I hope everyone slept well. I certainly did."

"Like a rock," said Sven.

"I didn't sleep well at all. I have a lot on my mind and am unable to sleep deeply," said Jean-Pierre.

"What could possibly be bothering you on a beautiful boat like this with all the amenities and good service provided?"

"I have a premonition something bad is going to happen to me. I don't know what it is or when it'll happen, but it worries me."

"Well, I don't know enough about you or your private life to offer any solace or comfort," I said. "If either Sven or I have said or done anything that's upset you, we're both terribly sorry."

"You've done nothing at all. I want to apologize to you both for not being able to participate in the activities the other night. I was just not in the mood."

"Don't worry about it," said Sven. "Some of us can party at the drop of a hat, or our trousers. We missed you but I had a great time."

"I think I'll go topside and begin my morning sun worship," I said. "Will you two join me?"

"I'll join you if you won't think me a prude for keeping my clothes on."

"You're free to do whatever you want, say whatever you want to say, and dress or undress in any manner. These are the rules of this boat, but you should know that well. How many trips have you made across the Atlantic?"

"Several. I don't remember the exact number. Maybe twelve, I guess."

"You must really like the sea to do that many crossings. Are you always on this boat or do you take others?"

"I'm always on this one. Pierre has been very good to me and accommodates my desires for the sea. On some occasions, he'll have a party on board similar to the one the other night. I'm not always such a boob. I like to party too. I just didn't feel good. It was my worrying."

"Well, if you should remember what's troubling you, let us know. Both Sven and I are good listeners."

Sven and I lay on our chaises while Jean-Pierre sat in a chair. His dark glasses prevented me from seeing his eyes plainly, but I could tell he was eyeing Sven's body, all of it, rather intently. Sven picked up on this also.

"Do you go to the Casino in Monaco often?" I asked.

"Yes, I do. I love to gamble. My game is Baccarat."

"So is mine," I said, "but I always seem to run out of money."

"You can always use your credit cards," said Jean-Pierre.

"I never use my credit cards for gambling. I'm prone to spend too much."

"If I were a passer of bogus bills," said Sven, "I'd play Baccarat too. As you know, the bills are placed across the slot and then pushed into the catch bin. I could be finished and gone before the house knew someone was passing funny money."

No comment was made, so the subject died.

"When you were introduced by your brother, he said you were quite an expert on forgeries. You've detected counterfeit bills?" Jean-Pierre asked Sven.

"Yes, once in Amsterdam, but the overhead light was quite strong on the table. I've learned to spot forgeries quite easily, mainly because counterfeiters never attempt to duplicate exactly certain features on the face of the bill, especially if it's a U.S. twenty."

"This subject fascinates me. Could you demonstrate your abilities?"

"I could if I had a bogus twenty to mix in with a group of the real ones."

"I have one which I always carry with me, so I can compare the real thing with any bill I suspect," said Jean-Pierre. "I'll get a few real twenties and put the one counterfeit in the group. I'll be right back."

I looked at Sven and appeared a little nervous about what was coming.

I began to mention possible differences like the crispness of the bogus and the slight coloration differences when Jean-Pierre quickly re-appeared. He dragged a small table toward us and sat down. He put a stack of twenties, possibly ten or twelve, in the center of the table. Sven looked through the group rapidly. Then he put each one on the table, face up. There were thirteen bills in the group. He picked up each bill, felt it and brought it close to his eyes. When all thirteen bills had been so inspected, he chose one of them and identified it as the bogus.

"You're absolutely right, Sven. You are fantastic. I'm sure you won't tell me your secret but I would find it fascinating if you would." Sven said nothing. "Oh, well, let me put these away and we can talk some more." He left the deck and went to his stateroom.

"Tell me quickly how you knew that bill was bogus?" I asked.

"All the bills were relatively new, but the bad bill had a slight difference in the color green. It was very slight, but detectable. As you may not know, I've been an expert on bogus art and currency for the French, the Belgians, the Spanish and the Dutch." Jean-Pierre returned to the table.

"Sven, you are absolutely fantastic. Wait 'til I tell Pierre about your abilities."

"I would prefer that you don't. I performed as a courtesy to you. I certainly don't want everyone to know of my talents. You look like an upstanding man and I like your style. Let's leave it at that."

You're good, Little Brother, I thought. You've got him on your hook. I recalled his looking at Sven's naked body earlier with a combination of admiration and desire, and this show of talent had been the *coup de grace*. I think I know what's bothering Jean-Pierre.

"Jean-Pierre, I want to ask you a question but I don't want you to feel pressured or obligated to grant my request." Sven asked. "Could I please have that bogus bill for my collection?"

"It's the only one I have," he said. "I don't know if I want to part with it. Let me think about it. You'll please excuse me, I must go below."

When he had descended the stairwell, Sven excused himself also.

"I need to go below for a few minutes," he said.

After about fifteen minutes, Sven returned to his chaise.

"I have the bill," he said.

"And I want to know the details of how you got it."

He smirked and said, "I've always been proud of my endowment and I always look for ways to put it to good use. Let's just say that sometimes I'll do anything for my country."

I got up to get some water. I noticed Pierre and Bruno approaching the yacht in the skiff. Paul, Sven and I greeted them. Pierre was carrying a package wrapped in brown paper and sealed with tape.

"I trust you had a successful journey," I said rather casually.

"Quite," answered the Ox. He handed the package to Bruno. "Put this in my stateroom." As Bruno was descending the stairwell, he passed Jean-Pierre coming up.

"Welcome back, Pierre," said Jean-Pierre.

"I hope you three had a good time while I was gone," said Pierre. Paul was standing by watching and listening with a look of anxiousness.

"Sven and I had a very good time. Last evening for cocktails, I asked Paul if we could have some red wine. He brought us a bottle of your Château Figeac. It was superb. Later, I asked Paul if we could have another bottle, which he brought. Sven and I were enjoying your wine and relaxing here on the deck. We could not entice Jean-Pierre to join us." I looked directly at Jean-Pierre. "He remained in his cabin the entire time you were gone." I paused and looked at Paul. He appeared to be greatly relieved. "I must confess that while Paul was out of the galley, I slipped down there and pilfered a third bottle of the Figeac. I know that Sven and I have been rather greedy and free with your wine, so when we get back to the marina, I'll call the wine store in Marigot and have a case of wine delivered to your boat. If they don't have Figeac, I'll get another comparable St.-Emilion."

"Thank you, my friends," said the Ox, "but that won't be necessary. You're my guests. You may have anything you want that might be aboard. I sincerely appreciate your kind gesture, but I must decline to accept it."

"We feel like we've been sunning and drinking your wine, eating your food and enjoying our stay possibly to excess. Is there no way we can repay your hospitality?"

"None at all." He turned to Paul. "What are you serving us for lunch?"

Paul recited the items we could expect at the table. "Lunch will be served in about twenty minutes, if that's acceptable."

"That's perfect," said the Ox. "I'll get comfortable and meet the rest of you at the table."

When he departed and Bruno had gone below, Paul looked at me and said quietly and sub rosa, "Thank you." Jean-Pierre walked over to Sven and said, "I sincerely appreciate your discretion. Thank you. Thank you, too, Philipp."

"Ca ne fait rien (It was nothing.)," I replied.

We four were already seated when Pierre arrived, nude, as were Sven and I. Jean-Pierre still had on slacks and a shirt. The Ox spoke.

"Jean-Pierre, we've got to get you loosened up before we get back to the marina. I would suggest that after we've finished lunch, we gather on deck *au naturel* for some sun." I looked at Jean-Pierre. He was uncomfortable.

"You know, Pierre, how uncomfortable I am being naked."

"Nonsense, my friend. You're a nice looking young man, well built and in good physical shape. Even I enjoy looking at you nude." The Ox laughed, as did Sven and I. Jean-Pierre looked perplexed.

"I'll do it, but you gentlemen will have to excuse my shyness."

We finished our lunch.

"Now let's all get some sunshine." The Ox rose and led us topside. We each lay down on a chaise on our backs. In just a few minutes, Jean-Pierre arrived, totally nude. For a man about my age, who allegedly spends little or no time nude in the sun, his body was remarkably well tanned. There were no tan lines anywhere. And his equipment made the rest of us feel somewhat inadequate. Without saying a word, he lay down on his stomach.

There was very little conversation while we sunned. Soon, Paul brought four iced teas and a dish of chilled white grapes. Bruno appeared and reported that all staterooms had been cleaned and the beds remade. The Ox thanked him and invited him and Paul to get some sun up on the bow, if they cared to do so. They both declined. Within the hour, the yacht began its return voyage. We four continued our sunning until the marina was in sight. We went below and dressed. Sven and I brought our toilet kits fully packed.

"You're not leaving us just because we got back to land, are you?"

"I really should check in at home," I said. "Mother has been sick and wasn't too happy about our trip. If it's okay, we'll probably see you tomorrow or the next day."

"We'll be leaving tomorrow for Monaco. Jean-Pierre says he must get back to attend to some business. Oh, how wonderful it is to be unemployed and carefree." He laughed.

"In that case, let us say again how much we've enjoyed meeting you and your friends and your crew. You are a wonderful host. You make your guests feel very comfortable."

As the yacht pulled into its slip at the marina, Sven and I shook hands with all aboard and walked down the gangplank.

When we arrived in the room, I called the boss immediately.

"How is life in St. Martin?"

"Wonderful and quite complicated." I told him everything that had transpired, well almost all; how we had located the probable site of the printing press or presses and about Louis Breville and his part in the operation. I gave him as much information as I could. I also reported that the Ox plans to leave tomorrow morning for Monaco. I told him about Sven's part in this assignment.

"You would have been very pleased to see my little brother in operation. He not only displayed talents that I didn't know he had, but he coaxed Jean-Pierre into giving him one of the bogus bills which I feel almost certain came from the Ox's printing press. He was a super agent and deserves to be cited in the records."

"Let me talk with Sven."

Sven got on the phone and listened as the boss thanked him.

"Thank you, sir. It's a pleasure to serve my adopted country and a greater pleasure to work with Philipp. He's not only a super guy but one of the best, the most well-trained and most effective people in your group."

I took back the receiver. The boss asked me to scan the bill on our private decoder. He also indicated that we should take the bill to Z and let him alert Interpol on all the facts I'd given him and on Pierre's expected arrival in Monaco. Interpol might want to wait until Jean-Pierre actually uses one of the bills at the tables to allow John to catch him red-handed. It'll be interesting to learn about their plan of action. The boss also told me he would arrange for both Sven and me to take the early morning flight tomorrow for London. The tickets will be at the desk. The flight departs at 9:00 sharp. He hung up.

I telephoned Arnauld and asked him to pick us up at 6:00 AM. I turned to look at Sven. He was smiling.

"You have a right to be smiling, Sven. Your actions in this assignment were absolutely flawless. What would you like to do now that we're home? Would you like to go see Eloise again before we leave, or would you like to rest a bit in your big bed? I know the stateroom bed was cramped for you; it certainly was for me. What's your pleasure?"

"If it's all the same with you, I'd prefer to relax, just the two of us, over a bottle or two of good red wine and a hearty meal here in the room."

"Are you sure you don't want another roll in the hay with Eloise?"

"I enjoyed both times with her, but to be absolutely honest, I'd just like to spend the rest of this evening talking with you. I have this feeling that this'll be the last assignment we'll work together."

"Is it another premonition?"

"Yes and I don't like it."

"Then the rest of this evening will be spent here in this room, just the two of us and a bottle or two of red and some dinner later. Did I get it right?"

"Perfect."

I went to the phone and ordered two bottles of the Hermitage Rhône that I remembered from the wine menu. We kicked off our shoes and took off our shirts. Bernard arrived shortly and opened the first bottle and poured a bit for my inspection. Then he filled both glasses. I signed the check and added a generous tip. He left the corkscrew and then departed. We raised our glasses, clinked them, and I said, "To the best partner I ever had."

"Tell me more about this premonition you have about us not working together again."

"I got it while we were sunning this morning. The details were rather fuzzy but the bottom line was clear: you and I would split up soon and never again work on the same assignment. I don't want this premonition to come true. I don't even want to think or talk about it."

"The subject is closed. Next subject? Shall it be about any of the characters we've met in the few days we've been in St.-Martin? Or would you rather just talk about sex?"

"Since you brought it up, I know that sex is on your mind. I felt so sad when you weren't able to make it with Barbara, especially since I was banging away in the next room. And I felt sad again on the yacht when the party broke up just when it was getting started. Philipp, I know how you're hurting thinking about Arlene. I know how much she meant to you and to everybody else in our group.

"When we were alone talking about seeing her again, you got so excited. You were obviously very much in love with each other. But, my friend, that was then, and this is now. If I could get you laid, you know I'd do so. But you're the only one who can take that step. I don't know when it'll happen, but it'll happen. You're a very virile man in good health. Your horniness is second only to mine. So quit worrying about not being able to take that step and concentrate on how you're gonna make it happen."

"You're an excellent psychologist and I thank you for saying what you said. I thought I had my act together when I met Barbara, but I wasn't quite ready. I have a feeling – maybe it's *my* premonition -- it tells me I'll meet someone soon who'll share with me the wonders of a sexual relationship like Arlene and I had. I really do feel the time is near when I'll meet someone who needs me as much as I need her." We finished off the first bottle. "Maybe this person is someone I've previously known or someone entirely new. I don't know. But I can honestly say to you right now I'm gonna do it just as soon as I meet that person, new or old."

Sven had tears in his eyes as he got up and pulled me close to him for another hug. This time I kissed him on the cheek. He kissed me on the cheek also. Then we sat down and opened the second bottle. We talked about the past experiences we'd shared. He pointed out how many times I'd given him good advice and instruction, by both word and example. After that, our conversations slowed down and became fewer and farther between. We slowly sipped our wine until the second bottle was also empty. We hadn't ordered any food; we agreed we really weren't hungry. We just sat and looked at each other and occasionally smiled.

I looked at my watch again. 10:20.

"I think we should turn in. I'll set my alarm for 4:30. That should give us plenty time for our exercises and showers before Arnauld arrives."

We stood up, shook hands, and turned to our bedrooms.

"Good night to the best little brother in the whole world.

"Good night to the best and the only big brother I'll ever have."

This time we both closed our doors.

TWENTY-FIVE

4:30. I did my triples and went into the bathroom. I opened my bedroom door and went in the drawing room. I got down on the floor near the double windows. As I was just ready to begin my push-ups, Sven came in and plopped down right beside me. He began his push-ups, two-handed this time. He was keeping pace with me. I re-started my count as he began. My normal morning tally is about forty or a few more, but I'd be damned if I'd quit before he did. Forty-one, forty-two... forty-eight, forty-nine, and fifty. We both stopped without saying a word. We sat facing each other with our feet touching and began our sit-ups. We counted together. Forty-three . . . forty-eight, forty-nine, and fifty. Again, by unspoken agreement, we stopped. We turned side-ways, lying parallel and began the nameless wonder. I deliberately lengthened the time for each one, allowing Sven to keep up. When we got to twenty-five, he stopped, as did I.

"You win," he said. "That's the only exercise I know where you can outdo me. I didn't feel like being humiliated this morning."

We got up and started the sidewinders. When we'd done fifty, we agreed to stop all exercising and sit down on the sofas. We were breathing hard and laughing at the same time.

"I'm gonna miss watching you doing the one-arms," I said.

"And I'm gonna miss watching you outdo me on the nameless one."

We got up, shook hands and went to take our showers. When we'd finished and were toweling dry in the drawing room, Sven spoke.

"When I get to be your age, I hope I look as good as you do."

"And when you get as old as I am now, I hope I'll still be able to do at least one push-up."

We popped each other with our towels and went to get dressed. I put on my crotch pouch, shirt and trousers. Packing was easy. I looked at my watch. 5:50. We left the suite. Arnauld was in the lobby to take our luggage and garment bags as I checked us out. We got into the taxi and began the drive to the airport. This time, he took the other route rather than going through Marigot. Arnauld said traffic there is very crowded this time of day. When we arrived at the airport, he got two baggage carts. I gave Arnauld another 100-dollar bill and thanked him for his service. He bowed low and thanked me profusely and wished us both a safe journey.

We had forty minutes until departure time. We went into the restaurant and ordered coffee, eggs, bacon, and toast. We were very hungry having missed dinner last evening. As we walked to the gate, we saw Barbara and Eloise waiting at another gate to board the flight to Paris. We stopped and said good morning. They both threw their arms around our necks. Barbara whispered in my ear what a super guy I was and that she hoped to have the pleasure of being in my company again soon. She kissed me on the lips. I kissed her back. When Eloise let go of Sven, she did the same. He reciprocated. We said goodbye and continued to our gate.

"I'll tell you what Eloise said if you'll tell me what Barbara said."

"Barbara said what a swell guy I was and she hoped to see me again soon."

"Eloise said I was the best lover she'd ever had and looked forward to next time real soon."

We smiled as we boarded the plane.

The trip to London was about eight hours. The movie was *Pretty Woman*. I don't remember it being so sexually arousing the first time I saw it. We landed at Heathrow on schedule. After we cleared customs, we went to the taxi stand and took one to Z's building. A new Secretary greeted us as we entered his office. We introduced ourselves to her. She said her name was Penelope Farthing but that everyone called her Penny. I thought she was joking but it turned out she wasn't.

When we entered Z's office, he stood up and welcomed us warmly and said how pleased he was we were home safely. As we sat I extracted from my briefcase the bogus 20. Z looked at it closely under a magnifying glass.

"This is good, quite good," he said. "Sven, how were you able to identify it?"

"The green is a shade lighter than the real ones. My eyes are quite sensitive to the shades of colors. But of course, you already knew that."

"I'd heard rumors about how good you were. I'm pleased to be able to see for myself. Well done, my young friend."

"Philipp, I received a call from Interpol yesterday. Through an informant, they learned the identity of the driver of the lorry that ran down Arlene. They found it in a London garage and the driver was arrested shortly thereafter. He confessed he'd been hired by a man named Marchidi to kill Arlene because she and Francisco had uncovered the Columbian group who were planning to set up the importation of drugs into the Emirates with the help of a man named Zanani. Both Marchidi and Zanani have been arrested and charged with both murders."

There was a silence in the room. Z finally spoke to me.

"Philipp, I'm sending you, with your American boss' permission, on an assignment I know almost certainly you'll find to your liking."

He turned to Sven. "Unfortunately, you won't be on the same assignment. You're being posted to Stockholm. We need to explore several troubling problems, all local, and I believe, on the recommendation of your friend and mentor, you're ready to attack them." He paused for a couple of beats; Sven said nothing.

"You're also being promoted to Agent, effective immediately. I hope you'll accept this assignment with the same enthusiasm you've exhibited on all your other training missions." Another beat. "Your father knows you're coming. He expects you to be on the six o'clock flight tonight."

Sven stared into the near distance, stunned. He looked at me with moist eyes.

"Philipp, you're going to take a one-month leave of absence at the Countess' villa. She specifically asked that you be given this leave and that you spend it with her." He almost smiled. "I hope this is acceptable."

"I could use a little R & R. The de Bollo villa will be a most pleasant place to spend some relaxing time. Thank you. You're most considerate."

"Your flight leaves Heathrow at six-ten for Madrid." He leaned forward with an envelope for each of us. "That should get you both through the next few weeks.

"Sven, I want you to contact me at least once each week, more frequently if you have some information.. I'll explain your first assignment when you call. And, Philipp," he said "don't you contact me unless you are ill or get engaged to the most wonderful and beautiful forty-five year old in my organization." He winked.

"Sir, when can I go through Arlene's personal effects?"

"Helga Schmidt has boxed everything. Arlene's mother's home has been sold along with all the furniture to the local Anglican Church. It will make a wonderful parsonage for visiting clergy. The boxes have been shipped to Washington and you'll find them at your house when you return. As for the finances of the estate, Arlene left everything to you."

We left his office at 4:22. Standing outside the office, I spoke.

"Let's go to Heathrow, check in, and have a glass of wine."

Sven avoided my eyes. After a moment he said in a choked voice, "I told you I had a premonition about this. It's final for us as a team, and what's worse, I may never see you again." The hitch in his throat was matched with real tears.

"My dear little brother, as a new Agent, you must learn to control any outward sign of emotion. Only when everyone present will fully understand your expression of your feelings may you do so."

"It's just you and me here."

"Yes, you get a pass this time. I too feel like tearing up at the loss of our companionship but I must restrain myself. Buck up. Let's go to Heathrow. We can toast and depart with a warm belly of wine."

We were ahead of the afternoon traffic. We checked in at the two counters and met at our agreed-upon spot carrying our briefcases. We ordered two glasses of the house red at a nearby restaurant. We clinked our glasses but didn't toast. Words just didn't seem appropriate. At 5:30, we stepped outside the restaurant and stopped, facing each other. This was the time for farewells, but neither of us could say anything. We looked each other in the eye and shook hands, turned and walked to our respective gates and to the next chapter in our lives.

During the flight to Madrid, I began to think of the Countess in a new way. Wouldn't it be extraordinary if she was the woman who would be the next great love in my life.

I remembered the desire in her eyes when just the two of us were on the deck of the *37* in the early morning hours, she wrapped in her robe and I in only my trousers. Even though darkness pervaded the deck, I saw her looking at my nakedness which caused me to have an erection. As she left the chaise and headed for the stairwell, she turned and said, "My dear Philipp, no need to be shy with me. Ever. Just because I'm a Countess doesn't mean I'm in any way prudish. To prove it, I'll let you in on a little secret. When I have dinner in my room whether at home or at a hotel, I always dine nude. Can you imagine that?"

Remembering that scene, I could imagine it and did so immediately. I knew I'd continue to imagine it until our relationship changed from friends to lovers and the imagining became a reality. I was determined to make that happen soon.

I like to think Arlene would approve.

THE END

Made in the USA
Charleston, SC
28 April 2012